THE PLAYERS

Also by Margaret Sweatman

When Alice Lay Down with Peter
Sam and Angie
Fox

MARGARET SWEATMAN

The PLAYERS

This is a work of fiction and does not exactly follow the chronology of the historical events.

Edited by Bethany Gibson.
Cover image after a photograph by Ignacio Leonardi, www.ignacioleonardi.com.ar, stock.xchange.com.
Cover and interior page design by Julie Scriver.
Printed in Canada on paper containing100% post-consumer fibre.
10 9 8 7 6 5 4 3 2 1

Library and Archives Canada Cataloguing in Publication

Sweatman, Margaret
    The players / Margaret Sweatman.

ISBN 978-0-86492-518-3

    I. Title.

PS8587.W36P53 2009   C813'.54   C2009-901429-7

Goose Lane Editions acknowledges the financial support of the Canada Council for the Arts, the Government of Canada through the Book Publishing Industry Development Program (BPIDP), and the New Brunswick Department of Wellness, Culture, and Sport for its publishing activities.

Goose Lane Editions
Suite 330, 500 Beaverbrook Court
Fredericton, New Brunswick
CANADA E3B 5X4
www.gooselane.com

For Bailey
and Hillery

I am a Fox.
I am supposed to die,
I already threw my life
away.
Something daring,
Something dangerous,
I wish to do.

Erdoes and Ortiz, *American Indian Myths and Legends* (of the Brule Sioux)

The PLAYERS

PART ONE

Birds of the air will tell of murders past . . .

Christopher Marlowe, The Jew of Malta

One

This was the beginning of Lilly's real life, the one she would invent out of thin air.

In the hour before sunrise, Lilly went out, walking past the bonfires on Tower Street all the way to Aunt Meg's place on Pudding Lane, arriving at dawn, when everything is revealed at its most uncanny, without the mercy of colour. Aunt Meg, who never slept, heard Lilly's fists on her door and went down to find Lilly standing there, a tall, barefoot waif wearing all three of her mother's skirts, wrapped up against the cold in both of her mother's shawls. Meg drew in a breath and said, "She's gone, isn't she."

Meg brought Lilly inside, banked the fire in the kitchen, covered Lilly with a blanket, and gave her a boiled egg with tea.

The sun rose and with it came prisms, rivers of amber in glasses left on the tables the previous night. While Lilly ate, one of Meg's girls, Susan, tried to tell her, in swerving, euphemistic terms, what she'd have to do to keep herself here. Susan was fair, with white eyebrows and lashes, and had a rash, a hot roseola running between her heavy breasts and up to her cheeks. She was kind-hearted and liked things to sound pretty, so it was hard for her to make any sense. Aunt Meg laughed, wiping her eyes with her apron. Meg was sad because her sister was dead,

13

but she laughed anyway. She said that you may as well. Then she put her hand to Lilly's chin and lifted her face.

Lilly's life took shape. By next nightfall, when she left her mother's attic room for the last time, she knew death by touch, a shock her hands would never forget. And she had a bed (to share with Susan and with Claire, Meg's other girl). Susan held her that night and told her the ways to keep from getting in trouble. "In olden days, in Eej-ip, the Queen put crocodile dung up there. Crocodile's shite," she said, dissolving into giggles; then she sobered and added, "Course, now we make a good paste of Nellie." Susan tried to tell Lilly what to do so that her pockets would never again be empty. Lilly whispered to Susan that she needed to sleep. She didn't want Susan to know that she didn't think her own life would be quite like that.

Two weeks after Lilly's mother died, Lilly steeled herself through the hour of dawn, and while she knew that she'd always be vulnerable to dawn's particular shade of blue, she would never again be helpless. She crouched to remove the pessary, the little cap of honey, baking soda, and cow dung that Aunt Meg laughingly called Nellie's plug. Lilly had been with boys before, but of course this was very different. She wrapped herself in her mother's shawls and crawled in beside Susan and Claire. Susan put a hand to Lilly's cheek, saying, "Lilly," her white eyelashes flickering in the first light. The bed had a childish smell of being sick. In Lilly's fist, like a seed, she held a coin.

Lilly didn't find it odd, but Susan and Claire certainly did, that what Susan called "the very first stranger" to put a coin in Lilly's hand had gold ringlets and a title. He was the Second Earl of Buxborough, but he said his common name was

Bartholomew. Bartholomew had a small but lively canker he didn't try to conceal, and, besides, he was too drunk to be effective, so they spent the time in conversation. He paid her despite that. He began to pay her often. After a cure, he proved himself capable of a certain energy, but he liked wine more, and while he admired Lilly's flesh, he soon became obsessed with her other qualities.

Bartholomew was a poet and quite glorious to look at — though it seemed he never really wanted to be seen; his clothes were a dazzling sort of camouflage. He was a real poet, with an ear for music and satire and a haunted mind. His wife was rich, but he had scant money of his own, though like any of his class, he could put his hands on a loan when he needed it.

Bartholomew was his wife's steward. And he was honest, except on those rare occasions when he was blindsided by desire. Bartholomew hoped that his mostly drunk experience of life (the sheer terror of experience itself) would qualify him as being *real*, though he didn't, he wouldn't quite believe he was. He *felt* unreal. He felt separate. It made him sad, but he chose to be sad in a gorgeous, modern sort of way.

He took Lilly up; he fed her oranges, and he bought her a pair of shoes. She served ale at Aunt Meg's, but she didn't need to go upstairs with any of the customers; she had enough to get by, as long as Bartholomew liked her. She didn't miss her mother by day because her mother never gave her much, but in quiet times she missed her mother's voice. It was as if Lilly had gone deaf in this one crucial area. But she would take things from here, from zero. Making Bartholomew like her called for patience and skill, especially since Bart was so eloquently wounded by his easy life, so falsely gay; he was what men called "witty."

Bartholomew knew that Lilly was performing for him. Whenever he saw that she was not entirely sincere, not completely absorbed by his company, he pretended to enjoy it, to be ironical and admiring of her talent for playing the courtesan. Yet he was obsessed. He made a bet with a friend that he could turn Lilly into a *real* actress, a wager that made his obsession seem more like a joke. He began to give her lessons in stagecraft; he taught her how to move and speak, and then he foisted her on the players at the King's Playhouse by telling them he'd pay her wages.

Lilly proved to be a very good player.

One night at the Playhouse, Mr. Baringdon was passing a stone, and the cues were in chaos because Baringdon was playing Vermin the Footman, a key role only because he served the entrances and exits. Baringdon was a sweaty mass of agony leaking bloody urine in the tiring room, so the action was up for grabs. And Lilly grabbed. Didn't she have to? Bartholomew wouldn't pay her stage wages forever.

Lilly was playing Bizy the Maid. Baringdon didn't come on to announce the arrival of Lord Pleasant (played by Mr. Shift). Lady Le Blanc (Mrs. Gordon) slipped the billet-doux to Bizy (Lilly), and Bizy was then to give it to Pleasant, but when Baringdon failed to appear, Pleasant failed to appear (Mr. Shift was too stupid to improvise). Bizy curtsied just a few seconds too long, her skirts just a few inches too high, tucked the billet-doux in her bodice, crossed right, passed close behind Squire Squint (Mr. Chesterton — good, handsome, and astute Chesterton, who even drunk had the best intuition of any player in London), pressed her bosom to his back, and spun an exit line out of the excess of the several plays that Bartholomew had already made her memorize: "I shall go, sir, to fetch a nosegay."

Chesterton spun around and met Lilly's eye with quickly gauged admiration. "And prithee, Bizy, why a nosegay? Have I asked for it?"

"Your nose wants it, sir."

Chesterton sniffed, plucked the perfumed letter from Lilly's bodice, said, "I haven't nose enough for my good wife," and tucked it back in again. Lilly smirked, made a curtsy (Lilly could make even a curtsy funny), Chesterton groped, she dodged and exited, and the audience bawled with laughter, missing Mrs. Gordon's next lines. Even the gentlemen in the boxes noticed Lilly then.

In the wings sat Bartholomew with quill, ink, and brandy. He looked up at Lilly as she passed and said, "You're good. Devil only knows, you're good."

As Lilly exceeded Bart's training, he began to laugh mysteriously to himself in her presence. He wrote plays for her, here in town or at his wife's house at Addenbury where there's nothing but rain and sheep, writing with an air of injury, almost of hatred.

She became a success. The King's Players began to pay her (a little) for her work, though she still had to serve as a barmaid at Aunt Meg's. And while Bartholomew couldn't find enough money to get her a house, he did give her enough to keep her for himself. Claire and Susan nursed themselves with worm fern, Whore's Root. Lilly never forgot Nellie's plug. She would look after herself; she would never bear a child. She would never forget, never forgive, and never stop missing her mother's plaintive, self-pitying litanies as she drank herself to death.

Lilly's ear for suffering gave her a talent for playing comedy. Huntington, the manager of the King's Playhouse, bustled the many gentlemen to Lilly's tiring room, where they'd kiss her cheek, linger over her breast, and coo, "Such a nice leg, Huntington, she must play a man, come on, Huntington." And Lilly would say, "Lord Mallet has the prettiest leg." The men laughed excessively. Because Lilly didn't find life very funny, the gentlemen found her *very* funny. Someone kissed her on the mouth. Then they all did.

In six months, when Lilly's reputation as a player grew fully beyond Bartholomew's control, he did what he liked to do: he inflicted pain on himself. He introduced Lilly to the one man in London who would have the most power over her.

One afternoon, after a performance of Dryden's *Indian Emperor* (Lilly, in maroon petticoats and gold skirt, playing Cydaria, daughter of Montezuma, emperor of Mexico), Bartholomew took her elbow as she came to the side-wing after her bow. Without a word he pointed up to a box. The candles in the great chandeliers were smoking in a draft from the clamour of gallants and masks leaving the pit, and Lilly could barely make out the profile of a gentleman seated there, a gentleman of obvious means. Bartholomew would later recall the backward glance she gave him as she hurried across the stage toward the stairs; he would remember her excitement, her victory, and he would savour the heartache it caused him.

Lilly stepped into the box. The candles dimmed and flared, and she was met by the spectacle of an enormous raven, a man with a raven's watchful stillness, a hunter's objectivity. He didn't move. She saw the white of his eyes, his black eyebrows, his black wig merging with the dark. He idly lifted his hand to touch his own wide mouth, and she heard lace, a fine, clean music. If she failed to please the King, she'd merely live out what years she could bargain from poverty. She settled into the chair and let him look at her. The fictions she'd tell would be told with perfect candour. She was, after all, a realist. King Charles and Lilly Cole would soon learn that this was one of several attributes they shared.

"Pretty girl," said the King.

She peered at him, then said, "Did you like our play, sire?"

King Charles made a wan face. "Much coming and going. Much *discussion* between tortured and torturer. Much stabbing." He examined her in her petticoats and spangles, gazing on her small feet, her white satin shoes, and added, "You got stabbed very well."

Lilly was flushed with the performance, and now she put her hand to her breast, recalling the vicious, vengeful thrust of Mrs. Gordon's dagger. When she looked up, King Charles was smiling at her. She unlaced her chemise and slipped it from her shoulders. She leaned back in her chair and let him look. She threw her arms over the sides of her chair, breathed deeply, and he looked.

The King liked her, this girl who did Dryden so well. For nearly a month, he came to see her often, onstage and afterwards. Twice he had her delivered to him at Whitehall Palace. But he didn't give her any money. It almost appeared that he didn't have any, not in the coin that she needed to live. But there was more at stake than a few small coins. She made him laugh; she pretended to the King that she didn't need anything, and she pretended so well, he treated her as a lady, as a friend. However, women who really befriend men might starve. Lilly worked and slept at Aunt Meg's, but she never told King Charles anything of her real life — she was only as he wished her to be; he must have wanted to believe she was *born* on a stage. She thought, if she could only be *good*, as a woman, not merely a friend, she would never sing the death song that her mother sang.

But the Plague rattled through London. It was hot, the summer of 1665. Three thousand, then four thousand, then seven thousand people were dying each week. With great reluctance, King Charles ordered that the theatres be closed. The Court was forced to move to Oxfordshire, where there was nothing to do. Summer declined to autumn, the smell of death drifting over the countryside, and then to winter, bringing only drizzle, without frost to slow the affliction. King Charles needed diversion, and it was Bartholomew, the poet, who again found an occasion to hurt himself by suggesting to His Majesty that the little actress, Lilly Cole, be sent here, to these temporary quarters. At Oxford.

Where we find her, in a private performance.

Two

King Charles pulled away, distracted. How like a plant organism is a woman, he thought, his slow-lidded eyes examining her flesh. He had pressed her till she was tender. She was growing pink simply because she was young. The flesh has a mind of its own: it will betray the most vigilant irony. Despite herself she gasped. She was dewy, smelled weedy.

The large geography of the King's face, with its southern pitch of cheekbone, was impassive, but there'd been a change of weather. Lilly, with a snail's trace of juice on her thigh, sensed the shift of temperature, though the King remained intent. He enjoyed a free range to his observations, and he liked Lilly from a little distance.

He held her still while he studied her. Her lips were lopsided; her mouth leaned to the right. How nice. His large mouth and thin moustache didn't respond to other mouths because a king will not present himself in correspondence with anyone; he is a man distinct. They looked at each other for a moment, both dark-eyed and unsentimental. The imperial eyes studied her pale tissue with its betraying blush. Yes, how like a blooded plant, visceral, fibrous, fresh. He compared the complications of his own hand, the large pores, the delta-lines of knuckle, decaying — though this girl — he affectionately slid his fingers along the silk string toward the silk-wrapped sea sponge (Lilly had advanced from Nelly's plug) — with what genius or wit combined with youth has on her person not the slightest scent of death.

She leaned her elbow on the pillow. Her breast, freed from the garment he'd unribboned, was abundant with the vibrant fat of a young animal — blood, fat, sap. He observed that the nipples were of a colour with her very luscious quim. "Veni vidi," he whispered. "I saw." Lilly obliged his long royal cockerel, offering him her warm mockery. She pressed, and the King entered her, twice, thrice, watching her face. How pretty she is and how lush, like a plant cut open. The green light seared the drapery, and when he closed his eyes the King saw greenery and the green sun.

King Charles sashed the curtain, raising a cloud of dust; then he stood in his silk stockings, stork-like, with enormous feet. The room looked to the southwest. His black furnace and all the tools of his chemical experiments were exposed and ugly in the wintry afternoon. Glass vials and stoppered bottles were filed in wood racks. He'd been fooling with his cousin Rupert's formulae for gunpowder. Passing the time, really. Though recently King Charles had been feeling certain small detonations in his own being — the sense that he was fated (and being *fated* is hard on the nerves) to play a tired, nearly ludicrous role. He was embarrassed in the company of the new scientists, Boyle and so on, that young man Newton. He didn't like to feel so — so *irrelevant* . His family was ancient, *ancient*. He sighed. Just so.

Lilly wrinkled her nose. "What is in those little bottles, Charles, that smells so much like Meg's awful ferret?"

Charles's face didn't reveal his irritation. But Lilly felt prompted to add, "I suppose it is the scent of Science, sire. Of

Discovery, is that so?" She spoke softly to imply that he need not listen to her, that she is music as well as woman. Demanding nothing. She settled back among the pillows and murmured, "Such a scent could banish the Plague."

Charles relaxed. He liked Lilly's black hair against the pillows. He sat down beside her and played with her ribbons. "Do you know, I dreamed of you, Lilly," he said. Lilly didn't answer but raised her eyebrows, an expression she knew would convey moderate, pleasantly skeptical surprise. "Yes," he went on, "I saw you in a dream. You were dressed" — he paused — "costumed as a little beggar. A street wench. On a cold night. The people had their bonfires burning, you know how they do, you were among them. Your feet were bare. I thought, even in my dream, how I do not like to see Lilly with cold feet." He reached under the bedclothes and took one foot in his hand, bringing her knee up, inhaling the scent of her. "I was riding by, and I stopped. I saw you. You lifted your hand, and opened it — like so. And do you know what lay there?"

Lilly watched the King's immobile face. She experienced the surge of energy she got when she knew precisely, magically, what to do onstage. "A coin," she said. "A penny."

Charles betrayed his surprise by dropping her foot. He laughed. "You are a witch," he said. And perhaps because she'd unnerved him, he slid his hand up her leg. Such a brave little thing, fostered on an empty stomach. She is rare, bold, funny, probably difficult. Rich mistresses, avaricious and addictive, have weaknesses, easily manipulated. Lilly Cole has nothing. Well.

Her lips were pressed tight in that crooked smile. She laughed, so *natural*, and then with mock solemnity she whispered, "Your Majesty. Should the Puritans return, you could always survive by telling fortunes."

King Charles absolutely never lost control of his facial

muscles. A smallest tic. Lilly touched his face, the bone below the eye. It was nice that Lilly didn't need to be obsequious, but a woman must be cautious with a man whose father had lost his head.

"Forgive me," she said. "I haven't come from nowhere, Charles. Or, that's to say, I have. Many times, I've palmed my last coin and thought what a small piece stood between me and starvation. So you are confirmed, Charles, you are an oracle." She touched him at his oracle. Then she was forgiven.

It began to sun-shower. Oxford was mossy and mildewed. If only a frost would cleanse the Plague from town. The last leaves were letting go. Lilly turned her cheek to the cool pillow. She touched her own breast, and Charles thought it possible that she compared him to other lovers. She breathed, as of course she must, her light chemise rising and changing colour. He disentangled himself. He will send her back to London, surely it's not too cold or too late.

Bartholomew, Second Earl of Buxborough, in the wake of Lilly's moment, moved in his chair in the anteroom, sensing the air. "Sir," said Charles quietly, knowing that Bartholomew would hear him, "you may come in." And Bart entered the chamber.

Six weeks ago, Charles had made Bartholomew Gentleman of his Majesty's Bedchamber, apparently, perversely, as a reward for some insulting poems on his mistress, Lady Castlemaine. To demonstrate Bart's ineffectuality. The duties of office of Gentleman weren't overly demanding: for a week of each month, every morning, Bartholomew helped His Majesty put on his first shirt; for seven nights he kept him company if he wanted to eat in private, and he slept by him on a pallet. He ordered the things of the bedchamber: thus, today, Lilly. For these services the young Earl received a thousand pounds a year. Certainly more than he'd ever make as a poet.

Bartholomew, at twenty-three — twelve years the King's junior — was an adoptive son of the Court since his stupid but loyal father, the First Earl of Buxborough, died of the stomach when Bart was twelve. The free affection given him by King Charles, combined with an addiction to novelty, had made Bartholomew outrageous and in need of increasing doses of outrage, until he'd reach that empty stage where a drunken fight, a naked dance with ladies of the Court, violence committed and forgotten by morning, all devoured all, created the pure white light of satire. Though today, Bart was nearly sober.

Charles felt cheered by the sight of Bartholomew in his yellow stockings and green coat that set off the gold ringlets. Bart said that there was a French Explorer who'd been awaiting audience since early morning.

Bart served wine. "He's an unusual sort of barbarian," he added, handing Charles a glass. "He waits as one who hunts, moves not a hair for the hare, neither contented nor impatient." Bartholomew tended to forget that he wasn't always writing, but Charles liked that.

Lilly gave one of her crooked smiles to Bart. Charles saw it and changed his mind. "You may stay to meet the French Explorer, Lilly," he offered. She shrugged in a gesture that seemed Gallic. Charles was taken aback, but then he thought, well, she's a mimic, of course, an actress. "You may if you like," he said. He went to the window to watch the rain, the low cloud portioning the sky. He appreciated that Lilly had provided him with summer, and here it was late October after all.

With a despairing attitude, Bartholomew went out. Rain turned to sleet and daylight turned to stone. Lilly and the King felt the chill of a winter dusk and that infestation of self-consciousness that, strangely, they both avoided with whatever was at hand, preferably theatre. They didn't speak; they were both accustomed to waiting; they both liked to look *out*. The smell of Science, of eggs, the sour scent of wine, Charles's perfumes. Lilly sniffed the air. The room shuffled as if with the pads of a cat. A stranger stood at the door.

Three

The French Explorer was thin as a walking stick. His suit was the colour of brandy. Lilly, with one foot bare and the other in a stocking, went to him.

The laboratory, with its couch in disarray, occupied one half of the apartment; the other half served as a receiving room. It was a temporary arrangement. Lilly took many small steps to reach him, but before she could make out the sandy drifts of his suit, she smelled him. The stink of clean body. Soap, a forwarding of the Explorer's Self. She let her weight sink back on her heels and stroked the tiles with her feet, toward the stinking innocent. She heard the French air expelled through his French nostrils.

She approached till their lips almost touched. He wore animal skin, its low collar trimmed with a narrow strip of fur. "Monsieur," said Lilly, passing her hand over his face. The Explorer's eyes were on the King. Lilly understood that Charles cut a terrifying figure not only because of his power. His breeding had forced his limbs long and his features so eloquent as to be baroque, but the terror was spawned by the fact that the King was only a man.

Lilly traced a deep scar that ran like a seam of iron on the Explorer's left cheek. He had a swarthy complexion, cracked and pitted. He wore no wig and no powder, yet he seemed wily, artful. His lank hair draped about his neck, his green eyes shifted to her, a proximate target. She reached down and fiddled with his fingertips, which were so strange that she lifted his hand to look. They were malformed, the nails sunk in splayed flesh.

King Charles took a chair, his leg displayed on a pillow, just as Sir George Rose arrived, followed by a school of English herrings drenched in lavender, Bartholomew trailing after. Several were chewing cloves. Jabots of the French fashion were much in evidence; lace frothed down their chests and foamed up through slits cut in their sleeves. Ribbons around their calves, bows at their ankles. Two or three were so well dressed that they'd not been successful in relieving themselves, which added a certain damp caution to walking already made risky by ill-fitting shoes on a stone floor. That acid scent of pizzle. Everybody bowed and then bowed again. Five spaniels burst into the room and Charles greeted his dogs happily.

Sir George Rose thrust his hands behind his back. It was evident that, even in lace and in late middle age, Rose was strongly built. He was an irritable old Royalist. With an eloquent lack of conviction, he said, "His Majesty has demonstrated the foresight that is the mark of his genius in granting us this audience."

"Yes, yes." Charles lifted a spaniel into his lap and viewed with distaste Sir George Rose's Scottish mouth. "Do get on."

Rose waved toward the driftwood figure. "Monsieur Radisson. Come forward, sir. And tell King Charles your news of the passage to China."

Radisson put his lacerated hands together and approached. Lilly walked beside him, staring. Her face mimicked his instinctively, a habit she couldn't shake. Radisson pulled the taut wire of his body back like a bow. The story, be what it may, would be informed by its target. Lilly knew an actor when she met one. She knew what was in his pocket.

But before the Explorer could let his tale fly, Charles raised his heavy curls and, looking past, said, "Cousin."

All turned toward the entry of a tall man with a dark, ascetic face. Prince Rupert tacked across the laboratory till he arrived at the King's knee. "Your servant," he said, his accent northern Europe, *all* of northern Europe, and all of the south. A family resemblance between them, in the dark colouring. Though Rupert had distinctly blue eyes, they were, like the King's, large and sardonic. The appetite for light pleasure that remained in Charles had been extinguished in Rupert, displaced by discipline.

Charles was most comfortable with exiles. Those who stayed home and flourished with Cromwell, the Roundheads who had, with Cromwell's death, remembered their devotion to the Royals, those greasy rogues had been treated to an uneasy conspiracy with the King, who was habitually good-natured. He'd hanged only a few. Even the convicted regicides died (hanged, drawn and quartered, burned, their ashes licked up by dogs) in a gentlemanly manner.

Charles loved Rupert. Rupert carried exile in every bone. He yearned even now for his lost kingdom of Bohemia; he suffered from lifelong homesickness. Elegant, occasionally ill with a tropical disease (night sweats, treacherous bowels, a rash that comes and goes), Rupert had returned from his wartime wanderings in the Baltic too late to enjoy the celebration at Charles's restoration in 1660. He'd felt belated ever since.

Rupert's head hurt; an encounter with a cannonball. He'd been drawn away from his experiments at Windsor by rumours — a Frenchman had arrived in London claiming that he could find the passage to China through Hudson Bay. He bowed to the half-dressed Lilly and turned to the Explorer. Rupert was six feet, four inches tall. Radisson straightened his back. "From France?" Rupert asked.

Radisson had too many answers: France, New France, Boston, the unknown land of the savages. He looked at the girl. At Prince Rupert's sad eyes. How to seduce a realist? With what will smell most real. Cruelty. And what will warm the cruelty? But of course. Poetry.

"Peut-être," the Explorer began, "it will most delight His Majesty to hear something of my travels in the rich land that lies between England and China."

The gallants recoiled. A French manner is evidence of good quality. Not to be spoken by this buckskin.

Charles looked at him, weighed and measured him. "If it be a pleasing tale, we will to business better inspired."

"Then I begin." Radisson squared his shoulders like a singer. "It is a land very bountiful. Many acres of grain, and this that we call Indian corn and turnip." He turned to Mr. Pretyman, a gentleman in dove blue. "Groves," he said, "orchards as of Eden, chestnut and the oak, and great companies of hogs so fat they cannot run. The sky, she is filled with fowl and pigeon."

Sir George Rose interrupted. "Metals?"

"Ah, oui," said Radisson quickly. "Copper, I have seen."

"Copper," said Charles. "Not gold."

Radisson bit his lip. Then he offered, "Something more precious than gold."

Inattentive blue Pretyman, the richest of all herrings, snorted with laughter.

Charles, feeling a pulse, a possible prize, nodded slightly: continue.

"I have myself brought to New France more than one hundred forty thousand livres of pelts, les castors. The beaver."

The London courtiers cast a glance at one another, embarrassed to be English just then. Somebody twittered. Fur. And the Spanish made themselves so rich in gold and slaves. They felt a spasm of self-loathing. All but Prince Rupert dreamed of the consolation of oysters, mince pie, anchovies, and claret.

Charles didn't want an audience for a conversation about beaver. Commerce must at times be commonplace, and he didn't trust these blockheads. His eye on Radisson, he said, "Thank you, Sir George. You may leave us."

Sir George Rose bit the insides of his cheeks. He gave a military sort of nod, and his powdered entourage teetered out behind him. "A charlatan," grumbled Rose, leaving, "a mountebank."

Lilly had retired to the couch, warming up beside three spaniels. Only an actress would be competent here. She saw how the Frenchman shifted about the room to maintain the actor's ratio — all: him.

"Monsieur Radisson," said Prince Rupert, glad, too, to be alone with the Explorer, "do we find ourselves in China at the close of your voyage?"

"Very near." Radisson would make them happy. "It is but fourteen days' paddle from the Bay of the North to the Ja-pan Sea."

"If this is true," asked Prince Rupert, "why have men not travelled there already? If it be so near."

"I have preserved this news for His Majesty alone," said Radisson.

"Does your King Louis know about this?"

"There is no one for to tell him. Only I know this country."

Bartholomew poured the King and himself more wine. He toasted Charles and said, "Even among the French, Your Majesty inspires loyalty." When Bart drank, he poured the liquor into the back of his throat through a wide-open mouth. He swung toward the Explorer, would touch him but, he recalled, it is wearing animal skin, it would not like my touch. "Mr. Radisson, you will find our King incapable of stupid action." He showed his ankles. "For real folly, you must seek out his advisers."

Charles observed fondly, "Bart will upstage the entire Court in folly."

"I swell," said Bartholomew to Lilly, "with the nectar of the King's approbation. Long may I swell. It overcomes me; I cannot stop."

Radisson gazed out the window, revealing his boredom. It brought them back to business.

"Fourteen days' journey," prompted Prince Rupert.

"That is so. By the river that flows to Hudson Bay. I have travelled far, yet it remains now to push on some degree farther to enter the Ja-pan Sea."

Rupert never drank wine. He was a chemist. Knew metals. Drank absinthe. Extremely sober. Because Rupert was still, drank little, expressed nothing, not even incredulity, Radisson directed his tale there.

"Why have you not simply pushed farther, but come here to the English Court?" Rupert asked.

"Oh, this passage is dangereux," said Radisson. "It is to be attempted only in the months of August and septembre. During these months only is the passage less block by ice. But if it please the King to provide a boat, I will go."

"Ah." Bartholomew clapped his hands. "He wants a boat. An *English* boat."

Lilly would never take down an actor when he was in role. Her questions were in the spirit of his tale, for she'd forgotten that it *was* a tale; she saw the river, she saw the Japan Sea. Sitting forward happily, she asked, "Is this the boat that takes you up the river to China?"

"No, no. For the river we take little gondolas made of bark."

"Little gondolas." She glowed. She'd seen pictures. "As they do in Italy? With the poles? Who will push the poles?"

"That is the service of the Iroquois."

Lilly mouthed his words.

"Iroquois," he repeated. "They are the savage of the place."

"Savage," she said and beamed at the King. "Savage."

"Well, then the Court will be most at home there," said Bartholomew.

"Tell us of these savage — savages." Lilly turned to Charles. "Will it please you, King Charles?"

Charles would have liked to tell the story of his own escape from Cromwell's troops at Worcester in '51. He envied Rupert his dreams of the Northwest Passage and felt galled by his own hunger for trade: how much money the Frenchman wants; how much money, if any at all, the Frenchman might bring in return.

Radisson wet his throat. How quickly they have dispensed with *la poésie*. "I have lived many years among them," he began. "I know their trade. I can get much fur from the Indian. Only *I* know of these affaires."

"How have you come to know Indian savages?" Lilly squeezed her knees together. She had never felt so confident in her role as courtesan, or even as *actress*.

"I live among them since I am a boy. I am out hunting and I am taken captive by them. When I escape, I must kill two of that party. When they find me, they torture me."

"Oh," said Lilly. "Your hands."

"If you will permit." Prince Rupert crossed to Radisson and held out his hands. "Give," he said.

Radisson placed his paws in Rupert's hands. Rupert recoiled. "How did you come to be so mutilated?"

"The Iroquois," Radisson said carefully, casting his cool eye among them to watch his effect, "they tie me to a post by the hands before a burning fire of the rind of trees. They put their hatchets and instrument of iron in this fire. Then they quench them on my flesh. They pluck out my nails. They draw the blood from my fingers, then stop the bleeding with a hot brand." He had a nasal voice and he described cruelty without inflection. "They squeeze the marrow from the bone and put my hand in a dish full of burning sand."

The King's face was expressionless. Lilly held her breath.

Radisson could feel Prince Rupert's dry, hot skin, milk blue, the numerous scars like star clusters. By comparison, Radisson's were two pieces of raw wild meat, just off. Though Rupert, too, could smell the soap, and he found it interesting that this little hound should be, of that company, the one most recently bathed.

Like a beautiful green bird, Bartholomew glided to get a better look at Radisson's hands. "These *savages* sound more like the Spanish," he observed. "Are you sure you have come from New France?"

Charles laughed dryly, considering. "Tell me, what is their purpose, going to all that beastly trouble? As the Earl has already said, such, what say, *activity* would be quite natural to the overly pious Catholic, bless my mother. Zealous, true. But one cannot censure such action, however dreadful or strident, any more than one can censure the Inquisition. Ha! At your peril. Though I must say," he added, almost to himself, "I prefer that sort of behaviour to the vomitous Scot purges." He took a good long drink and mused: if this strange story is even partly true, it stirs something more than mercantile interest. A boy kidnapped by savages, raised by savages, fostered by primitives. He felt a strange affinity.

To distract himself from the depression that would overtake him at the most unlikely moments, Charles examined Radisson's costume. Leather stockings will soon form the pattern of modern foppery. And the fur trim. Yes, the fur trim. It is time to serve notice to cousin Louis — Canada will be England's. "It is not my wish to be discourteous to any subject of France. Your tale has been entertaining, but if it is to be proved serviceable, it will be necessary for you to provide us something into which we may sink our teeth."

Rupert took a chair at a writing desk. "What further proof have you that the Indians know the passage to the Japan Sea?" He began to draw clouds, or land, a channel. A map.

"I know the language of them," Radisson said.

Bartholomew said to Charles, "Well *that* will prove a tiresome accomplishment. We may go and *talk* to the savages. I trust they match a taste for barbarity with some degree of wit or I will go mad. Or not go at all."

"I had not conceived of your going off to sea, Bart," said Charles. "I had not."

Prince Rupert's journeys had taught him that a storyteller carries his house on his back. It made him skeptical and trusting, both at once. To Radisson, he said, "You will have us believe that you are the only man in the world who can discover the passage to Asia. You come from the French Court to the English. What proof can you provide us that your knowledge of the place is veritable and real?"

Radisson sniffed noisily. He will not lose their interest. He will leave here with the promise of a ship. "I have seen them eat human flesh."

Lilly's jaw dropped, her tongue lay moist on her lip.

"My own flesh," Radisson persisted, "I have given them eat."

And Lilly gave one of those little gasps of an intimate nature so recently disclosed to the King's ear.

Radisson watched her through half-closed eyes. Yes. Cruelty will excite them, it will show them, I am Radisson! It is better than a dance! "The Indians cut pieces of flesh from all parts of my body and broiled them. Then they made me eat it, thrusting my flesh into my mouth. They hang from my neck six red-hot hatchets which roast my legs. I do not cry out but they make me sing. The whole village came to see. Even the little ones do exercise themselves about such cruelty."

"The children do," said Lilly slowly.

"Cruelty is a great pride. The children are given such by their mother."

Lilly was an actress of consummate skill. She'd performed more than two dozen roles in her brief career, never losing a line; every rhyme and metre, every jig performed with that excess of character, a duality — an uncommon talent in an actress, to be true to the role while also remaining herself, larger, more than doubled. She rarely (only when pressed by candour) spoke critically of another's performance. It was against her nature to reject this Frenchman's yarn, to sever the bloodline between actor and audience. But there *must* be standards, some integrity among liars.

Radisson looked on Lilly with patient hatred. He would not let her interfere. He scanned the gentlemen. The one in green believes in nothing. The northern one with his white scars, he offers more: cold proportions yet curious, a blood-hunger. Of the King, everyone knows he has no money. His influence is important, his purse is empty.

Radisson spoke evenly. "They burned a French woman. They pulled out her breast and took a child out of her belly that they broiled and made the mother eat of it."

Bartholomew pinched his upper lip. "Ah. We have come to the *mother*!"

"The *French* mother," said Charles, his large, immobile face.

"Monsieur Radisson," Bart said, not looking at him, "have you taken your tale to the French Court?"

"I have been much betrayed by the French. They are a superstitious country and do much lack the scientific. Besides that, they tax too much. They are a corruption of man on this fair earth."

"I don't believe you." Lilly now stood over Radisson, who faced her, badgered.

Bartholomew said, "Oh, I assure you, Lilly. The French are most corrupt."

Lilly poked a finger into Radisson's hide and spat out, "*That* was a load of dung! And *you* are a dunghill! A bladder! A bad, bad man, and a bad, bad — actor!" To Charles: "How *dare* he come to you with this, this load of fish heads? A foul tale, and *badly* told! Do you think the King a soft-headed fool? Shatterbrain! Liar!"

Bart, wistfully to the King: "I see your royal sceptre has pointed you once more toward a soft, complaisant sex."

"Hold, Lilly," said Charles. "He spoke as well he might. Perhaps something was lost in it being told in English. The French will speak ghoulish with a style we may never fairly emulate. I learned this in exile. Sanguinaire. Ensanglanté. It is heroic, quite. A matter of taste. Come and sit. You block my view."

"I want him proved dishonest!" Lilly circled Radisson, who had gone still, though his green eyes followed her.

Prince Rupert was a sapphire in this pissy bed of British ivy. Radisson dared to look away from his tormentor. Was the Prince for or against him? The Frenchman knew that the English King was scandalously poor, rolling whore to whore, preferable to the crazy Puritans but too easily ruled by his prick. But for money, a ship, victuals, a captain, a good crew, now, to get all this now, before spring. To go, that is what he desired, only to go, and for all of that, the prize, the novelty! Hudson Bay! Tell them it is China! Only give me a ship! He lifted his head proudly and met Rupert's blue eyes with that glance that said, Women! Pfft!

Rupert traced his map with a long finger. To Radisson he said, "At what latitude lies Hudson Bay?"

"Hudson Bay is at fifty-seven degrees of latitude," said Radisson, "and two hundred and seventy of longitude."

"Two hundred and seventy. Yes. And what is the longitude of Japan?"

"Only seventy-three degrees of the great circle intervenes from Hudson Bay to Ja-pan." His nose was shiny with sweat.

Rupert was calm but keen. "And how many leagues do you calculate from seventy-three degrees of longitude?"

"Only one thousand four hundred and twenty leagues, good Prince."

"The globe does shrink betimes," said Prince Rupert.

"Oui. And it does increase your country's riches, when you may lay your hand across the seas." Radisson approached the Prince. "Two seas, the one of the south and that one of the north, are known already. There remains only the sea of the west, which joins them, to make one great sea from three small ones. Only seven days' paddle will take me to that Stinking Lake, which is but seven days' more journey to the great Sea of Ja-pan. If we push some few degrees farther, we will enter the rich bounty of China."

"He *is* a charlatan, Rupert, really," said Bart.

Radisson's scarred cheek flinched as at a fly. He leaned into Rupert's table, saying softly, pressing home, "But, Prince Rupert, we must go quickly to prepare this great thing."

"Cousin Rupert!" cried Charles. "He's got you!"

Lilly leapt toward the King. "He cannot! I can't bear it! There must be something, *something* of quality! Charles, King Charles, have you *no* interest in true stories? Beautiful monarch, may there be no *art* to our tales?"

Charles considered the collar, which even on Radisson's scruffy hide shirt looked appealing. He imagined it transported to an afternoon coat. Or a hat! Beaver is alluringly parliamentarian.

King Charles would keep his head. The monarchy is a sacred cause — he would not say that even to Bart, because he means it. It is endearing that Rupert wants China, but in the scientific age it's mercantile interests that will bind the country and prove her power. And we will not, *not, never* let the French come anywhere near Hudson Bay and its parliamentarian beaver!

To Lilly, Charles said, "Sit." Even in a rage, Lilly on a lap was a soft spaniel, and he was amused by such passion in a little thing, though he was surprised at the heft of her. He observed mildly, "You are a lover of the truth."

"I am a lover of true artfulness," said Lilly. "This tale does not merit a king. It is a sham, Charles. And *badly* told!"

"Ah," Charles mused. "He is a rough chronicler. We will need better stuff for England."

"Oh yes, sire! We must have better stuff! A crow could sing with more effect! Besides, he's ugly and he stinks of soap!"

Charles pulled Lilly close. He needed a little entertainment. "We will miss you, Lilly Cole," he said.

"What are you saying, Your Majesty?" Lilly asked carefully, evenly.

"It has become obvious that Rupert is going to provide this *bad actor* with a ship. It will be a voyage of great significance for England. Now, we know that we cannot trust our French quack to sing a tale of proper proportions. We need — are you following me, Lilly? — a chronicler, a scribbler, someone to recount the discovery of this Indian land of Catholic savagery. So I say, Lilly, we will miss you."

Lilly put her small face to the King's large one. "My Lord," she said. "There is one small difficulty."

"You will dress as a man."

"I dress as a man in England, Charles." She hesitated; she

did not like to reveal herself, but perhaps he'd find this news sufficiently charming. "My problem is something more difficult to overcome," she said slowly. "I can't read nor write."

"Come, Lilly. I've heard you speak lugubrious Dryden as if it was Shakespeare." Lilly squinted, watching his face. He continued. "Rhyming couplets and sanctimony. You warmed the lines, you *knew* them, never prompted. Now you say you cannot read?"

Lilly opened her mouth to speak. Stopped. She glanced pointedly at the Earl.

"Bart!" Charles turned to his Gentleman. "What hand had you in this?"

"A wager." Bartholomew took a drink. "Etherege said I couldn't do it. Turn the girl into an actress. I even taught her to dance." He shook his head, amazed.

Lilly saw his pain and she thought, Bartholomew makes a habit of pain. But a crisis seemed to have passed. "He's a good tutor, Charles," she said. "Even drunk, he plays a better Graciana than I. Really, Bart, it's too bad you were born a man. You'd make a better actress than me."

"My wit, your leg, Lilly. The Devil couldn't make a better joining."

Charles heard the forced lightness in Bartholomew's voice. He realized, Bart never looks at Lilly. He stared at his Gentleman and put Lilly off his lap. He was irritated. It didn't matter why. She'd fucked him first, his friend. He didn't glance toward Prince Rupert. He no longer even *saw* the French Explorer. Then, the royal perspective, the kingly balance was restored, his feathers falling back into place. Lilly made a humble curtsy, standing at his knee, and said, "I can't perform a line without Bart's tutoring."

"Yes yes, you have said this, do not be tiresome, Lilly." It had been a jest, a pleasantry with a whiff of the vicious. But the

40

wench had proved to be quick. Well, we shall play a little harder. He reached up and put his hand on her throat. "England. Damn England. I lose a warm cunt," he said softly, "and my wit."

"Pardon?" said Bartholomew. "I missed it. Maimed old debauché that I am, I am deaf in the ear." He shook the ringlets from his narrow face. There was something of the hothouse flower about Bart, almost past bloom, though beautiful, a lush white petal.

"You heard very well. Warn your wife. It will be a long journey. A long and difficult journey. A cold cold voyage, and dangerous." Charles wanted to be alone. He would not look at Rupert, but it was to Rupert he spoke. "Money," he murmured, "the trade must bring us a great deal of money. Or we are thoroughly stewed." The company saw that he would go away and leave them there, Lilly, Bartholomew, even the French Explorer, standing, like children, Charles thought, like children who witness their father take a temper. At the doorway he forced himself to stop, to turn, to raise his voice magisterially and tell them, "Monsieur Radisson shall further consult with Prince Rupert." He waved at Bartholomew and at Lilly and said, "Go away."

Four

Radisson left Oxford and, despite the warnings of infection, returned to London, padding through its deserted streets. The Plague had advanced to Houndsditch, to the burying pits at Whitechapel. He had come too late to hear mourning at these windows, the lamentations from quarantined houses, the nightly clatter of the Buriers' carts. Now, the surviving English showed a grim self-interest. The lock on every house had been picked open, either by thieves or by servants scavenging the abandoned homes of their masters. On many doors, the Cross, painted carelessly in red, off-kilter, the signature of Mister X.

Pierre Radisson moved lithely in the wet wind. Plague is Judgment, he thought. There are so many English, they poison themselves by breathing on one another. They are too knowing. That's why they made Cromwell. Cromwell was the most smart man. He was without the blinder. Without the blinder we have no freedom. I must thank God that Cromwell is dead. They want me to go to China, so I will sail west, and is not China there? Pfft. They are pitiful. It is pitiful to live on an island. They must feed themselves on one another. Or feed on other lands.

He sniffed the scent of corruption from a lodging nearby, its door smeared with a callow plea, *Lord Have Mercy Upon Us*. They only pretend to ask for mercy. The English *chiefs* never ask for mercy. And even the common fools have the common genius. He approached the inn, its broken gate yielding a view of the yard, the dry, nearly purple turf, and let himself in at the room above the Pyed Bull that he shared with his companion, his brother-in-law. Two tallow candles were alight. The smell of mould is quite like blood. Radisson threw some coal onto the fire.

The glowing coals aroused the memory of the frog. The savage woman, she saw it with me at the bush not far from Trois-Rivières. All night, the fire burned so hot we did not need any cover, my bones were warm. In the morning when it was dawn and the wood coals were hot, a great frog crawled out from the coals. Green. Big. From that fire he hopped. The woman she saw it too. The big green frog lived in the red-hot fire. We took a stone and beat the frog to death. A miracle frog.

Radisson awoke from his reverie. "Médard. I bring good news."

Médard Chouart, Sieur Des Groseilliers, lay on the bed with his boots on. He always spoke quietly when he was angry, and he was always angry. "What do you know of a man named La Tourette?" asked Des Groseilliers in French in his soft, raspy whisper.

"Not at all," said Radisson. "I know no man of that name."

Des Groseilliers stared at the flickering light on the ceiling. He has a big nose as well. Everyone here has a big nose. Des Groseilliers's was aimed at the sky, an isosceles triangle. Radisson wondered if his brother-in-law was aware of his big isosceles nose. Médard is a good explorer, Radisson thought, he has a compass, he has *two* compasses, like all strong men, the nose and the prick. But Radisson cannot tell Médard of his two compasses — no, do not talk of this to a man who shows such quick offence. Still, Radisson loved Médard, and, he knew, to explore is the greatest thing for a man; it takes courage and flat feet.

"Médard," said Radisson, "tomorrow we will move to the castle of Prince Rupert."

Des Groseilliers shrugged.

"We will have a boat, or more!"

"We will need more than a boat."

"There is time for these arrangements if we push the English." Radisson turned to go back downstairs. "I cannot bear this place. I am going out."

Des Groseilliers lifted from the bed in one smooth motion. He was heavier in bone and build than Radisson but moved quickly. Radisson flinched. Des Groseilliers whispered, "I will accompany you."

They returned to the deserted streets. The wind had died, and there was dense yellow fog. Radisson's moccasins made no sound, but Des Groseilliers's boots clacked. They walked through the steelyard toward the river. Up the ramp from Dowgate wharf came the Dead-Carts with their cargo for the pit at Finsbury, unloaded from a barge moored at the dock. The Frenchmen moved aside to let them pass, covering their mouths with their handkerchiefs. The Buriers sat dangling their legs and drinking from a jug. One of them laughed.

Radisson and Des Groseilliers stopped at the edge of the wharf, beside an empty, deep-bellied barge. There were voices across the water from hundreds of boats at anchor, swinging in the dark, a feeble attempt at quarantine. A swollen corpse was jammed, rocking in the water, between the cribbing and the barge. Radisson felt a surge of excitement, the tug of the great fish, Prince Rupert, so recently hooked. Rupert, he thought, you have lost your Kingdom! You are too old! Now I am here to take the ship!

The two men rarely spoke idly to each other, but here there was the additional problem of their being French. What was an advantage in Court was dangerous on the docks. Despite the danger, or because of it, Des Groseilliers raised his voice. "There. That is the man, La Tourette. I spoke of him to you."

Radisson twisted around. At the top of the ramp stood a short figure, openly watching, with more than curiosity — as a parasite fixes on its necessity. "Is he a spy?" asked Radisson.

Des Groseilliers's lip curled. "He addresses me as 'uncle.' Perhaps the Jesuits pay him. I should kill him, but . . ." He wearily shrugged. How can a man obey his instincts in this Hell?

"Médard, we may leave England, after this winter. In June."

Des Groseilliers spat out, "June." He bellowed at his stalker, "La Tourette! Go your way!" The figure swayed a little, then attached himself again.

Radisson touched the thick muscle of Des Groseilliers's arm. "I, too, hate to walk this way, one direction up, one direction down the stinking streets. We are choked. We sleep in beds. Our enemies stalk us openly, call you 'uncle.' It is a chamber pot, England and the English. They are worse than the French. I must feign my credulity. Come," he said, carefully taking his brother's elbow, "and I will tell you the conditions of our keeping by the English. There may be some petite problème."

While they walked, Radisson told Des Groseilliers the stipulations of their voyage, of the possible attendance of a little whore and an English fop, as chaperones, as *historiens*. Des Groseilliers said nothing but listened with growing fury. Radisson's feet were getting wet, and he, who loved the cold as a musician loves music, felt yet again betrayed by England, a country of soggy winter.

At last, Des Groseilliers whispered, "Is this a farce?"

"Who can say among such people, what is real, what is comédie? They cannot laugh but through the nose."

Radisson knew Des Groseilliers would purge himself soon. Like any intelligent man with a temper, Des Groseilliers liked the simplicity of rage. Again, Radisson reminded him of the future, of their eventual release from this prison term of a winter in London. "In June," he said, "in June we will sail."

The rain returned on a west wind, and before they could make it back to their lodgings it turned to thick white plates of snow.

Five

When Lilly walked naked from the bed to the window in the sunny, chilly afternoon, the muscles of her thighs showed hard and thick. Her legs were strong; her arms and shoulders, round and firm. Normally, she kept the ridge of thigh muscle hidden beneath layers of petticoat. She was a big girl who had invented a more accessible body, and she gave the impression of being light. When she was lying down, her pelvis seemed like a basin of milk.

The garret, Bartholomew's current lodgings in an alley off Tower Street — his wife and mother remained at the country estate at Addenbury — had oak pillars that more or less supported the roof, and these threw long shadows across the room. Lilly leaned her elbows on the casement and peered down into the alley. A cool sun struck through crooked frames.

Bartholomew wore his breeches and shirt. A pot of ink and a carafe of wine spilled into the bedclothes; his golden hair strayed across the pillows. His monkey crouched beside him, wearing a ruffled collar, filching fruit from the tray. When Bart shifted, paper fluttered across the bed to the floor. "Say it again," he said.

Her downy haunches reflected winter sunlight. "I'm tired."

"Good. Now we'll see what you're worth."

"You know very well what I'm worth." Since the theatres

were shut, she was worth only the few pennies Bart gave her and the few she could earn serving ale at Meg's. They'd been sent away from Oxford. Now there was nothing to do but rehearse for a play that might never see footlights. But then Lilly's attention was drawn to the shady side of the lane.

She saw a red shirtsleeve in the doorway across the way; it disappeared and returned, attached to a man lunging out, pursued by a woman who pleaded with him as she tried to pull him back inside. He wore only the shirt. They wrestled. The man had the advantage of size, but he appeared to be drunk. Even from this distance, Lilly could see the sores at his groin. She felt the freezing sensation from witnessing pain. He had a skinny face. Once, he might have been handsome. His screams filled the alley. He fought the woman to the ground, grasping her throat till she was kicking against the stones. Then he let go. He fell. The side of his head hit the road. He didn't even shudder but was utterly still.

Lilly didn't move. The woman lifted her eyes directly to hers, crying out, "My love! My love! My love!" The lane was empty; all the shutters facing the bright street were closed. No one came.

Lilly turned toward the room. The sound of the woman's lamentations winged hard around her like so many cormorants.

Bartholomew's heavy-lidded eyes were cast toward a dark corner of the garret, his impassivity belied by his lips, ripe with almost childish injury. The monkey mimicked the woman's cries, pulling at its ears and laughing. Lilly took a step.

"Stand," said Bartholomew.

She didn't hear.

"Stand, punk."

"I do stand."

"As an actress. You pose as a heifer."

Lilly lifted her bare arms away from her sides, bent them slightly, and opened her palms.

"Give us the Prologue." Bart was too beautiful to look dissipated; he didn't look old, he looked ancient — as if, despite the liquor and the blackouts, he'd never had a chance to forget anything.

Lilly faltered, the merest ripple, then she held still. Outside, the woman was silent. The monkey settled. This room is all there is. The oranges sat on the tray, fleshy and bright. Lilly felt a roaring wave of terror at the thought of dying. In two months she'd be seventeen.

She felt her teeth in her jaw, her spine, the bones of her feet. Her flesh persisted. She willed it to be so. Do not stop, do not stop for anybody, don't get caught, make it seem easy. The room was freezing. When she'd got up from bed, she'd been heated by Bart's attentions, but that had worn off and now she was cold, yet she wouldn't withdraw.

Bartholomew relaxed a little. Something of his fondness for deceit came staggering back to him. It had to be a witty thing to dress Lilly finely. How much better to anticipate the joke, to undress her first, let her have a piece of costume, chemise, bodice, skirt, one shoe at a time so that she'd learn balance, each role accomplished from the skin out. But Bartholomew could never remove his hands from her without this awful yearning. He was training her to disdain love. She'd proved to be so good at it.

Still, she couldn't learn lines except through him; he was her book. When he'd first taken her up, she spoke like an urchin and fondled her clothing. Now, she was mesmerizing onstage, distinctive, charming. Other actresses were vain, seeing you see them, fancying how nice they looked up there. Lilly was complete, and she reflected you back to yourself. He'd made her swoon and sweat today, but afterwards, she shrugged it off, as if she was a friend, as if she knew him too well.

It was appropriate, inevitable, that Bartholomew had educated Lilly in the very skills she now used to injure him. He'd taken her to Tunbridge Wells in the early days of her training. It was early summer and the resort was bright with all the birds of paradise who dared to be out, their faces veiled with tulle, an elegant mask against the Plague. The party was in the park, playing a game of pall mall. They seemed to need mirth verging on hysteria.

Lilly was the youngest woman there, the freshest. A lean whippet wearing black kid gloves insisted on being introduced to her. "I am a dear friend of the Earl's," barked the whippet at Lilly while he kissed Bart's cheek and called him "my darling sin."

Bartholomew introduced Lilly and tried to steer her away, but Lilly was pleased to attract the attention of a wealthy Lord: Soby, Lord Metcalf. Soby had followed her, found her a glass of champagne and a cake. Bartholomew attached himself to her arm, putting himself between them, until Lilly finally shook him off and hissed at him, "What are you doing?"

Soby stood nearby, and Bart could only lamely say that she would miss the carriage back to London. Lilly turned on him with a sardonic grin. "Sweet, cowardly Earl, I can look after myself. In fact" — kissing him — "remember that you made me. You should be proud that a Lord likes my company."

Soby said, "Go away, Buxborough." Then he took the flesh of Lilly's arm between his gloved fingers and pinched, not letting go. She gasped in pain and tried get away, but Soby pinched harder, bringing Lilly nearly to her knees. She was crouching, watching his face now. Smiling, he said, "Imagine how good that would feel on your tit." Then he let go.

Lilly's hand was numb, her shoulder burned, she'd broken out in a sweat. Bartholomew pulled her across the lawn. "Don't look back," he said. He took her to the carriage and home.

Not long after, Lord Metcalf came into the tiring room after a performance, sent everyone out, and sat on the couch, wearing that smile. He didn't touch her. He watched. Lilly found herself unable to move. He stayed like that for an hour, saying nothing but slapping his hand with his glove. Bartholomew stumbled in, drunk, and found him. Soby stood up and left without a word. He did that three times. Then he began to send letters demanding that she come to his house. Lilly told the messenger that she would, soon, she said that she was indisposed but would come.

Lilly asked Bartholomew to keep Lord Metcalf away from her, and he'd had to refuse. "No one tells Soby what to do," he said. Restraint excited Soby. He'd murdered at least two gentlemen and one link-boy; he'd been indicted twice (he was not indicted for the link-boy) and both times got away with it when his fellow peers intervened.

Bartholomew couldn't have Lilly, and he couldn't protect her. He wrote plays for her. He would hear his own voice, the couplets manufactured in some anteroom of his too-familiar body: witty words, his witty skepticism.

"The Prologue," he said and filled his glass.

"I've run through it forty times."

"Another forty and you may see your dress."

"Never will get to wear it," she grumbled. "The Plague's never going to end, and the theatres'll stay closed forever. Anyway, your play is black, Bart. All of it. The Prologue's made of butter, especially the last bit. But it doesn't fit with the rest, y'know." Her arms were still raised. She could hold a pose longer than any actress in the stable.

"The Prologue is there to ease my entry, Critic, to make my point agreeable. Watch them in their boxes. When you speak, they feel themselves less foul-fed than the poet."

"Every time I look up at the boxes, I see Lord Metcalf."

"Never mind Soby," said Bart. He poured the wine down his throat. "I'll — take care of it. Soby's the least of your worries. What are you going to do about your exile?"

"I'm putting my arms down." She shook the blood into her hands. "What are you saying?"

"Charles. Your exile to the Orient. I believe I am required to accompany you."

"You don't believe Charles means to send us away. You don't mean that."

The carafe was empty. Bartholomew bayed sweetly for his valet: "Jack! The master will have wine!" Then he smiled at Lilly in a way that reminded her that she was alone in all circumstances.

"It doesn't fit him," she said. "It exceeds his spite."

"Ah. But it does not exceed his imagination."

She hadn't given the matter much thought until now; no man had ever said anything sincerely to Lilly, so she'd assumed that the King's threat was empty. A hole opened at her feet.

Bartholomew felt a flash of hope. He was always working to match the cruelty he felt in others. He tried to love this world as little as it loved him, and he tried to love Lilly as little as she loved him. But maybe she was vulnerable just now. "Come on, Lilly Cole, be good," he whispered.

"It amuses him, doesn't it? Charles will like the idea of sending me to China because it's amusing."

Bartholomew threw back his head. "Jack! I perish!"

"Of course," said Lilly unevenly, "I can use my — my influence to change his mind."

"Oh, that you must do. Your life depends on it. These are not sentimental times."

Lilly resisted the need to have Bart hold her, resisted.

"But who am I to advise Princess Punk?" he said. "I will, however, give you one piece of advice before I die of thirst. Jack! Never mistake the prick for a simple instrument. Ahh, Jack! My

52

fellow. My nurse. Put it here, put it down, pour, that's good."

Jack poured the wine and refreshed the tray. Bart's monkey snatched a cluster of grapes. Jack slapped at it, withdrawing his hand before he could be bitten, then he jerked his head toward the window. "Another one for the Buriers," he said without enthusiasm.

Bartholomew ignored Jack. He continued his lesson to Lilly, his speech thick and slow. "Charles is not in fact as easy as he would seem. You will find that he is quickly sated. The sex is but one entertainment among many. You must play them all, all at once, ahead of his tune."

Jack leaned on one leg, assessing his fingernails. He'd been with the Earl four years and was owed a lot of money. "Sang a death song, didn't she," he said. Again, he looked to the window and softly he chanted, "My love, my love, my love."

Lilly shuddered. "I've got till June, haven't I?" she said. "By June, the Plague will be finished and the theatres can open. He'll want to see me on the stage again. He won't want to send me away. He can't. I'll be too good."

Bartholomew put the tray on the floor for his monkey to feed. His movements grew more languorous; he was so tired.

"The way I see it," said Jack, "the Plague's the only bit of luck London's seen since May of '60 when the King come back." Jack looked right through Lilly, yet he seemed to need an argument. "Well, think on it! If all those servants had survived? We're rid of forty thousand people, don't care what the accounts say, it's prob'ly far more. And most of them turned off by their families. Would've made an unbearable burden to the City, to suffer the expense of that lot."

Lilly's teeth began to chatter. She willed herself to relax. Jack had an uncommonly narrow body and face, as if he'd been squeezed between two palms, a distortion that translated his low-born features into an unsettling parody of a noble's. She breathed deeply, staring at the crooked plane of Jack's cheek-bones till she stopped shivering. "You said you'd hear the Prologue." She raised her arms again, placed one naked foot before the other. "When did you last sleep?"

Bart was fainting. He wiped his lips, considering. "I haven't *slept* in five years. I do, however, pass out every forty-eight hours. Regular as a church bell." He raised himself more properly. "Which is not yet. So we shall work."

"Will the King like your play?"

She needed to know if she should persist in her affiliation with Bartholomew. She'd miss him. But maybe she'd have to get by somehow without him. He could sink her. He had habits. Lilly distrusted, she *feared* habits. She caught an echo of her mother's voice; it had been lovely when she stroked Lilly's hair, singing her melody of woe. Her mother's name was Beth, and she had been something like the Earl: they were both beautiful; they both worked hard at killing themselves, especially when they had a chance for success. Like with his new play, if the theatres ever open (please, God, let the theatres open). Bart always drank harder when he had a good play.

Now he had to play the pimp. "Give me the Prologue."

She began his verse. Bartholomew spoke again and she stopped. But he insisted: say the lines despite me, concentrate, hear what I'm saying and ignore me at the same time. So she did, and while she delivered the lubricating verse, he instructed her: be easy with Charles, let him forget his passions and jealousies, never stir his anger, never pretend to be other than useful to his pleasures, but with hand, body, head, all the faculties you have, comply with his desire, let him enjoy new intrigues, help him to swive and screw anyone he chooses, smooth him and arrange for him and he will relieve us from punishment, if you do this well Lilly, but oh, Lilly, you must do this well.

54

Prince Rupert was a towering figure at the top of a flight of stone stairs. At his side stood a pair of greyhounds. He wore a silver fox cloak with pearl grey satin lining. It was so cold in his chambers, he could see his own breath. At his ankle, silk ribbons, the shade of imperfect pearls. His black curls descended past his shoulders, framing a long nose and jaw, his large and baleful eyes, his sorrowful face. Rupert was a man who'd been deeply exhausted for many years, and his face was expressive of a certain self-reproach, self-distaste.

Radisson and Des Groseilliers climbed toward him. The stairwell was adorned with instruments of war, some of them quite old. Slingshots, a bow and arrow, pikes, and new inventions, a small pistol designed by the Prince himself, a fine thing that made Des Groseilliers stop and give an involuntary, heartsick groan. Positioned at the top of the stairs, his head at a level with Rupert's feet and within breathing distance of the dogs, Des Groseilliers saw that the little gun was made of gold and that beside it sat a golden needle.

"You admire my pistol." Rupert said this in French. He moved to descend to where Des Groseilliers had paused, fourth step down, but the greyhounds startled, skating backward and shivering, so Rupert pointed down to the instrument. "The little gun will shoot the needle through a piece of oak three inches thick."

"Joli chose." Des Groseilliers's whisper echoed in the stone stairwell. He climbed the remaining steps. The greyhounds bristled. The Prince backed up. And Des Groseilliers saw the suite, a large portion of which was occupied by Rupert's laboratory, the walls hung with designs for ships, architectural drawings, a charcoal sketch of what appeared to be a hollow cannonball, which the Explorer would soon learn was a bomb that explodes in the earth, the Prince's invention. There were three large tables laden with the instruments for drafting and cartography, charts both celestial and nautical, a sundial, four quadrants, and a case of flutes. Near the window casements was a sleeping room partially enclosed by Turkish screens. The furniture was elegant, but the table legs and bedposts looked to have been chewed, and even now a young white spaniel lay under a table on her belly with her hind legs stretched behind her, gnawing on one of the carved lion's paws.

It was an unfortunate barrier to friendship for the Prince: his extraordinary height determined that he'd always look down his enormously sad nose (even, by an inch and one-half, to King Charles). He offered a view of a dimpled chin and a sensuous though disappointed mouth. What he saw of Des Groseilliers was a broad, round, cantankerous soldier of about his own age, with a lot of wiry grey hair falling around his shoulders. Radisson followed him, pushing himself into the suite.

Radisson alarmed the blue bitch greyhound, the Prince's favourite. She whipped her body against him, stinging him with her backside. Tattooed on her shoulder, initials, *H H Pr Ru*. She had a scar on her hindquarter. Prince Rupert cupped her muzzle; the animal's nerves rippled up through his arms. "Do you like to race hounds?" he asked. The two Explorers looked at him blankly, as if the language were incomprehensible, though Prince Rupert continued to address them in French. The Prince was accustomed to being answered, and he waited impassively.

The walls, draped in tapestry, radiated cold. Rupert, whose old head injury had made things nearly intolerable of late, had white lips, and he rubbed at the pain in his temple with purple fingertips.

The shadow of a rook flew across the Prince's chambers. Des Groseilliers's eyes followed it. The rooms were richly vestured, layer on layer, like a silk onion with nothing at its middle. Emptiness always inspired him. He wiped his hand over his face.

Prince Rupert hoped that he might cast off the tedious metrics of Court speech. He had the awkward emphasis of a large body, but, like his cousin Charles, he was an agile tennis player. A negro child appeared at the top of the stairs. Rupert seemed relieved and put his hand on the little boy's shoulder. "My nigger from Guinea," he said fondly, and ordered the child to bring chocolate.

The animals (four spaniels, a fallow-coloured buckhound, the two greyhounds) were skittish, their toenails clicking on the floor. Rupert became almost ferociously serious, though, when the boy presented the chocolate; he poured it himself, this domestic nicety somehow evidence of a broader masculinity. He was most at home — now that he was in his late forties and too badly injured to fight at sea — in his laboratory. He'd never had a mother tongue. When he was young this seemed to auger an infinitely various future, but he'd since learned to see infinity on its own terms.

Radisson touched a quadrant. "A fine instrument, Prince Rupert," he said.

"Made by a fellow in Wapping." Rupert answered in French with a very English termination.

"Ah."

Radisson glanced impatiently at Des Groseilliers. It is up to Médard, as the elder and contemporary of the Prince, to steer the conversation to the acquisition of a boat. "A very fine instrument," Radisson said again.

"Oui. C'est fin," said the Prince.

All afternoon the men clung to the occasion, each convinced that the goal was just around the next clumsy phrase. The Explorers would win a boat and provisions, Prince Rupert would win security for his investment. They were all navigating by instinct, filled with a sense of inadequacy for a loathsome task. The disease of conversation, foul business. But it would yield — what? A country, riches, freedom. The wonderful violence of freedom.

They drank too much chocolate, and when darkness fell, they were sickly agitated. The men paced, the greyhounds climbed on the bed or clattered with the boy up and down the stairs to piss outside. The Prince played with calipers, drawing intersecting spheres on the terrestrial globe. All around them, night pressed and swelled. Africa, the West Indies — they traced old voyages on Rupert's maps, crossing the shrunken pear of ocean between Europe and Asia. Trajectories like comet tails seemed to trail behind Rupert's hands.

"Barbados sugar," said Rupert, "requires we take slaves from Africa." The calipers drew an arc from the coast of Africa to the Barbados. "Our negro trade feeds the Barbados sugar trade, the blackamores providing labour for the plantations. *Now*, we will take the money from slaves and combine it with the money from sugar" — his hands pivoted, Des Groseilliers saw a string of quicksilver to the inchoate northern ocean, ahh — "to pay for ships to take furs from Hudson Bay." Another sphere; Rupert's hand connected the north sea to the Sea of Japan, the path of an ocean current like an eye or a fingerprint, the silk onion.

"It is nature's course," he said. "See it in the circulation of disease. The negro has brought us syphilis, but Africa also provides the plants to create the ointments to cure it. The Plague, also from a Dutch colony, and that is where we must go for its cure. It is as natural as breathing. Natural revolution."

He put down his calipers. "The money from Hudson Bay will pay for the passage to the Orient. To gold, rubies, pearls, all the riches of an ancient empire. Which will build us more ships. To take more slaves. Like so. A complete cosmology. Perfect unity."

Radisson had scarcely been listening; he'd been surging through his memories of a hunt, an Indian war, the revenge we take on the enemy tribe. He was deafened by his memories, but the words *Hudson Bay* crashed through, splintering the last of his patience; his excitement broached, spilled into English. "Good Prince!" he cried. He did not know how to proceed. He was in love! How dark it is outside! "We will bring you furs, so many you will have all the fur in that country. I promise you this and more!"

Des Groseilliers laughed angrily.

For the first time in that meeting Prince Rupert, too, spoke in English. "You have not told me, sufficient to my curiosity and my doubt of your intent, why you betray France."

"Because they are a pack of fools," whispered Des Groseilliers.

"The French are sick with greed," said Radisson.

"New France cannot survive," said Des Groseilliers.

"Oui. Too many priests," said Radisson. "The Jesuits keep out honest trade." He trembled. A nervous greyhound rose from where she had been sleeping and sniffed at his back.

Prince Rupert said, "Stay the night at Windsor." He ordered the black boy to warm beds for the Explorers and tell the kitchen to prepare a meal. Then he looked at Radisson as if it were a brave thing to do, a high act of conviviality. He said, "England is overcrowded. There are too many vagrants."

"Ah, oui. It is terrible!" said Radisson. "But I say to you, fair Prince, we give you a warm mainland, one not occupé like the

West Indies. You must only cut away the Dutch, cut out the French. Cut *especially* the French because they gain, even now, day by day, greater power in the New World. Prince Rupert. I know something of you. You are the orphan of the North."

Rupert was startled by vanity, by newly remembered affection for himself, the product of being — oh, rare event in this lonely world — accurately named. "I feel," he murmured, "a curious affinity for the cold."

Radisson was inspired, magically clairvoyant, the words coming from the black air. "Ah, oui! You! On the one hand, a Prince, lost and kicked out at birth, sneaked from the back door of the Bohemian Castle just after Prague was defenestrated and only a small breeze before the Parliament came like the hurricane to blow the Royal from the Rhine."

"I beg your pardon?" The Prince was almost afraid, startled by love.

"Pierre." A warning growl from Des Groseilliers.

"I go too far. I apologize."

Rupert was clearly embarrassed, mystified, and pleased. He began to speak, opened his mouth, closed it, bent stiffly over a recent map, his long hand caressing the froth of northern sea, the Passage to the Orient.

Seven

Lilly entered Meg's tavern and found Susan. "Can you do for me? Can I have a minute to myself before I start?" Susan smiled and blushed and said yes, "O' course."

Lilly went upstairs to the room she shared with Susan and Claire, but Claire had a fellow with her. Lilly opened the door because she didn't hear anything, and there they were, in bed. Skinny Claire, on her back, her stringy black hair, her bloodshot eye trained on the door, no expression, blanked out, the man striding her, pumping himself between her breasts, with his hand; he didn't make a sound, the cords of muscle and veins on his arm, Claire's hands gripping the mattress; he stroked himself so fast his fist hit her chest bones. Lilly backed out and quietly shut the door, but she waited and listened. Quiet ones like that are most dangerous. Stray dogs.

She went to wait at the end of the hall, looking back at the closed door. She'd eaten oysters that Bart had provided. She'd made herself chew carefully, though chewing hurt her teeth. To be awake to it, the viscid creature, the surge of food. She could still taste oyster liquor in her mouth. Sacs of juice. She'd been stupid to have considered herself safe. The admiration of the King, a few coins if the stage ever opens, Bart's erratic patronage — why had she thought she wouldn't end up like Claire, like Susan? *Devoured.*

She was evermore aware of the silence at the core of things, a deep hollow from which we shout our death chants, like the woman in the alley bleating over her dead husband. *My love, my love, my love!* Lilly refused to be ashamed of surviving. The door opened and the man came out, running his hands through his hair. The smell of him. Hate, blooming in Lilly's blood.

XXXXX

Bartholomew woke up with a black hand running over his face, an oily hand with long, tapered fingers. It was quite dark in his garret. He was on the floor, his head serving as a doorstop. His monkey, perched on his chest, was investigating Bart's nose. At some point in the lapsed interval (an hour, five hours, two days?), Jack had tried to force open the door against the Earl's unconscious body, then had given up and gone away. The monkey kneaded Bart's chest with its hind feet. Bart said, "Get off," and the monkey gave him a dirty look but climbed down, chittering.

On the other side of the door was a steep flight of stairs that ran down to the lane leading to Tower Street. Bart stood up, and finding himself to be attired in his dressing gown, he threw a cloak around his shoulders and flowed, he ran like liquid down the stairs, wondering when Lilly had left and if he could find her.

A freezing wind on Tower Street. Charlatans, astrologers, and Doctors of Physic hung out their signs, offering salvation from the Plague. A skeletal, nearly bald woman in a white nightgown wafted through the vendors, protected from cold and disease by a sandwich board slung over her shoulders, scrawled front and back with a charm:

```
ABRACADABRA
ABRACADABR
ABRACADAB
ABRACADA
ABRACAD
ABRACA
ABRAC
ABRA
ABR
AB
A
```

Bizarre spells were best. Street vendors sold salves, incense, charms, half a crown, and many were willing to pay that and more, though they'd have no money left for food.

Bartholomew lurched elegantly through a crowd of citizens soaked in vinegar (a sure prophylactic), Tower Street's red-eyed, stinking offal. The individual, Bart thought, is a vile joke. A seething insect life. Each leg of the centipede wants to be immortal, each person seeking the delusion of a *soul*. Five hundred thousand centipedes feeding on the skin, on the scum that forms on the driving force, an appetite for heat and air. How he envied those who do not see this.

The Earl's gold ochre cloak was draped around a violet dressing gown and a rather simple white shirt with voluminous sleeves. Even after his dead-drunk sleep his hair spiralled into place. He surprised people with the light that shone from him, with his slurred waltz. He was different from other courtiers: he had a lighter touch and his immoral attitude seemed innocently wounded. When people looked at him, they often remarked that he wasn't a man who would live long. He was a familiar sight here. Tower Street and the theatre, these were his places of worship.

Potato peelings, rotting turnips, black cabbage, and excrement of every kind, dog, human, horse, raked into corners to bed the vagrants, decay and steam mixed with coal and wood smoke. Bart felt extremely well. The crowd's yellow faces opened around him like a field of sunflowers, a field of sunflowers rooted in shit.

It had snowed, and now the sun had dropped with that suddenness peculiar to London. Unlike most of the city, grieving and terrified and dark, Tower Street was lit up for the night. He saw the torches reflected in melting ice, each bright flame. A roan horse walking loose down the street, flesh-pink patches on grimy stone, people with their bird-flight motivations.

From a coffeehouse, wearing a cape of watered black silk lined with black mink, his narrow legs in black stockings, Lord Metcalf appeared. Bartholomew had the impression of Soby suspended by his patent heels, floating through the vapours. Soby's long, narrow muzzle pointed at Bart, the lips drawn back in greeting. "Buxborough, my darling sin, how fortunate to find you. Get me the girl tonight, dear, or I'll be vexed. Vexed, dear. Fetch the little actress. Haven't I been patient?"

Soby draped his arm about Bartholomew's shoulder, drew him, purring, "Do you think I'm soft? It's because I love you, Buxborough. But get the little cunt now, that's enough." Soby watched him.

Bartholomew said he would, but Lilly had been ill.

"Cunning bitch," said Soby. "I'll take my chances. Tell her to come tonight or I am not answerable."

Bartholomew slid away from Soby and swayed to the side.

On a bale of flax straw beside a small bonfire outside the Dog and Bitch sat a hunchback playing a violin. Bart flung himself on the man, pressed his cheek with kisses, tasting grease and salt, caressed the deformity and whispered in his ear, "All men must embrace their disease." He peered into the hunchback's eyes, and what he saw was the fine film of disbelief that shields the human race; the disqualification of a man's own circumstance lets him live. "Play, Your Honour! I demand that you play!" Maybe music would distract Soby. "Let down your dulcet tone!"

They attracted a crowd. They were well known here, the merry gang, the Court Wits. Among the crowd were a half-dozen shabby soldiers, starved and drunk. They'd come home from the War to find London infested with Cromwell's Roundheads, who'd got off, with those few grisly exceptions, scot-free, pardoned and advanced to positions of Secretary at Whitehall. In fact there was one here now on Tower Street, a Puritan spy who looked like Cromwell himself, a square-rigged blockhead, a blond mass of scruples so clean-shaven his skin flaked.

The soldiers knew the Puritan was here, they expected him to be prowling around. The habit of spying — more, the habit of being spied on — had been grafted onto Englishmen and it would never wash away.

"Play, Your Honour!" Bartholomew wrapped himself around the hunchback, lunging for the violin, which of course the man would protect with his life. Bart snatched the bow from his hands and the bow became a sword. He shouted, "Play! I insist, Your Lordship!" The soldiers urged him to beat the cripple. A hand moved eagerly to touch the Earl's glossy gown while Soby rippled with furious laughter and cried out in his thin voice, "Will you refuse him, fiddler? Do you dare?"

The fiddler was unafraid. He was calm, fatalistic, wanted his bow back.

Soby shouted, "Play! Or perish! Play or I'll cut off your ears!"

Bartholomew came between them. "I apologize for my unruly friend. Lord Metcalf's love of music exceeds reason." He offered the bow, withdrew it. "But satisfy his passion, I beg you. Play!"

From the Puritan came a low, swelling voice: "Pimp. Whore-monger. Whoremonger for the King."

The Puritan planted himself before them, a big, trembling man with tears of outrage in his eyes. He knew that he'd risked his own life. But his doomed protest aroused the crowd's bewildered sympathy, and they turned uncertainly to the Earl.

The liquor peaked in Bart's veins and retired, left him dry. The fiddler's deformity seemed refined, even purposeful, compared with Bartholomew's ornamental self. He hesitated.

The Puritan called the watch, who came promptly, armed with a bloodstained staff. With the appearance of the burly watch, the audience feigned boredom or industry; a squabble wasn't worth a broken head. The hunchback sneaked away to the gloom of the alley beside the Dog and Bitch, but he stayed in the shadows, unable to escape because the Earl had retained his bow.

Bartholomew smiled at the watch and said, "We love music."

The watch called out, "Humpback! Play an' ye'll eat tonight!"

"Come, gentle monster," said Bartholomew. "See? I return your weapon that you might slay me with your tune. Come, come out from shade, that's it, that's right, play the nightshade, pretty bat, that's a man, see him with his dirty hand, 'tis a sunny night, a humpback knight, Sir Lurch and Snatch. Ah."

The fiddler, prodded by the watch and under the scowling gaze of the Puritan, played. Played beautifully.

Bartholomew listened, removed and shadowed. The fiddler had chosen a folk melody, forming it slow and broad, refined beyond the tastes of Tower Street.

Soby was too drunk to hear the musician's integrity, but he knew that the fiddler mocked them by playing so well. "You'll pay respect, triple tripe. Pay respect!" He made as if to strike him with the flat of his sword.

The watch put a hand on the fiddler's shoulder and said to the Earl, "You owe him a sovereign, m'Lord. You know he's earned such."

"He has no money but from his pimping," said the Puritan.

"I'll not pay." Bartholomew turned his back on them. He had no money. He must have wine.

"We'll not pay the cripple. We did not like the music!" Soby had a frightened young woman under his arm while he swung his sword at the fiddler. The crowd, the hungry soldiers, drifted forward again, eager to see blood.

"Someone must pay, and let's be off," said the watch.

"We'll not pay! Damn you, hound's face." Soby pushed the girl away and snatched the bow from the fiddler. Now he was armed with sword and bow.

Bartholomew must have drink, his throat almost closed in anticipation, he will swallow wine, he wanted to swallow.

Soby flourished the bow at the fiddler, then thrust it at the fiddler's throat. The fiddler jerked his head away. Soby thrust again, aiming high, at the face; the bow swiped the fiddler's cheek and found his eye. Soby's wig slipped and he stumbled forward. The bow thrust deep, broke through, then farther. The fiddler's knees buckled and he fell, pulling the bow from Soby's hand till it was upright, planted in the fiddler's head, and then the body twisted and the bow dislodged and clattered to the ground.

A stunned, wary pause. The crowd vanished. Soby dissolved into vapour. The watch recovered sufficiently to look about. Bartholomew, too, was far distant, a dark plum, thirsting for oblivion. And trailing him, the Puritan, in a freezing rage.

Eight

When Des Groseilliers came down to breakfast, he found
Radisson seated in bars of light like the tines of an enormous
fork. Radisson was at a very long table in a very long hall with
tall, narrow windows, a style in that luxury of civilization that
lets men do away with the earlier function of defence while
keeping, celebrating its aesthetic. The proportions were so
immense, Des Groseilliers lost his balance and made a crooked
path down the hall's deep pink carpet toward his brother-in-law,
who was eating yet seemed about to be eaten.

Radisson chewed the fat from a rib. He raised one eye to Des
Groseilliers and indicated with an expressive nod that the food
is good and Des Groseilliers must sit down. The hall was so
quiet that Des Groseilliers heard the rip of tissue, the small
plucking sound of Radisson's fingers. He felt excited for a
moment, or it may have been only the memory of excitement
stimulated by the smell of roasted meat, an updraft of nostalgia.
Then dread reasserted itself. The Prince soon would be present
and *conversation* would resume. Today, they must win the
commitment of a boat. Des Groseilliers ate. A warrior must eat.
"Damn English!" Des Groseilliers said aloud. Radisson
understood this impatience, but, he thought, it matters not at
all, we must eat.

Prince Rupert appeared at the far end of the hall. Both men sensed him at once, put down their ribs, and stood, Radisson wiping his fingers across his britches. The Prince shyly pulled out a chair and with a small wave of his hand bade them be seated. He spoke so softly they had to lean to hear him.

Rupert took some herring and onion on his plate and ate with solemn measure, his wide mouth casually taking the food. Des Groseilliers felt the foreignness of this man, the strange northern pickled fishiness, and the way hunger and appetite were a matter of choice for him. The Prince's hand on the fork, like his hand on the map, would never be swayed by desperation. He was so long everywhere and his heavy eye seemed never to have expected anything more than disappointment. For some time, the three men continued to eat without speaking.

Radisson could be patient, but Des Groseilliers was litigious. Argument — what other purpose is conceivable for this armoury of words, words! Silver spoons and porcelain, carpets and painted ceilings, patterns upon patterns upon patterns! To battle! Even a paltry battle of words is better than effeminate mewlings. Let there be war, for in conflict there might be — if not truth, then what? *Life* is in conflict. Des Groseilliers gave way to an involuntary curse. "Vierge! Laitière!" He'd spoken aloud.

Prince Rupert looked up from his herring as if awoken from a dissatisfying sleep. He put down his fork, gazed out the narrow windows at the bright, cold day. He wasn't alarmed. He was never alarmed (except by disgrace). He blinked slowly, sad and handsome. Gently, he said in French, "Peace is indeed a prison." He was almost embarrassed by his great enjoyment of the Explorers' company. He wanted to prolong it. Besides, he didn't know how to get the money for the Voyage, as they obviously hoped he would. Quelling a sense of fraudulence, he said in English, "Gentlemen. I suggest that we join this morning's hunt."

Radisson and Des Groseilliers were confused. What game could this land yield? Is there anything left but chicken? But they agreed, of course, and without further comment, rose to the hunt.

✗✗✗✗✗

They left the hall with great purpose, fixed to the goal of killing fine animals. Radisson and his brother-in-law, skilled hunters, bowed to the Prince, who bowed to each in turn and showed them to the immense doors leading to the stable. When the two Frenchmen turned around to await their royal host, that good man was gone.

"This happens all the time," whispered Des Groseilliers in fury. "The English say, 'Now we will do some great thing.' We tell them we are ready to go, fight, hunt, what they like, but what do we do instead?" He glared about the yard. "We wait."

"The good Prince is preparing the men for the big hunt," offered Radisson.

Des Groseilliers spat. A thin crust of frost on the horse dung slowly thawed into bits of amber flake. There wasn't even a stable boy or groom to cheer them with preparations for the hunt. The castle yards were deserted. The castle itself seemed not to have been altered since the days of William the Conqueror. The day was getting dusky, cloud moving in. Then they saw an inconspicuous door open in the stone wall and let out a tall man wearing a pearl grey riding suit with a black helmet, like a hero of a past age. It was the Prince.

Rupert approached. The yard was silent, and the empty courtyard offered only an icy breeze across colourless air. Prince Rupert looked down at his boots, then, with a flick of impatience, he said, "Tsk." And everything exploded into sound.

The stable doors were drawn back, two grooms shouted

orders to the boys struggling with three rearing horses. A great baying echoed from the kennel behind them. Radisson turned to see the huntsman, his costume also of pearl grey, break out five couples of hounds, shouting at them and leashing them in. From the stable the horses surged into a high canter as the wind took them up from the frail hands of the stable boys. The Prince steadied his horse, easily fit his left foot into the stirrup and lifted himself up into the saddle of the tallest mare. Then, it seemed as if without any further movement of his own, he settled the horse to a four-square pace.

Radisson and Des Groseilliers each took a bridle. When the other riders, with perhaps thirty horses and as many yellow bloodhounds, appeared in the yard, their excited mounts spun from the stirrup, yet they leapt into the saddle. Radisson, in moccasins, knew his stirrups were too long, but he'd grip the horse with his knees and make him fly. His horse reared; he pulled down and to the right on the reins and the black mare was forced to spin, spinning while Des Groseilliers and Rupert set out with the baying hounds and the brass horns through the great gates to the Saxon woods. Radisson hurriedly kicked his steed to follow.

For two hours, they tracked their game through forest covert, Radisson urging his mare to overtake the hounds. The Prince's aged servant leaned from his own horse, to touch Radisson, to warn him, his accent so broad that Radisson couldn't believe it was English. "Let the 'ounds be thy mark, m'Looord," said the old man.

Radisson reined in. "We must teach the Prince how to hunt!" he cried. "The dogs will scare away the stag!"

"Stag! Stag, d'ye say?" The old man let go a laugh. "We're efter Lady Rufus, yer 'onour. An' she's a fox!"

"A fox!" These English are more stupid than I thought. To have a fox you must be quiet and set a trap. Then he saw her, the red coat running out of the forest to the gorse. The servant bolted, jumped a fallen tree, then a fence. Radisson's horse followed, winded. Out in the open now the hunting party zigzagged up a hill, grassy under a thin layer of snow. The hounds' tails like yellow snakes, their frantic baying, the horns' short, running blasts, "Tally-ho!" The pack closed in on the vixen, the huntsman soon on them. There was something wrong with Radisson's horse. Lame! He could not ride a lame horse! He dismounted, spraining his ankle when he jumped.

The pain was unbearable. How could an injury incurred in an idiotic game be so acute? Together, horse and rider limped across the furzy, snowy field in the direction of the hunting party, a great distance marked by agony.

Des Groseilliers was lifting the flask to his lips when he spied his brother-in-law approaching in misery. A band of servants was roused and the fallen hunter was carried to camp. He was made to rest, to warm himself and drink the proffered brandy. The Prince presented him with a prize: the fox head, which they call the mask. Radisson received it with feigned goodwill made possible by a quantity of brandy.

Like many a man whose own triumphs in the field blind him to the resentment of his companions, so did Prince Rupert mistake the Frenchmen's false enthusiasms for true. The short day passed, night was nigh, the Prince ordered his servants to build up the fire and prepare an evening meal on the spot, with torches made ready to guide them all to the castle when they'd had their fill of food and drink. The richness of his costume fed on firelight, and Prince Rupert seemed almost an incandescent giant. Protected from the wind by a hedgerow, he bade his companions rest and partake of the chops as they were roasted over the flames.

From where he crouched across the fire, Des Groseilliers studied the Prince in his pride. He whispered, "I see you as you were, when you did fight the rebel army for your liege. I have heard the tales. You were called Devil Robert, oui? And you dressed in many disguises to ride among your enemy."

Prince Rupert put down his lamb chop and looked through the flames into the eyes of Des Groseilliers. His sad eyes were full of trust for a comrade-in-arms.

Des Groseilliers leaned forward on his haunches. He liked the Prince, but he knew damn well that Rupert was dallying with them. "It is said you dressed as a woman and rode through the enemy lines this way."

Prince Rupert flinched. He tried to remember. It would be unusual to forget doing such a thing, and he instinctively trusted the word of a hunting companion. Still — no such thing took place. Is this Frenchman joking?

Radisson was drinking very much brandy to ease the terrible pain in his ankle. The fox mask was laid by the fire. He prodded it with his foot. "Prince Rupert," he said, "in the New World you would find such wonder, you would not desire to return to England, so dull it would seem. Even Ja-pan cannot offer such great wonders to your eyes." Radisson was a nurse trying to encourage an exhausted mother to suckle an ugly newborn. "No place on earth will give you more mystère and richesse. I myself have seen near the land of the Iroquois an animal that resembles a horse but has the cloven hoof. Oui. The cloven hoof and shaggy mane, a tail like that of the wild hog. With black eyes and a horn that poke out of his head. There, in the gloomiest wilderness are found these creatures."

Des Groseilliers whispered, "You never saw such a thing, Pierre."

"I do not say I saw; I say I heard that men saw. You must listen. This animal, in the dark forest of Canada, is very shy. The male he never feeds with the female. Except when they must" — Radisson knit his hands before him — "join for the

73

purpose of increase. Then, they put aside their férocité. But when the rutting season is over, pfft, they do not go one with the other again."

Prince Rupert asked mildly, "A horn, do you say, Monsieur Radisson? From its head, a single horn?"

"Oui, that is correct. One wild man, he tell me he saw the creature run her horn straight into a tree. Five feet long it was. He could not get dat horn out. He try to eat dat 'orse meat, but he cannot. And the skin is too 'eavy to carry so the t'ing mus' be lef' behind, everyt'ing, hide and horn. They lef' dat t'ing in dat dark forêt foncé."

His accent had thickened. Des Groseilliers quietly cursed. The three hunters gazed into the fire. A sickle moon ascended in the blue western sky. The Prince pulled himself to his feet. He could not delay these dreamers any longer; they had started to play with him. How will he raise the money for the Voyage? "Well," he said, resolute, "we will start back."

Nine

It started out all right, at least for the first half-hour. The men were maudlin, slobbering over each other, smacking and singing, filling their brains like bladders. They crowded around the tables, making it hard to swing the ale. And Lilly thought, They hate me, hate Claire, simply because they love each other.

Lilly had seen Claire come out from their bedroom, furtive, ashamed. She'd come to Lilly and let her hold her. It was like holding a bird, so fragile, trembling. They rocked each other, Lilly remembering the song her mother sang to make her sleep. *"Black is the colour of my true love's hair, His face as soft and wondrous fair . . ."* Claire got shy, pulled away, wiped her eyes, and said, "Not so wondrous, was he."

"No. He was a dog."

Claire gave a sad laugh. "Ugly every which way."

Meg said things were different from before. "Before what?" Claire asked, downstairs now to serve. She chewed on a strand of her hair and winced when the tray hit the bruise on her chest. Her bones were so brittle, she once broke her leg tripping on the stairs while half dragging a drunken fellow up to bed, and she finished the task before asking Meg to get a physician. Wiry Claire pretended she expected it vicious, but behind her gloomy aspect she couldn't hide the hope that things were once different, not as mean. Meg said it was so. Meg said, once, men and women were friends. They didn't call us whore then.

"What'd they call us?" Claire wanted to know.

"Claire, ye idjit. They called ye by yer name. Holy mother, ye're dim." Meg smacked Claire's skinny behind. "Put on some fat, princess." Handed her some bread and beef juice.

Claire batted her eyes, gratefully sat to eat, and asked, "What'd we do fer money then?"

Meg ran a rag over the table. "Was no money then," she said.

"No money?"

"Furthermore, if we didn't like their one-eyed wonder, we could say, No, Joe, it's not fer me. When it weren't to our liking, we'd say, Take it away, Joe. Thank ye, Claire, they'd say. Thank ye fer bein' so nice to roger, ye beautiful girl."

Claire laughed hard at this. She laughed as if she were hearing a story about herself as a baby, a fairy time when hands were gentle and she was loved.

Lilly had had a glimpse of what Meg said. Once or twice at the tavern, she saw the ruddy faces of Hal, Joe, or Jack look — for an instant — like a tissue filled with life. A few times, she'd met men who took an interest in a woman's comfort (Lilly didn't say "pleasure," an obscenity). For those small moments men and women could be mistaken for similar animals. She'd since used that onstage — it helped to have seen something mutual with men.

Today, they were drinking hard. Early, a soldier with purple veins showing on his bald skull, blue-eyed, northern, squeezed Lilly's breast, a brutal grip as if he'd tear it off. She was brushing past his table when this happened, with a mug in each hand. Her arms flew up, spraying the air with beer, dousing this pike-holder, this guardsman, son of a guardsman, he of the long lineage of royal defenders, out of work, having inherited nothing from his father but a weak liver. The beer had splashed his face, so he hit Lilly with the meaty flat of his hand.

He climbed on top of her. Everybody moved out of the way. Lilly made herself relax, forced herself to go still, to breathe and listen. He put his knee between her legs, held her by her hair, and pushed hard till she was arched up to him. He smiled, and he said, "Lick me." She did; she licked his chin. He said, "More." His voice was shaky with hate. She licked his face. "Say, I love thee, and lick my face like that." "I love thee." She licked his face. She breathed. "Say, I love yer cock." "I love yer cock." "Say, I love yer cock an' the way ye *hurt* me, ye stupit cunt." He yanked on her hair and kicked his knee into her. "Say it." "I love the hurt," said Lilly. The pain brought tears to her eyes. She breathed. He laughed and let her up. Lilly watched him. He was trembling more than she was.

Lilly couldn't get rid of the pike-holder's taste. It went into her nose so everything tasted and smelled like him, like burnt toast. She drank some beer to clean her tongue, but it made her sick and she put it back on the table. The barkeep nudged her, drink up. He'd never been kind before; Lilly figured that her injury appealed to him.

The barkeep was a grudging type, but he'd act as if he'd help you if he saw damage, till you got back up. Sitting down like a regular customer, Lilly knew she was in for one of the odious tales he insisted on telling. The only sex he knew was a dirty joke.

The barkeep didn't like the pike-holders. He was critical of Meg over her management of the tavern, believed that Meg had let the ruffians take over. He pointed to the inn at Newmarket as an example fit to follow, where the finest women in England could be had. "The Royals go there." he said. "In disguise. An' the husbints in the neighbourhood come with their wives and get so drunk, the Royals can tumble their women without constraint. Now," said the barkeep, warming to a tale, "one night, a rich old man comes late to the inn. He's marrit to a very pretty girl who's always left at home so's no one can steal her. But one gentleman, an earl, he likes the challenge, doesn't he. The earl plies the old man with liquor till he falls down, dead drunk. Then the earl goes to the old man's house and he knocks on her door, and the girl lets him in. She feigns shy first, then she complains that her husbint's too old so he hides her at home. And quick as you please, the earl has her." The barkeep laughed. "She's so grateful, she breaks open her husbint's safe and steals all his money. Then, the earl brings her back to the inn. On the way to the inn, who do they see but the old man wending his way back home. The earl and the wench hide behind a hedge and he has her again right as her husbint passes by. At the inn, the court gentleman have her, too. Then they send her out of doors. Go to London, they tell her. Find yourself another husbint."

The barkeep laughed. Lilly said, "So did she?"

A trace of fear on the barkeep's face. As if to an idiot: "Did she what?"

"Find another husband. How's it end?"

The barkeep took her glass and pitched the beer into a bucket.

"That's a quaint tale, Henry." Lilly looked at him wide-eyed.

The remains of the joke pressed up against Henry's palate. "When the old man finds his wife and money gone, he hangs himself from a beam." He laughed again, his mirthless eye uneasily on Lilly. He didn't even find his own stupid story very funny. His laugh didn't go down his throat. He was rangy. There was no room in his body for laughter. He looked, Lilly thought, like a walking roger. All the weight was in the head.

Ten

Charles listened implacably, playing with the paws of the spaniel on his lap. When the Puritan had emptied his tale of Bartholomew's incident on Tower Street, and after several depleted moments, Charles said, "You argue that Lord Metcalf and the Earl of Buxborough pose accountable for a street brawl between Tower Street citizens and a diseased fiddler."

"Lord Metcalf committed a murder."

"So you say."

"The Earl of Buxborough instigated the shameful altercation. After that, he fled into the night. He ran away."

King Charles barely flinched. (That he did flinch, only Sir George Rose would notice.) "Pretty one," said Charles to the spaniel, and he stroked the silky coat. He did not look again at the Puritan.

The Puritan understood that he was dismissed. He shouldn't have been surprised, yet he was — stunned — to discover his righteousness outshone by the King's radiant skepticism.

Sir George cleared his throat. "You are aware, Pilgrim, that slandering a Peer is punishable by the loss of one's ears and a night in the pillory."

"I slander no one," said the Puritan. "I speak the truth."

"Rancorous and low."

"There has been a murder."

"That is not our concern." Rose waved to a footman, and without further ado, the Puritan was ushered out.

When he was gone, Charles abruptly stood, sliding the dog to the floor. The Puritan's manner, his evocation of Truth, reminded him of the Scottish Covenanters in the most dismal season of his youth, the year after Father was decapitated. A year of grief and rain. Endless sermonizing, foggy women, dirty linen, oatmeal in the whisky. Insinuating themselves with their bullying cant until he was made nearly impotent by cold and by blackmail. Damn Bartholomew for trailing Cromwell's shades into our chamber. And something else: the picture of the Earl slinking away from a murder. To Sir George, Charles smiled and said, "The matter rests."

Rose's cheeks, framed by silver love-locks set above a cascading jabot, puffed and blew. "The matter," he said in a voice so neutral it could only convey a definite bias, "will come up before the Commons. The Lords shall need to step in."

"So they shall." Damn. He should have extinguished every Puritan. Hanged them all beside Cromwell's exhumed corpse. Now he'd be subjected to a petition from Soby's fellow Peers, in this particular case a constituency of fops as loose in the bowels as the Puritans are constipated.

Young Bartholomew had gone too far again. Send him to Hudson Bay, damn his eyes. Puritans, Presbyters, it all has the same old lurching stink of piety. Charles recalled the scent of shame over Montrose, faithful Montrose, executed by the Scots, his head on a pike in Edinburgh, his hands nailed to the Tolbooth at Aberdeen. Charles saw the withered blue hands, like a huge moth, that terrible summer. Montrose died for the greater glory. So it goes.

Sir George Rose sensed the royal despond, and his irritation with the Earl grew into hatred. He'd been a privateer in Charles's father's navy in the War, where he'd gained a reputation for personally throwing mutineers overboard, and his treasures from Morocco, capitalized many times over, had been keeping the Royal Navy afloat ever since. He'd resisted the wooing of the Parliamentarians and, instead, had designed and commanded a fleet of fast galleys to pirate Cromwell's supply ships. Then he'd sold the goods to France and had given most of the money to the exiled court in exchange for a great deal of prime Crown land handed over to him on the Restoration. Now he was a Privy Councillor and an MP and perhaps the richest man in England. Charles had spent many years prying money out of Sir George Rose. Rose was a fiercely loyal monarchist, but it was the monarchy as idea that appealed to him, whereas the monarch before him made him queasy with fears of bankruptcy and damnation. He did not like having to "cheer up" the King.

His mouth a tightly peevish line, Sir Rose dutifully tried for a light tone. "This matter shall not be in currency long. Look at what happened with that clerk, Curr, or Carr." Carr was clerk to a troop of Life Guards who refused to pay Soby, Lord Metcalf, two thousand pounds above the regular fee. Soby assaulted Carr's wife and children, and Carr went straight to the Commons. The Lords stepped in then. Fined Carr a thousand pounds, set him in the stocks, jailed him, burned his petition. "The peers shall take care of this matter. It will go no further."

Charles thought, Yes and no. It might dissipate now, but it will never go away.

"As for the Earl of Buxborough, it is naught but a poet's peccadillo." Rose hated poets.

"We have heard you, Sir George."

Thus the matter would be formally retired. Yet, yet the image remained: Bartholomew scurrying into the night.

The most sordid alleys of London can be transfigured by a single strand of a poet's hair. But if the poet is seen to be craven — more — if the poet is *truly* craven, the very wit who serves as Gentleman of my Bedchamber, this beautiful young man whom I have loved, who has — let's be honest — who has pre-empted us in bed with the sweet punk, the little Lilly — a golden-haired man, a libellous, satirizing monkey. Bart. I have loved him like a son. But if he proves base, we shall put him out.

And so it came to pass that the King ordered Huntington's players to appear at the palace that very night to perform Bartholomew's new play. If the play proved bad, if Lilly's performance fell short, King Charles would send them to sea, let them search for China with the French Explorers, indeed he would (and while he was inspired by nothing but pique, it had grown darker, become a more sombre pique).

Eleven

At ten o'clock, when Susan came downstairs, she discovered Huntington, manager of the King's Playhouse, in his red, tasselled fez and dirty red slippers, impatiently banging his fist on Meg's front door, though he could have come inside through the tavern. Susan went looking for Lilly. "Huntington's here," she said.

"Why?" Lilly felt a flash of hope, almost painful, like heat on frozen flesh.

Susan was picked by another fellow. Her rash flared brightly. Over her shoulder, as if throwing Lilly flowers, she said, "To go to Church!" And winked. Good Susan, heart of butter.

Meg said no, Lilly can't go, but Huntington glowered, It's for the King, and Meg backed off — she had to — but she gave Lilly one odd look. Lilly saw the resemblance to her mother in Meg. She kissed Meg quickly and ran.

Outside, Huntington sniffed her — "Clean enough" — making a sick face. Lilly's face ached from her temple to her jaw. Huntington saw the bruise, grunted, considering whether she was too spoilt, and then set off, trotting like a Shetland in a sweat. Lilly asked why do they have to walk? He raised his eyebrows. "Duchess Punk, know thy place." Through darkness, Lilly followed the sound of his slippers wheezing over the knucklestone.

They made the Playhouse. He lit a candle in the tiring room, threw a bundle of costumes into her arms, then shoved her back out to the street. Now they were rushing with their arms laden, toward Charing Cross. It was not to be at the Playhouse then; they were moving toward the palace. Lilly felt strong as a mare in harness; she could sleigh Huntington on his fat buttocks. Across Spring Garden, Whitehall was dark. Then a light at the gate. They were hurried inside, led by torch down a gallery to a hall and abandoned there without light.

Judging by the echo, the hall was very great. Cold as only stone will be. They stood in pitch black. Now and then Lilly said, "Huntington?" "Here," he said. Huntington was a good actor; he had the talent for staying calm, so calm the cold couldn't affect him, a toad in winter marsh. One by one, the rest of the company was led to the hall, where they got a look at one another before the torch was withdrawn again. Now there were thirteen. A skilful company of actors: all slowed even their own heartbeat and waited.

It was an hour before the light came back. Lilly had almost lost control. When the torch flared and lit the faces of her fellow players, relief gladdened their white faces. A play! At last, they were to do a play! They felt risen from the dead. They set to work.

XXXXX

Bartholomew didn't know that the company was presenting his new play to the King. It had been arranged and would occur without his knowing, a ghostly phenomenon because he was feeling so strange and so dead. If he'd known, he might have withdrawn it, the play. He didn't believe in the furious freedom so boasted by its inevitable rake. His witty, arch, caustic vision was a foaming sham. It was fast becoming impossible not to care about things. Having cared too little in the past, now he cared too much.

He was haunted by the death of the fiddler. He had confirmed himself unworthy, and he clung to his old belief that *everything* is unworthy, that it's a weakness to let anything trouble him, any feeble move made by man. He now knew that he wasn't strong enough for his own philosophy. He descended into the spirals of obsession. The hunchback's music didn't fade but resounded over the cries of gulls in the refuse, carts in the street.

The air smelled of mud and fish. He walked toward the Playhouse. At his back, a howling want, a wave of vacancy engulfed him, pushing him toward Drury Lane on a cold, full flood. Drink was like midnight; it ticked upright and cured him of himself, then ticked past again into need.

At the closed doors of the theatre, Bartholomew fell to his knees. He put his mouth against the door, his tongue to the lock, and left the vapour of his breath there, a white *O*.

XXXXX

It was at a conference with the Lord Treasurer and Sir George Rose, along with the Duke of Albemarle, Lord Bunkard, and Sir Harvy, that the naval secretary, James Hale, had painted such a dire picture of the King's condition for money for the navy that everyone had thrown his hands in the air and said, "What shall we do?" The implication being, "Why did the people loan so much to Oliver Cromwell when they loan so little to Charles Stuart?" Sir George glowered at Charles. Like many rich men, he couldn't comprehend insolvency. The King had blithely turned his back and let drop the news that his players were presently preparing a play, now that the Plague had cooled and the Puritans were nullified, a new comedy by the Earl of Buxborough, with Lilly Cole.

At the mention of a play composed by the scoundrel Bux-borough, with pretty Lilly Cole in character, James Hale had shuddered violently and splotched a moth stain of ink on an otherwise clean ledger.

> 22 tunns of beere for 32 men for 7 mo. at 28 dayes
>   to the month &
> <u>5</u> tunns more for 17 men for 3 mo. in all
> <u>27</u> tunns of beere at 3 quartes a man p. diem

Splattered and rived by the quill. A blob. Hale wouldn't sleep for two fretful, flatulent nights. Two days later, he'd rise at four in the morning and recopy the ledger.

James Hale was pragmatic and unfanatical. Under Cromwell, he'd affected the transparency essential for a man to prosper in a spy-ridden State, blandly adopting the prescriptions of the Puritan military regime. Of course he'd been through his radical phase: in his youth, he'd been a great Roundhead, enthusiastically, at thirteen years of age, witnessing the beheading of Charles's father and declaring that "the memory of the wicked shall rot." As he matured, he'd exchanged grand causes for one private one; at this moment he was worth a figure that he wouldn't tell his wife.

Huntington lit the candles preparatory to the performance. Each gentleman shrank into his collar, blushed, and avoided the others' eyes, yet they were hooked there, wriggling, impaled by a lust for show.

Puritan shame hadn't been effaced by the Restoration's lace and rouge, not among most of the solid Londoners. It was home to stay. Affixed to profit. Sir George Rose ordered coffee, his breathing tight and shallow. It was not only God at his back; he was stiff with misgivings, an intuition that his mercantile ventures were at odds with such "licentious" (he lisped on *s*'s) poetry as flows from the dissolute poet.

Outside in the dark garden, a trace of snow melted and revived the lawn into a vivid green; when the cloud withdrew, it showed a sky littered with stars. At last, King Charles removed himself from Lady Castlemaine's apartments, strode across the garden and into the light of the long gallery, nodded affably to his guests, and took his seat.

It was the best thing that Bartholomew had ever written. It was better than any play since Marlowe. That is, Charles thought, it is the most corrosive. The man has the courage to reject that moralizing equilibrium of Shakespeare, or what the current fools make of Shakespeare. Bart had let go of the tailing rope, that nautical measure of a ship's speed. This play has no measure, it sails in the dark. It is a play without — he searched — without ground. A rootless, beautiful black nightshade. Deadly. And taunting death.

It was weird to perform a play at night. It needed too much candlelight; the double-burners would set their skirts on fire. Though it was the first performance, Lilly knew her role so thoroughly, she could extend it, delay this line, take that line early; she *played*. But nothing could have prepared her for the thing in its entirety. In private repetition with Bartholomew, the role had been a delicious vehicle. Now, in performance (they'd had no rehearsal with the entire cast but had learned their roles separately), she was one leg of an insect life, and in her words there were shades of intention far beyond her immediate control. She spoke, she smiled, turned, smirked, her bruised face masked by grease paint. But Bartholomew's stark, bright vision was unbearable, it scalded, it filled her with loneliness. It had lost the last shred, the final glimpse of the congenial, bawdy mirth that Lilly had glimpsed so rarely, so fleetingly.

Lilly had earned the affection of most of the players because she knew that, onstage, listening is more important than speaking. She didn't wallow. But tonight nobody heard a thing before their own cues; everybody was only five words ahead. No one was willing to stand upstage, and they faced the King like bloody Romans. Yet the thing tripped forward.

The audience didn't cough, didn't move a finger. The actors listened to the drop of the lines, to the perfect cadence, to the word like a ship sailing tight to the wind, tacking on the breath, the accents of Town, meanly Town. They had to laugh. Wit is viciously true, quick as a weasel's tooth. The Princess and Prince (Lilly played the Princess against Mr. Shift's surprisingly credible Prince), the upper frame, were burnt to ash, as if they'd sucked poison from snakebite. The virginal Princess was not wise; she revealed just enough self-delusion to make her responsible for her own fate. There were no heroes, no heroes but a singular, unhappy victor, the false rake (played by Chesterton, who seemed to grow more sober, to gain gravitas with each passing scene), the seducer winning feint upon feint, like a bird crashing through the windows of the hothouse. The rake didn't pledge to love the sincere Princess sincerely; he refused to renounce his stoic and thorough disbelief in everything (everything, that is, but power for its own sake). He thieved the play, ripped it open, and the blushing Lords swooned for him, and no one would sleep lawfully tonight, there would be spanking.

Charles was alert. The play fed and, paradoxically, gnawed on his growing pessimism. Like it or no: it is new. And as such, new, he thought, there will be those who will cringe and fawn for it, crushed by the thrust, the stride, when the victims of wit are put in their place as they want to be. Charles was estranged. He would persistently, almost devotedly sharpen himself on Bartholomew's brave writing. Forget the actors, the Earl had written for the King.

This is the theatre that takes England to the New World. Charles felt himself flaring out across the void of ocean. To invent the future. To realize the very future for which Father was sacrificed, for which he was devoured. Out of the ancient darkness of Father's death comes this new darkness, and we shall show courage, shan't we, we shall greet empty night with the artifice of capital and power.

When the play was over, Huntington, chastened, a new, lonely resolve visible even through the fat, did an odd thing.

The players quit the stage, left the gallery to walk dizzily outside in the freezing garden. They didn't anticipate being feted tonight; the play had needed them too dearly, and they'd been paid for an undefined service. In the garden, for the first time in memory, the roses turned black. Their petals collapsed on touch. In the gallery, Huntington, either sleepwalking or inspired, crossed the playing area to the candelabras and with his fingers he extinguished the candles, every one, leaving the company lit by the night sky, in the bouquet of his burnt skin.

Sir George panted in obvious discomfort. Charles said nothing and moved not a feather. No one dared to speak or to look at His Majesty. They were statues.

From his dais above them, Charles surveyed their silhouettes. His limbs did not flinch from time or silence. He was thinking about his father. Before his execution, Father had picked up Charles's young brother, Harry, eight at the time, put him on his knee, and said, "Sweetheart, now they will cut off thy father's head." Charles could hear his father's voice as if he'd been there. He felt the man's hands as if he were the one they'd lifted. This is the way things are. All things are true. And all things that happen happen to the King. He sat still as stone in the gallery. If he were to move, the planets would once again be set in motion.

Twelve

Sir George Rose watched the King uneasily. Charles had adopted his majestic posture, his feet on pillows, legs aslant, immobile face. Rose hadn't been sleeping well — actually he'd barely slept at all these past three weeks.

Three weeks ago, Rose's wife died. She'd got sick on a Monday and died on Wednesday morning, right out of the blue. He was usually somewhat repulsed by his wife when she'd lived: she'd been corpulent, compulsive about trivia, and bored by everything that mattered. But now that she was suddenly and absolutely gone, he was shaken, lonely to the depths of his soul. And he couldn't sleep.

Rose's spies had been providing him with reports of a flurry of meetings among the Catholics — sickly papists, quickening with ambition. He felt the threat of conspiracy looming in the shadows. Not only attacks on the Church of England — full-blown witchery was in the air. It was impossible for Rose to trust Charles's judgment, even though Rose had risked his life and fortune for his father, the unfortunate Charles I. Quality so often cannot transcend generations. Charles caught him staring, and there was the merest deflection in his lightly sardonic eyes, a quick, deep gap of irony.

Rose forced himself to study the prisoner, La Tourette, a mis-shapen, stinking gnome. I should pick him up by the collar and throw him out the window, he thought. I could do that with immunity. No one would mark the disappearance. It's very doubtful that King Louis has had anything directly to do with this ferret's mission. La Tourette has more likely been set up by that Jesuit ambassador in France, Father — Father — some French name — and the French diplomat in Holland, yes, him, along with that cold-blooded Colbert, and they'll either assume La Tourette has slipped away with their money or guess correctly that he has been murdered but know themselves to be in no position to do anything about it. They won't even care. The filthy idiot should stop talking. Never say more than is necessary. A tongue flies loose, see the gulls get it.

"I am in paradise to find myself here, before you, Royalty," La Tourette was saying. (Charles didn't blink. He, too, waited for the stage of excess when he would harvest the lies.) "I only present the history of the two men from New France. It has been terrible to speak of spies in the celestial light of you." Then, to Rose, "And you."

"Speak, maggot. Earn your feed." Rose held his handkerchief to his nose.

"I dread to speak of my uncle's treachery."

Rose heaved. "Caterpillar. Speak of your uncle."

Tourette began to talk rapidly. "My uncle, he who calls himself Sieur Des Groseilliers, he and Pierre Radisson have escaped prison in New France by selling to the Jesuits their knowledge of that country between the River St. Lawrence and New Amsterdam, ah, hear me speak, the place that was New Amsterdam is now called New York, and you may be assured, everyone is most pleased with the success of England there." He spluttered, frightened, but he must persist. "The Dutch pay the two Frenchmen in gold to act as spies for them." He appealed to Charles. "Des Groseilliers and Pierre Radisson are in the pay of the Dutch to spy against the interests of England. These men have long conspired against Your Majesty's interests. In New France, in New Amst . . . York, and here in London." He sagged. "I am miserable."

La Tourette's body emitted an eerie whining. Sir George Rose, who had been passing his sleepless nights studying Joseph Glanvil's recent *Philosophical Considerations Concerning Witches*, felt a chill.

Charles's legs had pins and needles. As always, his voice was unhurried. "Sir George. Monsieur La Tourette will be staying for a day, maybe two."

La Tourette caught this bone, then fearfully dropped it. "Your Majesty, you do me great honour by this offer. Even one as insignificant as I, however, has duties elsewhere."

Charles continued, "Send word to Windsor we wish to see the French Explorers. I believe they are entertaining Rupert. Rupert must bring them here himself."

La Tourette fell to his knees. "Good King, I am waited for at Dover!"

Rose watched La Tourette. On his knees he is womanish. Perhaps he is indeed a woman and a witch. His rags are loose, sufficient to hide his teats. His nose is long and from it drips the clear sap that runs in his veins.

Charles saw the revulsion in his counsellor's face, and he re-examined the spy. "Sir George," he said, "remove it, but do nothing untoward, please, not yet." He didn't look again at La Tourette. "Show no violence, will you? We will have it meet with the Explorers. Put it out. Then return to me."

Rose stood at the doors to Charles's apartment, his shoulders drawn up to his ears. With his hand at his thigh, he snapped his fingers. La Tourette whimpered but followed, and Rose leapt forward as if keeping La Tourette on a leash.

Alone, Charles stood and shook his feet. If it is not too wet, perhaps we shall persuade Rupert to join us for tennis, though it's too damned cold to hold the racquet. He went to the window. Thick, firm rain.

A view of the square. The stone appeared to be of a different shade on each side. Why does the rain fall at a steady pace? But no. That is not how they phrase the question. They no longer ask Why, they ask How.

Everything was once one. King and country. The steady pace of rain. Bartholomew's play had left Charles with sharpened sight — the edges of things grew insistent and decided. He was aware that he must abide without dishonest sentiment. So he would. But not, *not* without beauty. He faced the room. Rose was already there, watching. He had been watching the King's back.

"Claret," said Charles.

"Of course." Rose poured.

Charles recalled his attention to the depressing matter of spies. "What do you think?"

Rose was surprised to be asked so baldly. "He's lying. But it doesn't matter."

"Unless the two Frenchmen go to the Dutch Court for a ship."

"Ah. However, such tactics do not affect us."

"Why not?" asked Charles.

Rose looked up warily.

"I find my counsellor lacks enthusiasm for England's interests in Canada." In the uneasy light, the King threw a huge shadow.

Rose said slowly, "Not at all."

"Good. I would be loath to doubt the integrity of any of my Privy Council."

Rose was attentive, nakedly exposed by Charles's attention.

"Tell us, then, why it does not matter that the Explorers go to Holland with their information."

Rose put down his glass. "La Tourette exaggerates. The Explorers cannot carry so much influence."

Aside from valuable Crown land, Sir George Rose had been given how many hundreds of thousands of acres between Virginia and Florida? He was joint overlord of New Jersey. There was his interest in the African negro trade and his interest in the East India Company. He was a master of the board of trade. Too much. It was time to rein him in. And get cousin Louis out of it quietly, with his own *patriotes*.

Charles's voice like incense filled the chamber. "I have recently had credible report that King Louis has provided a certain Dutch captain, a Van Heemskirk, with a ship. Van Heemskirk. A damn Dutchman. Working for France." It was rare for Charles to express personal anger.

Rose managed to look concerned for the right reasons, the King's reasons. His late-night reading, the news of Catholic cabals, all of this made him feel tainted, as if conspiracy were blindly contagious. Charles may be dissolute, but only a fool would discount the possibility that the King might resort to absolute power if he wanted to. Remember Henry Vane? Beheaded on Tower Hill for possessing *a wicked imagination*. Rose rubbed his jaw. Carefully, he said, "You think that the Frenchmen will in turn go to the Dutch for a ship and cut England out of Canada altogether."

"Louis has granted Van Heemskirk all the lands he shall discover in North America by entering Canada from above, all of it, extending to the South Sea. As far as he can reach. To a Dutchman. A Dutchman would have North America."

"This is certainly news, Your Majesty." Rose let himself be seen more fully. The candles were sputtering in a draught. He turned to a servant, barely visible by the door, and told him to pour coffee. He took a moment to drink it down, then said, "May I offer something, Charles?" The coffee gave him a moment

95

of blissful rationality. He spoke sternly, gruffly. "I believe that this is, in simple terms, a question of intelligence."

"I have better spies than even Cromwell."

"I am speaking of intellect. The ability to reason."

"Ah. You are in vogue."

"Where there is the ability to reason, you will find loyalty, discretion, a terra firma. But where the reasoning faculty is absent, and we just witnessed such depravity a moment ago, we find a monster, terra incognita."

"The charges against the Explorers must be answered."

Sir Geroge Rose needed to testify so that he might begin to believe it, to free himself from the terror of his own imaginings, to be *scientific*. "I believe that evil is born of a depravity of the mind. It's not a question of the *soul*. Yet, yet a deformity such as La Tourette almost makes us believe in a supernatural power. But, no. It's not possible. We must think reasonably. Life is composed of matter. A degeneracy of the mind, *that* is where *evil* hatches and feeds."

"Sir George —"

"I am not degenerate," said Rose.

"Heaven forefend."

"I do not indulge in wicked imaginings."

"Good."

"But I fear that there are some among us who do."

"Send a messenger to Rupert, and we will examine the Frenchmen."

"Charles." God help me, I must speak. "I believe that La Tourette may be a witch."

Charles's face revealed nothing. "That is somewhat *extreme*, Sir George."

"On the contrary. I limit my imaginings to what is reasonable, what is of service to the Church of England."

"Send a messenger to Prince Rupert." Charles took paper,

dipped a quill. "I will keep my eyes open for apparitions while you are away."

"If it pleases His Majesty to mock me . . ."

"It pleases us to investigate the spies. Deliver this. Go now, Rose. And do try to stay calm."

"Of course I'm calm."

"So are we."

For a moment Rose looked lost. Then, vaguely, he said, "I will send it by messenger."

"Do."

As Rose went toward the door, he heard the King's voice behind him.

"One small thing."

He swung back on the balls of his feet. Pain arrowed across his chest and down his left arm.

"Another errand, and we shall be gratified." Charles looked closely at Rose and said, "I will have the actress, Lilly Cole, sent here now. Do that also. Do it right away." Then he turned him off.

Sir George Rose stepped cautiously to the stairwell because there was, abruptly, no light about him.

Thirteen

Bartholomew's vision wasn't so much impaired as enhanced by liquor. The candle sputtering at an upstairs window at Meg's house was charismatic, mystical. He wanted to see Lilly. Dawn of a clear, cold sky. Why did this tallow burn so wastefully, if not to draw Bartholomew to the girl?

It didn't matter that he was in disfavour with Charles, that he wasn't here to fetch Lilly for the King's bed. He hadn't a thing to offer her, no money, no gain. All he had was obsession swirling in him in lush waves that altered the scenery. The street was a moat. The candle was Lilly's purity. His love was answerable. Its power would create a responsive chord in her and he could, at last, speak true.

A half-dead whore begged from her corner of the lane. In Bartholomew's eyes, the beggar became a hound barking at his heels. The romance lurched in his stomach, threatened to turn back into brandy. He moved toward the barricade of Meg's front door.

Just then a coach drew up before his lady's castle. Bartholomew swept across the lane, passing beneath the horses' frosty breath as Sir George Rose leaned out and Lilly emerged from Meg's. She wore the cloak that Bart had bought her with his wife's money (a rare fiscal indiscretion). How broad Lilly's face is, the dark eyes set wide apart, her full, childish cheeks that his hands longed to cup.

Lilly looked at Bartholomew in brief confusion. They'd been exiled together, banned from the King's favour. Now she was implicated in Bart's life, and she didn't like it. His play had proved to her that he didn't believe in anything. Bartholomew began to speak. She thought that he was here to see her delivered, his usual trivial performance as King's procurer, and she turned from him, gathered her skirts, and climbed in beside Sir George Rose. Bartholomew might be a strong writer, but he was a weak man. And now, once again, the King had confined him to the backstage business. She didn't look at Bartholomew again. She was being given another chance to make a success. She knew it was her *last* chance.

She was gone from him. Gone for her own good. Night flushed cold air into his blood and Bart was more drunk than ever. With what was left of his flickering self, he swayed past Meg's and on, to find a hackney, to get away, to leave London.

The poet of cruelty, the harbinger — if not creator? — of the modern age, undisclosed as the romantic he would rather be, his golden head weighted by a black void of drink, left the city to go home. Home? To his wife's house. To the likelihood of death by boredom, in civil peace, in Addenbury.

But, he thought as he staggered into the coach, he'd achieved one good thing. Huntington had told him about the performance at Court of his new play. *The Enchanter's Nightshade*. His caustic posturing in verse. Huntington, not one to spend flattery, had pronounced it "visionary," and he'd said that Lilly had been brilliant; he'd solemnly announced that Lilly had "matured." Bartholomew knew that Charles would not merely be amused by her now, as he'd been before: he would be enthralled. He and Lilly will not be sent away. Bart clung to this, though it hurt him, or because it hurt him. It had taken a pack of witty, rhyming lies to gain this fragile portion of grace.

Fourteen

The ankle is hurt worse than can be believed. How can this be? The effeminate nature of England, it has changed me into a woman! Radisson anxiously groped himself between his legs. Ah, they are still there! I was becoming alarmed. Today, I get the boat from the Prince or I die, I bleed to death inside.

Windsor Castle was eerily quiet. The long ascent to Prince Rupert's apartment was accomplished at a crawl, but he pulled himself upright to face the quivering blue bitch, her black lips rimmed with potently scented spit. Even the dogs had eaten! The serving plates were spread on the floor, licked clean. Radisson quelled his anger and impassively wished the gentlemen good morning.

Des Groseilliers and Prince Rupert watched Radisson limp to a couch. Neither man commented on his injury.

The Prince resumed a conversation that had obviously been going on for some time. "Well, the fact is, we're starving the Americans into revolt. They won't support export taxes that are two, nay, four times higher than their return."

Radisson leapt up, nearly falling. "I agree! Too much tax!"

Prince Rupert nodded. "Yes, Monsieur Radisson. The colonies need to be properly milked, if you will forgive a vulgarity."

"But not by you, good Prince." Radisson looked up at the

tall Prince from the corner of his eye. "You do not milk. You sail a ship of your own."

Prince Rupert's chest lifted and his black eyebrows arched hopefully, to concede: "I once did."

"I know a sailor when my eyes do."

"May I speak frankly, Monsieur Radisson?"

"If you did not ask, then you are not, and if you are not, there is no measure for to ask."

"Quite. Precisely my point. There is very little left a man might do that is not on one side of the Devil or the other."

"Except that such a man will find a new world to explore."

The Prince exhaled as if he'd been tapped. "I once planned to take Madagascar." He looked sheepish but proud. "Of course I was very young at the time."

"Europe is an old woman. Africa, she will be good for some time to come. But the North, Prince Rupert, ahh, the North, *she* is a crystal of ice that keeps men pure."

"I envy you, Monsieur Radisson."

"But why, good Prince? I am nothing but what I can find for your profit."

"To trace the paths of the stars. While we in England must satisfy ourselves by keeping ledgers and accounts."

With the briefest glance at Des Groseilliers, Radisson said, "I will find you the best beaver."

"Find me the passage to China, Monsieur Radisson."

Radisson liked this Prince; he did not like to lie to him. The passage to China? Why? The future is in beaver! He said, "I will make you very rich, Prince Rupert."

Rupert's sad smile. He was of an age at which he'd come to accept the weather patterns of his own life, the stamp of his destiny. He would live out his days in castles and fine houses, but he'd never be rich. It hadn't been written into his experience, and he was no longer in season. Ideas preoccupied him more and more. If the discovery of the Northwest Passage requires trade en route, so be it. His head ached. He saw mountains of ice rise up, cut open by ocean currents, revealing the path to Formosa. *How* will he raise the money to get there?

The black boy appeared at the top of the stairs carrying a tray in one hand. With deep disappointment, Radisson realized that there was no food on it. The boy quizzically opened his eyes wide, white on black against the oversized white wig. Prince Rupert waved him to come forward. The boy held the tray, a letter.

Rupert recognized Charles's handwriting.

> Rupert,
> Ride at once and do bring us Messieurs Radisson and Gooseberries. Do keep them close to you, as you cherish the Affection of your Cousin and your King,
>
> *Charles R*

Des Groseilliers smelled change. The impasse had broken at last. His right eye, its black pupil squeezed into the shape of a goat's: another minute of inaction and he would surely have taken *une crise de colère*, a falling-fit.

"I'll be damned," said Rupert. "Charles requests your company."

✗✗✗✗✗

By the time they arrived at Whitehall, nearly eight hours' ride, Radisson was faint from hunger. He had hinted to Prince Rupert that he must eat and then, in desperation, had asked him outright for food. The Prince was deferential. It was only in the denial of the most basic provisions that Radisson recognized that he and Des Groseilliers were prisoners.

Past midnight, they rode through the King Street Gate to the palace. The stable boy who took charge of Radisson's horse didn't help him to dismount and Radisson fell to his knees in six inches of water. Rupert had watchfully herded the Explorers to London. A bitter night, the east wind driving sleet into their faces as it drove floodwaters into London.

The King was in the Privy Chamber, the place lit by sparsely placed flambeaux, one of which stood either side of the throne. The effect was sacrificial, the atmosphere freezing in every sense. Radisson forced himself to walk, though he felt he might faint from the pain. Des Groseilliers's left eye throbbed to the pulse of the flames beside the throne.

Charles glanced over them with mild curiosity. "Rupert," he said, "you will be pleased to see Sir George Rose."

The three men turned to find themselves joined by Rose, who emerged from the gloom and said, "Rupert."

"We have discovered some unusual news," said Charles. "A matter of security."

"The French Explorers have been accused of spying for the Dutch," said Rose.

"Ah." Prince Rupert's face, his stalwart posture, gave nothing away, but he was cheered, remembering what it is to be *involved* with things.

"Forgive me," said Radisson. "I must sit or I will fall."

"Let him sit." The King's voice had grown more nasal with the severity of his current role as interrogator.

Des Groseilliers seemed to have disappeared in shadow but for the heat that emanated from his body, his gathering rage. The men sensed it. Charles told him, "Come forward into the light, Monsieur Groseilliers. That's better. You are not formally charged with spying, not yet. We do you great honour. We invite you to speak."

"It is La Tourette," breathed Des Groseilliers.

Radisson, who'd taken a chair far to the side of the room, moaned from either pain or hunger or recognition of the name. Rose shuddered.

Rupert removed his cloak and held it out for a servant to take. His gesture distracted them for a moment.

Rupert's attitude toward Sir George Rose suggested reticent distaste. They'd shared battles and prizes in their pirate days. But it seemed Rupert's lineage prevented him from gaining the great riches enjoyed by Rose and his ilk. Only three of the men of Rose's circle of colonial overlords, Hyde, Cooper, and Berkeley, were of high aristocratic stock. The rest were — as Rose was now — merchants: nine very, very rich men dominated England. Rose was nearly sixty, but he looked more pugilistic than ever.

"Who is this man La Tourette?" Rupert asked Charles.

"A greasy piece of tongue," grumbled Rose. "It claims kinship with that one," pointing to Des Groseilliers. "It is his nephew."

Des Groseilliers startled them all by bursting forward, as if his barrel chest had exploded. "It is no such thing! Nephew. Pah! Someone pays it to follow me." He moved to Radisson and raised his hand to strike him. "I told you, Pierre, it will bring trouble if we do not stop it."

"Why does he make claims on you if he has none?" asked Prince Rupert. Then, impatient, "Will no one take this cloak?"

Radisson watched the upraised hand without flinching and said, flatly, "I have been telling you, gentlemen. No one is more *valeur* than Pierre-Esprit Radisson and his brother Médard, Sieur Des Groseilliers."

Des Groseilliers brought his palm to Radisson's face and stroked the scarred cheek.

Charles laughed dryly. "Ah, oui, Monsieur Radisson. No doubt you are *valeur* if put to good use. But try our patience no longer."

"La Tourette is being paid to destroy us," Des Groseilliers growled.

"The Catholics are at the bottom of this, I'll wager," said Sir George Rose.

Radisson struggled to his feet. His hunger and injury were forgotten; his thin face showed an enviable objectivity. "La Tourette has been bought by the French Jesuits, not the Dutch. Though both countries want to cage us. This is so. They try to cage us, then let us out to do their bidding and take what profit we will bring. We could bring them much profit."

Rose said, "So you betray them."

"We betray no man," said Des Groseilliers.

"Tut! No man! But what of kings, Mr. Gooseberries?" Charles asked with a faint, indulgent smile.

Radisson answered for him. "Everything is become big and very small, both. We bring you the future, King Charles. We bring you the world. We will find the passage to that place. Then, when we do that, you will have everything."

At that moment Lilly appeared from an inner chamber. She was prettily if lightly dressed in white, her curly black hair evocative of children in sleep. She smelled of girlhood, newly plucked. The gentlemen, according to their various moralities, bowed, sniffed, ignored her.

Rose had conceived a deep hatred for the girl: he had been forced to play the role of King's pimp, God save him. He would assign a spy to her. His knowledge of witchcraft was modern and urban, a far cry from the village mischief and mean revenge that had affected his father's rude boyhood in Lancashire. If the girl is a witch, she has ingeniously attached herself to the most gullible atheists, a rabble of fops and wits.

She was leaning toward the torches at the throne, compelled toward the King. She appeared to be half asleep. Charles was charmed by her momentary, unguarded show. He let her press against him, his large hand stroking her. His voice trembled a little: "Is there a servant about?" But he himself had dismissed the attendants. "Rupert?"

Rupert was thinking about "everything." He who had lost his home at birth — could it be possible that he could invent himself a new one? Has a Prince without a country been found, redeemed by the French Explorers? He yearned for the passage through the North — through the ice, yes perhaps, or as some suggest south through the Californias. But would such a voyage to the Orient only be a perpetuation of his homelessness?

"Rupert?" Charles called again. But Rupert didn't hear. He stood transported by a new dream. To have again a country, not his place of origin, not his place of birth, that's true, but what has been lost, what has vanished — at least in function — from the face of the earth, may now be *discovered*. A land for Rupert, a Rupert's Land. Dare I hope? I dare.

Lilly shivered, awoke, saw the company.

Charles called softly for the third time: "Rupert. Did you bring the little nigger?" He liked Rupert's black boy.

"Say what, Charles? No," said Prince Rupert. "It is too cold for him." He laid his cloak on a nearby chair. His homeless soul wafted around the room. Rose started, his dewlaps shook.

Lilly pulled herself upright. She curtsied to Charles. The curtsy became a theatre curtsy, then a small bow, mimicking Radisson. Her lips plucked: "I do think I dreamt."

Charles kissed her elbow, a remarkably expressive and

vulnerable act. He turned to Rose and said, "Bring us the little man, the Jesuit's rat, yes? S'il vous plaît."

Rose hesitated.

"Fetch him, do. Here to us."

Lilly Cole stood by the throne like his daughter, like his Queen. Charles looked at Rupert and raised his eyebrows as if to say, Aren't we having a *serious* evening!

Rupert was indeed having a serious evening but in a way that pleased his King, a *properly* serious evening. And Charles thought, I am going to get Rupert some money.

Charles, using his domestic voice, spoke softly to Rupert. "My mistress is cold. May she use your cloak? You are not in need of it?"

Rupert fetched his cloak, draped it over Lilly's shoulders. She rearranged it.

"Thank you," she murmured.

"It is my pleasure," said Rupert.

Charles caught Rose's eye and feigned surprise that he was still there. Rose, rigid with anger and dread, bowed and left, muttering a prayer, while outside there was thunder, unnatural in the season of sleet.

Fifteen

Two attendants dragged La Tourette, his heels whining over the floor, dropped him before the King, and wiped their hands on their jackets. Lilly buried her nose in Rupert's scent.

Sir George Rose entered, shouting, "Make it stand! Stand up!"

La Tourette staggered upright and faced the King. Then he made an elaborate bow to Lilly. Rose sputtered, "Ha!"

Charles held a vial of scent to his nose. "Ask it to greet its uncle."

Despite his fear, La Tourette spoke clearly. "Your Majesty, I beg you, permit me a private word with my uncle."

Rose interrupted. "This is not fitting! Send it to the gate-house before the air swarms with beetles."

"It will speak with its uncle here," said Charles.

La Tourette sidled toward Des Groseilliers. The little man had a mink-like ferocity. "Uncle," he began. Des Groseilliers bristled. "Uncle, I suffer for you. Yet you turn me away. A current of blood flows between us. I am your familiar. Do not cast me off.

"King Charles," La Tourette continued, "I beg forgiveness on behalf of my uncle. He burgeons with the special knowledge of what men want. He cannot be blamed for spending that knowledge in foreign courts. He is only a pawn for the Dutch, who use him for their purpose."

"What Dutch?" Des Groseilliers growled. "What Dutch?"

"Ah, mon oncle Médard." La Tourette chuckled.

"It is quite plausible," said Charles, "that the Dutch would be interested in you, Mr. Gooseberries. We believe you are playing many games at once. A certain secretary informs us that he has seen you in Amsterdam."

Then Radisson calmly observed, "You speak of the Dutch sea captain."

"You know of this?" Charles asked with mild relief.

"Oui. I know a Dutch captain who has appealed to King Louis to give him a ship to find the Ja-pan sea," Radisson said. "If we do not hurry, the French will have first the North, then the way to China as well. Pfft. Even with a stupid captain who is Dutch."

"Why don't the Dutch provide the Dutch captain with a Dutch ship?" asked Rose, curious despite himself.

Radisson coolly appraised Sir George Rose. "The Dutch are kept busy fighting you at sea," he said. "You also beat them in Africa, so they lose the riches you gain from slaves." His English was good. His limp was statesmanlike.

La Tourette crouched. "Your Majesty, I must profess my gratitude for the divine comfort of my proximation to the warmth that emanates from your glorious person."

Rose burst out, "Do stop this thing from speaking!"

Charles said, "Dismiss the attendants."

The attendants withdrew. La Tourette smiled with mad confidence. "I beg you to forgive mon oncle Médard. Your divinity has drawn his compass."

"Indeed." Charles was concocting his own special version of these events. Rupert is enamoured of the Explorers or he wouldn't have kept them so long at Windsor. Even now, Charles could see in Rupert's face an emotion he'd almost lost sight of. Hope. Well. We shall put money to it. And bring Sir George Rose more closely under our wing. All in one fell swoop. To Rose, he said, "You may remove it now. Do."

La Tourette collapsed like bladder kelp. The smell was appalling.

"I will not go near the thing," Rose protested.

"Remove it — Sir George. Please will you."

Rose said hesitantly, "I will need some help."

"Monsieur Groseilliers will assist you."

La Tourette backed away in panic. Startled, Des Groseilliers and Sir George Rose looked at each other for the first, potent time. Rose was embarrassed. "Without even a single servant to carry it." He glanced cautiously, craftily, at Charles and then said, "Would Mister Gooseberries be so kind . . ."

So they went, Des Groseilliers towing La Tourette like trapped game.

𝄞𝄞𝄞𝄞𝄞

It was five o'clock in the morning. Charles never slept longer than four hours at a time, but now he'd been awake since dawn Tuesday. He wrapped his ermine robe about him and walked out to the garden for air. Radisson sat down and fell asleep.

Rupert and Lilly were left behind. Rupert had had few real friends in his life and, excepting Charles, they'd all been women. He indicated a chair and invited her to sit, pulling another chair up nearby and seating himself.

They listened to the watchman strike the hour on the walls below. Lilly shivered.

"Are you cold?" asked Rupert.

"No." She pulled her knees up and crouched inside his cloak.

110

"Do you know," Rupert began, "what I would like right now?" He put his fingers together and leaned forward. "Lamb's wool," he whispered.

"Lamb's?"

"Wool."

"Ah."

"Do you not know it?"

"Wool?"

"Lamb's Wool. Hot ale. Dolloped with roasted apples."

"It sounds nice."

"It is."

She smiled at him.

Encouraged — for Rupert was always afraid to bore people — he said, "It makes life worthwhile. Just to know that Lamb's Wool exists."

Lilly was shocked by the tenderness of such a confession, by such a guileless expression of delight. She experienced a wave of dread. In many ways, she was a Puritan. She felt gut-dread over desire, over yearnings.

Rupert's voice was low, deeply relaxed. He was with someone who couldn't possibly hurt him. "My mother liked the stuff. Funny. A woman who drinks ale. I fear she was eccentric."

Lilly gave a little hiccup that she covered with a cough. For the first time in her life she felt old, older than this middle-aged man. She said, "A mother who drinks ale."

"Of course that was in Amsterdam and very long ago."

"You come from Amsterdam?" Amsterdam must not be of this earth.

"I have been a traveller all my life." His voice was dry, a gentle whistling. "I went to school in Amsterdam, at Leiden. Then, to fight at Westphalia. And to Linz. Linz was very beautiful."

"Well, it sounds nice. Linz."

"Linz. Yes." They heard waves on the shore. It was still windy.

They heard the turn of a fish, an eel, a body. He looked to the door, then back at her, compelled to tell her more, to give her something, a story, his trust. He was so homesick tonight. "Linz was where I first fell in love. Well, one of the very few times in my life I've done so. Fallen in love, that is. I was in prison there, you see. And she was older."

A cold draft. Rupert willed her to speak. "I suppose you think . . . ?"

Bootsteps in the hall. Lilly, alarmed, said, "Yes of course."

"I'm sorry," Rupert said. "I am an old bore."

"No!"

He stood loomingly. The spaniels scrambled in, the room suddenly ripe with the spice of cold dog. Rupert gave her one stark look — abashed — and raptly greeted the dogs.

King Charles appeared with Sir George Rose on his heels. Rose was dishevelled, as if from a quick sexual encounter. His lace was torn and speckled with blood. Then Des Groseilliers arrived and even the spaniels sidled to face him, shrinking from his boot, his nervy smell. Rose breathed harder and better than he had in years; in his body, he showed a realignment, in his gruff manner, signs of recompense.

Radisson awoke, cheered. His brother Médard, he is finally feeling better. Everyone is feeling better.

"Let us have a drink, shall we?" said Charles. Then, playfully: "And speak about a boat to sail to China." The King had plucked each man's windpipe into a major chord.

Sir George Rose was refreshed; he felt avid for life. He poured everyone but Lilly a glass and raised his own in a toast. "To all the money in the world!"

"To money," said Charles. "Quite right. Messieurs Groseilliers and Radisson. Ha! Well well. To England! Pour my Lilly a glass, Rose, there's a fellow. Cheers! 'Tis thus we pledge our love aloud.

B'dod! A secret shared is a blooded bond." He studied Rose, amused by how easy it had been to satisfy, and to implicate, the old boar. A morsel of meat in his cage. "Well! To business. Rupert, you have applied yourself to learn the route to the Northwest Passage. Be so kind as to tell us something of this science."

Rose had not emerged from his blood ecstasy, but he retained sufficient reason to remember the charges against Des Groseilliers. He spoke closely to the King's ear, Charles drawing back from his meaty breath. "Are we to proceed in trust with the Frenchmen, Your Majesty? It may well be true that they are in league with the Catholics as well as the Dutch."

Charles appeared to be grateful for this caution from his counsellor, and he blinked sagely. "Thank you, Sir George. What say we simply outbid them all and capture the Explorers for our own profit?"

Rose didn't want to descend to ordinary reason, not yet. He was in love with Des Groseilliers right now; they had shared the darkest act. "Buy their loyalty! Quite!"

Radisson stepped forward. "Good King! Let me speak of the great Voyage!"

Des Groseilliers whispered angrily, "Shut up, Pierre!"

Prince Rupert walked to the centre of the gallery. His tall figure was lit with the moony light before dawn. "I have listened to the French Explorers," he said, "and what they tell is confirmed by my own calculations. The Hudson's Strait lies but a month's sail, six weeks at most, and from there it is an easy passage to Asia."

"The Bristol merchants lost money in such a venture some thirty years ago," said Rose.

"Ah." Charles brightened. "Captain James. His ship was the *Henrietta Maria*, after Mother." He gave Lilly an avuncular little nod on "Mother"; she seemed to be the stand-in for that role tonight. She stood stock-still, wrapped in Rupert's cloak, holding a glass of odious claret.

Charles, like Rupert, loved to collect narratives of sea journeys, and he rushed ahead as on a sea swell. "He got stuck in the ice, didn't he. Spent the winter in the bay. Lost three men. Or four. He sank his own ship! Ha! Brilliant move, in some ways. Kept her from being crushed. Then he raised her, sent his men diving to get the barrels out of the hold — and sailed away. In July. Barely made it back to England." He stopped short and gave Rupert a quick look. He did not wish to discourage Rupert from anything that might give him pleasure. "But Captain James was a terrible navigator."

"It's madness." Rose betrayed a grudging excitement. He loved high risk. The very improbability of the adventure had its attractions.

"La recherche est très recherché," said Prince Rupert. "The quest is greatly to be desired." A small play on words.

"It will prove more profitable than the slave trade, Sir George," Charles added. "Furs do not lose weight in passage as Negroes do." But he knew that Rose would back away if he felt that he was being coerced. To get his money we must appeal to his insubordinate nature and his competitive drive. "Sir George is aware that New England adventurers have been trying for a voyage to the northern bay. Shapleigh, I believe, a powerful family, from what they say. Captain Shapleigh. Powerful and rich."

"That fat man of Boston!" Radisson could no longer be contained. "We put out to sea in his ship in the spring for our discovery. But oh, what an incompetent buffoon. When we reached the very entry to Hudson Bay he was afraid. Alas! he cried. This is not Barbados sugar! These mountains of sugar candy, they are made of ice! Oh, I am afraid of that!" Radisson broke off into bitter laughter. Ignoring the growls coming from Des Groseilliers, he plunged on. "They break the promise they make to my brother Médard and to Pierre-Esprit. No man does that two times. Again they make proffers unto us for what ship we would go on in our Designs. But we answered them, No! We do not try again with you! A scald cat fears the water though it be cold!"

"Shapleigh?" In Sir George Rose recklessness came disguised as generosity: the two impulses seemed identical. "Oh, yes, indeed, he is fat, you know. But the Shapleighs of this world matter not. We stand to have much better."

Prince Rupert was keenly, and synthetically, English. He felt adoption in the marrow of his bones. The vision of Rupert's Land glowed in his heart, while his loins ached over a seductive phantom, the passage to the Orient.

Sir George Rose was exhilarated, but he was also exhausted. "God help me, Rupert," he said. "I'm in."

Their voices lifted a semitone. Greed had been refined by gamble. They were relieved of themselves in the winds of speculation. Prince Rupert gallantly kissed Lilly's cheek, and Charles laughed. Lilly stared at the blood on Rose's sleeve, at Des Groseilliers's unquiet satisfaction. So this is "politics."

Radisson looked at her speculatively. Has she tricked her way to a cozy bed? If the girl will keep under the covers, my brother and I will not be saddled with her and her green pimp on our great Voyage. But be sure, Pierre. "And the lady stays here!" he said cheerfully.

Charles hadn't forgotten that business with Bart, but things had transpired, he'd moved on. And of Lilly? Well, I'm in for a penny now. "The Earl of Buxborough wrote a play," he said to Radisson. "It was a very *good* play."

Radisson tipped his head. Charles slipped Rupert's heavy cloak from Lilly's shoulders, revealing her in her thin white smock as if he'd just then created her. He handed the cloak to Rupert and said, "Lilly was very *good* in Bart's play."

"C'est fait!" cried Radisson; then, to Lilly, "You will be warm!" Everything is wonderful!

Prince Rupert felt the affinity among the others, and he resumed his habit of loneliness. He walked to the window, looked out at the blear light of dawn. He saw their enthusiasm for the prospect of the voyage to Hudson Bay slip in value to a speculation, scientific, mercantile. I will not share its aspects poetical. My Rupert's Land. My unknown home.

Sixteen

It was sunrise when Charles took her to his apartments, where the valet waited to undress him. Charles's valet was more than blond; he was white as new snow. Lilly had never seen an albino before. She wondered vaguely if he hadn't been born of the unearthly rules of Court, where even a servant could be so pampered as to become almost invisible, a ray of sun.

The valet's arms descended and lifted the wig from Charles's head, a change so radical, Lilly almost shrieked. The sight of his blue-grey hair plastered by exertion (he'd walked at least ten miles yesterday), by oils and talcum, was new to her. Their lovemaking had been decorous. Her surprise was almost beyond her art to conceal. She coughed — "I have a tickle in my throat" — and grinned, feeling offstage and wildly childish. These kinds of men, Charles, his cousin the Prince, they live like *angels*. Angels, she knew now, are deadly if they want to be, and prodigious!

Charles closed his eyes with relief at the breezy day on his head. The morning sun struck Lambeth Marsh and made a crusade across his white shirt. When he opened his eyes, Lilly was kneeling on the bed, her hand against his cheek. "I have a favour to ask," she said.

"A favour now."

"I would like to have a bath."

Charles saw her glance quickly at his bleached valet. Something had passed between them. His court mistress, Lady Castlemaine, Barbara — needle-nosed, Catholic, rapacious, with five children underfoot — was losing the affection of his household. On the other hand, Lilly Cole — young, fresh, dark-eyed. "You are not Catholic, Lilly?"

"Shall I be?" she asked lightly.

"Oh! I think not." He saw that she was giddy; it made him feel unpleasantly paternal. He felt the gloomy shadow of guilt that was forever associated with his Catholic mother: he had loved Mother, but of course; he could taste, even now, the pink plaster of Mother's cheek.

He puffed, as he always did when vexed. I cannot deny it, she's, ah, so pretty. "Prepare a bath," he told the valet.

"Oh! Thank you!" Lilly kissed him.

Charles felt like a doting mate. "Now, Lilly, I advise you, whilst in the palace, show some caution. Particularly with your cup of chocolate. Barbara is a baneful physician, and chocolate has been known to be her favourite medicine."

Lilly obediently poured her lovely cup of chocolate into the chamber bowl. Over the next season, King Charles would come to associate *that* scent, milky and burnt, with his new thing, Lilly Cole.

King Charles had approximately ten illegitimate children, so far. He acknowledged all of them. He wasn't a philanderer: when he tired of a lover, he didn't turn her off; he supplied her with an allowance.

Charles stubbornly preserved a lucid portion of himself that let him live his life entirely onstage, even in his Privy Closet, with Cheffinch coming in to assist. Something at Charles's core remained private. And he'd seen this in Lilly; an aspect of her skill as an actress was an impermeable self that will shift and retreat from public knowing. He did not expect to *know* her; he really didn't want to — that would be disrespectful. He liked her.

Charles was objective, but objectivity didn't make him cruel in love. This agreeable, impartial quality would make him more of a friend than a passionate lover. He was, however, passionate about theatre. The theatre is *all*, whereas the bed can at times be overly specific. The *consciousness-in-death* aspect of Lilly's performance, the way she let her role be engulfed by a poet's night, had created in Charles the generous tenderness that, he knew too well, would burgeon into an annuity. While she spoke Bart's lines, Lilly had permitted herself one direct glance at the King, and that look had plumbed his soul. The girl fathomed the play, the ancient night that pressed on every word, keenly as the blade that severed Father's head.

Lilly spent the day in Charles's apartments while he came and went, coming rather often to look at her. He dined with Barbara, who was made suspicious by an alteration in him that could come only from fresh acquisition. He made his escape before Barbara could fan herself to flame, cheerfully descending, the dogs capering at his hems, to cut across the garden, returning to Lilly.

Lilly stayed in his apartment into the night. Tonight — though she would very soon be made to forget this — she knew intimacy. For the first and maybe last time in her life, tonight Lilly would be tempted to forget herself.

Lilly had never before experienced such generous admiration — taking into account that she hadn't quite reached her seventeenth birthday. In the sweet surfeit of the hours, she drifted down into nearly trusting desire, to the place Charles invented or knowingly sought out, where she, with the last shreds of separate mindfulness, thought, I will be what you like, let you do what you like; I'll even like what you do.

Seventeen

By the slender virtues of a new winter moon, of distant stars, Lilly stood at the top of sweating stone stairs leading down to the river. Even at this hour, traffic moved on the water in rippling paths of lantern light. At last, by a code that remained a mystery to Lilly, a boat was signalled to the dock. Far below, the boatman lifted his white face framed in smoke, his boat an open, floating pod.

Through her gloves, the wet stone staircase felt like the inside of someone's mouth. She stepped on her skirts and nearly fell, aimed for the boatman's expressionless face, the hot glow when he drew on his pipe. Lilly had been soundly asleep in the warm security of the King's bed when his valet came, like ice, to wake her. The King would arise by four-thirty; he did not like to awake with a woman. Now she dreamed that she was climbing down a man's throat, yet the goal was the hot dry pipe smoke. Nearly four in the morning. The tide turning.

The boatman took her a short way, to Temple Stairs. Charles had neglected to give her coin for a carriage or a link-boy to take her the rest of the way to Pudding Lane, to Meg's, back to sleep. It was a royal imperative not to carry money. And she'd felt too proud to ask for it. She'd have to walk.

At Wych Street, someone came from behind and wrapped his arms around her ribs, cutting off her air. He lifted her up so her feet dragged and carried her to a dark yard. Breathing fast, he pushed her, face first, against a stone wall. With one hand he held her there while he fished the other hand under her skirt, raised her to him, and knifed himself into her.

She climbed till her feet were almost off the ground while he drove her into the stone wall, and she bent back so only her chest and stomach would be scraped. She tried to breathe, to go loose — as she would onstage — tried to let it happen, turn it into some kind of animal reaction. She hoped that he'd think so too — that he'd not think. He was making rutting noises. When he was frenzied, she felt the most powerful disgust, rage, she'd ever let herself feel. She twisted over to the right; pinned by him to the wall, she reached down and dug her fingers into him. She loosened her grip and then reached again, almost fell off him, got his tight little sacks in her hand and dug with her fingers, but she was wearing gloves; finally she found a grip that served. He let go, she fell and staggered to her knees, and he took her head in both his hands to smash her against the stones, but first he wanted to see her face; he turned Lilly around. They saw each other, as if in broad daylight.

Soby. Bart's friend. Lord Metcalf. He stepped back, smiling behind his hand. "You have tried my patience," he said.

Lilly nodded carefully, as to affirm, that is so. She got to her feet as if rising from a curtsy.

Soby wiped the sides of his mouth, then adjusted his breeches tenderly. He was dressed à la mode, if just off. He saw Lilly appraise him and he seemed to sharpen, to point. Suddenly he put his hands around her neck, as if to admire her face, holding her by her throat.

Lilly didn't look at his face but over his shoulder. She wanted to see the next few hours, to see her way ahead. Soby wouldn't wait long; he'd act out of boredom if he didn't act from excitement. She met his eye, she forced herself to mimic his style of humour, sliding inside Soby's brittle comedy. She let him know, if he killed her, it wouldn't satisfy him because he'd have dipped into his own contrivances, killed within his own frame — it was the exterior that aroused Soby, so she made herself intimate.

He loosened his hold and tipped backward, breathing the night breezes, poisoned by cold night. He said, "Next time, come when I call, punk."

She nodded without seeming to; nothing would do but to snake alongside, looking where he looked. She took a chance and patted his chest lightly. If she didn't carry things forward, they'd go back. Soby resented her touch and then accepted it. She touched his lips and moved to the side so he felt as if he had moved, not she. She was just here just now, nothing had transpired between them; she took several idle steps here and there. He was watchful for a few seconds. Then he turned his back on her.

In the greenish illumination lay a piece of broken glass that seemed to rise to her hand. Her glove protected her. She paused for a second and looked out at the street, at the way things were before. Then, with a deep moan, she drove the glass into the pocket of flesh under Soby's arm from behind, like an oyster cut. She pulled it out before he could turn, so it wouldn't get stuck. She met his eye. He still didn't believe her. She cried out and drove it across the cords of his neck. He spurted blood, and while his hands were busy damming the flow, she struck once more, at the A of the ribs. She struck up. "Yes," she said. "Yes, do you see?" And left the glass there. She was sobbing. When she turned, she saw him go down on his hands and knees. He gave her a look of reproach. She slipped in his blood when she turned, fell, but got up and ran, the sea-bilge stink of Soby's blood.

Throbbing pain threw her forward; her pulse hurt. She

stopped running, aware that someone was following her, keeping his distance; she walked quickly to Pudding Lane. Someone walked behind her, there were footsteps on stone, the sound of authority, of consequence. She lost her nerve and ran the last few yards to Meg's.

She'd probably hang. But she wouldn't grieve, she refused to. That had been simple, her few hours of success with the King. That had been child's play. She'd be thrilled, she'd be true, she'd hate.

Lilly pounded on the door with her good hand, waking Meg from the light dormancy she called sleep. Meg came down in a yellow dressing gown, her dried-out peelings of hair coiled at her shoulders, called out, Who is it?, but knew, knew somehow; Meg was keen to the scent of blood. She opened the door, Lilly falling into her.

Dawn not a half-hour off, already the lane had a mottled-blue pulse. A man in a shapeless coat stood watching ten feet away. Meg pulled Lilly inside, threw the bar into place. "Go to my room. And don't wake the girls."

Meg lit the candles in her room, sick at the sight of Lilly peeling her glove over gashes in her hand, the forefinger cut to the bone. Meg gathered the soggy clothes in a sheet. Lilly was scraped from her ribs to her cheekbone, and her stockings were bloody. Meg fetched water, clean rags, and brandy. She'd get Lilly drunk before she sewed the finger. When she cleaned between the legs, Lilly hid her face under her arm.

She spit back the brandy Meg tried to pour down her throat, insisted Meg sew her hand without it. When she was clean and stitched, in Meg's bed, she curled up, her bloody fist at the centre, studied the brown smear of blood on the sheet. Maybe she'd always have the sensation that his blood was inside her. As if she'd consumed him. The bed sagged as Meg crawled in beside her. Meg curled her body around Lilly's and sang as she stroked Lilly's cheek. *Black is the colour of my true love's hair, His face so soft and wondrous fair, The purest eyes, And the strongest hands . . .* Lilly lifted her bruised faced and said, "Don't."

Lilly fell asleep and dreamed of her mother. Dreamed that Beth sank her teeth into her, clinging with a dead mother's grip, sucking on her daughter's blood. Lilly struck her mother, she beat her off, but Beth crouched, begging for kindness — and Lilly, in sleep, wished she could be kind but could feel only shame and rage. Her mother drowned in a tavern, on dry land. Lilly heard her mother say, "He's got a stick atween his legs," heard the words clearly as if awake, her mother's great joke, saw the words mixed with blood on Beth's swollen lips.

Eighteen

That was at the end of February. All through March, Lilly listened for the boot on the stairs and waited to be arrested. She listened for men's voices outside the door while she recovered in Meg's bed.

Meg gave Lilly what mothering she could, with a hand better suited to swiping tables and snapping dregs out of glasses. She kept a purse full of money tied at her waist, and the jingle of coins would break the sweep of clean sheets tucked over Lilly's feet; the coins would screen the sounds of children playing outside, making it impossible to mistake the low bustle of dishes and voices below for the sounds of home. Meg smelled of mildew and beer, but she was the right kind of mother for Lilly.

When Lilly failed to appear in Dryden's *Secret Love*, King Charles sent his albino valet to inquire as to her health. Meg met the snow-white man at the door and, without missing a beat, offered him a pint, drawing him into the tavern, where her patrons shrank from him, a queer thing like that dressed so lofty. Susan in all innocence said he looked like a lamb, and Claire slapped her ear, in case she was tempted to fall in love. Meg told the valet that Lilly had cut her hand picking up some broken glass in the tavern, that it was all her fault, Aunt Meg's, and she hoped the King would forgive her if "my niece is indisposed for some time" because the incident had led to fever and she would take a few weeks to mend. "That girl," sighed Meg, "she's made of finer stuff than what's her lot down here."

At Easter week — except for a scar on her hand that Lilly could say truthfully was caused by broken glass — her skin had healed, leaving no outward trace of Soby. She returned to the stage, and she visited Charles at Whitehall Palace. She discovered that she could make Charles believe that she was the same girl he'd liked, the one who felt the blade of Bart's modernity, who got on so well with cousin Rupert, who was so nice in bed, who had an artistic intuition as to when her scene was over, a real feel for the timing of an effective withdrawal from the stage or from his presence. She began — almost — to understand why Beth had drunk so much: perhaps it wasn't failure that had unnerved her mother, but success; it was the fact that it had been too simple, too easy; the negligible quality of Beth's success had made her thirst.

By June, Lilly had moved into that sphere of Charles's affections that suited her best, into a stately house near Lambeth Hill. She gained good furniture, wore graceful clothes, had several servants, a coach and four. Lilly maintained a calm dignity through these months by means of her own steely will. It was an act of vengeance.

The neighbourhood was familiar. There had been a time, when Lilly was almost too young to have remembered, when Beth had secured the affections of a rich man, a gentleman, a serious man who wanted Beth to raise her child in respectable circumstances. For a year or perhaps longer, they'd lived in a house not far from the one where Lilly was currently installed. It was a brief reprieve from impoverished widowhood. But her mother liked to drink. In those early days, the drinking was quite frivolous, an indication of a restless spirit, which the gentleman had the courage to admire. Then came the tantrums, the nights when her mother would shut herself in her room, and sing, and weep, and then a carriage at the door, her mother going out, returning at dawn to waken Lilly and embrace her, still dressed in evening clothes and her borrowed jewels. Everything about Beth was borrowed, and she seemed to tear at her own feathers, to throw them off. Eventually, inevitably, the gentleman lost faith and turned her out. He offered to provide Beth and her child with a small allowance, but Beth refused. She told Lilly this often, as if Lilly would admire her pride.

The house near Lambeth Hill that the King had found for Lilly was certainly gracious, but Lilly made it apparent that, unlike the increasingly rapacious Lady Castlemaine, she didn't aspire to ducal titles and an apartment at the palace. And she insisted on performing with the players. Charles agreed, and she thereby secured a degree of independence. Further, unlike other Court mistresses, Lilly didn't become pregnant. A sea sponge wrapped in silk, an elegant pessary compared with Nellie's plug, and serviceable. She wouldn't become pregnant, though it might have made her situation nearly secure. She didn't trust her hands, she did not trust her hands.

It didn't yet occur to anyone that Lilly would be associated with the murder of Lord Metcalf, which passed through London history like a politely suppressed sneeze. There wasn't a soul in town who would wonder at Soby's violent end. Even the peers, after huffing in Parliament for a week or less, dropped the matter. His passing was recorded in February's *Diseases and Causalities* as "Dead by bleeding." Only his mother missed him.

The lambs returned to the lion: Lilly to the King's bed, Bart to the King's antechamber. Charles declined Bartholomew's request to withdraw his brilliant, scathing new play. *The Enchanter's Nightshade* was in repertoire at the King's Playhouse, and Bartholomew was famous for being a man above common sentimentality, a poet who scorns love. Everyone admired him as one who refuses the crutch of morality. The audiences loved what they were afraid of, and they greeted Bart's play with the bright fever reserved for very new, less affable entertainments. All of London tried to conform to Bartholomew's excoriation of the heart, to anticipate, outrun him in cynicism.

Sometimes, when Lilly was onstage, she recalled Soby's surprising flesh. She was given bigger, more complex roles to play, and not solely because of her status with Charles. Her talent for mimicry helped her to stylish surface reflections, but it was the memory of the heat of Soby's blood that lent to her performances their deep, cold timing, which only Lilly knew had needed to be warmed for the public. She had, in a sense, become Soby's widow; she killed him over and over again.

At one time, before Soby, she would have brought audiences to congenial, condescending mirth. They thought they knew her better than she knew herself — maybe they did, then. She heard a new quality in their laughter now, in their gasps and barks: a ring of pain, the sweet poison of estrangement with its consequent element of respect. Now they knew they didn't know her. They said simply that she had matured. And she had. It was the summer of her eighteenth year.

Nineteen

In June, in a grand house to the north of St. James's Fields, a squat boar looked out at a sky full of blown petals, wondering where they came from, perhaps a late-blooming hawthorn. His wife would have known. In their rooms upstairs, his three chubby (oh, fat) daughters were bickering over clothes. Since his wife died, there'd been a buzz of aimless rancour among the girls. Sir George Rose had anticipated a period of decorous mourning, a tragic though restrained chorus of grief. He'd hoped that their spats were a female method of navigating the currents of sorrow over their mother's death, and he waited patiently for his daughters to break down into demure, pious lamentation from which they would rise matured, maybe even two or three stone lighter, and move on to good marriages, in their own houses.

But the world was in the hands of the wicked. The wicked and the blind.

Since his spy had informed him of Lilly Cole's evil act, he'd bided his time; for many anxious months he'd waited for the best occasion, when a scandal would cause the greatest damage to Charles's power. Soon, he would bring things to such a pass that Charles would know who was calling the tune. Then Sir George Rose would see a proper, sober court, faithful to the Church of England. But without appropriate conditions, his charge against the pretty Court mistress for the murder of the debased Lord Metcalf might strike a sour note; in fact, it might even make her more popular. If only the wench was a papist . . .

The caterwaul upstairs reached screaming pitch. Rose took a longing look at the pink petals drifting in the wind. He rested his forehead for a moment on the cool pane. When he closed his eyes, he felt trapped inside his own head, as if it would burst. And so, of course, he could not sleep. Besides, it was time to dress for dinner at the Pope's Head. The naval secretary would be here soon to collect him. He pulled himself up the stairs to his dressing room. His private world teemed with female mayhem and his public world with the horrors of the present age.

The King was in a cabal with the Catholics, that much was certain; Charles's sister was married to one, King Louis's brother. Henriette-Anne, yes, a sly little "diplomat" who would have us all denounce our true Church. England was under the sway of the Evil One. It was up to Sir George Rose to herald a great cleansing.

XXXXX

A footman closed the carriage door behind Prince Rupert as he settled in beside Sir George Rose, who turned himself on the broad platter of his buttocks and somewhat breathlessly introduced the naval secretary by name. "You have met James Hale," Rose said, as if pointing out an advantageous strategic position.

James Hale smiled at Prince Rupert, studiously ignoring the bandage beneath Rupert's wig, and said, "A chine of beef."

Precariously balanced on the seat beside Hale was a large tray with a roast the size of a small child, its juice running from its ribs. The coachman whipped the horses from a standstill to a canter.

"We are dining at the Pope's Head, Prince Rupert," yodelled James Hale. "I think that you will find it quite suitable." Hale, too, had the excited attitude of a conspirator, a tone of jocular but intense scheming. His smooth face bobbed like a cork above the pitching carriage seat, eyebrows raised, a tight, polite smile with a constant sort of hmm? implied there.

Sir George Rose bounced off Rupert and tried to take a closer look. The Prince wore a film of sweat on his grey face, and his eyes were set in bruised sockets. Between his greying hair and his black wig, the swath of bandage showed a limpid pink. Rose and James Hale exchanged a knowing glance. It had been said in town that Rupert had had the pox for years; far advanced, it appeared to have eaten his brain and gnawed its way through his skull.

"Are you well?" Rose inquired.

Rupert turned. "Quite well, thank you." He touched his head. "I have improved the methods of self-trepanning. A simple matter really, a question of reversing the handle of the drill and using a smaller, diamond bit, you see. With my assistant, I let out a good deal of corrupted matter a few days ago."

"Hmm," said Hale. "Quite so."

"A bit of bone in the brain."

"Hmm?"

"From the campaign at Guinea."

They arrived at the tavern dusty and in some disarray. The thick door closed behind them and they were stranded in the entry, like sailors in a greasy fog scented by roasted marrowbones. The Prince unsteadily made his way to a table set for a large company of men.

No others had arrived, but the cook brought forth a leg of veal with bacon and two capons to add to Hale's beef. Rupert continued to speak of the mechanics of drilling a hole in one's skull, while Rose and James Hale listened with assiduity stimulated by mulled sack. Hale offered a description of last Wednesday's meeting of the Royal Society, where they had observed a procedure by which a leg of mutton "in a most satisfying performance" was turned into liquid. There remained a simmering rancour among them, marked by insincere credulity.

A dish of fritters with sausage, three pullets, two dozen larks, and the marrowbones appeared on the table. But Sir George Rose, James Hale, and Prince Rupert ignored the feast, apparently free of appetite for anything other than blandly earnest speculation. They watched a servant fold linen napkins into the shape of swans. Dinner cooled, the day brightened through dusty windows, the gentlemen discussed the committee report (each man spoke of a different committee, but it didn't matter). The afternoon was then forced into constrained turbulence when a carriage was heard in the street and there arrived a gaggle of gentlemen. To a man, they were wearing, in the heat, tall beaver hats for which they each had paid thirty-four pounds, a promotional device of the nascent Company of Adventurers. There was much sneezing and sitting, commanding and drinking. The linen swans flew up and away, stained with wine.

They heard another carriage outside, and everyone turned to the door to see the King arrive, stooping in the low entrance. With him were Lilly Cole, wearing ash grey, modest and noble, and Bartholomew, beautiful in green. Rose gave a start, glaring. Charles placed the girl in a chair to his right, indicated to a gentleman at his left to give up his seat to Bartholomew, seated himself, and seemed to nod without moving his head at all.

James Hale couldn't restrain himself any longer so raised his glass and cried out, "To the great Voyage!"

With the exception of Charles and the girl, the company stood and cried right back, "The Voyage!"

Hale fit the occasion as a boot fits a stirrup. Rupert towered over him with his arm awkwardly raised, the wrinkle of blood on the seam beneath the wig. "To the King," Hale continued, "who sanctifies our quest with his blessing and with the granting of his vessel, the *Wivenhoe*, which he puts at our disposal. And the new frigate, the *Prince Rupert*, so gloriously named, so fit for glory! Tomorrow, gentlemen, will find us ready for the venture to the Northwest Passage. To China! To Cathay!" He turned to the Prince. "Please, sir, be seated, you are white as a ghost. On behalf of our Governor, Prince Rupert, may I say the adventure has begun!"

Sir George interrupted. "Sit down, Hale. All of you, sit down. If it pleases you, Your Majesty," he added with mechanical courtesy.

They sat, Rupert with evident relief. Sir George Rose had what amounted to a moral advantage in appearing to be the only serious man in the room.

"King Charles!" It was Bartholomew. With his yellow hair, his rich, damp scent of desperation, he could have been a model for a religious painting, though the artist would need unusual skill to mediate that lush, solid flesh. He was fatuously drunk, and he had no idea what he was about to say. "Sweetly strung wit, viol of England, I would hold thee 'tween my knees and pluck thee, and bow 'pon thy gut, by my honour. Merry monarch, scand'lous and — merry monarch, I love thee, sire." He hiccupped. "I absolutely do."

"For God's sake, take him out before his stomach stirs," said Rose.

Bartholomew straightened, focused keenly. "Well! It is the witch-hunter! Sir George! How sane you seem in these proceedings! You have tamed your fears sufficient to join us today? Do you not anticipate contagion, if not from Evil, from Unreason? Our business might prove so profoundly fantastical, you will go mad, like me. I am at a table of poets, am I not? No? Am I alone?"

"I have some new information that might sober you," said Rose, looking piercingly at Lilly.

"Oh, I do so yearn for a change," Bartholomew mumbled, smiling whimsically.

"Pardon, Bart?" asked Charles.

At that moment, the tavern door opened and two men entered, drenched in sunlight, their features indiscernible to those inside.

Charles was first to understand who'd arrived, and it was he who announced, "The French Explorers. Dusty with the dried brine of Hyde Park. Sir George," he added, "our heroes are come. Frenchmen! Frenchmen more loyal than a vineyard of Englishmen rendered or vintaged. Oh! But be assured, be *assured,* my devoted gentlemen, my *friends.* How well I know your worth."

Des Groseilliers strode toward Sir George Rose, with whom he felt the closest bond. The two men greeted each other with the small shudder normally associated with lovers. Des Groseilliers had tied back his wiry greying hair with a long leather lace. Behind Médard padded Radisson (he never relinquished his moccasins). Both men were dressed for travel, though of the two, Radisson, in his buckskin jacket with a knife sheathed at his waist, cut the more exotic figure.

James Hale stood, pushing his chair back till it fell over. The two Frenchmen recoiled, prepared for attack, and then recalled their genteel circumstance. Hale said, "Gentlemen. May I present Monsieur De Grozalleurs and Monsieur Ratizon?"

"Je suis Pierre-Esprit Radisson," said Radisson. "Et cet homme, c'est le Sieur Des Groseilliers."

"Quite. Mister Groseyey. Well! And his friend, Pierre. French."

James Hale indicated that the company should applaud. Des Groseilliers bowed to His Majesty, and with a flourish Radisson followed suit.

"We have good news for you, Mister Grosaleur and, ah," said Hale.

"Be seated, Hale." Rose cleared his throat. "Be seated, gentlemen." He felt almost disappointed by how easy it had been to take charge. But there were more sour plums to pluck.

"Have you been well?" Prince Rupert asked Radisson, peering at him with rapturous intensity. Rupert was deathly pale, and the bandage now was clearly soaked in blood.

"The French Explorers," Hale explained to everyone. "Marvellous."

Rose said, "Perhaps His Majesty would like me to review the prospects for tomorrow's Voyage."

"Tomorrow!" Des Groseilliers's hand shot out to grip a fork. He still found this success hard to trust.

"Demain!" said Radisson. "But I told you this will happen, Médard."

"A lovely vessel!" said Hale.

"Two," added Rose. Then he frowned. He did not like the role of Sir Christmas. "King Charles has once again most graciously granted one of his naval vessels. The other ship has been provided by the Company."

A dozen hats approved of one another.

"The ships have been victualled by our two French Explorers, who have provided us with the specifications." Hale looked fawningly at Radisson while he drew forth several rolled parchment sheets, an account.

"That is my account," Radisson affirmed.

Hale read, "Eighteen barrels of shot, five thousand needles, twenty blunderbusses, thirty muskets, and so on. Raisins, beer, prunes, peas, oatmeal, beef, etcetera. Pork. Thirty-seven pounds of tobacco. Cordage, anchors, cables, compasses, pitch, tar, axes, spears, saws, lanterns, hammers, hatchets . . ."

"We need many gifts," said Radisson. "For the Indian. We must have many gifts if we are to make them go to us. Tiny thimble. Combs made of ivory. Like that. Oh! The looking glass of tin. They like for to see themselve — it make them laugh! We must all the time make them happy, or no, we will not get le castor."

"You will need ink and paper," Bartholomew observed, pouring himself wine.

"Ah, yes," said Hale. "Paper, quills, and ink."

"That is true," said Prince Rupert to Des Groseilliers. "You see, monsieur, we are not only adventurers but men of science. We require that you record what you see. Tides, depths, winds, Indians, all. I find I must lie down." He stood and then swayed.

"Cousin Rupert." Charles's ringed hands stiffly gripped the arms of his chair. "This is a ghastly business."

"No," said Rupert. "I will rest here a moment. We must see the ships."

"I have arranged for a barge, Your Majesty," Hale gurgled at Charles, "to take you from Tower Wharf to Gravesend, there to see the *Wivenhoe* ketch and her sister ship."

"We sail tomorrow!" Des Groseilliers was still trying to confirm that this was indeed a fact — *tomorrow I will set forth on the Voyage to the Bay of the North.* He'd begun to think that he'd have to return to New France and face the wrath of his wife, should she still be alive.

The table was breaking up; the men were rising, preparing to go to the barge. Bart, Lilly, and Charles remained seated. Rose stopped and said, "I will see that everything is made ready."

"How very good of you," said Charles.

Rose heard the tone, hesitated, then having made up his

mind, he bared his teeth at Lilly. "For some months, I have kept this secret because I am reluctant to be in any way a messenger with news that might cause His Majesty pain." He stared so hard at Lilly that Charles looked at her too. She was rigid, but her face betrayed nothing.

Charles smiled a little. "Well well, we are most curious."

Rose puffed and continued. "His Majesty has been deceived. His Majesty has associated with Guile disguised as Woman. She on whom you have showered gifts, a house, even the reflected light of the house of Stuart, she with whom you have been, tush, that is to say, friendly — this, this *fe*male — brews evil in her very blood. To speak plainly, King Charles, if I must: the wench . . . is a witch."

Charles burst into laughter. "She most certainly is!" he said fondly.

Rose closed his eyes. "Capable of an action so far from her natural power, she could only have performed it in confederacy with the Devil."

Bartholomew turned to Lilly and kissed her cheek. "The sweet scent of sulphur is on you." Lilly jumped, looked at him in horror. Bartholomew, astonished, thought, My God, I do not know her.

"Absurd," said Charles.

"Verifiable," Rose continued. "I am sure His Majesty will want to address the matter with the woman herself. We are fair men. She shall be permitted the chance to confess and thereby, perchance, save her soul!"

Lilly straightened and stared at Sir George Rose with such cold will, he blanched with fear, not only of her wickedness: he sensed that he might lose.

He anxiously lisped, "Succubus. No child? Your Majesty, the woman brings forth no child. Do you not wonder why? Only a sorceress has the power to inflict such wounds upon the fetus that he will return to God sooner than be born unto Satan. 'Tis a secret treaty with the Devil — and may it lead the country to search out other secret agreements, with the Catholics, say? His Majesty's cousin, King Louis, appears more congenial than is natural even in a brother-in-law. They are whispering in Parliament, King Charles, whispering. But," he added, "I shall leave you, that you might digest the matter." Rose turned his back on them, opened the door to the white sun and the budding breeze of early summer. He snapped a fly out of the air with his fist. He would walk out.

"Don't dare do that, Sir George," King Charles said quietly. His command, like a well-thrown knife, nailed Rose to the door.

Rose's age showed in the curved spine; he looked like a vole. The Adventurers were silent. The King let the moment steep.

Softly, Charles said, "Do not lay scandalous accusations at our door and then leave them there as a cat will leave a mauled bird. We shall deal with your issues in due course, in a proper way. George, I am surprised at your lack of occasion. Are you feeling quite well?"

Sir George Rose wanted to confess: I cannot sleep.

"We are most unpleasantly surprised," Charles said. "In your haste to stir trouble you have forgotten an important matter. Rupert, cousin." He indicated with his hand for Rupert to approach.

Rupert came forward. This little crisis had cleared his thinking.

Charles resumed, addressing Rose. "It is surely your prolonged grief over your good wife that seems almost to have un*manned* you, Counsellor. Otherwise, you would not have been so neglectful of your immediate responsibilities to the Voyage. Prince Rupert, Governor of the Company, must today, even now, appoint his overseas representative to Hudson Bay."

Des Groseilliers gave Radisson a meaningful, miserable look: Governor! Pah! There is no freedom on earth.

"Ah yes," Prince Rupert agreed. "Before we send our ships to sea, we must have an overseas Governor, but of course."

"Let Rupert be an example to you all," said Charles, revolving in his chair and appraising the Adventurers in their hats. "There is more at stake in this enterprise than trade and profit, though indeed, these are admirable goals, gentlemen. My gift has been generous, as it is in my nature to be. We have given you Canada — and we are happy to grant you this, even with the possibility, as you may surmise, of there being some strain in our future relations with King Louis, who has, it may be argued, preceded us in generosity by giving the very same territory to a Dutchman, this Van Heemskirk." Then, "Rupert," he added, "would you be so kind?"

Rupert stood at Charles's side; he seemed in full command now. "Gentlemen of the Company! We will go to meet our overseas Governor!"

"Marvellous!" said James Hale, glad to be on firm ground. "When will he be here?"

Rupert looked to Charles. He was saddened to realize that this business with his head had interfered with his mind: he'd forgotten to confirm with Charles the appointment of the overseas Governor. He waited patiently for a clue.

"He awaits us at the Tower," said Charles.

"At the Tower of . . .?" Hale looked like someone who must laugh at a joke he doesn't understand.

"The Tower. Quite. Our man is in the Tower."

"He is a guest?"

"A prisoner. He is a prisoner."

Rose found his voice. He was fighting to regain his outrage, but in his tone there was an element of chagrin that he could not disguise. "The overseas Governor of the Company of Adventurers is a prisoner in the Tower?"

"He has been in the Tower for this last year."

"On what crime?"

"Treason," said the King.

Sir George Rose and the Adventurers gasped. Des Groseilliers's spirits lifted.

"Of course," Charles added, "he must first meet Rupert's approval." To James Hale: "Accompany the Prince. Take a carriage." To all: "The French Explorers will go down to the barge and await us there. And we, Gentlemen, will go to the Tower. Go!"

The Adventurers milled about in some confusion and then muddled out the door. Rupert insisted on walking to the Tower and took his leave, enlivened, curious. The Explorers bowed and departed. Dust floated through the oily air.

Charles, Lilly, and Bartholomew took a short, truant breath. The fine ribs of a lark were sitting in an orange sauce. Charles pushed his chair from the table and stretched his legs. The three stared, snagged on a moment of despond. Rose's lurid accusations against Lilly felt indecent. Charles considered whether he might simply wish them away. He liked things as they are, or as they were only a few minutes ago.

He roused himself. The "whisperings" in Parliament were a concern. There was a possibility that word had got out over the secret treaty with France. Charles's sister, Henriette-Anne, had shown herself a brilliant diplomat there and made great gains toward securing France's assistance in the war against the Dutch. But open affiliation with Catholics was always a risk. Charles thought, I will not permit my country to blunder into another disastrous rebellion. His beloved sister, with the memory of Mother, not to mention James and his own Catholic Queen, the whole damned lot of them made life difficult. But what on earth would the mad old witch-hunter intend by attacking Lilly? Seated gracefully beside him, the girl seemed dozy with the suety remains of the meal. Charles softly asked, "Did the mason arrive and repair the garden wall?"

Lilly peered at him to see if he was serious, then answered slowly, as if reading code. "Yes. Yes, he did, actually. Perfectly well."

"Good."

The muffled din of kitchen pans, and outside, a cart clattering over stones, all sounds engulfed by the rising afternoon heat. Bartholomew wore an abstracted look of listening.

"Are you writing anything these days, Bart?" Charles asked with decided, even measure.

Bartholomew said, "I supposed, I'm — it's hardly the time to discuss . . ."

"Ah." Charles nodded.

Lilly put her hand on his arm. "Shall I speak, Your Majesty?" Charles didn't immediately respond. "To these — charges — against me."

"Well they are not 'charges' in any legal form, now are they?"

"Still . . ." she said.

"Sir George Rose is old and unhappy. Aging men often make mischief as they lose influence. An unfortunate display of impotence."

Lilly and the King looked at each other carefully. "All right," said Lilly.

"Your soul is your own concern, Lilly," Charles added. Then he sat up as if turning the page of a book. "Did I tell you? My darling sister is expected to see us very soon. We have pried her out of France, with Louis's blessing and the curses of her puling husband."

"How nice for you, Charles."

"Yes. We are very pleased."

A fly discovered the remains of the pie.

"Well," sighed Charles. "I suppose we must introduce the witch-hunter to the overseas Governor."

Lilly laughed nervously. She found her parasol and waited for the gentlemen. An attendant opened the door and they went out.

"A carriage?" asked Bartholomew. He was on the windward side of his veering sobriety, now that they were out in the fresh air. For the first time in his remembered history, he wished he weren't drunk.

"No." Charles pushed at the open carriage door so it banged against the steps. "We will walk." He looked down at Lilly's feet. "Or would you prefer to ride?"

"No," she said. "I'd like to walk with you."

Charles studied Lilly's profile, her determined, womanly expression. He couldn't fathom what she might have done. She seemed capable of anything. He felt flush with desire. "Perhaps we shall speak later . . ."

Lilly bit her bottom lip. "Yes."

They began the journey up the hill to the Tower, Charles at his customary gallop and Lilly at a dogtrot. Bartholomew fell behind and then, lifted on the wind from the river, beat ahead. Soon they passed the waddling Adventurers, who tripped to catch up, and the ensemble arrived at the stairs to the Beauchamp Tower in a flurry of lace and rosewater. Prince Rupert, attended by a sweating James Hale, was already pacing in the execution yard.

Twenty

The prisoner normally resided in one of the northeast-facing rooms in the White Tower, but he'd been brought here today, to Beauchamp Tower, to the beautiful butter-blond stone room with a view of the gallows. This June morning it was a sunny space but cold: the stone kept winter's chill. He had been escorted here, politely, without explanation, had been told only to expect some very important visitors, nothing more.

Since he'd left the colonies, Prisoner Brown had been in fifteen gaols and two madhouses. Dungeons. Torture chambers. By ratio, very few courts of law. This was certainly the most comfortable imprisonment he'd ever known.

Magnus Brown was born not in the colonies but in England. Long ago, when he was twelve years old, in August of 1642, he was kidnapped — stolen from the palace yard. He'd wandered out of Whitehall to see what a war looked like and got snatched into a coach and carried off.

Magnus's mother was inside, hiding in the palace. She was officially the Queen's lady-in-waiting, but the Queen was in France at the time, trying to sell her jewels. The boy had been cooped up in the nursery with the younger children, and he was sick of it so he'd slipped outside. Magnus's friend, Prince Charles, was having all the fun; he'd gone off to Nottingham with his father the King to wage war against the Parliament.

The stolen boy was secreted aboard a ship bound for Virginia, where he was sold. For nine years, he worked as an indentured servant on a tobacco plantation — his term exceeded the customary term of seven years because he was disobedient.

Virginia was a Royalist colony; its people had no time for Oliver Cromwell. The boy was sold to a master who tolerated the King, sure, long as he stays in England, but who didn't believe that Magnus was a chum of Prince Charles. Besides, he'd paid for a hard worker, hadn't he, not stolen gentry, and he didn't want any trouble on his own head. He beat Magnus till the tales of life in a palace, of beautiful women, of fathers with different names, till all that flummery dried up in blood.

When the boy was quelled, his master let him read the Ten Commandments. Before he had been stolen, Magnus had been reading Dante's *Commedia*. But the Bible was better than a beating, and the boy took whatever learning he could get. Very soon he'd memorized great swaths of the Old Testament. Without the distraction of other literature, Magnus found that the wind that blew the words to Moses filled his own lungs. He began to know that his master didn't own him. Magnus Brown felt his growing body fill with the breath of God.

At twenty-one, Magnus Brown was paid in corn and a suit of clothes and became a free man. He walked away from the tobacco field and into the woods. In the woods, he encountered more than a dozen people sitting on the ground, speaking passionately in hushed voices. They were Quakers. Most of these people were women. They greeted him and let him join them. Over a fire bubbled a pot of green corn and walnut soup. While Magnus Brown sipped the sweet, silky soup, they began to lecture him on the evils of a talkative tongue. They talked about that for hours, till the sun set and the bush went dark. Then they walked back to their houses without light.

After that, he sought the company of Quakers, who always

spoke in feverish argument on the virtues of spare, simple speech. The women were especially expressive on this subject. He especially liked the company of the women.

Magnus Brown remembered his own mother as being very beautiful. She had seemed pleasantly scandalized by her effect on others, and she liked to exert her control over men, though she also knew how to play to the proprieties of Court, in particular to the subdued tastes of a Catholic Queen. His mother adored being Catholic. She loved the Mass, she loved the smell of it. She loved what guilt can make men do.

Magnus Brown was illegitimate. His father was a Scottish Earl who claimed to be a descendant of Fergus the First. He was a Presbyterian and a Covenanter. It was strange for a fanatical Presbyterian to spawn a child out of wedlock with a Catholic woman, but Magnus Brown's mother was so beautiful. She had a flair for transgression and a taste for revenge; she knew that the old Scot Presbyter would suffer Hell's pains for his fleshly weakness.

Magnus Brown's Scottish father would indeed grow huge with guilt, which he learned to ascribe to women, especially debauched Royalists. He would be among those Scots at Aberdeen, in the drizzling cold summer after the King's decapitation, who would make life so unhappy for young Charles.

The Civil War in England ended, and Charles was restored to London and the throne. In Virginia, Magnus Brown turned thirty years of age, and he was widely known for his knowledge of mathematics and the science of navigation. That was when the incident occurred, an event as simple as an apple falling from a tree.

He did not love, surely he did not love Sarah, the wife of Samuel Bedford, his neighbour, his friend. Sarah Bedford, with black hair, full of unruly joy and achingly in love with Magnus Brown. When the women gossiped that Sarah had kissed

Magnus and sat on his knee, the local magistrate ordered her husband, Samuel, to discipline his own wife. Sarah could have been imprisoned or publicly dunked for her offence, but the canny magistrate understood that his method would be far more effective. Samuel maintained a rational exterior, refusing to denounce his pretty wife, but he was raw inside, and when he began to discipline Sarah for the sake of form, his blood rose up and blinded him and he didn't see that she was dead until his hands had cramped closed around her throat.

Magnus Brown left Virginia by ship the following day. He was God-struck by the ferocity of love. His life was no longer his own. At night, in his undersized bunk, he was awakened by his body's vibrating. His burly body trembled in ecstasy. He was quaking. It was no longer simply a word. He was transpiring.

Magnus Brown sailed directly for Brest, then made his way overland to Rome. He was called by God to cleanse the Pope, "the High Priest," "the idolater," the "Fornicator with the kings of the earth." (He drew on Dante.) He spent that summer in a madhouse suffering the brain fever brought on by burns from boiling oil stroked on the soles of his feet.

Released from the Italian madhouse, he stumbled back to France. Along the way, his antithetical preaching offended the authorities in Genoa, Lyon, Vichy, Orléans, Fontainebleau. When he was released from a Paris gaol, he had no shoes, so he walked on his scarred bare feet to Calais, en route enduring almost solicitous torture in prisons in Rouen, Amiens, Lille. When he arrived at Calais and its prison, he persuaded a warden to find a ship's captain to provide him passage back to England. Arriving at Dover, he refused to take the Oath of Allegiance and was imprisoned in a madhouse run by nuns, who quickly ascertained his sanity and submitted him to gaol. Subsequently, he saw the gaols in Chatham, Gravesend, Erith, Woolwich, Greenwich.

And then Newgate. Magnus Brown was unravelling. He began to write letters to King Charles warning him that, unless he renounced his wantonness, his kingdom would be razed by the whirlwinds of the only Lord.

The somewhat elevated charge of treason was not enough to take Magnus Brown from Newgate to the patrician confines of the Tower of London. Charles remembered his childhood friend. His very bowels remembered the brilliant, excessively curious son of Mother's favourite lady-in-waiting.

Charles was afflicted by conscience. He'd provided well for Magnus Brown's mother, and, with his help, she had survived the war in relative comfort, dying of toothache just after the Restoration. But the restored King had indulged himself with Brown's Scottish father. He'd had the old Presbyter hanged, gutted, and burned, back in 1660. It had been a rare indulgence.

XXXXXX

Retrieved from Newgate and installed in the White Tower, the prisoner was interviewed, at Charles's request, by Sir John Robinson, Lieutenant, who reported that Magnus Brown was extreme in his passions but capable of reason, if not altogether sane, and, further, that Brown demonstrated certain qualities of genius.

Charles heard these reports with his customary impassivity and ordered that the Quaker be treated with the respect due to a man of condition. On hearing that the prisoner suffered from sore feet, Charles told Robinson to provide shoes. Ever since the war, when he had run from Cromwell's forces in borrowed boots, Charles had felt compassion for men and women with sore feet. Robinson had paused, then carried out the strange order. No one dared to breach the moratorium surrounding the Quaker.

Magnus Brown received new shoes and retired into silence broken only by interviews with the Lieutenant, when he would express himself in simple speech of unquestionable honesty and astounding intellect, especially in the areas of navigation and accounting. In addition to shoes, Charles provided Brown with a fine bubble quadrant and a compass of moscovia glass and with charts dating back a hundred and twenty years. At Christmas, he sent Brown a copy of Hakluyt's *The Principal Navigations, Traffiques and Discoveries of the English Nation.* Volume V. Voyages. Martin Frobisher. John Cabot.

No one but Charles connected Magnus Brown with the dangling, befouled gallows fruit, the dour Scottish Earl, one of seven men hanged in a single day. Charles never visited Magnus in prison.

But if the King should visit, Magnus Brown had decided, he would not inquire after the fate of his father. This was healthful. It was said that the people had bargained for the old Scot's gallstones, left behind in the ashes.

Twenty-One

The cold in prisons had been so chronic that Magnus Brown had learned to live in it through quaking. If he were a fish, the cold would be water. When he was alone, he sat upright at his table, his beard the colour of frosted barley, feeding on the cold, throbbing at first, then experiencing it as a substance essential to himself.

His stay in the Tower had been calming. He'd quit calling himself a Quaker; in fact, he'd quit calling himself anything at all. No more canting, no more thee-ing and thou-ing, gone were the Quakers' tortured (ha!) cadences. He'd given up names and naming. Though he'd been christened with five names, he had retained only his first and his last — Magnus Brown.

It is a mutable world defined by declining and ascending light. Magnus Brown kept a ledger of these (and all) events. The forces of disorder will be met by the forces of order. With white hands the span and strength of a dove's wing, with purple veins like pinfeathers and long yellow nails, he calculated the motion of the stars he saw at night through his prison window. He observed the transformations of things to devise the integer of stability. He folded his hands before him, but not in what most men would call prayer. Here, in this room awaiting his visitors, Prisoner Brown resided in bliss.

A shadow flicked over the floor. He went to the window and

saw a maw, what they call a seagull, flying from the Thames. And in the yard below, a retinue of hats.

The room was at the top of a narrow staircase. Magnus Brown heard the crowd climb toward him. He left the window, having no special appetite to be thrown out of it, and went to stand before the empty fireplace.

A gley-eyed courtier, of obvious means and testy as a wild boar, entered first. Prisoner and boar were alone for a prolonged moment. The boar said, "King Charles." Promptly, the cell filled with men. There was a girl, a strangely self-possessed girl with a white face and black hair. Magnus Brown trembled with the revival of an old disquiet. She slipped into a corner, to a short stool there, and closed herself, wing to wing, nearly invisible. Brown focused on the men. The girl sat at the back of his mind, a small dark spot of foreboding.

The courtier was squat beside the man who might be Charles. But there were two such men, very tall, swarthy, richly attired (and perhaps not rich at all). Magnus Brown watched carefully. The taller of the two, wearing a bloody bandage beneath his wig, stepped aside, taking himself out of the circle. The man who remained at the centre did not move his head. Now it was apparent who was King.

The King was a black star devouring light. He was so ugly, he was beautiful, an enormous raven, and his eyes betrayed an intellect so remote and free and dangerous that Brown, who only moments before would have refused to fawn before any mortal, dropped to one knee.

"Brown," said the boar, "tell us your true and full name."

"Brown," said Brown.

"Magnus Brown," said the King.

In Charles's mouth, a sudden taste of cod-liver oil. Magnus Brown was, after all, a Scot. He met Brown's eye. How much does the man remember of his childhood? And could it be that a prophesying nature creates a prophet-sized body? The beard, the sunburned cross of nose and cheekbones, a voice like wind and thunder.

"I am Magnus Brown," the prisoner declared. His long white hands hung at his sides. "I have no past of my own but only a fluctuating present."

Sir George Rose snuffled impatiently. "Pugh, give us no metaphysics. Where do you come from?"

Charles, unblinking.

"Out of bondage, which is nowhere," said Magnus Brown. Then, reluctantly: "Virginia. But I am by and large a foreigner."

Rose stepped forward. "For what reasons have you been imprisoned?"

Brown showed them his blue eyes in a brightly bearded face. Not innocent and not young, his face had taken the colours of this cell and the colours of the flagstone shores of the northern seacoast he'd never seen. Charles remembered Brown's father's ruddy face, saw the resemblance. He detected the boyhood friend in Brown and he knew that Brown remembered, too. Magnus Brown's history of dissent didn't particularly alarm Charles. The man seemed to have been calmed by imprisonment, the food, the peaceful periods of study. Charles could sense no rancour here.

He began to enjoy himself and said, "Magnus Brown is a Quaker, Sir George. A colonial dissenter. Do we smell corruption?"

Rose honestly considered this, sniffing at the room. "No," he said with all seriousness. He, too, experienced a wave of enthusiasm — the familiar urge to attack. "His Majesty the King, with Prince Rupert of Palatine, has undertaken to recommend you to us, Magnus Brown. You must tell us why."

There it is again, thought Brown. Are they stupid? They

want him to explain the motives of other men? Magnus Brown's reticence was so eloquent, Rose felt himself a fool.

Prince Rupert brightened. What is it about the man that's so remarkable? *A foreigner.* He had not expected to be impressed by this fellow, of whom the Lieutenant of the Tower and even Charles himself had made such a fuss. *I am getting emotional.* Excitement swelled the glands of his throat.

Charles glanced at Rupert, and Rupert did an extraordinary thing: he *smiled.* Rupert hadn't smiled since 1641, when he was in love while imprisoned in Linz. It was a strange, rare smile, and Charles was reminded of how unusual it is to have a dog who will smile. In fact, Rupert's poodle, Puddle, used to smile; they'd smiled at each other, Rupert and Puddle. Perhaps then Rupert had not smiled since Cromwell's forces murdered the dog back in '45. Yes, he did smile during the War, until Puddle died. Hell and damnation, Charles thought, I cannot resist the old pirate.

Magnus Brown had not yet responded. Charles felt a sudden joy. A rebellious colonial who had joined with dissenters in Virginia. He could not have devised a better means of easing his pinched conscience while thwarting Rose. And besides, Brown makes Rupert happy.

Charles said, "Sir George, you have met our overseas Governor, Magnus Brown. Arrange the prisoner's release, that he might undertake the navigation of Hudson Bay."

"May I speak with you in private, Your Majesty?" Rose moved to the stairwell.

"Hudson Bay," said Magnus Brown. "West-northwest. Round the coast of Greenland at fifty-nine degrees north."

Prince Rupert walked slowly toward Brown. "Thence to Resolution Island. West, half a point north."

"Sixty-one degrees twenty minutes north at the island's

south end," said Brown, his voice gentle with compassion for the Prince's head injury.

"Lest we grow prematurely enthused . . . ," Rose dryly interrupted. "King Charles? A word?"

Charles indicated that Rose must speak here, not in private.

"I am providing a substantial sum toward this adventure," said Rose.

Charles put this aside. To James Hale he said, "Acquaint Magnus Brown with his duties in the expedition. We may spare no time."

Hale, as naval secretary, had heard the Lieutenant, Sir John Robinson, speak fulsomely of Brown's ability to navigate and — what interested the secretary even more — to keep accounts. Magnus Brown was said to be a genius with figures. "The Company has the perfect boat," said Hale, his gurgling voice. "A ketch, Master Brown, built in '65 at Wivenhoe by a man named Page.

"She's seventy tons," continued Hale excitedly, confidentially, to Magnus Brown. "Eighteen in the beam. Draws eight. And carries eight guns." He was pleased with his numbers.

"May we not spare a moment to question this man's loyalty?" demanded Rose. Even as the words left his lips, it dawned on him that Charles had chosen Magnus Brown precisely because Brown had been, in a rather sublime sense, disloyal. Rose didn't skip a beat. "As you yourself point out, Your Majesty, the man is a Quaker. A dissenter akin to the Puritans. Worse than the Presbyterians."

Charles wavered very slightly.

Rose thrust home. "A Scot." Expanding, and to the astonishment of the entire company, he recited a homily oft heard from the lips of his deceased wife, herself a border Scot: "You may fry an oyster, wing a partridge, thigh a woodcock, or lift a swan. But you'll never cook the Presbyterian out of a Scot. Ha ha ha." There. He could do no more. The men looked at him as if he'd taken off all his clothes.

Bartholomew laughed so sadly that Charles felt a dim, ominous sensation of fear. "Go out and get some air, Bart. You are unwell." Bartholomew cast one look at the prisoner and went. Charles's unease grew; he saw envy in the Earl's eyes. Dejection, even in the young man's footsteps, sounding down the stairs.

Magnus Brown looked out at the sunlight, at the ravens feasting at the eyes of a traitor whose head was impaled on the gates to the armoury. He was filled with wanderlust, a hunger for the purity of the sea. Surely he would find redemption in work; he'd find the grace he'd longed for since leaving Virginia.

He'd been studying the charts brought to him by Robinson, a gift of the King. He had grown peaceful in this prison, satisfied by the travels in his mind, but now it was time to be off. Among men. In an eight-gun ketch. To Hudson Bay. And beyond. To the Japan Sea. Below, the effeminate man in green was moping around the gallows. And behind him, a fluttering of dark wings, the light pressure of her will. Brown returned his attention to the King.

Charles looked him in the eye. And Magnus Brown instantly knew: the Earl, his father, was dead. He felt oddly purified, as if the estranged father had paid for the sins of the bastard son. He knew that the execution, which had been of dubious legality, for personal expedience, gave him some leverage with Charles. But of anything on earth, Magnus Brown hated bondage. He did not want to be bound to Charles; he did not want Charles bound to him. Still, the connection between them swung in his heart, and he saw a future for himself, a destiny unfolding.

"I may have Scot blood in my veins," he said, "but it matters not. I was a Quaker. Not a Puritan. Not a Presbyterian. Now I am nothing but a lowly servant of God and King. I navigate well, and I will take a crew safely to the Japan Sea. We will make profitable trade there and at every place where we choose to make land." He closed his mouth. It was obvious that he would say no more.

"Glorious," murmured James Hale. Despite the chill in the cell, Hale felt himself grow warm. He will go to see Bradwell's wife, yes he will, she'll let him do what he likes, yes she will.

Charles found his path to the stairs blocked by Rose. He towered over him and said, "Sir George, we are satisfied that we have found the man to govern the adventure."

Rose let long, discouraged wind through his nose and stepped aside as the King passed him by. The Adventurers heard the newest royal shoes, a coloured pair from Flanders, clack outside and away.

Rose withdrew his purse from his coat and threw it to the startled naval secretary. "For further victualling." To Magnus Brown, he said, "They tell me you have a talent for figures. See to it that you keep an honest account of every transaction. Leave nothing out. Let no man enter private trade. You are answerable to us. Should there be the merest indiscretion in your ledgers, you shall be recalled and will face punishment."

Magnus Brown answered with a twitch of the brow. It was enough. The sunlight cut his figure into two hemispheres, half light, half shadow. Then he moved so his body was wholly lit, bright as brass. There were seven visitors remaining in his cell. The cell was twelve feet by eight feet, giving an area — calculated despite the irregularities of its shape — of ninety-six square feet, which provided twelve square feet per man, yet each man did not occupy so much space, each man required four square feet, if cloaks, hats, wigs, and ribbons were taken into account. Four square feet times seven is twenty-eight square feet, leaving sixty-eight square feet of empty space. Brown sat down at his table and waited. As each man departed, he calculated the increase in emptiness. Until at last he felt the room was void but for one, she, a silent presence. He placed his dove's hands before him, and it seemed he would vanish into the chilly air if he hadn't been constrained by her, the woman with black hair.

Lilly watched Magnus Brown's back. She felt his resistance to her, she felt his bliss calling him out to sea.

In the gallows garden below, there was a hue and cry over her absence — Charles sent attendants back to fetch her and to bring the new overseas Governor of the Voyage to Hudson Bay. Lilly Cole waited for them. It had been a dream, these past months. This prison cell, the beatific bulk of Magnus Brown, here was the hinge to the future. The voices below grew louder. They were coming, all the more insistent because they'd forgotten about her. She watched Brown. He obviously heard but didn't respond. These were the last few minutes of what now seemed to Lilly to have been a pretty play, borrowed for a time, then stripped away.

Twenty-Two

They hurried to the mud-shingled wharf, sweating in the wind. A barge tilted, sucked at the waves, the oars squealing in their fittings. Twelve Adventurers, sans chapeaux but wearing the season's bright fabrics and coats with full skirts, were seated there on deck chairs, some of them mildly seasick. The new, rich blue velvet much in evidence, though several would persist year-round with sombre oxblood. William Pretyman, the Company's first subscriber, wore seashell pink. Prince Rupert lifted his pale face to them in greeting, his wig floating on the blood-soaked bandage. "Charles!" he cried thinly. "It is marvellous to be on the water! Come, come!"

"Rupert," Charles said, "we must get a physician."

"Nonsense!" Rupert waved his hand. "I am on my way to Gravesend!"

Charles pulled fretfully at his own earlobes. The lines were cast off. Sixteen sailors double-manned the oars against the wind, and the barge lurched upriver. At the bow of the craft, the French Explorers, joined by Magnus Brown, stood with the prospect of the River Thames unfolding before them and their backs turned to England. Seeing this, Charles felt galled by resentment, a chary regret for his own generosity.

They rowed through the afternoon, into the evening. There was a lot of traffic. The boats were various but generally well

157

appointed, and movement itself made them lovely. Perhaps it was the effect of being an immobilized passenger, but Charles grew increasingly depressed. The commerce so much in evidence on the river seemed more a betrayal than an augmentation of the Kingdom. Lilly was serenely watching the scenery — no — it was *as if* she were serene. Sleep — sleep in the constant wind — abruptly sealed his eyes. His head fell back, the barge jolted forward and he awoke from a fathomless, infinitely short dream of himself standing alone on the moors while merchant ships rose up on airy laughter.

They were coming into port. The two ships appointed for the Voyage were at anchor. Nearby, countless rickety docks shambled up the shore. Bartholomew and Lilly were seated beside each other. Lilly's hand lay palm up on the bench, as if she had just relinquished Bart's touch. They looked out in opposite directions but seemed conjoined, tight lipped. They appeared to have reached some uneasy conclusion and would sit with their secret lodged in their throats.

Charles reached out to touch Lilly's shoulder and asked her if she was cold. Lilly distractedly said she was, a little. Charles gave her his coat. There was a band of freckles on the bridge of her nose. Around her and Bartholomew, a veil so fine it could be made of sea spray.

It took nearly two hours for the pilot to guide them to the quay nearest the *Wivenhoe* and the *Prince Rupert*. Light wind. Gulls and terns weaving through strands of purple cloud. King Charles had adopted his waiting pose, perfected by years of mandatory tedium. The depression deepened like a chest cold.

He anticipated the night. They would take a room at Gravesend, have supper alone, perhaps the three of them, then Charles would send Bart away and have Lilly to himself. Perhaps it was time to learn what "evil" was lurking in that dove-white breast.

He was startled to realize that someone had moved to sit beside him. Sir George Rose, breathing rapidly, his damp breath condensing on Charles's black wig, whispered, "Have you been watching her?"

Charles regarded Rose with dread. Mist drifted between them. The barge rocked. Ships' lanterns smudged by dusk.

"It has been well attested," Rose continued in his phlegmy undertone, "that a Soul fretted with Vice makes a meal for Evil. We must not discount the susceptibility of the, that is, the girl, the player . . . she . . ." He drifted off anxiously. Let her even *begin* to conform to the shape of a hare and Rose will be on her with no weapon other than Divine Reason. "Transport is too soft a penalty for such as she. The woman must be made to stand before a judge and accept her proper punishment, to save her own soul."

"On what charge, Sir George?"

"My Lord, the girl is a murderess."

"Murder? Murder? My Lilly?"

Rose rolled his eyes.

"We are intrigued. When do you say this act took place?"

"Last winter."

"Yet you only raise this now?"

"The urgency has been compounded by a certain restiveness of Parliament over your treaty with France."

"Ah." Perhaps it is best to focus our attentions on Lilly. "And whom do you say she has murdered?"

"A man."

"A commoner?"

Rose said grudgingly, "Lord Metcalf."

"Oh. Well." Charles realized that this could well be true. "A man? A beast. How many had Soby himself murdered? How many times was he convicted of manslaughter, and how many times did he bully and buy his way out? Tut. Listen to me, I sound like a very moralist."

"It could have been anyone. It could have been Sir Colleton. It could have been *you*. It is not safe — even in your sleep, it is not safe."

"One must be cautious, Rose. If we are to start throwing about charges of murder, who knows where we shall stop?"

Rose froze and then burned furiously. "The world was made safer by the extermination of that evil rat," he hissed.

"Perhaps. But the Jesuits seem to have liked him. It took some effort to discourage them from a more zealous investigation, quite an effort indeed. And for all that, we certainly feel confident that the world is much safer with Lord Metcalf dead. He was a rogue. If your absurd suggestion is true, we can only acknowledge that Lilly showed good sense." This situation was more dangerous than he had first thought. Parliament, cursed penny-pinchers. Rounders.

"Such a woman could kill a man just by thinking it."

"Do not be vulgar, Sir George."

"Vulgar, Your Majesty? Was Abraham vulgar when he witnessed three Angels? Was Lot a vulgar man? Jacob, speaking to the Angel, is this what the King calls *vulgar*? Or perhaps your Royal Majesty would argue that Moses spoke to the burning bush in a *vulgar* fashion? She will hang! She will burn! God's will be done! You know that a witch in Essex was burnt to ashes on the left side of her body when there was no fire near her?"

"Stop!" Charles would have shouted, but he didn't want anyone to hear. He turned toward the bow. And there was Magnus Brown, standing directly behind them. He must have come aft to speak with the King when he was interrupted by Rose. The big man had obviously overheard; he was standing as if gripped by — what? Fear? Unlikely. No. Brown met Charles's eyes with undisguised shame. The man was in an agony of shame. Charles distractedly watched Magnus Brown lumber back to his post.

At last, the barge was brought to dock. It was dark now. The company gathered limbs and, with sour exhalations and stiff joints, clambered to the dock. Bartholomew and Lilly remained sitting in a place apart from the general confusion. Lilly was whispering to Bart. Sir George Rose gave Charles's arm one meaningful squeeze and joined the others, his missionary zeal defeated by the cold.

Twenty-Three

Tide rising, ships' bells clanging. Movement — watchmen overseeing kidnappings from the taverns for service aboard the merchant ships, the discreet stowing of private cargo — secretive, restless movement between ship and shore, at the threshold to the simple purpose of the sea.

On the sea reach of the Thames, they waited for the turn, a confluence of ebb and wind. The Adventurers had been tucked in with their brandy bottles to dream that they were still on the barge, sleepily lurching west, back to London. Only Mr. Pretyman had a nightmare and woke up naked at an open window. The wind had veered, blowing hard down the river, forming whitecaps in long, broken scallops. Mr. Pretyman, his cold, fleshless body the colour of thin milk, felt a piercing, indiscriminate stab of abandonment.

Charles, Lilly, and Bartholomew took rooms at the Cormorant. They ate their meal by the hearth downstairs with the ordinaries. The beer and hen were good. Bart was queerly hectic. He insisted that Lilly perform the Prologue to *The Enchanter's Nightshade*, and when she complied, he watched her, fascinated, applauding too loud, for too long. "How easy it is," Bart said, "to speak cruel." Since the success of *The Enchanter's*

Nightshade Bartholomew had dashed off yet another sexual scandal comedy, which he titled *Virtue Eschewed*; the poison seemed to flow ever more freely from his pen.

Charles put his hand on Bartholomew's, preventing him for a moment from taking a drink, and said, "It is far from easy to see the world clearly. I love you for it, Bart."

Bartholomew threw his head back, his throat seized in a sob, but he smiled, the tears streaming. "Do not love me, sire. Or if you will, let it be for something worthy."

Charles frowned. "You are worn out. Go to bed."

"I would, Your Majesty, but that I am not yet drunk enough." He stood unsteadily. "I bid you, good friends, sweet sleep." He went outside, to the wind and rain.

Charles was embarrassed for Bart. He observed lightly to Lilly, "The poet is soulful tonight."

Lilly stood and waited for Charles with an attitude of obedience he found unsettling. She had never looked so beautiful. Her shiny black hair was curled by the damp heat of the kettle, her soft white neck and bosom, symptoms of her sex.

Charles's hand guided Lilly to the stairs. He counted the elements of an evening: food and drink, his young friend, his beautiful mistress. How changed it all was, how strangely transfigured by news of Lilly's powers.

She preceded him up the stairs, her small foot in a fine grey shoe, a glimpse of white satin on her instep. Charles's entire body was stiff with desire, rampant — as in ferocious, as in standing on its hind legs. He threw off his wig, his coat, everything but his shirt and stockings, and went to her, seated on the bed where she could look out at the waves on the black water of Gravesend Reach.

Charles made love to Lilly in what might be called an unceasing way; his lust was iterative, in ascending riffs, all night, through the hours, compelled by greater, more delicious pain; he fought his way only to find another way, and another. He was too conscious of everything, it seemed, so conscious that he'd never *get there*. When she got drowsy, exhausted, when she lay on her side on the pillows and fell asleep, he jealously waited for her to be aware of him again.

He hadn't even asked himself how he'd protect her from the judiciary. Perhaps he'd not be able to do so. Especially if it was true that word of the secret treaty with France had leaked out. Parliament would want a sacrifice, a public reprimand of the Monarch. He practised running his hand a fraction of an inch from her body, hovering beside her.

Then he, too, slept. Because he slept so seldom, he slept deep. Lilly opened her eyes at the moment she felt his breathing undulate, a ground swell. One long, swarthy hand rested on her hip. His face was a third longer than hers. His sinewy body with its coarse hair was hot; he was a huge felled bird. She felt his ribs beneath his shirt, each rib like the archer's bow. She moved her hand over his loin to his hip, over his hip to the damp heat between his legs, then again to his hip. Very gently, Lilly pushed Charles onto his back and placed herself above him. She didn't even awaken him; he thought he dreamed.

"She is a swan, Your Majesty," cried James Hale. "An utter swan!" Hale strutted up the dock to greet the King. He pointed at a three-masted ketch. The *Wivenhoe*.

Charles hesitated. She *is* small. Not old but, judging by the mass of hemp stuffed in her planks, not sound. "Then our trade goods must go in the *other* swan," he said.

"Quite! A jest!" Hale waved toward the farther dock, where there was moored a small frigate, the *Prince Rupert*. Hale had acquired a pipe. Onlookers would be impressed with his nautical expertise; that sailor over there likely mistakes him for a pilot.

Charles felt melancholy, he felt remorse, so unfamiliar to him that he couldn't name it. Some private portion of himself had been brought to light, and he felt debilitated, shy to greet the day. His tenderness toward Lilly seemed distastefully avuncular, a burden on her, something boggy and shapeless and lacking in dividend.

The *Prince Rupert*'s deck extended not more than seventy feet. He turned to review the *Wivenhoe*. A deep-waisted boat, she'll founder in the first storm. Both ships were as small as, no, surely they were *smaller* than Captain James's *Henrietta Maria*. And Captain James had called *that* a small ship.

Charles became aware of Rupert beside him, wearing grape velvet stitched in gold thread and a fresh bandage beneath his wig. Rupert hummed something Italian. At least Rupert could appreciate the deadly ratio between the Voyage and the cockleshells provided for it. He was examining the *Wivenhoe*, her staves and ironwork and rigging.

"Small," said Charles.

"Hmm? Yes, she is rather," Rupert agreed, as if surprised by his cousin's acuity.

"Small and weathered."

"Hmm?"

"She reminds me of Mother."

"I was thinking of your mother when I awoke this morning."

"I think of Mother whenever I am worried."

"Your mother was a wonderful woman. You know, Charles, I owe all of England to your little mother."

Charles sighed. Rupert was often at his most elevated when he was in pain.

On shore, a rooster crowed. It was what a navigator would call "a change day," the day of the new moon. Auspicious, in an obvious sort of way that would please the pamphleteers. A beak poked up through the *Wivenhoe*'s hatch, Radisson's long nose.

"Monsieur Radisson!" Prince Rupert called out. "What do you think of our ship?"

From the tilt of the snout, Rupert and Charles assumed he'd shrugged. They heard sibilance. "S'b'n, p'rs'qu'c'p'tite."

Rupert turned to Charles. "He said that he likes the ship because she is small." Rupert put his hand to his mouth and bellowed, "And why do you prefer that she be small?"

Radisson took a step up. "She can be made to, like so, esquiver la glace."

"To dodge the ice."

"Oui. You cannot force a big ship through big ice."

"Quite." Rupert confided to Charles, "There will be a great deal of ice. That is what Captain James saw in '32."

Charles said quietly, "James also said that there is no possibility of there being a passage south of sixty-six degrees."

"Yes. I know."

"Why are we pretending?"

"A habit of mind?" suggested Rupert. "It's rather hard to give up."

"We cannot make the land disappear because we want China."

Charles saw Rupert's tongue rise to the roof of his mouth, like a seabird's, an expression of ineffable longing. "But we will find Rupert's Land," said the Prince.

Charles looked away. Why is everyone so, so *peeled* today, so nakedly *evident*. Is it the sunlight? "Monsieur Radisson! Come here!"

Radisson leapt over the pump and stood at the gunwale peering down at them. He lifted his eyebrows politely.

"Do you really believe, Mr. Radisson, that you will paddle only ten days from Hudson Bay to the Japan Sea?"

Radisson pulled back. "The savages say it is so."

"But what do *you* say?"

"We must get first to the bay. Then we will see what is what."

"You will need a better plan than that," said Charles.

"That is Discovery, good King. We do not know before or it would not be."

Charles sighed again. Another philosopher.

Bartholomew approached with Lilly. They looked like a pair of hummingbirds. James Hale rushed at them as if he'd catch them in a net.

"Shall we go aboard?" shouted Hale. "Do go aboard! Mr. Gooseberries is already there. And Mr. Brown. Mr. Radishes! Make way! Make way! We're coming aboard!"

The King, the Prince, the Earl, and the murderess were ushered up the gangway by the gladsome naval secretary, pipe gripped in his teeth. Sir George Rose was there, seated on a coil of rope. Even Rose had caught the stir; he was reminded of his pirate days off the coast of North Africa.

"This is a momentous occasion for England." James Hale beamed.

"One of so many, it is quite dizzying," Charles agreed, eyeing Bartholomew, who was looking decidedly fatalistic. Charles couldn't bear it if anything were to happen to Bart. "Dizzying, quite," Charles repeated. "I am put in mind of the performance of the Earl's new play, *Virtue Eschewed*."

"Gesundheit," said Rupert.

Bartholomew raised his heavy mauve eyelids. "A delectable pastry, Your Majesty. What is there possibly left for a scribbler to do after such achievement?"

"Have you had another bout of the disease?" asked Charles gently.

"Yes. Yes, perhaps that's what ails me. The disease."

Rose shook his head and said, "Impotent, vain, sodden piss-head."

Lilly watched Bartholomew. She seemed to be connecting Bart's mouth with his hands, his hair with his shoulder. Her apparent objectivity frightened Charles.

A fine black thread of blood purled down Rupert's forehead. "I have provided our new Governor, Mr. Brown, with a journal to record the events as they unfold. I am rather excited about it. I believe Magnus Brown is a man capable of composing an important document of Natural Philosophy, admixed of course with observations of a mercantile aspect."

The halyards started to hum. The wind was brisk; there was a broken crust on the water.

"The tide, she is turning!" shouted Radisson.

Des Groseilliers emerged from the Captain's cabin, where he'd been studying the charts with Magnus Brown. He sniffed the wind. It was time for him to leave the *Wivenhoe* and board the *Prince Rupert*: he and Pierre-Esprit would *each* have a ship for the great Voyage.

Magnus Brown had spent the night recalibrating the quadrants and semicircles. He came up from the companionway like Neptune, his massive head of hair blowing in the wind. Radisson called out to him, "We must away!"

The sky was full of widgeons, curlews, plovers, flying hither and thither and swooping low. Magnus Brown surveyed the river, the wind, the tide. Then he cast so eloquent a look at Lilly that she startled, as if he'd called her. With his eyes on Lilly, Magnus Brown gave his first order of the Voyage. "Call the crew to deck."

"Marvellous," said James Hale.

Charles wanted to retreat. He didn't want to be with anyone he knew.

"King Charles!" Rose's querulous, jowly voice. "We will first have the blessing!"

Bugger. Old woman. Despite the high wind, the cracking of unfurled canvas, the presence of twenty sailors on the ketch, and the shouting from the *Wivenhoe*'s sister ship, Rose was playing his Church of England card again. Des Groseilliers merely growled and descended the gangway to make his way to the *Prince Rupert*, to *freedom*. But the King must kneel, painfully bruising his knees.

"Go forth!" Rose was only pretending to kneel; he'd never get back up. "Profess the true Christian faith in your wanderings. Take the true gospel to the lost descendants of Ham who swarm and increase in the wilds. Bring them out of wickedness into the Light!"

"Amen," said Charles and stood. "We have had quite enough of that."

"Goodbye, good King!" said Radisson. He bowed, then bowed again to Rose. How I love the world! Get the fat English off the ship! But Radisson would ask one last question. He stopped Rose. "Monsieur! Sir George! What is this ham? The savage will spit out salt meat. Pah! I ask you this for my sake alone, and not to put you to the test."

"Ham, Mr. Radsen? The swarthy son of Noah who wandered to Arabia and spawned the wicked roe of barbarians with whom you will make trade!"

"The Noah tale! Ah, oui, I know that. But I forgot he had a son. We do not tell too much the Noah histoire to the savages. They get the bad dream that the white man will flood them encore."

James Hale called out, "The ships are ready!"

"Loose the topsails!" In a wink, the mizzen-top was sheeted. The maintopsail and the top gallant were raised, the small canvas slapping, blocks rattling. The ketch heeled to starboard.

The cables had been cast off. She was tearing through the water, out toward the sea reach of the Thames.

Charles stood on the dock, ribbon billowing at his arms and rippling at his knees, all in motion but for the head, on which even the long black curls were immobile, framing the large, immobile face. Then he saw. Bartholomew's golden hair shining by the bowsprit, where he was crouched out of the wind, Bart's fine head and the brave way he looked back toward London. Tears spilled over Charles's face. Under the great sky, he whispered, "Goodbye, my boy. God speed."

Hale shouted out, though surely he knew that the Earl couldn't hear him: "Should you see a narwhal, I beg you, make me a drawing. And the sea horse! And the cliffs of fool's gold!" Hale realized that he was standing beside the King. He lowered his voice. "It is not only for the Society, my Lord. My niece has such an appetite for exotica!"

Charles gave a start and pivoted, seeking Lilly. But he already knew.

Rupert gasped, "Oh," then with fear in his eyes for the sorrow he must share with cousin Charles, he said, "Lilly."

The *Wivenhoe* tacked into the east wind. There, a small figure in a dress on the quarterdeck. Charles shuddered with helpless regret, jealousy, and envy. The cloud that fetches the wind is a quill. The zigzag path to the sandbanks, to the Kentish Knocks and the Long Sand, the Black Deeps and the Shivering Sands, that which is called the Shipwash, and the Galloper. East, then north past Foulness Point and on, past the Scottish coast, past the Firth of Forth, Moray Firth, rounding Orkney. The signature, the *V* of Voyage, then, snaking north. Snake. Betrayal. Lilly Cole had defied the King of England. Lilly Cole had chosen her own fate.

PART TWO

O you that follow in light cockle-shells,
For the song's sake, my ship that sails before,
Carving her course and singing as she sails,

Turn back and seek the safety of the shore;
Tempt not the deep, lest, losing unawares
Me and yourselves, you come to port no more

Dante's Paradiso *Canto Two*

One

The *Wivenhoe* tacked out past Foulness Island, dodging the shoals and sandbars of the estuary. The reef-topsail wind, from the northeast and gusty, took them wide of Yarmouth. They made the starboard tack at fifty-four degrees north, for Orkney. Squally, but the seas not so high as to reveal the difficulties of her low waist; that would show up later in the storms off Greenland. For now, she was sailing pretty well and the crew already had a sense of her: a bit stiff in the keel, like a hard-mouthed mare, but she'd do. And the bilge was drier than any man had expected.

They'd almost rounded Yarmouth before they took the time to look around.

No denying it. There was a woman aboard. Lilly in a billowing dress.

She gripped the shrouds and yelled when the ship veered up and plunged. Her knees buckled. A hand gripped her arm to haul her up. It was Magnus Brown. Governor. His blue eye like a clearing in clouds, a face as big as judgment. She ground her teeth. Let him throw her overboard. Better than prison, better than hanging.

A scrawny, freckle-faced sailor slid down the shroud nearly onto Lilly's head. "Topsails hoisted and braced, sir," he said to

Brown. There was a trace of contempt in his tone. Brown wasn't Captain; his role, and his rule, hadn't been established aboard the *Wivenhoe*. The sailor leaned into Brown and said, "Course, we'll let the girl down at Stromness, Gov'nor, her and her buggering Royal."

Lilly stared at Magnus Brown. Where is Stromness? She is going to China.

Brown said, "Captain Newland wants to see you, Mr. Frost. Don't stand there, man. Be quick." The sailor gave Lilly a snide glance and went.

Magnus Brown turned to her. "Get below, get out of sight."

"I'll be sick if I go below."

He stopped. She has a crooked mouth. The northern winds brightened and defined her. God save me. A murderer, deeply innocent as a hawk.

"Bartholomew, the Earl, he's sick," she was saying. "He's going to fall into the sea."

Bartholomew was clinging to the pump, his yellow hair slicked to the sweat on his face, brandy-laced vomit flinging up on sea spray. Magnus Brown, with stolid patience, bundled Bart and tied him to a gun. Soon, swaddled, Bart was lowing like a calf and soon he'd fall into the first sleep he had known since adolescence. In the ten days till they'd see the islands of Orkney, Bartholomew would turn into gristle, travelling north, in euphoric withdrawal from alcohol, along the east coast of England, trailing the persistent spool of his half-remembered Self.

Bart had a new life. A new purpose. A sacrifice. For love. He would protect Lilly. He was sick, but he was happy. He had a role to play. He was squiring Lilly to China.

It was nearly solstice when the *Wivenhoe* passed the cliffs of Noup Head on Westray. They'd not had sight of the *Prince Rupert* for three days and didn't expect to see her again, the ships having arranged to wait for each other at Salisbury Island, at the west end of Hudson Strait. Now the *Wivenhoe* must sail west-southwest to Stromness or steer westerly for Greenland.

At Stromness, they could take fresh water and let Lilly and Bartholomew off the ship, though the crew, except for the freckled sailor called Frost, admired the Earl and liked his presence here. They talked about him in respectful tones. He was beautiful even when he was sick. The girl, however, could be dangerous through her affiliation with the King. It's obvious, the sailors said, she's running away. Must be a felon, 'cause she chose transport, they said among themselves, grinning. But then they shrugged and went back to work. The rhythms of sea life were making them cheerful. And a young whore is better than an old one. Jimmy Frost said a woman brings bad luck to a ship, but no one wanted to talk about bad luck. Only one sailor agreed with Frost, a tall, dour Orkneyman who grumbled, "The whore will mak' the winds gae fickle."

Brown had to keep peace aboard ship. As Governor and Chief Navigator, he would demonstrate his generosity and let the sailors decide the first course to sail. If they agreed to free the girl at Stromness, they couldn't argue if he sent the Earl ashore with her for protection; then she could hide in the northern isles. How could he refuse help to a mortal soul suffering a sin that he himself suffered? He remembered the *Christian Epistles* almost word for word — *Oh! love the stranger and be as strangers in the world, and wonders to the world . . . and condemned by the world.*

He'd take her as far as Stromness. Her unlikely presence here, her crime, was God's way of offering him a chance at redemption, slim as a wishbone.

He asked Newland to call the men on deck. Everyone gathered aft around the wheel (to starboard, the green-eyed sea; to larboard, the face of Noup Head and the birds — razorbills, herring gull, kittiwake, guillemot, puffins, oyster catchers, falcons, and always cormorants — veering in the surf off its reefs). Lilly's grimy dress, worn for fourteen days straight, made her look like a black-headed gull perched on the gunwale, beady-eyed, biting her lip, oily feathered.

An old sailor with a high, sweet voice spoke in her favour. His name was John Sparrow. A man made old by fortune, built of copper wire, so wiry he vibrated in the wind — from the first, Sparrow had felt a paternal fondness for Lilly, a high-pitched affection made painful by the loss of his wife and four children to the Plague. "I say, we let her stay if she likes. Let 'em both stay, and why not? If they choose it." A year ago, a cable snapped and broke his jaw and nearly all his bottom teeth, and now his chin moved athwart like a half-hinged door. Lilly felt a blood-flush, hearing his gentle, wheezy speech. She worked her jaw like his, mouthing his words and staring at him hungrily.

The ship's dog, a shaggy hound, galloped from below decks with a guilty manner. The crew regarded the animal with resignation, knowing that he'd relieved himself in the galley. The dog leaned heavily against her leg while she cupped the mangy ears. She asked its name. "Dogg," said John Sparrow, proudly spelling it for her. "I don't know the letters," she said. The old man blinked, but he assured her he'd teach her to read before they reached the Labrador Sea. Sparrow saw that she yearned for something, a hunger she couldn't quite hide. For kindness, perhaps; kindness most likely.

It was a beautiful day. The cliffs were lucent in the sun. Magnus Brown gave his instructions: each man was required to vote yea or nay for the continuance of the "uncommissioned pair of Londoners," as he called them. But before anyone else could speak, Bartholomew lifted his face and said, "See the layered stones." His voice had the hopeful, redeemed tone of the recently nauseated, a boyish penitence and lyricism. "Each layer is time's signature, musical in its form and in its intent." Out of sheer habit his hand reached for a glass. "In its intent," he said again, and without any show of disappointment, he laid his empty hand on his knee. "Stacked staves of music," he resumed. "And the birds, lighting on the staves, they are the notes."

There was a swooning pause.

A sailor lives by poetry. They are at peace, they are at sea, they will have song.

In unison, every sailor — every sailor but Jimmy Frost and the Orkneyman — voted Yea, Ay, Fine, Right, Let 'em stay.

Magnus Brown went down to his cabin in fearful and utter astonishment. They'd voted a woman aboard. And a fop. Dear God.

Bartholomew nodded his golden head. He was sailing to China with Lilly. Lilly, uncertain as to whether she was included in 'em, clutched Dogg close. The *Wivenhoe* steered westerly. Tonight, they would lose sight of land.

Hour	Knots	Lat. N.	
1	3	59° 23'	*Topsail wind, stars shining. Six inches of water in the hold.*

Magnus Brown kept the ship's logbook. At every hour he dipped into his ink and tracked the wind's variations and the ship's response.

> *Light wind. Cloudy. Set topsails, hoisted foresail and main. Squalls. Rain. Carrying topsails, foresail, mainsail reefed. Made a larboard tack. Strong reef-topsail wind. Clewed up the mainsail. Reef-undersail wind. Clear with passing clouds. Topgallantsail wind. Stars shining. Made the starboard tack.*

Every several hours, the sailors registered the ship's speed, spilled the spool of knotted hemp overboard, its wooden paddle like a spoon. One and a half knots. Two and a half knots. Four knots. Five and a half knots. Three and a half knots. Three and a quarter knots.

Brown turned the hourglass. Recorded the winds and sails.

The latitude. He marked their path with pegs on the wooden quadrant hung from a hook in his cabin. The other pegs in the holes marked the ship's speed.

Mull Head on Papa Westray is at 59°23'. They were steering for Cape Farewell, at the southernmost tip of Greenland, 59°49'. Due west. More than four hundred leagues. Twelve hundred miles of open sea.

Nights lit with powdery haze blending into long, translucent days. In those first weeks, there were few storms, nothing violent. Lilly found a shirt, some hose, and mittens. She worked in the galley, helping to boil the beef. She didn't like to cook, but Magnus Brown said she had to do something to earn her passage, and it didn't seem likely the ship's crew would pay to hear her Florimel or her Cydaria: Dryden didn't write his plays for sailors — neither did Bartholomew, for that matter. No. They wouldn't like Bart's arch Prologue to *The Enchanter's Nightshade*. Best to stay out of the way, counting the raisins for Duncan the red-headed cook.

When he wasn't busy, old John Sparrow talked to Lilly. He told her about his family, how they got sick and died. Lilly didn't tell Sparrow about Beth; she never talked about her mother to anyone. But she liked to hear him tell his story over and over again, as if the retelling of catastrophe would affirm that loss is a general condition.

Sparrow tried to interest her in an alphabet he scratched with charred wood on a piece of slate. He perched beside her and carefully drew *A, B, C,* chewing on his tongue while Lilly looked on skeptically. Bartholomew did her reading on her behalf. The alphabet seemed to her a necessity of Bart's, something that only worked out loud. But she was compelled by Sparrow's voice.

"*A. A* is for Atlantis," said Sparrow. "Was Plato in a book, tells us of that great kingdom. Nine thousand years before

Plato's time. Though they reckoned a moon for a year, in those days of old." He put down his slate and sniffed the wind lovingly. "Atlantis was greater than all of Africa, greater than Asia, Lilly. It had great princes what governed from the Straits of Gibraltar all the way to China. Imagine. All of this was once a paradise." He turned his bony face to her. "And then come a mighty earthquake, and the sea rose up and the rain streamed down from the floodgates of Heaven. And the Kingdom of Atlantis was swallowed up forevermore."

Lilly was stunned. "Swallowed up?"

Sparrow pointed down, beneath the ship. "All was drownd'd." He put his nose close to hers. Sparrow smelled sharp, like dried fish. "But girl — there still be a parcel remaining. Aye. A piece of Atlantis. Do ye see what I'm saying?"

She nodded and said, "No."

"What we call America" — he waved to westward — "the Western Isles is the last dry land of the lost Kingdom of Atlantis. When we find America — we've found Atlantis."

Lilly stood up. She smiled vaguely at the old man. And answered gently, not wishing to hurt his feelings, "But we're not sailing to America, John Sparrow."

She walked away and did not see the pity on Sparrow's face.

The sailors' yarns, like swallows' nests of string and grass, assembled certain facts: she was a famous actress; she was the King's favourite whore. But Lilly felt freed, for now, from the necessities of either profession. There was a sort of pall over her sex. She felt like a cabin boy, exempt from manhood yet somehow, by default, male and therefore a person. This was a delusion, a mirage. Magnus Brown had let it be known that any man who touched Lilly Cole would be lashed and fined. Besides,

180

he added, they'd answer to the King, back in England; the King would want to hear how his mistress had been treated.

The sailors' desire for the sea was very great. They were insulted that Brown would think they'd jeopardize their first love for a bit of wagtail. Only Frost and the tall Orkneyman were troubled by her presence. Though Duncan the cook could gladly live without her "help" in the galley.

For the first time in her life, aboard a vessel the size of a decent dungeon, on a seventy-ton ship with twenty men, one dog, six pigs, ten hens, and a rooster, Lilly felt freedom. She'd had only one or two nightmares about Soby since she'd been at sea; she felt almost new.

She went to tell Bart. He and Radisson were in the Captain's cabin. Captain Newland was sound asleep, his head in his palms. Five feet tall, he fit perfectly into his bunk.

Radisson paced the tiny space, talking on and on while Bartholomew took notes. When Lilly and Dogg came in, Bart stopped and sharpened his quill. He and Radisson listened politely to Lilly. "I believe I am, I don't know, *happy*," she announced and sat close to Bartholomew, Dogg throwing himself down on her feet.

Radisson raised his eyebrows. "Ah," he said. "You are go through the mirror. You have gone through the looking glass, oui, I am correct. You are an ecstatic. I see such, all the time, when the sea is calm."

"We're never going back," she said, "are we, Bart?"

"You stay here on the boat and cut the onion, la la la," agreed Radisson.

Lilly clapped her hands and laughed. "I don't mind," she said, then took the sheet of paper from the table and studied Bart's script. "John Sparrow wants to teach me letters." The page swarmed with creatures, a cursive ocean.

Bartholomew placed his knife and quill on a tin dish on the table. He hadn't lost his conviction that he'd done the right thing, the true thing, in helping Lilly to escape England. The exhilaration, however, was fading. He had been in a sensual state of horror, all these three weeks since she'd confessed her crime aboard the barge on the way to Gravesend.

He was caught in a double bind. He'd finally made a selfless move, performed what some might call an altruistic act. But he wondered. Lilly murdered Soby. He couldn't help wondering. It was a weakness, he knew it was — but *shouldn't* she be — what? Remorseful? She exceeded him, she looked sideways and smiled hummingly, "Ggeee," a confident bubble of spit on her lip. Here was Lilly's flesh. Lilly's self-evident flesh.

Bart's genius had resided, like the genie, in a bottle. Now his spirit scattered over the heaving infinite, the Atlantic. Beneath his eyes were fine, sandy bumps of a greenish hue, but otherwise his skin remained pure. The ringlets framed his cheeks, the Roman nose with its high span, the swollen lips, his dimpled chin, a strong, if chubby, jaw.

"Bart," she said. "What will *you* do when we reach China?"

He shook his head, nothing. Yet he was full of information. Lilly was abruptly avid. She looked at Radisson. Something was wrong. "We're sailing to China," she insisted. She couldn't make anything out of Bartholomew's gorgeous writing. The *C*s, an *f*, or *J*. He took his pages from her hands.

"I am tell the Earl what sufferings I have endure in Canada," said Radisson, rather cautiously in his distracted English, studying Bartholomew's face.

"But we're not going to Canada," said Lilly.

The cabin tilted; the ship was changing tacks. She heaved Dogg from her feet and swayed to the galley, where the cook sighed patiently as she salted the stew.

Three

Lilly awoke in the dark, alone but for Dogg. She sat up, hitting her head against the upper bunk, waking the dog, consoled by his rich dog funk. Rats travelled the deck beams.

Dogg sniffed their way astern till they could see, the night was so light. It was early July. A topsail wind, a southwesterly swell, warmer than it had been the entire voyage. They were southwest of Iceland. Moonless. The sky was a pale green cup, a sieve filtering the stars.

They don't have green nights in London. Everyone was gathered around the shallop. Even the ship's surgeon was here, wide-eyed Luc Romieux. Nearly everyone else was named John. The First Mate (named John), Second Mate (also John, though they called him Jimmy, freckle-faced Jimmy Frost), Boatswain (Richard), the Gunner and the Gunner's Mate (John and John again), ship's carpenter (William) and cook (Duncan), and old John Sparrow of the broken jaw. Captain Newland didn't tell the crew his first name. Everyone, Radisson and Bartholomew included, was above deck. Everyone but Magnus Brown.

Brown listened from his cabin below. He always knew where Lilly was. She was his surprising redemption and she mustn't be mislaid. Magnus Brown took out his journal to make his daily record in an addendum, which he wrote from the journal's back page forward: she awoke, she ate, she looked out at the sea. Does she mistake this for a simple day?

The gunner's mate played a three-stringed fiddle, and the carpenter blew an old hornpipe. Some evenings, if the sea was calm, the captain would give them a dram of rum. It was so early in the Voyage, they hadn't yet run out of a smaller, private hoard, so there was more than a dram in some of the sailors tonight.

Lilly sat on the deck and felt John Sparrow's coppery heat beside her. The sailors were showing off a long canary, a made-up, showy dance with a lot of high kicking. They'd dance themselves off their feet, have a drink, and get up again, till they were finally exhausted and settled down to the ballads. Then Duncan the cook sang "The Valiant Virgin," a song about a rich maid disguised as a ship's doctor, and where she kissed, and where the wound. The sailors drank and thought about the maid kissing such a wound.

Then out of the dark to the larboard side, from a faceless man with a deep voice, came a song in the northern tongue.

> O the lass left aff a guidly auld mon
> Tae chase a sailor tae sea.
> She left 'er mon and e'en her bairn
> And run efter the gallant tae sea.
>
> O the winds that blaw did shrike the boat
> 'Twas cold as a witch's flanny.
> The ship did flame tae ribs an char
> Frae the shore ye'll hear the bitch cryin'.

Lilly was careful not to stir. It was the Orkneyman singing.

O the wench wha whored fer the sailor mon
Broucht daith tae the men who sailed 'er.
She curs't the ship frae stem tae stairn
E'en she pra'd gob's wouns tae save her.

Now there was ripple of disquiet among the crew. She felt the axis shift to isolate her. The men laughed casually, crossing then uncrossing their legs and chewing their pipes.

O the tittie gaed efter the sailor lad,
She didnae see Hob's hornies.
The ship gaed doon off the Orkney skerries,
Aa hauns gaed doon i' the nicht tae flamies.

Ta'nicht ye can hear her cryin'
Beyon' the far away lantern.
May the devil take tha whorin' slattern.
O may the devil take efter tha switherin' slattern.

On a starboard tack they sailed at four knots toward a purple horizon. Somebody hummed it again, "O the wench wha whored fer the sailor mon, broucht daith tae the men who sail 'er." The sailors gripped their pipes in their teeth to sing another chorus, a little louder, and somebody sat up to see where she was. "May the devil take tha whorin' slattern, may the devil take efter tha switherin' slattern."

Old Sparrow reached out, put his hand on Lilly's, and whistled, "Ye'd best go below."

"No," Lilly said. "I'm staying here."

Sparrow looked so tired then she nearly relented and might've gone below if the Orkneyman hadn't come to stand so he was looking down on Sparrow and Lilly. Several — four — of the other sailors stood and joined him. Sparrow said, "If ye touch the lass I'll kill ye. Now, or t'morra'."

The sailors knew Sparrow as a survivor — but survival doesn't always guarantee respect. Living close as they did, they'd long since learned to take small interest in their mates beyond what they shared aboard ship: boredom and crisis and sentiments of home. The Orkneyman announced that he didnae want ta touch tha whore; he wanted to give her to the fishies. Lilly saw that the others had in mind first to make sure that she'd be worth nothing but fish food. Her heart was pounding and she thought that the assault, when it came, would indeed make her worthless, so worthless they'd feel no prick of conscience about throwing her overboard. Now they looked as if they had in mind to piss on her.

A little man — later, Lilly would never be sure who it was — gripped her legs and pulled her toward him. Bartholomew stood and tried to force through the sailors, but they restrained him, as if it made them sad to do so, with almost apologetic determination. Others pushed the Orkney sailor aside and began to form a line, one man's hands on another's hips, with the Orkney behind. Lilly thought, he'll be worst.

Bart was shouting and pushing at the sailors who held him. Sparrow drew his knife. He crouched beside her and waved the knife at the men as they tried to get near. Captain Newland, unarmed, bursting with fury, pushed them back. "Get below," he hollered, "damn you, damn you to hell. Get!" The noise raised Magnus Brown from his cabin. When Brown walked on deck, William the carpenter, who'd watched it all, uninvolved in either outcome, took up his hornpipe and blew the last few phrases of a tune. A few sailors laughed, the incident was over. Radisson casually took a seat near Sparrow. Bartholomew stood where they'd left him, his chest heaving. The ship's doctor whistled nervously on his way down the companionway.

Captain Newland and Magnus Brown were careful not to look at Lilly. If they let on that they saw she'd been nearly raped and killed, they'd have to deliver punishment. And the ship was too far from shore for punishment now — the Captain knew it, Magnus Brown knew it.

Lilly woke up to fog, the Witch's Milk. Rolled in a grey blanket, she was lying beside the shallop, looking at the white planks of its cleanly painted hull. She felt sick. The sea, the ship, everything was shrouded in mist, vacant and too close at once, a vast blindness.

A figure was seated beside her, leaning against the shallop. In one fist he held a sheaf of paper and in the other a quill. The breeze shifted and she saw Bart's face, his hair spindled on fingers of fog. Then she became aware of that plangent voice, and she strained to see Radisson straddling the shallop, his beak in the air, his hair hanging on his collar, talking, reciting his histoire. Bartholomew's paper was smudged; ink seeped into its seams. Radisson intoned while Bart inscribed.

"I beseech Him, the Almighty so and so," Radisson was saying, "to grant me better success than I have had before and give me the grace, you know what to say, everlasting so and so, what men need far more than the world, and so like that."

Bartholomew said, "Pierre. I will serve as your amanuensis. I will record your Voyages as frankly as you tell them. Even the most cruel and bizarre facts, I will take at your dictation. Your ambitions, your schemes, your self-pity, your aggrandisements, only speak, and I will copy, costumed in English, yet true to the French gut that heaves them. Boast, lie, exaggerate. But hear me: if you insist on preaching pap, I quit, I'm out of it. Hire Lilly. She's learning her letters from John Sparrow. Utter one more sickly phrase about your soul and I'll jump overboard and take you with me."

"Just do and I will say," said Radisson, or something to that effect, but the fog thickened till he was obscured from sight, leaving a faint shadow.

Bartholomew shouted, "I will not live in Canada! You beast! You barbarian!"

A gull burst into view and settled on the pump. They ignored it for a moment; then, jolted awake, they called the alarm, "Land ho! Look out! Prends garde!"

A cannonade, thunder, cascading water. Lilly could see the staysail full of wind. The *Wivenhoe* must be moving quickly, though it was impossible to gauge speed in a world without form and void.

In the cabin below, illuminated by a single candle, Magnus Brown was calculating their position, or making a calculated guess, because until the weather released them he couldn't take a proper reading. His pocket watch had failed and he wasn't sure of the hour. He heard the shouted warnings, he heard seven thunders, the dragon with seven heads and seven crowns. His head bent over the chart until his beard rested on the table. "Fifty-nine degrees north," Magnus Brown whispered, "and maybe forty degrees longitude." He peered into the fog, which had seeped below decks, into the compass, infiltrating its glass, rendering the instrument useless. "Amendment," he wrote. "Longitude forty-three." Brown regarded his logbook as a dissatisfied husband will regard a distracted wife.

The first ice hit amidships just forward of Magnus Brown's cabin. A corner piece struck. The berg was forced alongside and struck again. The *Wivenhoe* was fifty-six feet long. It felt like the ice would shatter its spine. Brass, wood, glass, veins, nerves snapped. The sailors were flushed up to the quarterdeck, Jimmy Frost barking at them.

Through the porthole, Magnus Brown saw the Spirit of God move on the face of the water. He left his cabin and went up.

The ship was surrounded by ice, pieces big as churches, higher than the mast top-head, the colour of cold, their jagged corners jutting over the gunwales. The crew took oars and poles to fight it off. Someone swung an axe against an edge, failed, swung again, found a green seam, and ice hurtled to the deck, barely missing his crewmate. The ship groaned. She'd be stove in.

Captain Newland ordered the men to fasten a kedge anchor and a grapnel to keep the ice close, keep it from smashing against the ship. Two men threw the anchors and hauled, winched the cables, winched the ship in tight to the berg. But the ice turned, broke away; hemp thick as a sailor's wrist frayed like cotton thread; a cable snapped and both anchors were carried away, a loss the ship couldn't afford. A piece of ice sheared four of the main shrouds. The ship was pounded so hard, they saw a piece of her planking adrift nearby.

The captain ordered the men away from the pump, shouted at them to lower the shallop and go out to retrieve the anchors. Huge green floes collided and split into pieces. Lilly was afraid to go below, afraid to be drowned in her bunk, the size of an ill-fitting coffin. She vomited.

Bartholomew stood beside her, absently patting her back. He felt the ice as something deeply personal. He'd kept himself safe from God, never felt that cardinal point on the divine compass, never — till right now — *believed*, believed in anything really. Thirst, yes, anguish, yes. But here, in the faces carved in ice, Bartholomew saw Him. Bart saw God. And He was angry.

For the first time in his life, Bart saw the nightmare of a single force, an indifferent, a malevolent force, negligent in its power. He felt cast out by a vindictive will. "Oh, God," whispered Bart. Until now, liquor and the pleasures of melancholia had protected him from the Almighty.

Ten sailors lowered the shallop into the water and rowed so hard they were standing up. When their path was blocked, they climbed onto a berg of startling emerald blue, hauled the shallop up and over it, then jumped back in, disappearing into the fog. Two hours passed before the boat reappeared; the men called out, they'd found and retrieved both anchors.

The implacable Captain Newland ordered the crew to throw the anchors again into the ice. Bartholomew was furious, torn by envy of the sailors' strength. He was too inept to be of service and too weak to rebel against his newly perceived God — he didn't *feel* like a fallen angel. He wasn't even fit to be damned.

The small anchors kedged the ship around a piece of ice, and this time the hawser held. They tried to winch the boat up to the deck. The capstan bar came loose and hit the gunner across the chest, threw him into the pump so hard everyone heard the bones break. They ignored him. They hauled up the shallop, and another sailor was hurt when the boat was turned over, crushing his hand between the two gunwales. No one looked after the wounded. Even the surgeon was hauling the shallop.

The *Wivenhoe* swung toward a green mountain of ice. They set more sail and slowly they came about. The mist was clearing. The sailors forced the ship into the narrow passage and out to open, choppy water.

The gunner recovered enough to sit up. He was lucky to have broken only his ribs. The sailor's hand was mangled, his knuckles bent backward, his skin ripped away, the flesh already pulpy with blood. Without prompting by the Captain or by Magnus Brown, the sailors fell to their knees and gave thanks to God for His mercies.

The *Wivenhoe*'s rigging was slick, its canvas frozen. Lilly stayed as small as she could make herself in a corner at the stern. Then she stumbled below and lay curled in an acid bath of her own sickness, under a blanket in her bunk. She buried her face and waited for ice to smash open the ship's seams.

Lilly willed herself to stay sane. The sea is a beast, a mother who eats her own, a bitch of loose tits, a gaping mouth, riding the ship, gripping the keel between her legs. Lilly tried to conjure *good* things; she relived her brief reprieve, the pleasant admirations, her brilliant scenes as Charles's pampered — murderous — mistress. Soby with black blood flooding from his throat, how his flesh had resisted, resisted. *Black is the colour of my true love's hair, His face so soft and wondrous fair . . . Yes I love the ground on where he goes . . .* Let Beth go to Hell, for no mother has the right to die. How Lilly missed her, that silenced woman. And then it came, a slow and terrible dawning: this wasn't just seasickness. There was a thing taking root. A little mass of want, gathering inside her.

That night at Gravesend, the last night with Charles, she hadn't used a pessary. She couldn't exactly say why. She'd needed to steal something from him, to have an element of power when she felt most powerless. She wasn't sure, then, that Bart would carry through with his promise to help her get aboard the ship. She hated to acknowledge to herself just how much she'd demanded of Bartholomew. If she didn't escape England, it would have been an advantage to be pregnant with the King's child, wouldn't it? And now — in China? Lilly burst out in a wet, sobbing laugh and wiped her mouth with the back of her hand.

Tomorrow she'd hear the far wind and think it was land, that it was trees moved by wind. She went above, where the waves split open, spilling over slate grey, where the rolling ocean became a place once again, not an extension of some infinite, terrifying moment. She and Dogg staggered around and around the ship. There was no progress in this journey, only the broad

191

sea. I'm pregnant, I'm not, she repeated, putting it on, taking it off. I've never known a mother I liked. Not true. I loved Beth. Lilly felt in her pocket. She had stolen an oyster knife from the galley, a two-edged thing with a curved blade wrapped in a swath of leather. If anyone tries anything, I'll kill him. She realized she felt bliss. Then she was terrified.

On one circuit, she and Dogg encountered Magnus Brown. Brown lowered his head and looked at Lilly from under shaggy brows. He was mute but appeared under pressure of some potent message. Lilly dreaded men's revelations. His size made him dangerous, and though she couldn't discern a violent aspect here, he was haunted by something, and a haunted man wants a woman to save him. The bloodless lips of Magnus Brown parted, a wet opening in a field of beard. Maybe he saw her dread. There's always the inextinguishable desire to be appealing, and even Brown couldn't bear the sight of the girl's flinching from him. He closed his mouth. He made a slight, gentlemanly bow and passed her while she and Dogg ploughed forward into his wake.

When she had stomach enough to go below again, she caught Bart on his knees and she gripped his shoulder. When he looked up at her, his face was unspeakably sad. "You're not praying, Bart?" she asked. O, God of Naught, she thought. Don't let Bart go lunatic. "Tell me no."

Bartholomew did not tell her no.

Four

The end of July, they were trying to beat around Cape Farewell at the tip of Greenland, pestered by ice and fog. There were no songs at night, not anymore, no dreaming, or all things became dream in the bitter dark.

Lilly shuffled in her blanket, up from her bunk, Dogg leaning on her even when she walked. Freckled Jimmy Frost sucked on his bottom lip. "She's got nothing to fear from Frost's yard," he said quietly, retracting his chin in thin, veiny pleats. "Gone back inside, he has. God a'mercy, I may survive, but old whisky dick is gone for good." He stretched his long, lumpy gullet and then, blinking fast and with a desperate smile, he slid a crabbed hand down her britches.

Lilly gripped his wrist and said, "Touch me again, and I'll cut it out o' ye, like I'd pit a fucking prune."

Frost breathed, "Try, little bitch, try."

Then Sparrow came, and something of his small-boned decency sent Frost back to work and Lilly into meagre silence.

The sailors' hands were raw, blistered by salt. They cursed the ice on the rigging, the frozen canvas. They cursed their lack of sleep, the salty water they took from the bergs. They cursed the cold, and again they cursed the cold. Many times they were forced to drive an anchor into the ice, to hang on through veering winds and erratic floods. The *Wivenhoe* would be broken between grinding plates of ice, and they'd curse. But when the flood peaked, the anchor was retrieved. A passage opened to the west, then the sailors gave thanks to God in His great mercy. They would never attribute to the Almighty any of the fickle cruelty of their circumstance. Any relief from pain was an occasion of thanksgiving.

Bartholomew watched the sailors in their prayers, their gladness when they rose and resumed their cursing. He was a feeble impostor among very muscular children. How he wished his newfound, vengeful Overseer could be more like theirs. One who would answer to a pet name: God. He wished he wouldn't question but merely trust His cruelty, His dalliance between safety and suffering.

In ice and wind, in the pitch and roll of wood and brass, Bartholomew's highly developed sense of irony came into its true power. Here, No-Place, a slow, elegant suicide is not amusing, isn't audacious or eccentric. He would have to survive until he knew where he was dying, under what contract, with God or Devil. He knew he'd most likely damaged himself beyond repair. But the Sea of Japan, China — what perfumed grace lies on the other side of the icy straits, what peaceful (maybe even sober?) pleasures await him?

Let Radisson tell his cannibal tales of Canada. The *Wivenhoe* will avoid that savage land. Magnus Brown will discover a route through to the richly appropriate occasions of the Orient, where even an exhausted poet will find rest, will know an interval of peace before his final nullification. For Bartholomew hoped to be nullified, that remained his best option. God is too awful for man, yes, but in his last years, before Sin and Death took possession, Bartholomew, Second Earl of Buxborough, would find rest. In China. In silk. In poignant unhappiness.

The weight of freshly apprehended Sin descended on Bart like hot wax, and it made him burn with a reproach he couldn't conceal from Lilly. She was with Dogg in her bunk, being sick, when Bartholomew found her. Bart hefted Dogg off the bunk and curled up at Lilly's feet. "Not feeling well?" All the ship's rigging was moaning and shrieking, men were bellowing above. Braced on his wrists above her, he looked down into her white face and said, "Lilly, you know I'll never judge you."

"What are you going on about?"

"It is myself I judge."

"Piss off!"

"I schooled you, I taught you how to please men. My God! I *introduced* you to Soby!"

"I told you to, Bart. What the hell are you talking about?"

"How — I need to know how —"

Lilly rolled over and covered her ears with her arms. "Bugger!"

"I don't doubt you had to do it. I know what he was."

She kicked at Bart, trying to force him out of the bunk. "I hate you!"

"Was it — I can't stop thinking about it! Was it quick? Did he suffer?"

She scratched his face and pulled his hair. Bart protested, but finally he had to get out of her range, crawling out, a fine cut on his eyelid from her nail.

"It was Soby!" she shouted. "It was fucking Soby!"

"I don't judge," Bart said, weeping now. "Don't curse! Please don't curse!" He turned away, bumping into Sparrow, who had come down to look in on her.

She let Sparrow wipe her face with a clean rag. She thanked him and pretended to fall asleep. When Sparrow had gone, she slipped out of her bunk and went to the Captain's cabin. Captain Newland would have gin.

Lilly took gin from the Captain's cabin and found a pack of seeds there, too. Mustard. The Captain hoped to plant mustard in China? She put the seeds in the gin and drank it off, gagging, but she wouldn't let herself vomit. She drank several tin cups of gin with mustard seed, forcing it down. Bartholomew judged her, he'd abandoned her. Oh for Whore's Root, for worm fern; she should always carry it, why did she not carry it?

It did not take. The thing remained like a barnacle. Her gut was in knots, but she didn't bleed. The gin didn't take, and she was poor for want of Whore's Root. She'd never been so poor.

Bartholomew judged her. She killed seven mice with a broom. No one was in the galley. She filled a kettle with seawater, boiled it over the cook's fire, and threw in the mice with another handful of Captain Newland's mustard seeds. A bad garden being planted here, she thought, a Sinful garden, and furiously stripped off her britches and forced herself down into the steam. She couldn't stand the pain and pulled off. Steam rose around her in the cold air. Several of the crew came in from their watch, saw her there, turned on heel and went back up to fetch the Earl. She tried again. Bartholomew found her there, gripping a rope between her teeth, squatting in a fog.

He dragged her off, and they fell onto the floorboards. She smelled of boiled cabbage; her clothes were soaking wet. He held her, buried his face in her hair, rocking with her. "What is it, my love," he said. "Tell me."

My love. He shouldn't call her that. It's a death chant. She told him, "I'm pregnant."

Bartholomew went cold, but he held her. After several minutes, in a steady voice with the timbre of his old, stoic indifference, he asked, "With whose child, Lilly?"

"It's mine."

"Whose child?" he persisted.

"Oh. Charles. It's — Charles's. But what will that matter in China —"

He released her. "Of course it is," he said in wonder.

She looked at the mice floating in the scummy water. "I don't think it's going to work," she said. She was beginning to realize how badly she'd burned herself.

Bart didn't have much to offer. Abortifacients weren't his field. He felt new, poetic courage. Now he was doubly a protector. Oh, this was a broad stewardship. Lilly and her infant. He thought maybe he would go and have a drink soon.

"Do you want it to work?" he asked.

"No," she said. She was too sick to lie, even to herself. Still, it astonished her; she was proud to be pregnant.

He kissed her cheek. "If he looks like Charles, they'll be afraid of him. In China."

The child would be born in China. The pain from her burns was terrible now. Bartholomew held Lilly and told her about the birds in China, how they fly on jewelled wings and sing such melodies the people grow like children there and no cruelty is known among them.

Five

At last, on the evening of July 30, after four days beaten back by headwinds, the *Wivenhoe* rounded Cape Farewell. She sailed forty leagues northwest, following the ghostly coast of Greenland up to Cape Desolation. Now, due west, lay the next leg of their journey — Davis Strait and the Labrador Sea — their passage to Resolution Island at the mouth of Hudson Strait, at 61°20' north, or so the charts said. One hundred and fifty leagues away, another four hundred and fifty miles.

Across the Labrador Sea, with the bergs floating down Davis Strait, came crowds of walrus, lying on the floes or bobbing in the water as if they were standing on rocks below the surface. The walruses looked like elderly generals, with drooping moustaches and tusks, with drooping English eyes. The *Wivenhoe* sailed all the way to Sir Thomas Button's Isles in their baleful, excremental company.

Jimmy Frost distrusted the womanish quality of Bartholomew's mouth and wouldn't let the Earl on his watch. It was too risky. An injury could be fatal; in the surgeon's kitbag was a razor, a needle and thread, a saw, and a flask of brandy. The seaman with the smashed hand lay in his bunk, hallucinating, his sweat soaking right through his thin mattress.

Bartholomew had reconciled with liquor, finding it more approachable than God, kinder than Lilly. But even when the

Earl was drunk, vomiting, talking to God, streaked with tar, he was the most beautiful man the sailors had ever seen. A *poet*. Some of the more sensitive among them had begun to wonder if he was inhuman, an angel.

Through the evening, in a light topsail wind, the crew worked with subdued contentment while they listened to Bartholomew sing Monteverdi.

> *Ohimè dev'è il mio ben, dov'è il mio core?*
> *Chi m'asconde il mio ben e chi m'el toglie?*
> Alas, where is my love, where is my heart?
> Who conceals my treasure and who takes it away?

This evening, Magnus Brown came on deck, scanned the ship, and located Lilly standing on the forecastle deck and Sparrow, warily, nearby. Brown took his place by the wheel.

> *Dunque ha potuto in me più che'l mio amore*
> *Ambizios'e troppo lievi voglie.*
> Thus more power than my love had my
> Ambitious and too trifling aspirations.

The sky weighed on the earth, revealing stars from far latitudes, impossible to see from land. Off the mainmast shone Polaris, that point around which the other lights revolved, Primum Mobile, and beyond to the Empyrean regions, to the swift stillness of Heaven.

Magnus Brown would later record that, despite the eerie grinding of ice floes, despite the smell of walrus excrement and the injured sailor's calling for his mother from his marshy sleep below, the ship was orderly, sober, tonight.

Brown filled his lungs with the freezing air, permitting himself a modest sense of pride for having brought them this far. He navigated by dead reckoning, using the stars, the hourglass, and the spool of knotted hemp. Time passed slippery as fish in his hands, but he had counted the hours and the ship was not lost. A tower of ice passing a cable length away suddenly broke into several pieces, and these swiftly passed the ship on the current. Shards like that have hidden spurs, spikes as long as the ship, hidden beneath the surface. Brown quietly told Jimmy Frost to double the watch, and then resumed his own watch over Lilly. Soon, soon they would needle safely through; they would leave the Atlantic, the Labrador Sea, Hudson Strait, and, despite the odds, they'd find their way through to the Pacific, to the Asia.

> *Ahi sciocco mondo e cieco, ahi cruda sorte*
> *Che ministro mi fai della mia morte.*
> Ah, stupid world, and blind; ah, cruel fate!
> You make me executioner of my own death.

Radisson squatted near Bartholomew, listening to him with growing impatience. Finally he stood and said, "Now it is my turn to sing something for you." A few sailors moaned because the Earl's voice was such a pure tenor. But a ship's deck belongs to the ship's company, and no one would dominate her well-scrubbed stage.

Radisson had been chafing under the Earl's quill. As his secretary, Bartholomew refused to translate Radisson's strangely yoked English into elegant Town, not even into good stolid prose; instead, Bart was faithful to Radisson's peculiar accents.

More silly still was the Earl's girlish mewling over the wars we fight with the Indians. "So, alors! We do not fight from ships, we do not shoot the little cannonball from a safe distance," Radisson had grumbled at Bart. "We burn our enemy in the bark of birch, we make soup of human bones. C'est fait! The bounty of the New World belongs to the man who will wage war among the trees, without a pretty hat, without cognac. This is the world to which you venture, you idiot fool!"

Bartholomew had shouted, "You are a savage, Radisson! We sail to China!"

Radisson always shrugged with irritating carelessness. The argument had been chafing between them for weeks. Now, Radisson, giving Bart a defiant look, bared his throat.

The song came from a place in Radisson's neat (however voluble) frame that no one but Bart had imagined existed. It was a wail, a lamentation, painfully courageous and solitary. It was without words, or of no language that the sailors knew, but the ghostly call of an animal, or a heron; or the entire, forsaken earth was crying out.

It made everyone afraid. Many sailors were skeptical that they'd make it to China, yet they couldn't relinquish all their hope that they'd avoid a winter on the savage islands, that somehow, by miracle or genius, they would sail through to the Orient, to grateful, tawny virgins, to golden lanes lined with fruit trees. Radisson's song made them doubt their own capacity to survive. No one spoke for some time.

It was lusciously, frigidly stunning for Lilly, Radisson's wild dirge, which was so unlike England, unlike Bart's mean wit and ink, unlike the organized violence of theatre and theatre's scribblers. And there remained the dawning presence of the thing inside her. A small sum, adding up. She might die, the baby might die in an unknown land.

The night was overcast. Then a white shadow loomed out of the night and quietly passed inches to larboard. The Captain bellowed at Jimmy Frost. Frost sent John the gunner's mate scrambling up the shrouds. The *Wivenhoe* had sailed that afternoon into freezing rain and the shrouds were covered in ice.

John slipped and dangled from his ankle. The ship was in the midst of sea ice. All hands were called to fend it off. Frost's freckled face leered into Radisson's and he said, "Ye'll do well to keep your savage howls to yerself."

Lilly was trapped under the swinging torso of the sailor hanging from the shrouds. Magnus Brown lifted the man free, and then he palmed Lilly's back to push her aft. It was the first time he'd touched her. She seared his hand, his entire mass, lighting him up like a mountain in a storm. All night his veins would feel scorched. He stood, deeply shaken, looking out to phantom shapes of ice till the sun was well risen and Sparrow appeared beside him with a mug of tea, and Magnus Brown realized he'd fallen asleep standing up.

But he couldn't know what had just happened to Lilly.

For the first time, the touch of a man's hand had an effect so provocative, so magnetic, so new to her she couldn't name its simple name, as trite as "God" for all the aspirations and bewilderment it would pretend to encompass. *Desire. Desire.* At the touch of Magnus Brown's hand, Lilly had felt — not the obedience (or power) of sex, but something more haunting, more like a blood poisoning. Desire. Desire without dread. Lilly Cole wanted the touch of Magnus Brown.

Six

Hour	Knots	Lat. N.	
9	43/4	61°10'	*Took third reef in maintopsail. Squalls, heavy snow. Ice. V. Cold. Sailor John D. lost his right arm. God be praised.*

Small, wiry John Sparrow was a practical man in his life before the Plague. And his sturdy reason was not broken by his family's death. When he watched their bodies carted off by the Buriers, their corpses scarred by tumours and boils, by murdering fingerprints of the Affliction, he did not break. But Creation's surface thinned, as hide is stretched to make parchment, and through its transparency, Sparrow saw a watery transmutation of one form into another. After that he knew the ground on which he walked was no different from the illusion of the surface of the sea.

His inclination was to love. So his discovery that appearances are a sleight of God's hand led him to optimistic speculation. It led him to believe that under the ship on which he sailed, commonplace and rank with unwashed humanity, under the aristocratic walruses, deeper than the secret roots of ice, there existed another world, determined by laws as natural as ours yet fundamentally different. There are no words for such an original world, though Sparrow listened for them all the same.

August 14. They were at the east end of Hudson Strait. Resolution Island was visible, a dark stone, twelve miles away. Late afternoon. Clear weather. Magnus Brown was making the watch nervous; through all the rotations, he was almost always standing near the helm with his telescope, forsaking the coordinates of his charts for the distortions of light and air.

In his long black coat, with his frosted yellow beard and his long hair beneath his hat, Brown may have looked like a Prophet, and it may be that it was as Charles had dryly observed — an inclination to prophecy will grow a man to a prophet's size. Magnus Brown was all too familiar with the extremes of passion. (He was so wary of Lilly that she assumed he despised her.) His very bulk made him yearn for proportion. His greatest hope was that things would be simpler than he imagined.

Magnus Brown was subject to the dream of first days, and he lived in hope sustained by disregard of current circumstance. He'd been a wanderer for as long as he'd been a man, that lonely moment of awakening aboard a ship bound for Virginia. Now his right hand, the bare yellow fingers with their long blue nails, pointed west. To Salisbury Island, to the North West Channel. Brown would soon know if they could sail northwest and, by reason of the sphere, find a passage to the blossoming East, or if they would have to travel south-southwest across Hudson Bay to the forests of a barbaric land fit only for sand flies, to console with furs their merchants of England.

He needed to record their bearings, here on the cusp of

north and south. The Adventurers had requested that he make such observations: currents, tides, depths. The night before the *Wivenhoe* had departed from Gravesend two months ago, Prince Rupert had approached Brown with the shy deference that occurs when one solitary gentleman meets what must amount to a soul mate. Rupert had been wearing an embroidered coat less ornate than the current fashion. The two men shook hands solemnly, their faces lightened somewhat, as by November sun. "Good," Rupert had said. Magnus Brown had nodded, Good. "Ah," said Rupert, "I have brought a small gift." And he'd put a heavy bound journal in Magnus Brown's hand. It had been a private ceremony, with only Brown and Rupert in attendance. "How I wish I could go with you," Rupert had said frankly, touching his head. Brown nodded his own enormous head. "Well," said Rupert. "I look forward to reading this when it is full of Rupert's Land." Magnus Brown had met his eyes, and their bond seemed a firmament. Two Governors, one in name, the other in the peculiar likeness of action, of "life."

Brown kept a richly informative journal for Prince Rupert. (He could not say, even to himself, for whom he was writing its candid, unofficial, backward-paged addendum, his oddly composed Book of Lilly.) The ship must be slowed; he would order Sparrow to take a sounding. At latitude 63°15' north, there is a rippling clarity. The sails were furled, and before too long the *Wivenhoe* drifted on the strait's indifferent current. Without the crackling of sails, the ship's sounds felt lush to their ears, like the sighs of a sleeping woman. Sparrow went aft, carrying the ninety-pound sounding lead, his muscles spindled around the bones and up his crooked jaw so his head seemed set on a broken tripod of cartilage.

"'Tis armed?" Magnus Brown asked Sparrow. Brown was fond of the old man, shy of him in a way.

"Aye," said Sparrow, his keen eye asquint, his heart trilling.

He'd pressed tallow into the hole, by which means he intended to raise a sample, a clue from Atlantis.

Sparrow carefully measured the distance between his hand and the swelling surface of the strait; then he let down the line, counting the depths and marks and praising God in His Providence for this brightest of days. The leather marks ran smoothly overhand, then the knotted white rag mark, the red rag mark; at ten fathoms he passed that piece of leather with the hole punched in it; at thirty fathoms he palmed three knots in the line, thought of crabapples, thought of calf gizzards, thought about the secret connection among all things; ten knots measured one hundred fathom and another two, and the line stopped. Sparrow called out, "One hundred and twenty fathom, Gov'nor." The line hummed with celestial voices shouting Gloria through the spheres above Atlantis, music, something like what he heard that time from the great organ at St. Sepulchre's Church. He scarcely had strength to hold. "May I raise the lead now, Gov'nor?" he called.

Lilly knelt beside him. Through the long weeks, listening to Sparrow's many tales, she'd never believed in Atlantis. She believed in the story, though. It was a wondrous story he was acting out. She stayed close by.

Sparrow trembled. His forearms were braided in cords of muscle when he lifted the lead to lay it heavily on the deck. There was white sand in its hollow. Fine and white as powdered wings. He did not touch it till Magnus Brown knelt and put forth his hand. Sparrow stole a glance at Lilly to indicate to her that everything, every sunny grain, was to be counted infinite in mystery. So it is. Thank God for His great abundance in small things.

Magnus Brown scraped a bit of sand into his palm and sifted it dry. He opened his hand when he stood, the sand blowing away, Brown's shadow thrown across the deck, the uneasy land on the southern shore of the strait, too quiet, it was quiet. *And the Word was with God and the Word was God. And He withheld it.*

Seven

The rendezvous with the *Prince Rupert* would be made at the west end of Hudson Strait, at Salisbury Island. Then the two ships would prepare to bear northwest through Foxe Channel. To the Orient. Magnus Brown would attempt to navigate the passage so unnerving to John Cabot that he'd turned back. Brown would surpass Luke Foxe, who gave up at 66° north and ran for home.

The sailors sang songs and told stories through the night, inspired by the feeling that their fortunes were ordained by the northern sky, which soared in crackling waves of silver and green, arcing over the path to China. They took wagers on whether they'd make it there. The younger men were more hopeful, tantalized, while their elders were simply desperate to avoid a bitter-cold winter among savages. John Sparrow kept mum on the subject; he was unafraid of America, the lost kingdom. But he worried over Lilly and the pretty Earl, as he would have liked to worry over his own children. He tried, as often as he dared, to suggest to Lilly that she needed to prepare herself for a tent in the bush rather than a silken hammock in a Chinese garden.

The *Wivenhoe* sailed the strait through the third week of August. A steady gale from the east was breaking up the ice, so they were able to force the ship through it if they put up enough sail. On August 17, they saw Salisbury Island about seven leagues away, separated from them by masses of ice. There was no sight of the *Prince Rupert*. Then the wind failed for twelve hours. They lay becalmed while ice rolled in around them, grinding in the dark.

Out of a fog at the fourth hour, a roaring sea rose from the southeast. The Captain bellowed to the men to take in the spritsail and lower the topsails. The wind grew high, with needles of sleet that iced the decks. The ship couldn't make headway and so was blown laterally. The sailors' frozen hands could barely hold the sheets. And their feet slipped on the ice so they fell in the heaped tangles of cordage. The Captain shouted at them to set the mizzen with the main. Their hope now was to ride directly into the wind. But the *Wivenhoe* wouldn't hold her course.

Four hours later, the gale veered at north-northwest, a white wind blowing sideways across the ship so full of sleet they could barely see one another. They were afraid the topmast would splinter and took down all sails and lashed the helm alee. They could only let the sea do what she would; they abandoned the upper decks, fell down the companion ladder to their bunks, and waited, praying for a dry death.

Sleet turned to snow. For two days, except for a rotation to man the pumps, the crew huddled over two fires, fore and aft, rolling with the ship when she keeled over in the wind. Above their heads, blocking the light through the companionway, snow swept in and drifted.

Lilly sat between Sparrow and Bartholomew in a circle of men around a big kettle burning coal in the galley. A sailor with a rosary was saying his Aves over and over. Duncan the redheaded cook handed biscuits around with sugared tea. Jimmy

Frost eyed Lilly with such animosity, the biscuits went dry in her mouth. As if she were not a victim of the weather like the rest of them, no — as if she *were* the weather.

The cook said, "Give us a rest from prayer and tell a tale, John Sparrow."

Sparrow had been dozing, but he opened his eyes and lit his pipe. "Well, I'll tell you the story of Jonah and his whale," he said.

The Orkney sailor grunted, gave Lilly a hard look. "There be a Jonah richt here, tae ma mynd." The sailors nodded, aye, but half-hearted, too cold, too numb.

"No," said Sparrow. "Was God Hisself who raised the tempest. Why? To frighten them what do not believe. Was a storm far worse than this 'un. They were sure to drown. So the sailors cast lots to know who was the sinner on that ship, who had wronged the Lord and made the sea rise against them. And it fell to Jonah, for as you know, Jonah was on the run from God. Jonah confessed, he said, 'Cast me into the sea!' he said, 'Throw me to the fishes! For it's on my conscience ye all might drown.' The sea seemed to answer, Aye, for the storm rose e'en wilder and tossed the ship most pitiful. So they threw Jonah off their ship. To drown. An' appease the Great Almighty."

"Ah," said the Orkneyman, looking around. The sailors, huddled in their blankets, twisted their necks to look at Lilly.

Sparrow went on, "The sea grew calm right off. But God is not to be so easily known by man, and in His great wisdom, He looked on Jonah drowning in the sea and He said, Jonah's body might be saved, but how to save his soul? So God sent Jonah a whale. A great whale swallowed Jonah whole. For three days and three nights, Jonah stayed inside the belly of Leviathan. He felt safe, in the whale's gut, safe from the sea, and hidden from God. Jonah was so grateful, he started to sing. Jonah lay in that whale's belly and he sang out God's praises. And he made vasty promises to do whatever God asked. But I think Jonah was a poor singer, for he caused the whale to vomick. Jonah was vomicked up onto land. All because he sang in such poor tune."

Sparrow reached across Lilly to catch a dock spider in his hand. He pulled out his handkerchief and put the spider inside it. There were several spiders in Sparrow's handkerchief, all of them dead, or merely watchful. He settled down again, pulling on his pipe.

"It's small and quizzical, Jonah's tale," Sparrow resumed.

The cook looked at his biscuits in some disappointment and said, "A fickle sort of Saviour then."

"A powerful God," said Sparrow. "We're not to be given shelter under Heaven. An' if we find it, it's sure to be a death trap."

Radisson shook himself and pulled tobacco from a beaded hide pouch they'd never seen him use before. He handed the tobacco to John Sparrow. Everyone watched the two men stoke their pipes.

Lilly stood up. That we are given no shelter, she knew of her own account. She poured a mug of tea, then walked through the circle, brushing by the long legs of the Orkneyman. She went aft, knocked on the door of Magnus Brown's cabin, and went in.

Brown's cabin was colder than death. She handed him the tea and sat on a stool beside the navigation shelf, bracing herself with her feet against the bunk. The colour had gone from everything, all was stark and sallow.

He let her sit, as if entertaining an ostrich, and when in a sudden gust she lost her balance and flailed out with her arms and feet, he cringed and knocked things over, his tea and his inkpot. He was bruised and cut, not only by sea squalls but by the squalls of a heart made clumsy by love.

Lilly felt exposed and assailable in a new way. Magnus is as big as an oak tree, she thought; he reads ocean currents, he reads wind. She could read his big head. He might be twice her age, and he was certainly three times her weight. She wanted to touch the windburnt bags under his eyes. The *Wivenhoe* keeled to starboard. They didn't talk. The silence between them curdled and made her ache.

On the third day, the storm declined to a low, unceasing howl. Newland ordered them up. They spent nearly an hour digging their way up the ladder, then emerged to find snow three feet high on the ship. The *Wivenhoe* was jammed in broken slabs of motionless ice. They shovelled the decks. Then Jimmy Frost, Sparrow, Brown, and Captain Newland climbed down rope ladders to the surface of the sea — which was like a sky fallen down in giant pieces under ribbons of yellow cloud in blue sky.

Slabs of ice jutted upright twenty feet high, or lay flat, puzzled into pieces a thousand paces long. They pitched the quadrant in snow to take a reading. They were at 63°4'. Maybe Mansel Island was over there, over the bowed horizon to the south. The *Wivenhoe* had been pushed nearly ten leagues off course. Salisbury Island was somewhere to north-northwest, a passage blocked by packed ice.

For another five days they tried to reach Salisbury, only occasionally under more than reefed main and foresails. In all that time, they advanced less than five leagues and lost that again, pushed back by headwinds. It wasn't only the cold and the snow on the decks; the sound of the futile wind and the grinding ice was wearing them down.

On the sixth day, Magnus Brown chose a passage from Job for the morning prayer. "He stretcheth out the north over the empty place, and hangeth the earth upon nothing." It was perhaps a poor, an unsettling, choice of text. The crew remained on their knees. They were wet, frozen, and mutinous. Captain Newland calmly, as if casually, told them to sit easy and speak their minds. The carpenter said that he didn't think the *Wivenhoe* could sustain any more pounding. He said her fastenings were loose, and it was a miracle she wasn't losing more planking. Others testified the ship's seams were leaking. They were exhausted, pumping water from her bilge; it was coming in faster and faster. They displayed their cuts and bruises from trying to lash cargo down in the hold. One of the pigs had been killed when a cask of water rolled free. Radisson had said nothing these many days. Today his restraint was most eloquent.

Magnus Brown hadn't intended to give up until that moment. He looked once at Lilly, a stricken look of apology, turned toward the relentless ice, the stretch of north, and bowed his head. Captain Newland simply nodded, then gave the order to steer south-southwest. China was lost. They sailed for the destiny of fools and failures.

Eight

At the end of August, at the lip of Hudson Bay, the *Wivenhoe* lingered, searching the horizon for her sister ship. Magnus Brown fought hard with himself to overcome his jealousy that the *Prince Rupert* might be successful finding the Passage where the *Wivenhoe* had failed. When at last they spied her, the *Prince Rupert* was sailing close to Digges Islands. Brown gruffly observed to Captain Newland, "She'll have no sea room on that tack." Newland felt the subtle compliment to himself and agreed. "She's luffing. She'll run aground if they keep on that way." He shrugged. "Somebody must be sleeping."

The two men parted company, mumbling something about pressing tasks, must take a bearing while the sun's out, see to mending a spar, embarrassed by their mutual need for reassurance, though of the two, Newland had more quickly recovered from his disappointment — he'd never put much store in finding the Northwest Passage. Magnus Brown, on the other hand, could barely move his limbs for a deep, almost paralyzing understanding that his deepest wishes had been betrayed.

The two ships met off Mansel Island, on the east edge of the great bay. Now the *Wivenhoe* swung beside the *Prince Rupert* on a tidal current from the west-southwest.

The crews from both ships met to make a hunting expedition to the island. Lilly stepped aboard the *Wivenhoe*'s shallop and sat beside Sparrow. They'd been sailing for nearly three months, *three months!* She would feel the earth under her feet. Radisson was excited to see his brother-in-law again; he gaily insisted on collecting Des Groseilliers to go in their boat to the island. Des Groseilliers roused himself and climbed down the rope ladder from the *Prince Rupert*. He blinked in consternation at seeing Lilly there, taking his place in the shallop like a big, sleepy cat.

The *Prince Rupert* crew leaned down over the gunwale and eyed Lilly. She was not quite three months pregnant; she might be able to hide it for another few months. She pressed her shoulder into Sparrow's and squeezed his hand.

They landed in surf over long pads of shale broken by boulders, with twelve aboard (and Dogg). The *Wivenhoe* crew was quietly awed by Jimmy Frost's skill at the helm, though the taut, thin, freckled skin of Frost's face flinched irritably when they tried to flatter him. Sparrow leapt out to guide the boat ashore. The stern swung on the waves and would have snapped Sparrow's stringy legs but for Frost's skill at the tiller.

Mansel Island is low-lying as a sandbank, but they all lurched when they landed and lunged dizzily, as if they were climbing a hill. Even Dogg was on sea legs, leaning on an invisible leash, leaving puddles of transparent puke in the pebbled sand.

There was a friendly reunion among the two crews. The captains of both ships had picked sailors born and bred; many of them had sailed together over the years, though none had come farther northwest than the coast of Newfoundland. The men took a brief look about them, finding the island more tedious than the sea. They roamed a while, then, one by one, returned to sit beside their boats to have a pipe.

Lilly walked over the dune, into the quiet of the bushes. It was the first privacy she'd had since leaving England. She went into a grassy place sheltered from the wind. The sandy clay showed the prints of birds. Grasses and moss felt cool and alive. The sounds of land, a rustling of leaves, and the voices of the ships' crews far off. She spread her arms side to side. Space. She pulled off her clothes. It would be the first time she could see her own pregnant body.

She found herself changed: not much of a belly, but it seemed her feet were more splayed than ever. As if to keep her still. Beth was never far from mind, Beth's body in the bed, like a pivot, with Lilly going around and around.

What lay ahead? Motherhood? How on earth? She was never to *have* shelter, so how could she presume to *be* shelter? Beth never was; Beth wouldn't be trapped, not by a man, certainly not by her daughter. She'd been an almost madly restless mother, absorbed by her own wants, her terror, her poverty, her beauty, and her falsehoods, her fakery — even to herself, she was a fake. Drink was the only cure for one so completely discontented.

Motherhood. Lilly Cole. Good actress, terrible cook, murderer. What if she can't love? How would such a one as she dare to put her hands on a child?

Des Groseilliers stretched and disappeared to hunt in the low brush, passing Bartholomew as he crawled up the beach to a little patch of scurvy-grass, a scrap of green.

Radisson discovered Bart kneeling before it. "Like the stag," he said, "we are drawn to what our stomach needs." Radisson plucked the scurvy-grass, offering it to the Earl. "You must eat the green leaves."

Bartholomew smiled wanly. "Shall I? 'Twill be nicely salted."

Radisson thrust the leaves to Bartholomew's lips. Bart said, "You're not serious."

"If you do not eat such things, your gums will bleed. Your

216

mouth will rot like the dead, and your joints will melt like hot bear grease so one bone will break against the next and you cannot walk without such pain you never knew could happen to you. Soon the pain will grow so bad you will die like the animal, wanting we should shoot you. Eat the green leaves, green Earl."

Over Bartholomew's face passed the shadow of a cormorant. His gums had been bleeding for two weeks. He took the scurvy-grass. "You have such skill in evoking torment, Radisson."

Radisson turned his back. He knew that the Earl would not like to be watched while he chewed like the sheep.

Radisson had seen fox tracks and a few birds but no other signs of life. There were fireplaces on shore — these could have been ancient heaps of stones in purposeful, indecipherable arrangements — but no wood anywhere.

Bartholomew joined Radisson at the water's edge. He'd eaten only a few of the peppery little leaves; he never did like green vegetables. He wanted to throw the rest away but clutched it politely to his side. Birdsong, wavelets lapping the shore, these small sounds, estranged from the low, constant roar of the ocean that had been with them for days, beneath the slamming of ship's rigging.

Ice moved like clouds over the bay and inverted the light so they felt as if they were standing in the sky looking down on the remotely drifting bergs. Like priests, thought Radisson, like monks in white robes who move about the Garden careless of themselves. Beside him, Bartholomew reeked of sobriety. The Earl must live; every man must live, but especially the Earl who is loved by the English King.

Radisson wanted to engage the Earl in friendly discourse, to prepare him for the New World. "You must make a tea of cedar for your bones. You are to look after yourself, and Lilly too, as I know you want to do. At dawn," he said, "we traverse Hudson

Bay. I go in the *Wivenhoe*, southwest, to the mouth of the river Nelson, called Kawiriniagaw, which means 'the dangerous.'" He pointed south. "You and Lilly go that way with Governor Brown, in the *Prince Rupert* ship, to the bottom of the bay. You will have a nice time at this place."

"We are to be moved to another ship?" Bartholomew swooned toward the horizon, a plate of white feathers, a bulging surface. His mouth tasted sweetly rotten. He didn't see a way to live through the winter. He certainly didn't want to have to do without Radisson, now that it had come to this. "It seems somehow promiscuous to change ships now," he said.

Radisson clutched Bart's sleeve and pulled him upright. "You must go with Lilly in the *Prince Rupert*, to the south. It will be better there. Magnus Brown will build a house for you. I go in the *Wivenhoe*, to make trade at Kawiriniagaw. We must make good trade, or your King will be unhappy." He removed his coat and draped it over Bart's shoulders.

Bartholomew, who despite his taste for ornament had in fact never been a vain man, sucked absently on a corner of Radisson's hide jacket, finding instinctively that the salty taste of deerskin quelled his nausea. He said, "We have come to the ends of the earth." He tried to smile. "Now we descend into Hell." His dry lips made a popping sound.

Des Groseilliers's spirits were improving with the prospect of good hunting once they reached James Bay. Why were they not on their way? Mansel Island was obviously barren. This was a stupid delay, and he wondered why Pierre had insisted on it. He was about to complain when he saw what looked improbably like a deer in a sunny glade. He crept up.

He saw Lilly through the thin branches of aspen. The girl was lifting her naked arms in a dance. He watched and admired her, in the way that he'd watch and admire a deer, but he didn't feel the consequent impulse to fire an arrow or a gun. He would like to lie with her. He stepped out of the shade, presenting himself with a quizzical May I, Mother? on his broad square face.

Lilly leapt for her clothes and then crouched with her britches tucked between her bent knees. Des Groseilliers came forward. His body retained the rocking pleasures of being at sea; he wasn't yet the critically contentious man he would once again become on land, and he didn't hurry. Lilly drew her knife, wrapped in a leather rag, from her pocket, shook it free and held it in front her, waving it in the air. To Des Groseilliers, she was a blur of woman and sun and brush. The knife, though, was affecting. He recalled his politic life and remembered that Lilly belonged to the English King. *Merde*, shit, *calice*. Yet again, happiness, freedom, enjoyment, all that makes life sweet, would be deformed by timid *law*. He sighed, turning away with one last, admiring look.

Lilly got dressed. It was unsettling how such a heavy man could walk so silently through the brush.

At the shore, the sailors were disturbed by the beating of wings and Dogg, fully recovered, galloping after a grey bird (a black cap, a blood-red bill). The bird dropped out of the sky even before they heard Des Groseilliers's gun. Dogg sat, wary of Des Groseilliers, and fell over with a sigh. His hopeful tail thumped the warm rock, a forgotten pleasure. Des Groseilliers came over the dune, picked up the bird to toss it into the boat. No wood on this island; they'd have to boil the bird on the *Prince Rupert*. Des Groseilliers shrugged at Radisson, as if to say, Why do you like to wait so much?

Lilly came out from the shade into the bland glare of beach and ocean. How far away England was. The rich house by Lambeth Hill, Charles's friendly affections, performances with the players. If she survived the winter, surely England would not be there when she got back; it would have vanished, like smoke.

Thick clouds were massing; it was getting late. They launched the three boats to begin to row back out to the ships. The evening sea wind blew them onto shore and they had to row hard to gain enough momentum to turn about. The boats were in tandem, following a promontory that could serve as a windbreak, where they could get pointed off shore. Sparrow, at Lilly's side, stood up suddenly and called out, "There! Oh! Look!"

Very near their shallop the dead body of a fish rolled in the surf. It was more than twice the length of a man, fourteen or fifteen feet long. Its skin — not fish scales but skin in shades of silver and black — was battle-scarred. At Sparrow's urging, Jimmy Frost manoeuvred the boat closer. The fish had a horn at least seven feet long. A gnarled, torqued horn, discoloured, as if by tobacco. "It is the unicorn!" cried Sparrow.

"It's the narwhal," Des Groseilliers growled. "A dead whale."

Sparrow leaned out to touch its horn. He grunted and reached into his pocket, took out his handkerchief, carefully opened it. Then, one by one, he inserted his spiders into the ringed hole at the tip of the horn. They disappeared. Sparrow triumphantly stood and announced, "It is the sea unicorn!"

The sailors gave a disparate shout. There was laughter, a surge of celebration. Even Des Groseilliers gained a sense of unruly enthusiasm. It was only a narwhal. But narwhals are never seen so far from Davis Strait — he'd heard of one such sighting and that was a lie.

Magnus Brown stood at the stern to contemplate this sign. Does the sea unicorn show himself, make sacrifice? The sky fell flat, its brown cloud laden with snow, broadly horizontal. This is so. We will gird our loins and be men; we will not be desolate. We are given disappointment, nothing but cold, repetitive, fretting tasks, but we will hold, we shall ask for nothing but the grace to endure.

The sea, the great mother, held them to her breast. They heard the booming of her heart, the crying gull. *Gulls. Far calls.* To make resolve. Magnus Brown whispered, "I abhor my ambition. I repent in dust and ashes. I repent in sand and snow."

They rowed back out to the ships and reached the *Prince Rupert* at nightfall. The shallop surged beside the ladder. Des Groseilliers jumped to the first rung, turned to Radisson to bid his brother-in-law *au revoir*, then disappeared over the side. Jimmy Frost went next — Brown had retained him to work at James Bay. Magnus Brown indicated to Bartholomew that he must follow.

"I prefer not," said Bartholomew. Magnus Brown looked altogether too much like God.

"Lilly Cole." Brown refused to look at her, but waved. "You also — go aboard the *Prince Rupert*." He turned to John Sparrow. With great reluctance, he shook Sparrow's hand goodbye.

Lilly swung into Sparrow, into the smashed jaw, into the heat of his raspy face, inhaled the sea salt, fish, the smell of wet hemp, tar, father. "I'm staying with you!"

Radisson said, "You will be safer at James Bay." Lilly was surprised at the kindness of Radisson's voice. She was being nudged toward the ladder. She clung to Sparrow.

Sparrow pulled away sufficiently to insert his hand before her face. "See this?" he said. "It's gold, a coin of gold. The Spaniards found it in America. See that face on it? That's the face of Augustus Caesar. The great Emperor Caesar of Rome. It's older than Plato, from ancient times, before the calamity, before the mighty earthquake and the heavenly flood. It is my greatest treasure. You must have it." Sparrow kissed her forehead.

Magnus Brown called out for them to hurry. Radisson lifted Lilly up, put her hands on the ladder, somehow inspiring her to climb. Bartholomew followed. He was very frightened now, almost ecstatic at the difficulty of his role. Magnus Brown nodded to the rest, then ascended the ship's side.

John Sparrow and Radisson rowed the shallop clear of the ship and struggled back to the *Wivenhoe*. A cold night followed. In the morning, the wind veered southwesterly and the *Wivenhoe* beat her way toward Nelson River. Far away, she sailed from sight.

Lilly stood all night on the *Prince Rupert*'s deck and clutched the coin from Atlantis. The *Prince Rupert* was a hermit crab. Crabbing southeast, to the dregs of James Bay. To the New World.

It is not new.

She heard the earth cry out, the plaintive call of an empty place, she remembered the lamentation, she heard Radisson's ghostly song.

PART THREE

Hath the rain a father? or who hath begotten the drops of dew? Out of whose womb came the ice? and the hoary frost of heaven, who hath gendered it?

The Book of Job: 38: 28-29

One

Early September, the *Prince Rupert* sailed cautiously through the shoals of James Bay. After nearly ninety days living in a barrel, except for the afternoon at Mansel Island, the crew watched the shoreline with the sensation that they in turn were being watched.

The sailors aboard the *Prince Rupert* regarded Lilly Cole with lupine interest, but they weren't overly optimistic: Magnus Brown's warnings against meddling with the King's mistress had spread among them. No way to avoid getting caught, and though it was unlikely anyone would be flogged while the ship was far at sea, it was a certainty when they reached land. Besides, Brown said, the King would have them hanged in England. Yet they watched; no harm in watching.

For three months Lilly had washed thoroughly only twice: once northeast of Ireland when the sailors were distracted by a school of halibut, and once off the shores of Labrador, by the kindness of Sparrow, who beat everyone out of the galley to let her heat some water for "a proper dook." Sparrow had cut Lilly's black curls in celebration of their sailing to Atlantis. She had two shirts. Sparrow would wash one on Mondays and the other on Fridays. Now he was gone to Nelson River. He was No-Where.

She bathed with seawater. Sparrow would say that this was a bath in the floodwaters over the peaceful kingdom. She could smell the sea life. On the foredeck, beneath the main bonnet, she, with a bucket and pumice and stripped to her shirt, furtively scraped at the tar on her arms. Magnus Brown, on a tour of the *Prince Rupert*'s rigging, came on deck and nearly put his foot in her bucket. He mumbled apologies, backed up, and thereby, with his bulk, eclipsed the sun. Then he moved, and she was blinded, as if he'd swallowed her whole.

Magnus Brown went directly to his cabin to bind himself more tightly to his left thigh.

On September 7, the *Prince Rupert* sailed into a swampy estuary swarming with geese feeding on eelgrass. Behind them, north, James Bay was a flat blue plane. Above, the sky whitened, disproportionate, and descended heavily on the ship's exhausted crew. Magnus Brown strolled the deck. By Lilly's measure, he seemed actually to be growing. The nights extended as the sun sank farther into the forests to the south.

At the mouth of the river, the ship ran aground on a sandbar. They raised more sail, double-manned the pumps, and waited for the tide to bring her off. For nearly four hours, she was pitched on her keel, surrounded by creamy orange sand littered here and there with boulders on a long spit stretching between forest and ocean. Behind the sands, rows of spruce seemed afloat, rippling between two long, watery blue lines.

"We have fallen short of China," observed Bartholomew to Magnus Brown.

Brown said, "Aye," standing straight, with his arms behind his back.

Magnus Brown weighed more than seventeen stone. His head weighed more than a lamb. He wasn't fat, he was a living *fact*. Posed beside him, Bart reminded himself of his pet monkey.

"So," Bart said, "we are to pass the winter here, in such a, such a *spa*." He'd grown so addicted to backchat, and here, he lived a life unspeakable. "And if we survive," he said unsteadily, "we'll sail merrily home to England, like the heroes we are."

"We will survive," said Brown.

"But of course."

Brown softened. The two men shared a lost hope. "We will make good trade with the savages. In the spring, we'll return to England with a ship full of furs." He glanced at the shabby Earl. "We will survive," he said again.

A brutish landscape in frank, unspectacular light. In the shoals, the sea turned red. They could see no signs of human life ashore, a fox, once, and many deer. No smoke, no villages, no Indians. East by south lay the river, a mile broad, filled with shrill blue geese and surrounded by sand spits that bear no benefit, with an incoming tide Magnus Brown gauged to be nearly two fathom.

In the last hours of the Voyage, they tidied the ship, spliced a frayed anchor cable, and prepared the longboat. That evening, a flat, elongated moon, the colour of a bloodied egg, sat over Meta Incognita. They raised both topsails, the jib and the spritsail, but the breeze was so slight they could only move off the bar, drop anchor to wait out the night, drifting, dragging. At dawn, a north wind would take them to a narrow channel through the rocks, warping up the river, till at last, at noon on September 8, the *Prince Rupert* anchored in two and a half fathoms of water before the bleak shore that Magnus Brown, deadpan procurator, named "Fort Charles."

✗✗✗✗✗

Someone, someone from England, or France, or Holland, had been there before. There was a derelict cabin inhabited by squirrels and barn swallows. They found a mouldy scrap of paper with ink markings too faint to decipher. Skunks had burrowed a den beneath one corner, and hornets had built a huge hive, like a paper head, above the front door. The Earl poked at it with a willow stick, watched five hornets drone into the air, and said to Des Groseilliers, "See your proud escutcheon."

Des Groseilliers silently took the willow from his hand, set it into the snare at the opening of the skunks' den. This would be the tossing pole, the last piece of an elegant, double-bar choke-toss snare with a noose of spruce root. Des Groseilliers stepped back to judge his work, frowning. He'd sniffed at the small, seedy bush berries. It had been a hot summer and fall: the spruce root noose was dry — it could break. *Calice*, shit. He was a fool to make it a choke-toss — but the noose could snap, too, on a toss snare. Shit, bloody English. He used no bait. He didn't efface his smell from the snare, as if his hands had no human scent. He walked away. He wasn't even ignoring his audience.

On Bartholomew's sleeve travelled a hornet as heavy as a guinea. When he brushed it off, it tumbled to the ground and crawled in the grass.

At water's side, where a narrow band of sand dampened and dried with the tide, Lilly made herself scarce. On a sunny day with a gentle wind, violence can be eerily disclosed. Waves are always beginning, never ending, forming a fish-scale pattern of burgundy and blue in the sand. Magnus Brown raised his arms toward the sun. Lilly, half a mile away, wondered if the tracks — a small pad with four long claws — denoted the kind of creature that would attack a smaller animal by daylight. She was watched by silence itself.

Magnus Brown's voice travelled over the broad green river,

over the sands and around the forest. He cried, "Praise be to God! Praise be to God! Praise be to God!" His voice shot off the far shore. He turned toward the shelf of peat that stretched like an eyebrow, where the spruce, cedar, tamarack, aspen, dogwood had been torn at the roots by ice and tide.

Jimmy Frost appeared above him. "Master?" said Frost. "You called."

"Take the boat and eight men. Go to the ship. Fetch the rum, a table, and cloth from my cabin. Bring tin mugs. Be quick." Where is she? Get this over with, then go find her, but don't let her see you, coward, fraud, protector. Magnus Brown had developed the habit of talking to Prince Rupert, his confessor inside his head. He told his imaginary Rupert: the crew is behaving as if they're on leave. We will show the men a ceremony, to remember their duty to England. His imaginary Rupert agreed, Good idea.

Far down the shore, Lilly stopped suddenly, feeling a hand touch her shoulder. She spun around, saw no one.

The crew assembled at sundown, at the site Brown had chosen for the building of a dock for the *Prince Rupert*. He faced them from behind an oak table resting precariously on the narrow beach, his back to the river, a jug of rum forming a ring on the linen draped over strands of dulse.

Magnus Brown stood like a sundial. He'd laid a sheet of parchment on the table before him, and now he clasped his hands across his chest, resisting speech. Suddenly he bellowed, "Let there be no whoring after strange gods!" Twenty heads bobbed up, twenty Adam's apples flinched from the invisible rope.

Bartholomew watched from a tangle of dogwood. He was becoming faerie-like, always ravenous, always starving himself.

This place was a shambles, fish bones and flies buzzing the beach, a saturate smell. The scene rippled in the wind, like a paper landscape. Bart was coming undone by its awful name-lessness. Even his wretched bucolic verse in Addenbury now seemed neoclassical, an achievement of mind far, far beyond his current idiot capacities.

Down by river's side, Magnus Brown filled his sails with Law. His beard dipped in shadow thrown by his magnificent head. He scratched his nose; the men felt an itch. He pointed one long fingernail at the scroll. "Ye be called by God to perform a sacred service to the King of England, Scotland, and Ireland." He gestured to Frost. "Fill their cups, man." The mugs were filled, appreciated, held aloft. "We are here to serve the proprietors of this new land, called Rupert's Land. In the name of Prince Rupert, Count Palatine of the Rhine, Duke of Bavaria and of Cumberland. Drink! By the grace of God, drink to the health of King Charles the Second." He was cheerfully obeyed.

Magnus Brown had memorized the Royal Charter, but he pretended to read from the parchment. "Ye be servants of the Company of Adventurers of England, to whom is granted all seas, straits, bays, rivers, lakes, creeks and psalms — and *sounds* — in whatsoever latitude, with all the lands upon the coasts and the confines of the seas, straits, bays, lakes, rivers, creeks and . . ." on and on, till he could feel himself lose his audience, then, furious, to Frost, "Fill their cups, man!"

Glad gulping. A Prince wants this fucking place? Crazy Royals.

The sun peered over the forest on the other shore.

At that very moment, far away across the sea, by candlelight in his apartment in the cold stone tower at Windsor, the Prince opened an ironbound chest and removed five sheepskin parchment sheets, the original of the Charter so closely memorized by Magnus Brown. Embarrassed by his own greed, embarrassed even to permit himself to feel any hope that this was not greed but patriarchy, Rupert searched for that passage granting him all the Fish, Whales, Sturgeons, all the Royal Fishes and all the Gold, Silver, Gems, all the precious Stones to be found on our Plantation, our Colony, granted our Company of Adventurers in England Trading into Hudson Bay, in this unknown place, my Rupert's Land. He looked up, he caught his reflection in the glass.

Magnus Brown raised his eyes from the parchment. He was overly conscious of its dermatological nature, the split skin of the sheep, its exposure to the air, its incipient decay. He saw Des Groseilliers appear over the ice-torn riverbank. The crew, anticipating rum, kept their eyes on Brown. They saw the face of Magnus Brown cloud over and they grew parched.

Brown gripped the table, partly because the earth was spinning so rapidly. "Ye be naught but servants of God. Servants of the King. Servants of the Body Corporate and Politic, the Company of Adventurers. This is a savage land. But you shall not yield to savagery. If you stray from your duties as Christian men, I will have you flogged, and you shall be fined. I give you my word, as Governor. It will go hard for you here. But you will *hang* when you return to the Kingdom of England!"

Des Groseilliers came into view. Unconscious of their presence, deaf to Brown's sermon, the French Explorer lumbered like a bear over the bank down to the freezing water. Strung from a noose on a long willow yard bent with the weight, a full-grown skunk gasped and kicked. Jimmy Frost snorted.

Des Groseilliers walked out to his groin to thrust the pole and skunk under water. Only way to kill a skunk. Once, just once, when he was a boy, he'd tried to kill one with a club to the top of its spine, and the devil had dug in its heels and pissed in his eye. Now the skunk was fighting like a big fish, but Des Groseilliers never let its feet hit the ground, and his muscles strained so forcefully they ripped the shirt on his back.

Two

The sailors were lonely for the sea and unnerved by the silence of the forests. They scouted in an eight-mile radius but found no human trace, not even human bones. The ruined cabin might have been only two or three years old, but it told nothing other than that its inhabitants had got away.

At night they stoked the fire and speculated on how they'd fight the Indians when they came. They cleaned their guns, and when they went to relieve themselves, they didn't go far from the flickering light of their campfires.

Lilly laid her blanket outside the circle of fire. It was cold, dark; she mourned for Sparrow. She even missed Radisson, who had, for whatever reasons of his own, behaved as an ally. This is what comes from giving our affections. Lilly felt her estrangement from men more than ever, now she was pregnant. But Bartholomew approached and insisted on building a fire specially for her, and she was glad when he set himself nearby, to drink while she slept.

Bartholomew asked her if she was afraid. "No," she said, and Bart said he wasn't either.

Bartholomew threw dead pine brush on the fire, sending a shower of sparks crackling into the night. They sighed audibly, and in tandem they murmured, "Nice effect." "What did you say?" "Nice effect?" They laughed. Then Bart said, "It's real, though, isn't it. It's not a scene."

"Don't be pious, Bart, or I'll kick you out of my chambers."

"I keep wishing I could make it all go away, make it turn into something else. Like a spectacle we can change between Acts. Someone would build a machine to fly us to Scene Two. Mexico. Montezuma's Chamber. But nicely done, like at the Royal, like at Drury Lane." He moaned. "Maybe theatre is gone forever. God, how I miss it. How I miss it."

Dread rose up in Lilly, or heartburn; wistful talk made her sick. "I'd be in prison, in England."

"Not when you're carrying the King's child."

"Probably, yes. Then, when the baby comes, I'd be burned."

"I wouldn't let that happen."

She gave a derisive laugh and turned her back, huddling in her blanket.

In a small, humble voice that Lilly tried to pretend she didn't hear, Bartholomew said, "I'm sorry about China, Lilly. But I won't let anyone hurt you. Or the child."

She didn't even have the art to feign sleep but lay on the ground and looked out at the shadows of the sailors against the firelight. After some time, she said, "Except if it's a bear, Bart. I'd like to see you fight a bear."

Camouflage became essential to Lilly's life; to be quiet, unassuming, provided her a certain privacy among the men. Bartholomew hovered and drank fretfully. She told him she was fine. "I feel well, Bart," she said. "Why don't you get some sleep?" But Bartholomew had given up sleep altogether; it seemed he rarely even passed out anymore.

She tried to persuade him to take up writing again, but he

resisted. He missed Radisson, too; he missed the arguments, he missed Radisson's boasting, sanguinary tales. Now Bart had nothing but his own fear. His ears had gone deaf to satiric verse, the mainstay of a London playwright.

Since being overtaken by his God, Bartholomew couldn't shake the idea that he should write for a purpose other than entertainment, so he approached the page in a panic. It took until the end of September for him even to begin to dip the quill and make a few calligraphic sketches, drawings of rocks or simple representations of animal prints in the river mud. Slowly, clay yielded to letters, and letters yielded sound. Eventually he had a series of sounds, chants, that soothed him. It was a strange new venture, certainly not theatre, not quite song, affected by Radisson's weird performance, and really, Bart thought, I am no longer a writer except in the yearning for it.

In those first days and weeks at Rupert River, while the company was unsettled, the crew liked to stay close to one another. Magnus Brown set up a station of command but found that he couldn't command even himself. He certainly had trouble commanding his desire for Lilly. He watched her furtively, but he couldn't make her out; she seemed like a cloud of moths the colour of winter brush. By now, Magnus Brown was having long chats with Prince Rupert in his head. Rupert rarely disagreed but met Brown's observations with frank, fond approval. It's true, said the phantom Rupert, she will be grateful for your protection, and God knows she'll need it — but may I add, Governor Brown, she will love God more. We all, for that matter, love God more. Then the phantom Rupert would disappear and a crow would caw four times. It was something like boredom, Magnus Brown's confusion in this place. Boredom is an awful affliction; it's Hell.

Magnus Brown was afflicted by a capacity for seeing the flux of things. Things breaking up. Things breaking up into pieces, then into ever differing pieces, Unknown, in constant change. Unknown, but without a deep Mystery. But this is a terrible way to think. It's not Christian. It is not the way a Governor should think. Lilly walked by. She will never love me. I don't even wish for it, that would be stupid; I may be odd, but I am not stupid.

Magnus Brown followed her. She heard the twigs snap. Thinking it was one of the sailors, she rushed ahead, trying to keep to the shore but led inland by the narrow streams that cut into the bank. Magnus Brown ran after her, he galloped, his pockets containing a knife, a spool and thread, an awl banging against his great thighs. Persuaded by its modest cotton swaddling, his manhood grew — all his efforts at restraint seemed only to excite his mutinous body. He had spent so many years in prisons, and he hadn't been troubled by the confines of the ship because his yearnings were so pure, so planetary. But now his tasks were to govern a colony for merchants and to capture, surely to redeem, Lilly Cole's soul. He followed her for nearly two miles, tracked her to a creek where the water hurtled down. He trapped her among broken red rocks. It was not at all what he wanted, and it was also what he wanted beyond recall. His heart pounded so fast, he thought he might die.

He stopped where the rock, spliced by ice, formed a high pink cavern crusted with lichen. Lilly stood, panting, below him. He'd come to this unprepared: ecstasy had always been solitary. For the rest, he would try to assign things to their proper place, in ledgers with summaries of gain against loss, the columns like dams powering his glory.

His voice trembling, he called out, "I know what thou hast done, good Lilly Cole."

Lilly blinked in confusion. Magnus. Speaking Puritan (she did not know Quaker). Brown started to climb down the rock toward her, too breathless to speak until he reached the ledge of rock nearby. "I know what thou art," he gasped and clutched his heart. Lilly stiffened, yet couldn't entirely resist her curiosity. What am I? "Murderer," whispered Magnus Brown.

She jumped off, slipped around him and up the other side. She almost made it. He reached one arm to grip her around the waist, finding her surprisingly hefty, struggled to pull her down, to make her be still. He could barely keep his hands from striking her, as he'd strike the hawk from his hands, the foreign flesh. Lilly could hear the shudder of a private torment. He cried, "Murderer!"

Lilly went still. Brown straightened, ashamed to have held her after she'd stopped fighting him. He saw her round cheek, the fair, childish skin against her black hair. He smelled her rank female scent.

"Who told you?" she asked without looking.

"I overheard. Aboard the barge before we left England. The short man, Sir George Rose, he told the King."

"Then why didn't you put me off at Stromness?"

"I — because I share thy sin."

She looked up at him full in the face, squinting. "You killed somebody?"

"A woman."

She winced. He added, "Nay. I killed her, but not with my own hand. It was my fault she died." This was not going as he had imagined. He was confessing to her. How did she twist it so? He looked down at her crooked mouth. "You must atone for your sin."

She gave an impatient sigh. "Time for that when I'm back in England. I'm a witch, see? Rose says so. He wants me burned." She looked hard at him to see whether that registered. "Do you believe I am a witch?"

"No. But a woman will suffer eternal damnation on her own terms," he said. "God is just." He stared at her. She has a beautiful complexion, grimy but beautiful. His blood hurt him, absolute, inflamed.

She said, "You put yourself in danger, keeping me."

Brown couldn't control himself. He touched her face. When Lilly moaned, he pulled back in horror. Her eyes were closed. She opened them. She wanted to put her head against his chest, then she did. Magnus Brown stood with his hands at his sides. He heard her panting. Lilly shook her head, No, against his chest. His hands came to her hips, her shoulders, her face between his palms. She felt the coiling heat between her legs, brought her body into his, and even in this, his kissing, his touching her, his face she could span with both hands, even now she thought weirdly about climbing a tree. She climbed up into him, and he held her. They staggered back against the rocks. They would have to unbutton, they fumbled with their clothes, her hand was baffled by the bandage.

Brown had never felt such lust; he was familiar only with shame, so that was how he described it. Overcome with shame, he fell back in the excruciating thrill, trying to withdraw from her. Desperately, he conjured sums of account, a list of bills to be paid: to the salter, the cobbler, the oar maker, the joiner, that one to the pewterer, a bill for the tinman. He imposed a grid of ink upon his painfully blooming pulse; he grasped penmanship, he lurched from the lure of dissolve to the straight black lines and firm calligraphy of a merchant's audit.

He pulled himself away. It was unbearable to look at her. His breathing slowed. The world, the real world of separate (however fluctuating) objects reaffirmed itself before his eyes. He looked around in fresh bewilderment. The lichen's spidering tendrils, soft brushes of the tamarack turning gold, an amber teardrop of sap from a band of green on the bark of the balsam, distinct, God-fashioned, and he, a man, well, as of now, I will suffer forever.

She waited in dread. "Magnus," she said.

"No." He bit his lip, his eyes filled with tears. "No."

Lilly's skills in survival had perhaps been hampered by Sparrow's brief paternity. She assembled herself.

Brown's lust clung to him, but he would overcome. His genius veered from this act. The memory of that afternoon would be refashioned and redeemed. He would remember that he'd stumbled against her, that she'd clung to him, that he'd had a moment of physical, manly weakness. Her crooked mouth. Should Magdalene be cleansed of seven devils, would she seem as innocent as this?

"Be invisible," he told her. "Please."

Lilly thought that soon she would be evermore visible.

"Come," said Magnus Brown wearily. "It's getting dark."

"Magnus!" She tugged at his sleeve, stopped him. "Will you tell anyone?" He looked so alarmed that she added, "About my past. My — crime."

He answered with an injured frown. For her mortal security, Lilly would have to make do with his hurt feelings. So it goes in the brave New World. The lords give and the lords take away. Chivalry. Fragile as the spider's web.

He turned his back, and she followed him in a rage to the settlement. Brown trailing a wild creature by the wavering Word; Lilly following a man driven mad by his cock. Has a life of its own, hasn't it? Hell and all Hell's bells.

She had one request of him. And he complied. He ordered a tent built, separate from the men. In her segregation she would let Brown's vigilance restore an imaginary virginity, on which all mankind depends. In this, Lilly proved wise. Brown would rebuild his strength, though he had trouble remembering its source.

When his strength did return to him, it came as the resurrection of his own rigid restraint through which he would scry the other world, the place of desire, unrest, woman. Only Lilly — and every man at the settlement — knew that Magnus Brown was fatefully in love.

Three

October. Frigid love snapped through the air, hedged by Brown's ardently chaste *virilia*. The masculine world grew industrious, working in earnest against the coming winter. Cold seeped up to meet a gunmetal sky and sealed them in. They built the dock. Within a month, they'd dug a cellar twelve feet deep, cut down eighty white spruce, bound them upright and chinked them with moss, and built a two-storey house. They'd built a good oven outside and a fireplace inside, at the centre of the house. They'd set the malt in the cellar to brew and buried the good beer to save it for the return voyage. The pigs, hens, and rooster were penned for the time being, though soon they'd have to come inside.

Bartholomew lay in the weak sun to watch the men cut timber and dig the liver-purple clay. As they did at sea, the land-bound crew supported Bart's indolence, exempting him from work, exempting him even from envy of his access to liquor. He doodled and drank brandy. Many of the sailors considered Bart an angel, and for the rest, he was a hazard, would just get in the way; it never occurred to anyone that he should take to wood-cutting, carpentry, masonry, though one day, he did help out the master thatcher. Thatching made Bart happy for an entire afternoon. It was like writing poetry, only — nice. He admired the weave of it, the laying down of the seasons, ripening, drying, ripening. It filled him with nostalgia for sartorial hours with his tailor. He worked with intense focus until after dark, until he got too drunk and fell off the ladder. After that, he returned to his primary preoccupation with brandy and ink, not as one who homes to a good and proper occupation, but as one destined to live on the sharpened point of the quill, waiting for the ink to sing.

Bart was warped by the magnetic pole. He dreamed about Soby; sometimes he dreamed that he *was* Soby. He stared at Lilly's hands, the muscles of her wrists or the way her childish fingers were changing, becoming decisive, like tools, rather than the pudgy, pliant hands of an actress with almost translucent skin.

Bartholomew loved Lilly because it was far too late to do otherwise. He wished he didn't. It was an awful condition. And Lilly was an awful woman. He sat with her in her freezing tent, his reticence so reproachful, she finally burst out, "Would you have me dead?"

"I don't know." Then, "No! Don't be daft."

She bit her lip and squinted at him.

Eloquence had come easy in London, where there was nothing to say. Here, in Rupert's Land, words were unmasked; even their voices had grown ugly. Bartholomew's conversion was permanent (he was a man of deep-seated habits), and his God wasn't one who laughed. "You've grown so *earnest*," said Lilly bitterly. "Next I know you'll have me hanged. Am I to grovel for what I've done?"

"Do you not feel any guilt at all?" Bart poured a long drink down his throat.

"I feel *sorry*, of course I do." She remembered the reproach in Soby's dying body. But the memory didn't pain her like it used to. Revenge. She'd had revenge. And she felt satisfied.

Faced with the demise of all art, Bartholomew refused to relinquish his tattered stockings and tarnished brass-buckled shoes. He drank as much as possible and squelched through the boggy woods, singing, "Where the bee sucks, there suck I." He counted each day as his last: his last October 7, his last October 8. There was a shrieking pain in his kidney, pain galloping at his crooked heels. This would be the last season of a silly life (forget the poems, forget them, except perhaps that one "Ode to Nothing"). Now that China was out of the question, he would experience death on its own, sere terms. He would try to expect no mercy.

Lace grew on Bartholomew like worm-eaten aspen leaves. Flittering down a narrow path, he came face to face with the French Explorer, whom he discovered standing in the gloom of black spruce. Over one shoulder, Des Groseilliers wore a sleek black animal, a mink. Des Groseilliers was startled. Bartholomew mistook surprise for culpability and he tripped forward to greet him, saying lispingly, "I am Keeper of the King's game. What have you, my good fellow? Oh! I daresay you have been poaching!"

Des Groseilliers didn't respond but slid the mink from his shoulder, crouched over it, and pinned its front legs while he gripped the creature's heart beneath its fur and gave it a sharp yank. The mink's paws splayed when it died. Des Groseilliers shook his head with mild consternation, saying in English, though not particularly to Bart, "I think the mink, she was dead."

Into this precarious world fell the snow, bluing the dawn, melting at noon, covering the shore till the tide rose and swept it out to sea, where it stayed, thickening, until the river and the bay were coated in grey-green slush.

Only the presence of Dogg kept Lilly from freezing to death in her sleep. She struggled out every few hours, waking herself up in the night to bring in more wood. Sleet, hail, snow. It was so cold in her tent that a kettle placed against the fire was too hot to touch on one side but covered in an inch of ice on the other. She wore everything she could find, and no one but Bart was yet aware of her changing shape. The baby had started to move. She thought about Charles. His size, for one thing, his extremely long feet. She was amazed — how intricate was this growing thing, like a magnificent ship inside a bottle. But how does one get the ship out of the bottle?

At last, she couldn't stand the cold at night. She was worried about the health of the baby. She didn't ask Magnus Brown if she could move into the house — she told him so. And he quickly obliged, shocked that he'd not realized how uncomfortable she must be, upbraiding himself for his lack of imagination.

In the morning when the men went out to hunt and cut wood, she'd sit by the fire. There was little to do. Her culinary reputation had followed her here, and the *Prince Rupert*'s cook wouldn't let her near the soup pot. She heard every move Magnus made, saw him worry over his ledger in the blurry light of the windowless house, saw the bright day strike him when someone opened the door. She liked his shape, the hesitant, persistent bravery he showed in every gesture.

Magnus would not look at her. Later, he'd not be able to say when it was he realized that Lilly was pregnant; the knowledge would eventually seep into him through the quiet afternoons. He didn't permit himself to wonder whose child it was. He, too,

244

considered it Lilly's. And quite unintentionally he thought, It balances: she took a life; she will bear one. Minus one, plus one. And thus Lilly was transmuted, by numbers.

The ledger of trade was not so satisfying. No Indians had appeared bearing furs. With a sudden flash of impatience, Brown slammed his fist down on his table. Both Lilly and Jimmy Frost jumped. Des Groseilliers, back from a dawn tour of his trapline, didn't even blink.

"We have made no trade," Brown said, as if accusing Des Groseilliers of hiding Indians in the woods.

Des Groseilliers said, "They are trapping now and will trade after. Anyway, the animals do not have good pelts until the cold of winter. The furs will be no use to us before it goes cold."

Lilly, crouched by the fire, gasped. My God. So this is not called Cold.

Jimmy Frost had a grovelling manner tainted by sarcasm. He liked to stay by Brown's aft quarter and make snide observations, just true enough to poison everyone's self-respect. He looked up from his corner where he sat oiling his gun. "Well, it's gratifying to see you sleep, Mister Gooseberries, I'm sure, an' the King wants you fat and drowsy, it's what you be paid for, that alone. No profit without our health, I say."

Magnus Brown let him go on like this. Corrosion serves a purpose, scours the surface. Though even Frost could read Magnus Brown's heat and never spoke too loudly about "the little whore."

With a smooth, angry motion, Des Groseilliers stood and said, "Ignorant weasel. I'm going out to set my snares in the forest." He shouldered his coat and his bag.

Lilly couldn't face another day blinking at smoke. She stood up. "May I go with you?"

Jimmy Frost smirked, commenting nasally, "O Law, the filthie wants to work."

Magnus Brown, stricken, "But you must stay here."

Des Groseilliers looked at her, such a pleasing face; he remembered the pleasant, warm sensation of seeing her naked. Lilly fingered her knife in her pocket.

"Do you know how to snare the small bird?" Des Groseilliers asked.

Then Lilly remembered something wonderful. Small birds, larks? Their feet tangled in thread. Who would have shown her that? Beth? A day of sunshine, the smell of grass, her mother with Aunt Meg, snaring birds. "I think I used to," she said in awe. She had been a child once.

Des Groseilliers shrugged. And looked almost happy.

Brown's thighs nearly knocked over the table when he stood. He didn't know that he moaned aloud.

Des Groseilliers had been afflicted with headache for many days, but now he felt excited — over such a small thing, snaring birds with a young woman. He threw a sack to her. Pain needled into his left eye. "Do not come hungry," he told her. "We will walk far."

When she turned to pull the door closed, Magnus was seated again, looking at her blankly. And there was Jimmy Frost in the corner, his slick arms nut brown in the dim light, his fingers black with gun oil. Frost clicked his tongue and smiled, the peevish lines of his face pulled up into Vs.

XXXXX

They set dozens of perch snares, then circled back to bag the birds, six firm-fleshed grey jays, two grouse. It was a cold day, the sun darting through branches. He showed her how to make rabbit snares, spring-pole, of willow, using only birch branches for bait. He made the noose of balsam-fir roots. Then he took a pouch filled with bloody meat and rubbed blood on the root,

246

speaking in a low voice as he worked. "Fox liver. The rabbit thinks it tastes very bad. So he does not bite away the noose and be free." He offered this without being asked. Together they set thirty snares, maybe more, kneeling in the snow to set them, quietly proceeding.

They remarked on the dryness of the snow, how it wasn't so cold out of the wind in the bush. To Lilly it seemed that his commentary came at some expense, that he was obliging her. He loved to be here in the woods, but he didn't love talking. She smiled at him; she wanted to thank him.

They tramped through the woods, out of the wind, with frost on their eyelashes, in blinking patterns of light, by the shoreline, near the dock. Des Groseilliers hadn't said anything for some time. He staggered now and then. She asked him if he was hungry, but he didn't respond. He stood stock-still. And then he fell, crashing down in the bush.

Des Groseilliers saw branches stippled by sun through a narrowing aperture hot with pain. The ground disappeared under him. His spine arched, his thick torso contorted backward, torqued, till his head almost touched his feet, his hands sawing the air like fins. It would strip his muscles from his bones. Then he lost consciousness.

Lilly watched, horrified. Des Groseilliers lay in thick brush, maybe dead. At that moment she heard voices out on the slushy river. There was a boat with a single mast, rowed by eight men, close enough for her to call. She slid on the snow down to the shore. The rowers struggled toward her, fighting the tide with Christian mulishness. She recognized Radisson by his hat, on a slant as if to correct the crooked angle of his shoulders.

It was extremely cold in the open. A rack of clouds covered the sun, the wind carried sleet. Radisson twisted his bare neck, calling out, "We are come!"

She waved. Then she heard Des Groseilliers groaning, and

she floundered back up the snowy embankment to kneel beside him and wipe his face. His yellow-green eyes were occupied by a sickness with a character of its own. His arm lashed out and struck her, broad and hard as an oar. She was thrown several feet into the brush; blood ran down into her throat. Again she crawled to his side. He was so sick; he was sickness itself, and not a man. She felt terribly sorry for him. She said, "Médard."

She'd never said his name before. It awoke him to a passion that had been evoked only for the wife he'd left in New France, Pierre's terrible sister, she who railed and bickered, doubted, complained and criticized with perfect aim, she, *wife*, with whom he'd left eight children and his debts. Lilly had succeeded. He was again a man. "Médard," Lilly said again. Des Groseilliers felt as if he was hearing his name spoken for the first time. He reached his big hand to her face and gently touched the blood. And then again he fainted.

Below them the boat had beached with some difficulty, the wind blowing from northeast. John Sparrow was not aboard.

Radisson was the only cheerful one of that crew. He stood at the shore and looked up at her expectantly, taking in her smeared face and bloody clothes with raised eyebrows. And something else. Her shape. A square making a circle. "I must speak with mon frère, Sieur Des Groseilliers."

"He's . . ." she hesitated, then leaned over, spit up blood, and waved to where Des Groseilliers lay.

Radisson scowled. "Pah. Je connais. La crise de colère." He clambered up the riverbank, his crew following. Lilly wiped her face with snow and followed them.

"Médard," Radisson grumbled, "I say you must keep busy. I tell you, you will not be so fall-down if you do not sleep so much. No one can say too many good things about being busy. Oh là, Médard."

He slapped at the bristled jowls. Someone offered a flask.

Radisson shook him and said, "Wake up and have the brandy. We have many tales, but no time. Already two men are dead."

John Sparrow. Lilly lifted Des Groseilliers's head, pried open his jaw, took the flask, and poured. Des Groseilliers looked around him, dazed, seeing his brother-in-law, the other men, then Lilly. He stared at Lilly as at a miracle. He wanted to hear her say, Médard.

Radisson laughed. "Like the bear, he wakes up. Oh! Here is the honey! It must be spring!"

Lilly, fiercely, to Radisson: "What men have died?"

"Ah. One who is named John, what, I forget his other name, and the other, the gunner, which is a sad thing, he was a brave man." He saw the mucus swill with the mess of blood on Lilly's face and he added, "The man with one hand, he is the one who died. Not John Sparrow. Monsieur Sparrow is en bonne santé." He smiled. It occurred to Lilly that he was glad to see her. "You don't look good," he said.

Four

Radisson and his crew headed out in the single-mast boat, followed by the *Prince Rupert*'s shallop, back to where the *Wivenhoe* was anchored, at the mouth of the bay to Rupert River. Water froze around their oars. As the two boats made their way toward the *Wivenhoe*, they heard the ghostly moaning of her rigging, thickly coated in ice; all the ship's sounds were off-key, belated. They called out. Sparrow appeared from below and began to hack at the ice.

The *Wivenhoe* had been at Port Nelson for eight weeks before giving up and heading along the coast of Hudson Bay, one hundred and thirty leagues southeast to Cape Henrietta Maria, at the entrance to James Bay. There the crew had lost heart, with two corpses stored in the hold and Captain Newland stricken with scurvy, unable to rise from his cot. Radisson had taken over then and navigated the ship this far, before seeking some assistance with the river shoals.

All day they cleared the rigging to prepare to sail to Fort Charles. Des Groseilliers had insisted on accompanying his brother-in-law on this expedition. The falling-fit had left him with a murky depression, moodily circling Lilly. Lilly had tried to assure him that her nose was not in fact broken; she could almost breathe through it. He always felt thieved by the loss of control that accompanied his falling-fits. These fits were humiliating; he considered it a streak of cowardice in his deepest soul to act without volition. Now into this gap in his consciousness had entered a woman. He could not escape. He even *liked* her.

Des Groseilliers was rarely troubled by a woman; he never let his affections interfere with his passion, which was for freedom above all else — as it was for Pierre-Esprit, as it would be for any true adventurer. What others might call selfishness was in Des Groseilliers's terms an abnegation — he refused to look away from an abiding awareness of his own inevitable death, his own vital privacy. Love, when he'd allowed it, had been a sort of homely animal that sat on his chest. But *this* love, now, ate at his heart.

If it could be said that Des Groseilliers had a religion, it was independence — his own and others'. He did not delude himself that because he loved he should be loved in return. There was no logic in that. So he was silent on this journey.

Darkness fell. They didn't dare to navigate the river until morning's light. They built two fires and tried to thaw the sails.

Captain Newland was lucid while his body steadily decomposed. Sparrow never took his eyes from Luc Romieux's fingers as the surgeon clipped dead flesh from Captain Newland's gums and feet or soaked a rag in a bath of cedar, herbs, and beer, dripping this over the Captain's sores. The cabin stank of scorched canvas and pus.

Magnus Brown concentrated on writing an inventory of the trade that Radisson had made while the *Wivenhoe* was uneasily moored at Nelson River. He elicited from Radisson the number of beaver pelts he'd got from the northern Christinos and the cost in knives and kettles in exchange. Radisson answered in a monotone, without his usual arabesque. Captain Newland's eyes ran with tears, but he did not cry out.

Brown closed in on the finest details, splintering facts in

obsessive multiplication. "Needles, thread, hammers, awls, how many? Five? Ten? Why so much? Profligate. What number hatchets? For what number hides?" The figures were so profitable that Brown, who was shocked at first, felt his first glimmer of avarice. "How could you leave such rich trade?" he asked of Radisson. "You must return. Or will they find their way here?"

Radisson regarded him philosophically. "It is far. Even for the savages, it is too far to travel by canoe."

Night endured. Magnus Brown twice fell asleep, startled awake when his ledger slipped to the floor. The third time, when Radisson again put the book back into his hands, dawn's light formed a scrim that obscured their vision. Magnus Brown began to speak as if he'd never been asleep. "You must go back. Stake the claim for the Company. Why did you not stay as you were told?"

The shrug. "A big storm rises, and it forces the ship from the River Nelson. Then the men get sick. I tell them, Don't *wear* the tea of cedar, *drink* it. But they say, Oh, we do not drink your savage mud. Maybe they think I'm joking."

The surgeon Romieux's hands stopped, then somewhat shakily resumed their ministrations.

Magnus Brown burst out, "You betray your own country! And now will you betray the English?"

Des Groseilliers stood up. Brown's eyes flicked in his direction to see if he was under attack. Brown didn't know himself, speaking so rudely to another man. He wanted to leave the ship, with its stench of death. He hated himself this way.

Radisson took his time. Through the porthole, he saw the sun seep over the trees with that curious refraction. "I belong" — he gestured vaguely — "to all of this land. I belong everywhere. But — Governor Brown — you must be assured, your merchant interests are secure." He looked at Magnus Brown so remotely that Brown felt his glance like a punch in his stomach. "The Captain nailed a piece of brass to a small tree at the river's mouth. It did bear the English King's arms. He took possession of all that land for King Charles. Everywhere at river Kawiriniagaw, Nelson River. 'All this land belongs to His Majesty,' and so like that. Did you not do this, Captain Newland?"

Radisson turned his attention to the sick man. Luc Romieux stepped away. In a soft, bruised voice he said, "Captain Newland is dead."

Morning brightened only to be extinguished, like a sodden rope of match.

✗✗✗✗✗

At Fort Charles, three days later, they buried the three bodies as deep as they could in the frozen earth. The service was conducted on a gaunt day. Magnus Brown's scripture was brief, inconclusive, and from the Book of Job, his favourite.

> *Have the gates of death been opened unto thee? or*
> *hast thou seen the doors of the shadow of death?*
> *Hast thou perceived the breadth of the earth?*
> *declare if thou knowest it all.*

Bartholomew was reminded that he really didn't like his new overseer, God, an intellectual bully. Asks questions only He can answer.

> *Hath the rain a father? or who hath begotten the*
> *drops of dew? Out of whose womb came the ice? and*
> *the hoary frost of heaven, who hath gendered it?*

The men couldn't stand still in the cold, and Magnus Brown had no wish to perpetuate the new sense of himself as the tyrant "Governor Brown," so he soon dismissed them.

Sparrow stayed a moment at the graves, nodding as if hearing their answers. When it was his time to die, he thought, he'd wish his body to go to the sea. He pitied the dead buried in matter solid and immutable. He'd go to the sea, he would.

Lilly went to Sparrow, held out her mittened hand to him, opened it to reveal the coin from Atlantis, the magic egg. "You may have it back," she said.

Sparrow closed her hand around the coin. "Nay."

Sparrow was thinner than ever. He had a frostbite blister under one eye. He tightened his grip, looking with quiet awe at the youthfulness of her face. His familiar, whistley voice took on a singsong tone, and he gently shook their hands together while he spoke. "Keep the coin, Lilly. Let it be the mark of a safe place for you, a place that knows no death nor sorrow." He touched the curls that showed under her hat. "Shaggy doll, you could use a trim." He could see very clearly, the girl is with child. Six months gone. He patted her shoulder and went inside. He'd have a cup of tea. A quiet joy was all he sought in this world, and sometimes he had to fight very hard to keep that.

XXXXX

Radisson directed the building of several tents for the *Wivenhoe*'s crew. It was too late to build them another house. They used sails. He was the only one confident that the canvas wigwams could be made comfortable. He showed the doubting sailors how to use a spruce tree for a ridgepole and to build rafters, then swing the big sails over top and drape them to the ground on either side.

"The Indian will be most impressed," Radisson predicted,

and he flung aside a sail and went in. The smell of sea and canvas, a deep stillness inside. He said, "Now, we make a place for to sleep," and patiently ordered the crew to release the bonnets — the swaths of canvas, like pleats, unlooped in light winds to make the sails bigger. "I nail them, just so, and you have the hammock for to sleep." The men were impressed by his ingenuity. But it was Radisson's tender patience that moved them more; they watched him set spare sail into the hammocks, helping him when they saw his intent, thanking him in subdued voices. They mimicked, following him in his fastidious preparations, setting green brush, then packing snow high against the exterior walls.

As in the house, a fireplace was at the centre of each tent. In Radisson's tent, he fanned fresh spruce boughs at the doorway and on the floor, and he brushed and relaid these every other day at dawn. He set a new domestic pattern in the *Wivenhoe*'s crew; they even smelled better, though of course they didn't have to contend with the pigs and poultry like the men in the main house. The men carefully hung their belongings from the walls beside their beds. Radisson reserved the west side for preparing food and for forming snowshoes when it was too cold to work outside. The sailors would pop in on any pretence to inhale the warm, sweet-smelling space. And to study his domestic management.

Radisson made snowshoes. He said to anyone who would listen, "You would be a wise man to learn this for yourself. You *need* to do so."

Lilly followed Sparrow into Radisson's fragrant tent to sit where she could follow Radisson's hands. "Do what I do," said Radisson. She tried. She smoked a pipe as Radisson did, with French nonchalance; she adopted his accent for hours at a time. She used all her talent as an actress to do as he did, but to no avail. The snowshoes warped and bowed. The needle pierced her hand before it pierced the hide of a torn moccasin. She could mimic his style, but she didn't have his hands' swift assumption.

Lilly was a Town girl, a Londoner. Clothes, when there were clothes, came stitched; food, if there was food, came plucked if not cooked. She remembered when she'd felt she had "skill." She could freeze to death a dozen steps from a tent. She lived in a bubble made by men.

The returned sailors from the *Wivenhoe* had greeted her with subtle tremors of surprise, seeing her bulk and her new waddle. Only the Orkneyman made comment in her hearing, and then it was more like a gasp, as if she'd beat him. She'd slipped out of range, become a perplexity rather than a target and not terribly desirable.

The wide-eyed surgeon Romieux hadn't even approached her concerning her pregnancy; he didn't *see* her. He had three deaths on his conscience, and he sought out *other* work, helping the ship's carpenter build a new pinnace out of the *Prince Rupert*'s old one, blinking at his tasks with a look of baffled, ever-renewed innocence. There was no conversation whatsoever about the obvious fact that Lilly Cole was carrying a child, at least not within her hearing. They didn't seem to hate her. They just liked men better.

Five

The Indians did not come. Winter was the only, the final, season. Snow set in waves frozen against shores of stark black sticks of spruce, grey groves of aspen, red knots of dogwood. Still, the Indians did not come. Magnus Brown worried through his ledger like a hulk adrift among reefs, imagining hypothetical trade.

Gun-worms	10 pair	for 10 Made-Beaver
Flints	100	5 M-B
Guns	10	100 M-B
Pistols	20	80 M-B

The ledger was for material goods, while the journal was for observations, scientific and objective. At the back of the journal, written back to front, was Brown's addendum, his apologia to a phantom Prince, the perfect listener.

December 22nd. It has become so cold I send the men out to hunt in groups of five. Yesterday they shot a moose, which we have dressed in preparation of the holy day. The sun mimics the moon, or it is the moon wearing the mask of a sun, for there is no calendar of days where such a scalding cold could radiate from that source. She goes out to her traps even on such a day, when to breathe is to burn.

✗✗✗✗✗

They came in a brief mild spell, on Christmas Eve, on snowshoes three feet long. Thirty Indians or more, wearing decorated moose and beaver skins, with French wool blankets. There were among them perhaps a dozen women, some old, some with young children.

They came silently, just before dawn. The wind had veered from the north to the south, making the snow heavy, so it was better to travel at night. They pulled ten toboggans, their runners quickened with bear grease.

Even if the Indians had made noise, Magnus Brown wouldn't have heard them. All night his dreams were in tumult. Strands of the canticle of the Virgin — *My soul doth magnify the Lord* — entwined with chaotic computations of trade. Dreams exhausted him, and he often fell deeply asleep in the last hour of dark.

Perhaps it was the smell of bear that aroused Dogg, who woke up Lilly. She lay there feeling the baby tumble. The silence was heavy-laden. She got up and went outside. This was the kind of light that most saddened her, the lifeless light just before sunrise. But she wanted to check her snares. She'd grown compulsive about doing this. Soon, she'd have a child to feed. She found solace only in a desperate practising of the skills Des Groseilliers had so casually shown her.

When the men awoke, Lilly's bunk was empty. From the woods far off, they heard Dogg baying.

Des Groseilliers stopped Magnus Brown and Bartholomew

258

as they were rushing outside, and he said, "I will go. I will find her more quickly."

Bartholomew recognized an ardent need in Des Groseilliers's concern for Lilly. He took a deep breath and followed him.

Magnus Brown reluctantly stayed behind to work, as a Governor would. Surely she would appear soon. He paced the house.

Bartholomew and Des Groseilliers stopped at Radisson's tent, to see if she'd gone there. Radisson shook his head and said, "Lilly is disappeared?" Dogg was madly barking. He began to sharpen his knife with a stone. "Maybe she has gone out to check her snares," he said. "She always do that now. Maybe she think the animal will come when she calls." He sheathed his knife and tucked it into his leggings. "One time," he said, deliberately appraising Bartholomew, "my brother and I are fighting among the Iroquois at Madawaska, do you remember, Médard? We took ten prisoners that time." Radisson handed a pistol to Des Groseilliers. Des Groseilliers grunted, yes, he remembered, and put the pistol in his jacket.

Radisson filled his bag with shot. "The enemy pursued us, so we made a barricade of dead trees."

Bartholomew asked, "What do you think is the matter with Dogg?"

Radisson put up a warning finger. "Only dead trees, for we do not want our enemies to know our presence by the fresh strokes of our hatchets." He stood, shouldering his gun. Bartholomew and Des Groseilliers waited for him to go out. "They never found us there, we were so well hidden. But to be sure we would live, we killed our prisoners —"

Des Groseilliers pushed forward. "Go. Go, Pierre."

Radisson blocked their way. He gave Bartholomew a strange look, and repeated slowly, "We killed our prisoners. Then broiled their flesh to show our great victory."

Bartholomew tried for skepticism. "You have peculiar appetites, Monsieur Radisson."

Radisson finally pushed open the tent and said, "In Rome we must do as they do."

Des Groseilliers pressed past him. "Pfft. In Rome they eat the Indian. Pfft."

Radisson smiled enigmatically, letting Bartholomew precede him.

The savages were waiting at the edge of the clearing. Dawn spilled across the sky like cooked egg. Magnus Brown opened the door to the house and came out. Dogg was hoarse from barking; he stayed twenty feet from the savages, who were impassive, but one young man clucked his tongue and held out his hand and Dogg began to creep toward him, timidly enthusiastic.

Blinking, shivering, all the men came outside. Everyone stood in the yard, a great company, thirty Indians and thirty-eight white men. Des Groseilliers could feel the Earl's liquorish breath on his ears and turned; Bartholomew was staring into the bush where Lilly hid, a speckled hen.

Magnus Brown began to clamber through the snowdrifts. But Radisson handed Des Groseilliers a pair of snowshoes, slipped his feet into another, and the brothers had moved to the centre of the clearing before Brown could make it past the clay oven. Radisson held up his hand. "Stay!" he cried. "Do not come toward now! Await me here in the snow without apprehends. I go to speak to the savages!"

"I go too, Pierre," said Des Groseilliers.

"No, Médard. I must go alone."

Baffled, the company watched Radisson stride on his raquettes to stand before the Indians.

A motionless scene but for the flick of Dogg's tail. There was no evidence of enmity or mockery. (As Radisson would later explain, "The wildman, he will tease like all men do, but in his own genius and not unless he hates you, or he loves you. At that time, the chief did not know I am like a son.") In Cree, Radisson cried, "Who is your chief?"

Those who were watching saw a handsome Indian raise his chin. The forest and river seemed to yell, as if a roaring chasm had briefly been revealed. Then he bowed his head, and the English would assume that they'd heard the wind. The Indians around him pointed and shuffled. *He is our chief.*

"Good chief!" said Radisson. "I am come!"

The chief peered at him politely, as if trying to put a name to an unfamiliar face. This whiteman spoke a southern dialect.

Radisson alarmed them all by falling to his knees. "Be of good cheer! I will be thy son! And I have brought thee a father!" He waved for Des Groseilliers to approach. "Here is thy father!" He patted Des Groseilliers on the belly, aiming for his heart.

Des Groseilliers knew that he must strike a grand pose. He scratched his nose. He was, somehow, commanding.

The chief mildly inquired, "Do you have guns?" He used the French for "guns."

"I have good guns and excellent fish hooks. You will be fat."

And the chief smiled. He was powerfully built but not young; his face had been creased by his good nature. He nodded to his young men, who pulled a toboggan forward and unloaded four robes of white beaver. Radisson raised his eyebrows. The white robes would make a man go blind, they were so brilliant.

Radisson fired his gun into the air. The Indians shrank from the noise but held their ground; the women collected their children and faced the whitemen. This family needed the weapons, too bad but true. The ugly instruments were not graceful and quiet like a bow — no good for hunting because they took too long to load and made so much noise the animals ran away. They could be used only to kill enemies and intimidate people. Still, they knew that the gun, useless in so many ways, was already a necessity. Radisson handed the chief the fowling piece and the chief cradled it in his arms, his hands stroking the barrel.

Magnus Brown ordered Jimmy Frost to fetch a case of guns and open it.

At the sight of so much machinery, the chief felt a knife of ice in his heart — no, not ice but European metal, a brutal sensation, not the death he had expected, which was by drowning. The chief was fascinated by Frost's freckled hands touching the guns. He had seldom seen men like this among his own people: cunning, and powerful because they don't care for the common good. He met Frost's eyes. *Pwaatich*. Not quite human. The spotted whiteman smiled without happiness.

The chief looked to Magnus Brown. This Englishman is the size of a moose, and he has something of the moose's morose discomfiture. Not evil; without a scent for it. An English trader, perhaps a lost sorcerer. The damage to my people will be accidental, almost without blame. So much the worse. "The guns are here to stay," he said. "Our neighbouring nations have them. We have to have them too or our wives and children will be stolen from us in war. We need as many as you can get. We will give you five beaver for one gun. Ehe. You will never wish to trade with any other nation."

The chief's face grew younger with the pleasures of tactical deceit. "But you should be careful," he added. "You must trade with us and avoid the river on the other side because those people over there are very treacherous." That being said, he opened a package of beaver pelts.

Magnus Brown counted. Twelve. The savages packaged by the dozen. The Indian took five beaver pelts, placed them on the moose hide that served as a table, then held the gun to his chest as proof of ownership.

Brown had been preparing for this. Five pelts for one gun was outrageous. The Indians packed the skins into bundles of twelve because they already knew their value. He took one gun from the case, placed it on the moose hide, took a bundle from a sledge, put it beside the gun. One gun: twelve beaver pelts.

The chief picked up his bundle and reloaded it for the journey back to his territory. Radisson had brought out tin looking glasses and trinkets. Cold light flitted across the faces of the wildmen. The women laughed, rolling the baubles in their fingers while the whitemen hovered uneasily.

The chief opened the hands of his people, removed the tobacco and mirrors, bells, ice chisels, combs, spoons, egg boxes, needles and thimbles, and dropped them at the feet of Magnus Brown. "Your tobacco looks better than that goose shit we get from the whites at Saguenay, but other than that, we will be happier trading with anyone but you."

Radisson quickly appeared at the chief's side and said, "I am grieved to see you destroy yourself and your people!" He stooped to repack the guns. "We have put our lives in danger to cross the great salted lake to bring you guns and flints. And now you will not make honourable trade. I have never felt so betrayed, except by the Ministers of France."

"You are a cunning man," said the chief to Radisson. "A real European. But maybe not as weak."

Radisson wiped his face as if there were tears. "Hélas!" he said, "I am sad to death! Your nation will be condemned to misery and famine when I leave you."

"I appreciate your concern, but we will trade with the nations to the east who go to the big river below the lake. It will save us a lot of trouble with your English strangers."

"I am surprised that a wise man like you would make such a big mistake. If you do not trade with us, we will trade with nations from farther away. They will travel over your territory to reach us. They will kill your animals and take your women. Your nation will perish from famine and war."

"Ah." The chief pulled his robe around him.

"It is so."

Late afternoon. The wind persisted from the south. The chief hated a south wind.

"Sometimes it is lonely to be the man who leads," said Radisson sympathetically.

Then Lilly emerged from the bush and hurried toward the house, her hands filled with white rabbits. Bartholomew and Sparrow followed her.

The sight calmed the chief. Women always calmed him. "Did you bring your women?" he asked Radisson.

"No," said Radisson.

"If that is not a woman, you are not a man."

"She is one who belongs to the King."

"The English King keeps slaves?"

Radisson hesitated. "She is young. But inside she is tough like the old hen. She is not weak and contemptible like a woman is weak and contemptible. So in this way, she is not a woman."

"Can she cook?"

"She is a terrible cook."

"Lace the snowshoe?"

"Very bad at that."

The chief drew back. He knew of many slaves, and he didn't like it. Nations to the south take slaves. Here, he thought, where we must account for every breath we take, a slave is excessive, wasteful, and will bring bad luck.

But nowhere had the chief seen a slave who was useless. He

wanted to meet her. "Is it the English King's child she carries?" he asked politely.

Radisson's knees buckled. It took all his guile to conceal the shock. He looked across the clearing, where a pregnant woman waddled to the house. What sorcery is this? Has she bewitched him? No man has said Lilly is with child. Radisson studied the crew. What of his brother, did he know? Every man must know but Pierre-Esprit. Embarrassment pierced Radisson to the quick.

The chief stood expectantly, waiting for Radisson to take him to view the English King's pregnant slave. Radisson marshalled himself. "I have been neglectful of good society," he told the chief, his voice trembling. "Come." And he took him to the house to meet Lilly Cole.

Six

Lilly came into the house, threw her rabbits on the chopping block, then anxiously began to chisel the fur from the flesh. The pungent odour of the pigs and hens rose through the floorboards. She was frightened and cold from hiding in the bushes, and she attacked the rabbits viciously. There were women among the savages. Savage women would know how to get the ship out of the bottle better than would poor Luc Romieux, in whose hands so many men had died. Lilly's hands shook as she threw a rabbit half-skinned into the cooking pot, stoking the fire. She had to find a way to speak to the Indians. Des Groseilliers, Radisson, they must help her get to the women.

Bartholomew and Sparrow came inside to find the place filling with the stench of burning fur. Sparrow quietly took the pot from the flames. "Wheesht, Lilly."

Lilly took up a knife and started to hack at an onion. The door opened. There stood the chief. His nostrils flared with revulsion at the vile smell in the house. He waited cordially. Radisson's beak appeared over the chief's shoulder. "The Great Chief has come to see the English King's slave."

"Pardon?" asked Bart.

"She who is big with child," Radisson added, giving Lilly a wounded look. And now he has the English King's baby to keep alive!

266

Lilly put down her knife. She thought, Radisson is sexless, in a way. She met his eye. And felt confused by a brief impulse to apologize to him.

To the chief, in Cree, Radisson said, "We will make you a gift to show our love for you." To Bartholomew, in English, he said, "You must sing. Sing the song you sang on the ship! Sing for great profit!"

Bartholomew began to sing. "Ohimè dov'è il mio ben, dov'è il mio core?" His voice was well seated by alcohol.

Ahi sciocco mondo e cieco, ahi cruda sorte
Che ministro mi fai della mia morte.

The door blew open; a sunny wind swept in. White sun bleached the crumpled velvet of Bartholomew's costume, whitened his curls, vanished the lines from his face, erased the sore on his lip, so he was perfected as marble was perfected by Michelangelo, as bones are perfected by seasons on the sand.

Tears filled Radisson's eyes. There is hope in this! Hope, trade, and adventure. Pierre-Esprit will protect Lilly and the English King's son too. Born in Canada! Life is beautiful! So full of wonder it will make you laugh!

The Indian chief tipped his head. The singer is dying. The chief sensed that Bartholomew had no disease that could harm his people but was dying of some personal and contrary inclination of his own. He regarded Bart fondly. Like all his people, the chief respected death, but he alone felt such tenderness for error. He was known as a witty man.

He examined the others in the room. An old man with sinewy courage and a pregnant slave. The English King's slave, fresh as a young tamarack. But what is her purpose here? Women (without words) tell all there is to know about men. He smiled at her and said in his own language, "I am called Weaabinakaabo." (Or that is the way it will be written.)

Lilly wiped her nose with the back of her hand and curtsied. The chief mimicked her, wiping his nose and making a most astonishing curtsy. She brightened. She curtsied with greater flourish. The savage copied her with perfectly gauged exaggeration. Again, she curtsied; again he mimicked, generously embellished — generous mimicry is by far the most difficult to achieve. What kind of man is this? Only a very great player can do physical comedy. She felt relief, happy relief running through her like a summer rain. Here is theatre!

Weaabinakaabo knew that he had made a conquest. It is always compelling to be admired, even by a white woman. He beamed at the slave and the dying man. "These people are comely as the dogwood blossoms, or the pouting flower that blooms on rotted wood," he said to Radisson.

Radisson couldn't follow all of what the Indian said, much of it being peculiar to the region, of local botanical nomenclature. But he stepped up to Bart to say, "I must confess, I am astounded at the charm you make. I should have brought my guitar." To Lilly: "Keep smiling. The wildman likes entertainment as much as a feast, and we know too well you cannot make the feast, so keep smiling."

John Sparrow's heart darted like a tern in the surf. Weaabinakaabo heard Sparrow's bones vibrating. Three months ago, Weaabinakaabo dreamed that he discovered a nest filled with new birds, their gaping mouths set on blue necks. He remembered that they were motherless and were either sustained or devoured by a great black raven, it could be either one. The people here inside aren't hairy-faced; that's another likeable thing about them. He went to the open door and looked out. The unusually mild day was fully dawned.

Weaabinakaabo watched his people mix with the whites.

Then there was a quickening, like a dog fight; the figures clashed and parted, someone breaking away and running. The whitemen were running after two of his people. Weaabinakaabo ran out after them.

He was nearly out of breath when he caught up to one of the whites. He threw his body against him, and the whiteman, caught by surprise, fell to his knees. Weaabinakaabo kept running. By then he had his knife in his hand. He reached forward and cut the leg of the man ahead of him, not so cruel, at the calf, not the tendon. The man fell and Weaabinakaabo sprinted past. The whites were chasing two women, one very old, the other young, carrying a young child. The women couldn't run anymore; they were falling and struggling in the snow. The whites took the young woman and forced the child from her arms. The child, about two years old, tried to stand. They shook the woman until something dropped from her hands, shining. Weaabinakaabo reached them at last, and he leaned his knife into the ribs of a whiteman, who released the young woman and fell to the ground. The woman picked up her child. She left the shining looking glass in the snow.

Several whitemen forced the old woman down onto her back. She kicked, but they caught her feet and pulled off one of her shoes; she wore buskins with strange, thick bone heels. When the old woman's foot was bare, they shouted to each other and pointed. The foot was cleft.

Weaabinakaabo's men and the whitemen milled about. Magnus Brown bellowed at his crew to retreat, to go back to where their trade goods sat, where the Indian women stood so defiantly. Weaabinakaabo's men were taut, watchful for a single move from their chief that would tell them when to strike. But Weaabinakaabo and Magnus Brown held them back and held each other by the eye.

Radisson had eased himself among them all. It was his

instinct to be close to an enemy if he couldn't be far from him. He embraced Weaabinakaabo, an act of recompense that also served to pin the chief's arms to his side. Weaabinakaabo understood him well; he stood still. He would speak for peace before attacking. Radisson kissed his cheek and released him.

The old woman tried to reach for her shoe, but the whitemen wouldn't give it to her. Someone said, "It's a Devil's foot!" Even Luc Romieux, attending to the wounded men, stopped and looked for the Devil's foot.

Weaabinakaabo spoke to Radisson with keen disgust.

Radisson listened to him, then turned to the whitemen, his face neutral, his voice calm to mask his anger. "When the old one was young, an axe falls on her foot, and — pfft! No toes in the middle. Just like the goat."

"Let her up!" Magnus Brown's chest heaved. "Take these fools to the house." The wounded men were carried away. Brown turned to Radisson. "Tell the chief, he is to be indicted for attempted murder. And the woman is accused of theft."

Radisson said something to the chief; between them they seemed to agree. "We must speak about this in my tent," said Radisson to Brown. "The Earl and old John Sparrow will attend us, with my brother. Just like a council. Yes?"

Magnus Brown thought, No, but it would have to stand as one.

Weaabinakaabo ordered his people to wait beside their toboggans. He walked proudly between Radisson and Brown, the jury following, with Jimmy Frost scuttling after carrying Brown's writing tools, while the nervous sailors slipped back to the house for their guns.

Seven

Radisson had swept the doorway and put down fresh boughs yesterday. The chief orbited to take his place on the north side, while Des Groseilliers seated himself opposite. Bartholomew and Sparrow came in, circled, and sat down. Radisson remained at the east door. Brown had waited outside for Jimmy Frost to collect his ledger; now he lumbered across, Frost at his heels. As his bull-like body settled on the spruce, Magnus Brown felt plagued by a sense of trespass.

The sun tipped into the tent, the air swarmed with bright green dust. Brown felt excluded from something quick and pure, he felt himself falling, like water over a mirror. But he had gained an advantage. Prince Rupert would congratulate him. The terms of trade had abruptly inclined in his favour. The savage had almost inadvertently transferred power to the English. A woman's thievery, the chief's attempted murder, these crimes might be exonerated if the Indian pays a penalty, serves out a contract. A winter's worth of fair trade.

Magnus Brown said to Radisson, "Tell the chief that his people must leave as soon as possible and not come back. Only three or four older men — no young men — will be permitted to come here to bring furs for trade. My crew wants revenge. I will try to protect his people, but he must be obedient."

Radisson spoke in Cree to Weaabinakaabo. "The English chief says he regrets the bad manners of his tribe."

"My young men want to fight you," said Weaabinakaabo.

Radisson turned to Magnus Brown and said, "The savage says he wants peace and good trade."

"Tell the Indian that we are open to trade if his terms are fair. No — wait — tell him, tell him, If he is obedient we will make a fresh start. We will make him welcome in the King's territory." Magnus Brown looked expectantly at the chief while he waited for Radisson to translate his greetings.

Radisson said to Weaabinakaabo, "We are come to bring you weapons to destroy your enemies. You and your wife and your children shall never die of hunger. Your nation is saved."

"Tell him," Magnus Brown said, "that he is on the King's plantation. Say, We are the Lords and Proprietors of this territory."

Radisson nodded and turned to Weaabinakaabo and said, "We have the power to make war all over the earth. We adopt you for our children. We take you under our protection. Our thunders will destroy anyone who does not submit to our will and desire. You should make good trade or we will take our friendship to your enemies, though that would be lamentable. Now we will smoke."

"Why are you among the English traders?" asked the chief, mildly, of Radisson. "How may we put our faith in you, when you do not show brotherhood to your own nation?"

Radisson opened his pack of tobacco. Very steadily, he said, "The English King is the most powerful king in the world. His power comes from the sky. He is powerful, but he is kind. He loves me. As I love you."

The chief winced at Radisson's display. "I worry that you are like the muskrat. A great liar. But we will smoke." He took out his pipe, a wooden thing fourteen inches long, decorated with spruce grouse feathers.

The tobacco was cut, the pipe lit. Magnus Brown had marvelled, as he listened to this exchange, at how many Cree words it took to pass on a direct order in English. He was particularly alarmed by the solemnity with which the Indian raised the pipe in the four directions, then smoked and placed the pipe in Radisson's hands. Brown had never lost his fear of idolatry.

Jimmy Frost was seated at Brown's elbow, at the very edge of the tent, where he could watch, as he liked to do, at a sardonic angle. Brown didn't pass the pipe to him, and Frost found himself evicted from society. He fixed with hatred on the Cree's stocky, powerful form, his white teeth, his shining hair flecked just so with grey. Frost would flag this day in his own declining fortunes, his diminishment to Governor's valet.

Magnus Brown's Quaker instincts were aroused. The pagan pipe was worse than coffee, though similarly cabbalistic. Brown was habitually dissident, yet transgression made him feel ill. What does God desire? A simple exchange.

Ask of me, and I shall give thee the heathen for thine inheritance, and the uttermost parts of the earth for thy possession. Thou shalt break them with a rod of iron; thou shalt dash them in pieces like a potter's vessel.

O Lord, forgive me, but I do not want to inherit the heathen. I do not want to break them and dash them, I do not want their broken shards in my hands.

When it came to him, Sparrow raised the pipe just as the chief had done. Beyond and above, Sparrow heard echoes of Atlantis. At last! At last! He had met a survivor of the beautiful Isles!

When it was returned, Weaabinakaabo held the pipe out before him and began to sing. His voice rose in melodious pitch.

273

Even Jimmy Frost felt the intensity, and he snorted with derision.

Magnus Brown put his palms on the ground, fingering the cool green boughs, seeking relief from Hell's heat. A rhetorical savage. What next? A Parliament of Beaver? He looked to Radisson, reminded of the Explorer's song aboard the *Wivenhoe* while they sailed the Davis Strait. How well savagery suits the disobedient Frenchmen, loyal only to their own freedom. The dirge went on and on. Radisson and Des Groseilliers listened patiently, even respectfully. They treat this gibberish with far more deference than they did the King's Charter.

Magnus Brown's English voice boomed like a church bell. "Frost, give me ink." Frost moved lazily to open the inkpot. The song was unending. Brown could feel Frost twisting into ridicule. "Get on," said Brown to the Explorers. "No more of this pretence."

The Explorers were delighted by the chief's performance. They heard from the broad cadence that the poem was ancient, older than the chief's great-grandfather's great-grandfather. The brothers had landed on their feet. It was obvious — this chief is a great hunter, a powerful man. There will be big profit. Good things come when we are trading with a man who isn't pretending more than is necessary for sprightliness.

Magnus Brown gripped his quill so tightly it snapped. This Indian had powers that he himself had lost, that he'd sacrificed out of duty to God and the Corporate merchants. The tent was alive. *Everything* was alive. The tobacco curled into smoky flame. Brown felt a sickle in his heart. Grief choked him for his rectitude (his timidity) with Lilly, for the loss of Asia, and for the lowly task ahead. He did not want possession of the uttermost parts of the earth and certainly not its swarthy strangers. The Indian's song sent Magnus Brown into the wilderness. *For I am a stranger with thee, and a sojourner, as all*

274

my fathers were. Destined to wander forever. Smoke engulfed him. From the frozen river came the sound of waves, beginning and beginning. The China Sea is lost, the China Sea is everywhere, you will never find the China Sea.

Eight

On New Year's Day, Magnus Brown awoke with the dream of a baby vivid in his mind. A fat, calm baby, who seemed to expect something from him, domineering, in a fat, calm way. He'd not held a baby since his Quaker days in Virginia, where the women liked to place their infants in his arms in a kind of milky seduction. He remembered the smell. He opened his eyes to the glow from the fireplace, to the snores of unwashed men. The injured sailors were snoring most greedily, submerged beneath Romieux's sticky syrups. From behind her protective blanket, Lilly, asleep, seemed phosphorescent.

Magnus Brown could see his own chest, a mountain. He saw the frame of his own face, the bridge of his nose, the bramble of his beard, winter red in the low firelight. His haunches flattened against the bedding, the moist groin valleyed between his stomach and thighs; he wriggled his clammy, stockinged feet. His heart accelerated its churning drive that persisted in spite of him, and his bowels groaned, an unusual time for this. He lay a little longer. Had he always been encased in such a hide?

It was at least two hours before sunrise, clear and cold without wind. A fine crescent moon dangled Jupiter from its spur. He pushed open the door and was astonished yet again by the range of snow, by the forest in the distance, a rippling of the

276

land as if it were awake in the dark, preoccupied by its own grandeur, by silent traces of lynx, wolf, fox, all of this withheld from him. After the mild spell at Christmas, the weather had been brightly cold. He went to where the snow was hemmed by the breathing trees, down to the shore of the river. He needed ecstasy. He needed to pray.

Lilly heard the latch. Her pack was hidden beneath her hammock. She'd hidden a cache of dried meat and pea meal in a snowdrift beyond the woodpile. She climbed out of bed, collected her pack, took the snowshoes Radisson had made for her, and she and Dogg began to run to the woodpile. Then she stopped. There, moving toward the river, was the massive, diminishing shadow of Magnus Brown. How could she go away from him?

Magnus Brown wore his watch-coat. He felt the cold only on the patches of flesh on his bearded face. At the shore, he sought prayer, as always without words. But words strand together of themselves; and that morning Magnus Brown staggered under a web of sound born of nothing, of a weakness of will. His soul was bored with him, a carcass bound in corruption, belly, bowels, blood. He prayed harder, begging his mind to be silent. Silence poured down on him, but he ruined it with words, words pearled like the white fat on moose kidney.

Listen, listen. How may he guide anyone without succour, without a schism of peace in the noise blood makes?

Then it overtook him. The cold breath of his God. The infinite is detailed infinitely, and Brown went out, searing his soul in a broad, inclusive space, an endless, rampant disclosure of creation. He was pierced, struck through, awestruck; awe was what Magnus Brown's stern destiny served him in the name of joy. He was on his knees in a garden of ice, a great, floundered man among petals of turquoise, violet, carmine, in silver fronds of frost on watery green stems. The ice bloomed in many colours.

Lilly stood on the riverbank and watched Magnus Brown in all his mystery.

XXXXX

The sky was deep blue — two hours before sunrise.

Sparrow emerged into starlight. An owl swooped over the passage to the woods. Then Radisson padded out to the brindled light, a grotesque shape with pack and raquettes; he turned and waved to where Bartholomew was standing. Bart, too, carried a pack. Radisson gestured toward the house. Nobody moved. Magnus Brown came out, stood on the threshold, and then travelled down to the river, a broad band of ice that boomed as it buckled with the tide. Brown's shadow descended the riverbank. A moment later, Lilly emerged from the house, Dogg at her heels, his tail tucked earnestly between his legs. She and Dogg began to run to the men hidden in the forest, Radisson murmuring, "Yes, run like the fox." Then Lilly suddenly swerved, heading to the river, toward Magnus Brown. She would give them all away. Dogg would bark and ruin everything. "Merde." Radisson turned on Sparrow. "What does she mean to do? Kiss the Governor goodbye?"

Lilly was running toward the river.

"Maudite femme!"

Sparrow shoved Radisson. "Quiet!"

Radisson cried, "No! I am away!" But he didn't go.

Lilly stopped running; she stood on the bank of the river. Then she carefully stepped back, put on her snowshoes, collected her cache of food, and began to plod clumsily to the men in the forest, Dogg racing ahead of her, bounding out of the snow like a deer.

Radisson nodded, as if he'd known all along. "She comes."

Silence swept the woods, then the owl's beating wings.

Nine

Radisson, Sparrow, Lilly, Dogg, and Bartholomew followed a bear path southwest in the early light. The terrain was fairly even, except when they came to creek beds broadening to the tidal flats, where they slid down and crossed on snow-covered rocks like big white turtles, then dug with their hands and feet up the other side. Lilly gripped Dogg's loose hide to steady herself.

Sparrow was resolute. Not long before, his dead children had come in the night to put their little fingers into his mouth. They were slick, oily, mortified, and Sparrow had vomited in his sleep, choking as he woke up. On this journey to Moose River he will forgive death. And see Lilly through her time. On a journey through Atlantis, there are only the laws of quick invention. And trade. Maybe he won't die of starvation in his old age, maybe he'll have some money. Sparrow felt purified by hope. There was no fault, no guilt in saving himself from a poor and bitter death; he was invigorated and peaceful, knowing these to be his last days, his last effort; he felt as if he'd come through fire, and now he knew the lovely ash of last resort.

They emerged onto a frozen bay. Across the bay were dark green hills of spruce, their branches patched with snow. The estuary was frozen in thick blocks of ice driven to shore from James Bay, with dry sprays of snow raised by the wind.

Bartholomew sat down on a fallen balsam. The winter morning light was sage green. His ringlets framed his white-rose face, his thighs trembled with exhaustion, and when he drank from his flask, the brandy hit his empty stomach with a joyful burn. Radisson cleared snow from the cleavage of two rocks to strike at the ice with his hatchet. Clear water bubbled up. He filled and drank off several cups, saying, "Do as I do." But Bartholomew kept to his blood-stiffening liquor. His pack was heavy with a casket of brandy. When it runs out — but don't think about that. Remember your role as saviour, protector. He smiled bravely at Lilly. It was a smile that didn't fit his face. He must proceed without knowing himself, almost in an absence of himself. So he sipped his brandy.

Wending his way through trees and brush to the east walked Weaabinakaabo, the handsome chief, his head up, his shoulders square, towing a loaded sled and carrying a pack on his back. Sounds in such a snowy forest are rearranged so what is close resounds and what is far comes close. He was dressed entirely in beaver skins, the fur to the inside, a jacket with a hood and tail, and supple skin hose, sewn with sinew, reaching to the knee. From the ankle to the knee, in place of garters (as Bartholomew would make a point of learning) the hose were held up by the tibia of a deer.

When Weaabinakaabo reached them, he set down his pack and opened the bundle on the sled without acknowledging them in any particular way. He removed a small item, recognized the Earl's fair curls, and said, "Here is the beautiful fool to whom I bring a gift. I make you a present. Maybe you will take it to the English chief, if you live to return across the salted lake, though no one can predict if you will survive longer than a blue butterfly."

He pushed a knotted piece of hide into Bartholomew's chest, indicating that he should open it. Bart withdrew a disk of highly polished turquoise, the size of a dung beetle. "My people took this and others like it in wars with the Nation of the Beef," said the chief. "It is to give you thanks for your song."

"You hang that thing at your ear," Radisson said cheerfully, if a little jealous.

Bartholomew was moved. He was briefly tempted to lessen his self-hatred, but he resisted.

Weaabinakaabo said to Bartholomew (Radisson didn't translate), "This trip will maybe kill you. But everyone eventually dies." When laughter left his face, it was displaced by indifference — not unkind but disinterested.

Lilly watched Weaabinakaabo's breath condense in the air. He turned, first to weigh her stocky legs, her bulging belly, her heavy backpack. Then he smiled at her. She could see that he doubted her ability to survive this journey. This was not the brilliant clown she'd seen a week ago — or he was greater than that, as the great actors are. It's always fascinating to watch a comedic talent when he's being serious. He turned to study the wind.

They travelled over the frozen bay, sometimes on shore and sometimes in the wind out on waves of hard-packed snow spiked with yellow marsh grass. Weaabinakaabo moderated his pace for the sake of the stubborn old man, the dying singer, and the pregnant slave.

They made unsteady progress. They had to take advantage of the cold; it made the snow good for travel. Radisson was painfully impatient. He'd been stationary for a lifetime, it seemed, aboard ship and at the Charles Fort. Now, the English dragged on his laces.

Yesterday, Radisson had watched Weaabinakaabo snare a fox, skin it, then put the mask and pelt in his pack, all in the time it took to smoke a pipe. Radisson had waited while Weaabinakaabo worked and sprang up quickly when it was done, Weaabinakaabo smiling at the muskrat's eagerness. He told Radisson, If they kill a big animal, maybe a lynx, he'll cache it for the return, but for the rest of their journey, they'll hunt only for food.

Then Weaabinakaabo — for the first time — stumbled over his words: he promised that the people of the land of the muskeg would bring furs plentiful and lush, like nothing the whitemen had ever seen before.

Never in his life had Weaabinakaabo been a speculator. Radisson felt saddened when he recognized the mangled sentence as an utterance of obligation. Sometimes the business of trade did not feel so good.

Weaabinakaabo was new to the concept of debt. As he walked, he thought how smoothly and easily the Europeans create slaves.

He had told his young wife (his third and his last; this one would surely outlive him) and his old sister (of the cleft foot) to stay away from the whitemen's camp. The Frenchmen had persuaded him to take along the pregnant woman. Weaabinakaabo had posed as reluctant, then generous — certainly he liked Lilly; she had spirit. But what he wanted above all was to pay his obligation to these whites and keep them far from his own people. Let the Moose Cree help the white woman deliver the English King's child. If the woman and infant die, let it be on the head of the Moose Cree. Certain hungers invite evil spirits who will come one after another with greater and greater hunger, needing more, devouring all without satisfaction.

They were tracking the banks of the frozen river that cuts parallel to the southeast of Rupert River. Lilly was proud of her strength. Often when she walked, her womb went hard as wood. Gradually, Radisson and Weaabinakaabo put a mile or more between themselves and the others. Weaabinakaabo left blazes with a shard of a French hatchet laced to wood, a hard swing with his left arm, chest-level — leaving Sparrow to read their trail.

Radisson wished he could take the savage with him and leave the others behind. He felt ready to strangle Lilly, she was so slow. And the Earl's ringlets disgusted him; here in the unmade forest, the soft Roman profile seemed contrived. Civilization will seep into everything, it will mimic, steal, atom by atom, yes, like that, so nothing evermore will be free of falsity. These thoughts so pestered him he began to speak aloud. "In my world," he grumbled, "if we take prisoners who are too slow they are very soon roasted and eaten."

He'd spoken in French. Ahead of him, the chief hesitated, moved forward again, and said, "The birds of the air will tell tales we do not want to hear." He twisted around to look at Radisson, covering his ears with his hands. "Their songs make me ashamed."

Weaabinakaabo let Radisson scurry past him, and then he said, "I think that you have travelled with the brutish nations to the south. Among my people, we show respect for those we kill. If we must kill a human being, we do it cleanly. Without unnecessary suffering, without happiness."

Radisson heard the threat in Weaabinakaabo's voice. He turned, half-expecting to be attacked. "My father, why do you talk of killing?"

Weaabinakaabo pointed to the northwest shore of the bay. "Over there," he said and then pointed at the northeast, "and over there, men eat the meat that is not cooked."

Radisson stood above Weaabinakaabo. With no cloud cover, the snow was blinding bright. Both men wore snow glasses carved from charred wood. Masked, Weaabinakaabo showed not a trace of laughter. He seemed a different man, as if a stranger had come upon him and taken his place. Or perhaps it was

Radisson who'd been stolen, and a spirit used his features now. A narrow, high-pitched band of sound slowly growing louder vibrated from the west, cut through the two men, across the land and on, fading into the forest that rolled in the distance.

Radisson felt his face pinned to his ears. He heard the pretence in his own voice. "Men must first cook their meat."

"Tell me why." Weaabinakaabo stalked toward him.

"If they do not, they fall sick and die in agony."

Weaabinakaabo was now level with Radisson. "What is this meat that men cook?"

Radisson was surprised to realize he'd collided, one world into another, and let himself be observed in aspects unintended. The wildman has some understanding of French. And he may hear more than is spoken; even some whitemen can do so, and how much more a powerful hunter.

A veil of cloud approaching from the west edged the sun. Then the shadows that were starkly blue turned pale and disappeared.

Radisson felt the change in the weather. His head snapped to the right to look back at their trail. "We must go back for the English," he said.

Weaabinakaabo stepped away. The wind was veering from east to south. Soon it would start to snow. They turned to retrace their steps. Weaabinakaabo removed his mask. He moved so quickly that Radisson nearly broke into a sweat, a potentially deadly mistake. When he caught up to the fleet figure, Weaabinakaabo had almost changed back into himself; the good-natured face looked more familiar. But his eyes didn't smile. Radisson hoped that he was mistaken when he heard Weaabinakaabo mutter, "Atuush. Pwaatich. Atuush."

Atuush. Monster. Cannibal. And *Pwaatich*. This may mean several things. Radisson, too, had removed his snow glasses, but he couldn't shake the sensation that he was still wearing a mask, that his human face had been separated from his true and monstrous shape.

The temperature rose with the wind. It snowed harder. Radisson was amazed at how fast the chief could move. "You exert yourself." He tried not to show his fatigue.

"Snow from the south can kill men too," said Weaabinakaabo.

In the afternoon, snow rose around the trees, Weaabinakaabo's blazes descending into the blizzard driven off the bay while he homed to the place where Sparrow was nervously building a shelter for Bartholomew and Lilly. Radisson had never in his life seen such tracking. What kind of man remembers the fallen tree so well? Such a hunter is always at the centre of the world. Radisson was glad to be in his company, though this sensation of subservience was most tiresome.

In the last light Weaabinakaabo walked to Sparrow and, without comment, helped him to cut the boughs. Within a half-hour, the travellers were in a nest at the base of a tree. Weaabinakaabo closed his eyes to rest, to listen. The wind backed to the north and blew stronger; the snow got hard, a freezing sandstorm on their backs, stiffening into frozen drifts.

When the wind died, the temperature dropped a little, steadied, and Weaabinakaabo slept. Radisson slept only on the second breath of the sleeping savage. And Lilly, too, made sure the chief was sleeping before letting herself relax. Then Weaabinakaabo was taking a deep breath on the rise, saying, "Remember what it is to sleep, my friends, because now we move or freeze to death."

As the geese fly, it's seventy miles to Moose River, but, Weaabinakaabo explained, we are not geese. At the shores of Hannah Bay, they had to walk south fifteen miles to cross the river narrows. The crust on the surface was brittle, cutting their legs when they broke through and making it impossible to get close enough to kill the few deer they saw. Weaabinakaabo was unsure whether to admire or fear the flushed vitality of the pregnant slave, the dying singer, and the grandfather with the whistling jaw. At times he wondered, Are they already ghosts? *Ehe*. He had always loved eccentrics best. These strangers are not innocent; their hunger is not innocent.

Their store of peas and pemmican would run out unless they killed a deer. They went for two days, then three without enough food and finally had to stop for a day to hunt. But the snow wasn't right, and the hunt failed. Weaabinakaabo snared several rabbits and a grouse and made a stew. It felt like a feast. Weaabinakaabo teased the three English, and they brightened under his musical chafing, their faces shiny with fat.

Weaabinakaabo was most skeptical of Radisson. When Weaabinakaabo held up the *cimutuwaan*, the stick from a beaver lodge he'd found in a creek bed, Big Nose had followed him just like the muskrat follows the beaver. This Frenchman is loyal solely to what is new, to action that will burn hottest. He wants trade, but trade is not something to keep, it is not memory. Trade is excess, and excess makes us forget. Weaabinakaabo had seen the ciphers of Magnus Brown's ledger; the big moose can't remember anything!

Radisson caught Weaabinakaabo looking at him, and he felt himself peering back through eyeholes, his breath hot and confined. He'd tried to be very serious, he'd tried not to speak, but there was no remedy for this argument between his pretending self and his true. It was only good to move.

Sparrow climbed a steep creekbed and pulled Lilly up after him. "Do you need to slow down, lass?" She gave a tight smile. This hunger was different from hunger in London; it stalked her with such a presence she'd turned around, several times, expecting to see it following. Sparrow waited while she caught her breath. They were on a barren hill where the snow was thinner. "Empyrean," he said. "That's what the cold is, Lilly. It means God. So we needn't have any fear."

Lilly said, "I'm not afraid, John Sparrow."

They descended the slope into deep, soft drifts where it was nearly impossible to walk, and they rested there. She stood as soon as she saw Weaabinakaabo move.

They walked for four days with little more than water and tobacco for sustenance. Bartholomew drank brandy increasingly diluted by snow, so his sobriety wheezily sneaked up on him. That night they rested for three hours and then moved on in the dark.

On the eighth day, in the midst of forest, with no river in sight, they reached the winter camp of several families. Bartholomew, Sparrow, and Lilly saw their own shapes reflected in the eyes of the Moose Cree. They'd been living in a membrane. Now the sac was ripped open. They passed from timelessness into mortality.

Ten

Radisson and Weaabinakaabo, with a delighted Dogg, went ahead to greet the Moose Cree. The two men turned around to wave toward their trading partners. Even they were shocked to see how ragged the English had become. The Moose Cree retreated to consult with Weaabinakaabo.

"Are they diseased?"

"They are Europeans!"

"Please be serious."

"Ehe. I don't wish to make light of death. They are diseased, sure, but only in white ways. Otherwise, how could I have travelled so far with them and look so good?" He wagged his head and danced from one foot to another. It was a very old dance, this pantomime. Watching him, Radisson was reminded of seeing a travelling troupe, Comédie-Italienne, when he was a small boy in Avignon.

The Moose Cree watched Weaabinakaabo impassively. Then they agreed, the Europeans could stay. But they had no food to give them. The animals were hiding, and the snow made it impossible to find them. They sadly held forth their empty hands.

XXXXXX

Before the change in weather, the hunting had been good, and this family had been staying here for some time. Bear paws and many antlers decorated with small skulls hung from a tree stripped of most of its branches, its trunk decorated in horizontal slashes. The lodge, partly made of skins supported by boughs strapped with roots, looked at first like a mound of snow with one eye. Skins stretched on hoops of tamarack were racked beside a thick wall of firewood, which protected the lodge from the north wind. There was no distinction between efficiency and ornament. In the snow-baffled eyes of the English, nothing had ever seemed so elegant.

The furs were as rich as Weaabinakaabo had promised. He negotiated the terms of trade for what the Cree already had in their camp, but they'd have to wait until the hunting improved, until there was food again and they had the strength to venture out to trap or to travel to another family some distance away. For now, they must be quiet.

The Moose Cree studied the misshapen group with its strange patterns of behaviour: the woman does no work other than going out to set snares, like the children do. Whereas their children have caught five rabbits this past week, enough to keep them from starving, the white woman has caught nothing.

Three brothers, the leaders of this camp, went to Weaabina-kaabo and asked him why the white traders have a pregnant woman who is so inept.

Weaabinakaabo had been expecting this. He told them, She is a slave who belongs to the English King.

The Moose Cree raised their hands in mock alarm.

"Our wives have been talking," they continued, with some embarrassment. "Our wives have asked, What kind of woman is she? How does she live without skills?"

Weaabinakaabo shook his head. "She must have some kind of skill," he said vaguely, "or these men would not keep her."

The men narrowed their eyes. "What skills are these?" They waited for his answer.

Weaabinakaabo was embarrassed by the innuendo. Grief turned in him. The Europeans were effectively destroying his grandfathers' power, with sorcery so potent it fit inside a tin thimble. The singer's illness was evidence enough, but the slave's incompetence told him more. The whites trained their women for dependency and death. Weaabinakaabo's daughters or his granddaughters will be for sale; their knowledge or their weaknesses, like too many furs, will be sold, an excess. So he learned Lilly as he learned the gun.

He told a lie that he knew was partly true. "She is the wife of the yellow hair. And daughter to the crooked face."

Weaabinakaabo's hosts asked, Why do her men not discipline her? The youngest brother, whose wife had been fractious this winter, persisted. "She must be capable of something."

Of what is she capable? She survives. She'll give birth and maybe survive that, too. Could she not be a fool? Fools are brave; must they also be useful?

Now that the ships have appeared, of what will we be capable? There must be joy or we might as well be dead. As he had grown older Weaabinakaabo had grown more impatient with pessimism, the judgment of this way or that. Will excess necessarily destroy us? Excess was the only word he knew for luxury. He felt the pressure of the new word hot on his thigh where he held his gun.

✗✗✗✗✗✗

The temperature rose and snow fell for two days, creating drifts five and six feet high. There were no deer, no lynx, no mink, no moose, no grouse, no rabbits. The animals went away. Sometimes animals go away, but rarely do they all go away at the same time. On the sixth day, Lilly found a rabbit in her snare. She stripped the hide over the sleek haunches, and Weaabinakaabo strung it over the fire to roast, but the aroma tormented them and they divided it nearly raw. Radisson boiled the skin and they ate that too. Weaabinakaabo took the rabbit's feet and tied them to a tree.

The Cree children were kept inside, in their lodge. Only the strongest people moved about, with such ghost-like lassitude they looked into one another's eyes to confirm that they weren't dead. The old ones remembered starvation and the illnesses that will come in its shadows. So they avoided the white people, though the women eyed Lilly warily, torn between compassion and contempt.

There were twenty-three people at the camp. They all could die in the cloudy forest. The three Moose Cree brothers journeyed to the river, which was normally only four hours' walk. They brought back some fish, but the expedition nearly killed them. If they could have moved the entire camp to the riverside, they could survive on fish, but it was impossible to transport the old ones and the children through such deep snow.

Radisson and Weaabinakaabo heard the brothers' story. Both men, in their different ways, thought, Stationary, that is how we die badly. We devour the small yield of *home*, then poison ourselves with our own refuse. They both knew that without the weak English, they, too, could travel to the river. So then, why did they not? Why did Radisson and Weaabinakaabo stay with Sparrow, Bartholomew, and Lilly?

Lilly was lying by the fire, her eyes closed. Weaabinakaabo, perhaps to see if she had died, leaned down and put the tip of his finger to the tip of her nose. She opened one eye and grinned at him. He patted her face.

Radisson refilled his pipe, lit it with a stick from the fire, and passed it to Sparrow. When he did this, he felt a shift in the room, a recalibration. When Radisson sensed Weaabinakaabo's approval, the self-conscious, wooden sensation in his face relaxed a little. He didn't permit himself a smile, no facial expression at all. Death is nothing. It is more wonderful to play a part in humankind. It was good to regain respect in the eyes of Weaabinakaabo. Radisson wanted to embrace him and kiss his cheek, but he did not. He showed dignity. Happiness flowed through him like trout in late summer, deep beneath the surface.

✗✗✗✗✗

They boiled the rind from the balsam trees, dried it to a powder, then boiled it again into a broth. It made them unbearably thirsty. Radisson boiled any hide they could afford to lose: his moccasin laces, Weaabinakaabo's hide sack, Sparrow's spare stockings. Lilly kept Dogg close, her hands sinking into the greasy coat. Radisson muttered that this was decadent, unsuitable to the conditions. But for several days, the chief supported her in protecting the animal.

Hunger made them always cold. Lilly lay as close to the fire as she dared. She ran her tongue over her painful molars, pushed, and spat a tooth into her hand, a rotten nut. All her teeth were loose. Her hair had been falling out, too. She could pull out hanks of it.

Lilly closed her eyes and tried to go away in her mind. She heard the men moving around the shelter, she felt the weight of Dogg at her back. She fell asleep and dreamed that she was in bed at Meg's, that Claire had been sleeping beside her and got up to work and soon Lilly would have to wake up, but she was stealing sleep for a few minutes. Then she dreamed that she was eating. She opened her eyes. A kettle simmered on the fire. The shelter filled with the smell of boiling bones.

She sat up slowly. The water was topped by blue and yellow foam. It smelled like boiled knuckles, a poor man's stew. Weaabinakaabo squatted over the kettle, stirring with a stick. He met her eye, then returned his attention to the stew.

When they gathered to eat the dog, Bartholomew burned his fingers in the steaming water that leaked from the cracked bones, from the lean, tough meat. Lilly did, too. She sucked on the meat to make it soft. Weaabinakaabo chanted a brief string of words. "We thank the animal," said Radisson.

The food cut through their empty guts like broken glass. Later, when Lilly crawled outside to try to relieve herself, she saw that Weaabinakaabo had tied Dogg's feet to the tree near their shelter.

XXXXX

Weaabinakaabo was mending his moccasins at night by the firelight when he gruffly observed, "I am getting old. I shuffle now. See how I wear out my moccasins?"

Sparrow understood him well enough, and he said, "I'm an old man too. It's not just my sore back and this searing pain in my left shoulder, or having to go out to piss five times every night. I'm old because I don't like the world as much as I did when I was a young man. And the world doesn't like me much either. Sometimes," he added tenderly, patting Lilly's knee, "I feel rage at the young."

Radisson translated this to Cree. Weaabinakaabo nodded and said, "Yes, they can really irritate you."

Weaabinakaabo burned the shoulder-blade of a porcupine over the fire. When the bone was charred, he ran his fingers

294

over a fine crack running along its thicker edge, to see where they would kill an animal. Maybe to the north. Maybe tomorrow or the day that follows. Maybe a moose. There's no certainty. He sang quietly while he did this.

𝕏𝕏𝕏𝕏𝕏

For days now, poems had been singing in Bart's head. They might be very good poems. He will write them down to see how they look. He thinks they might be sonnets because they feel so well shaped and happily aimed.

Bartholomew has a cough from drinking snow; now he coughs more than he breathes. But he can still stand. He can even walk. He is under the impression that he's tumbling down a steep hill in England. Weaabinakaabo has given him a lightly loaded sled to pull. He's startled to feel it slamming against his ankles or cutting him off at the knees when the rolling English pasture turns out to be a creekbed, but he walked on. Lilly is struggling with her pack, and he takes it from her and easily shoulders it. Now when he smiles, the smile fits his face. It may be a small accomplishment, to survive this journey, to keep Lilly alive — he has no idea; he has lost his measure. His God has shattered him like one of Rupert's glass drops, but he is too exhausted for self-hatred; in fact, he feels a sort of evenly distributed ecstasy.

There came a ringing in the fog that sat over the forest, and the temprature dropped sharply. The air around the camp cleared, diamond sharp. Weaabinakaabo brought rocks from the Moose Cree lodge to put them on the fire. He brought birch pots filled with snow and threw snow on the hot rocks, filling the shelter with steam. Bartholomew's cough subsided. At last it grew quiet inside their shelter. Lilly fell soundly asleep.

When she awoke, Bart was sleeping quietly. Sparrow was

295

sleeping *too* quietly. Weaabinakaabo and Radisson were gone. She touched Sparrow's gnarly blue ear and he opened his eyes. She turned and caressed Bartholomew's beautiful, ravaged face. He was cold, waxy.

She threw herself on him, shaking his narrow shoulders, then beating him, hitting his chest with her fists until Sparrow pulled her off.

The hunters travel lightly over the hard surface on the snow. Two deer try to run away, but their feet break through the crust. They try to dance out of it but only sink more deeply. Radisson and Weaabinakaabo glide to them without loosing an arrow. The deer lie down and let the hunters slit their throats. Their sorrel coats, rich patches of blood on the snow.

That night they all feed on venison. Weaabinakaabo puts some meat into the fire to thank the deer. Lilly sucks marrow from the bones. Tomorrow, they'll have a ceremony for Bartholomew and place his body in a tower built of sticks, Radisson says. How lonely he will be, never to go home.

Lilly thinks, This glassy ring of grief has been with us always. A fine shadow around every detail of the living world; Lilly remembers it clearly now, she'd let herself forget. Bartholomew died for her. The weight of that is too much to bear. Besides, she doesn't quite believe it. In death, Bartholomew is perfect. But he was no Jesus. And Lilly thinks, Thank God.

Weaabinakaabo is repairing his moccasins again. Death shapes the green bough and the fallen tree. It's the difference between the needle, hide, and hand; between light and flesh. As if flesh can only hope to follow light, its go-between.

Eleven

She lay for hours in saturated clothes, on soaked robes stinking of salt water and blood. The pain roared out of her. In the sallow dawn, she was alone in the shelter. This is how the ship gets out of the bottle, by breaking it. Something must be wrong; birth can't be so violent. She knew she'd felt love for the unborn baby; now it was going to kill her, she was helpless to stop it — what a genius, what a plan, the perfect murder. She clearly remembered, even in such pain, having loved her baby. Now love was far distant — she could see it, but she couldn't care, she couldn't care about the baby's fate, she could do nothing to save it.

Screaming helped. If she opened her mouth wide, bellowed deeply, pain moved in close, and when she fought close to the pain, it was her familiar; she gave over to it, entered it completely.

Lilly thought she heard the shuffling of feet, of dancing, Bart's beating heart. Women arrived, the lodge women. When first she felt their dry hands on her, she was enraged that they'd interfere in her dying. They spoke and put their hands on her. Lilly felt them lift her by her face out of a pool of shattered glass. She followed their voices and their hands as they lifted her up. They put their hands on her legs, and Lilly thought, they're organizing my dying, because where they touched and pulled, the surface returned to her skin, and she followed their hands. The pain that had been snakes became horses; the women's voices showed her, it was possible, barely possible to ride them if you dared.

The dancing went on, the beating heart. The women's tongues sounded like wooden sticks. Now they put their hands on her baby, her killer. A hand pushed down on her, a new pain joined the old ones. One woman lifted her by sitting behind her while the other woman pulled her until she fell forward to her knees. Rage flooded in. She raised her head and met the eyes of the lodge woman. Steady eyes, no fear, no alarm, no hatred, no pity. Then Lilly understood, this is what birth is, this violence, this daring.

Lilly had nothing and so, in fury, she rode the horses, guided by the hands, the voices, the dancing. She was going to lose. The battle went on too long, she had no strength. But then the women shouted and hailed.

She saw her long, spindly, wax-blue baby lifted from her. Love could not quite encompass the passion she felt then. So this is what is meant by ecstasy. She nearly went under another rogue wave of pain, but she rode it. And then the pain rode on, and she was left behind in joy.

The midwives heard the baby cry in English. It would be two or three days before anyone permitted themselves to acknowledge out loud what a funny-looking baby this was. The Moose Cree would talk about it for many generations. The grandmothers would tell the story of the tawny English baby with the longest nose, the longest feet, and the longest dingus since the great flood.

She was falling, a visceral plummeting into love, but she was afraid of the baby. With her eyes closed the baby seemed bigger than she was. Lilly undressed him to look and found him gawky but otherwise impeccable. In the instant when she first saw his face, she was shocked by recognition, as if she already knew him. She repeated to herself, *My son, my son.*

He looked like Charles. The dark complexion, eloquent lips, features inherited through Charles from a Moorish strain in the Medicis. She would have to show him to the King, of course, if she survived this and found her way back to London. Charles acknowledged his bastards.

She didn't want to sell her son to secure her safety from the pursuit of Sir George Rose. She didn't want to sell herself and her son to the Court. To coyly start the campaign to get her son a ducal title and an allowance.

She had fooled the Town, had fooled the King himself, by being quick with Bartholomew's scripts, Bart's words. She would have to do this again with a noose on her neck, without Bartholomew, without his wit and his melancholy love.

She'd lost two of her molars. She loved the touch of Magnus Brown. Something like love had happened in many ways, some deadly; she felt the full weight of Bart's sacrifice in the middle of the night, though by day she remembered him on his own terms, Hell-bent.

What had she gained from notoriety, from her season of fame as an actress? Dependence. Dependence on Charles. Dependence on Bart; gone now. Dependence — obscenely, perversely — on Sir George Rose. Rose will be her son's enemy, the child that is the product of a witch, evidence of the King's decadence. Rose will tell the people her child is Catholic.

The better part of her performance was in her bosom and

her leg; her talent lay in the timing. She wasn't as talented as Weaabinakaabo, but she did have good timing. How to pivot. How to exit. Exit. With son.

She had no milk. He bent his long, skinny legs, brought his long feet under his hard blue belly, and cried. He was the English King's son. His cries could be heard through spruce walls and snow, across the snowy clearing, through a patch of aspen, through the stack of firewood, through beaver pelts on tamarack hoops, through the hide door of the lodge, through the otherwise peaceful dreams of the Moose Cree women and their children and the elders who stayed behind when the men went out to hunt.

No one could escape the English King's son's voice; it infiltrated the fat dripping from the beaver's tail into a French kettle over the fire; every stitch was stitched through the noise of the English King's crying baby; his English wailing was on every hair on every hide, in every wisp of smoke.

And there was shit everywhere. Lilly didn't know how to manage the yellow ooze that the baby miraculously created out of nothing. The shelter filled with imperial *excrementum*.

Lilly held her infant in a mess of hide blankets that trailed into the snow. She forced her way blindly through the confusion of hides at the entrance of the lodge of the Moose Cree and kneeled by their fireplace.

The women's spatula fingers pulled soiled clothing from her baby, muttering contemptuously. He woke up, chilled, and let out a feeble cry. They cleaned him, put him in a moss bag, and wrapped him tightly in a sheet of deer hide. They held him and laughed at him tenderly. A woman was nursing her year-old boy. She put the child down and took up Lilly's son, indicating she would nurse him.

Lilly held out her hands and the woman gave the baby back to her.

It would be a reasonable choice, to give her son to the women in the lodge. He might learn all the things that Lilly would never learn to do — to survive, for one thing. He might become wise, in a way, wise as Radisson was wise — in the ways of contending. She had nothing to offer him. She was terrible at everything but mimicry. She was more surrogate than this savage woman, who knew how to make a moss bag for a baby. But if Lilly gave her son away, she would die. It was selfish, but there it was: she would take the baby back to her skinny breasts with their fine, yellow milk. If she couldn't be a real mother, she'd be a damn good fake.

Gradually, strength returned to the people of the forests of the tributaries of the Moose River. The famine had been consistent in their trading radius, though strangely there were remote families here and there whom the animals hadn't abandoned.

Weaabinakaabo guided Radisson to meet other families among the Moose Cree. Sparrow grew strong enough to join them, and they slowed their pace to accommodate the steadfast old man. By then, Weaabinakaabo had memorized several routes around Kesagami Lake. He moved about the land with a map in his head. He was quiet; he put all his effort into seeing.

In this way, they persisted and waited to see if Lilly and the King's son would live.

Twelve

Soon, the pelts brought back to the Moose Cree camp had been singed by the sun. The winter trade was over.

The sun was too warm, so they had to travel at night, hauling their loads of fur and the remaining trade goods that Weaabinakaabo would take back to his family. The greased runners of their sleds crackled over half-melted snow. Lilly carried with her the brilliant blue stone, Weaabinakaabo's gift to Bart. This much light remained of him.

The smaller streams swelled with spring runoff. Rabbits were motley, sap was running. Weaabinakaabo pushed them as fast as he dared. They'd waited too long at the Moose Cree camp. Weaabinakaabo had never liked men who forced their women to pack and move very soon after delivering a child, but he was embarrassed at having taken such a chance in leaving so late in the season. He looked back now and then to where the woman struggled to follow them, carrying the infant with the big nose. It hadn't occurred to him that the English King would be dark-skinned. He marvelled at his own budding affection for the ugly baby.

If he put the child to death in an honourable, deliberate way, he would demonstrate his power, he would protect his family. He would say, You may come and take what we don't eat and use for ourselves, but you may not bring your incompetent women here, you may not have children in this place.

Weaabinakaabo gave the idea back to the blackbirds. He wouldn't kill either the woman or her infant. He let himself enjoy his fondness for his travelling companions and prayed that he was not permitting the end of the world.

Weaabinakaabo was more relieved than he let on when they reached the north shore of Rupert River. The morning after their crossing, they looked back to see the river ice mottled and bruised. By noon, the ice was shredding, pulled apart by the current, compelled by fresh water rushing down from the east. Broken ice crashed into the bank, snapping off trees. It was so loud, they had to shout to be heard. This was where they separated, Weaabinakaabo and the white travellers.

Their leave-taking was in a high wind under a changeable sky, the clatter of thaw. Weaabinakaabo was in a hurry to be off before the river burst the banks. He took Lilly's arm and pulled her aside. From his pack he drew what Lilly at first mistook for a piece of porcelain. He held it on the palm of his hand, just so. It was a white mask of bone. She didn't understand.

Weaabinakaabo held the mask to his face. It was the skull of a fox. He placed one foot, then the other in a circle, inscribed around her. Like a Court Masque, in a way, except that he let himself disappear into the animal; he had a beautiful tail, of which he was proud, knowing, as a fox will, how foolish and necessary it is to be proud. No English actor could disappear into the cadence of another body as Weaabinakaabo could. He stopped his dance, removed the mask, and put it in her hand. Fox. He touched his forehead to her forehead. Then he capered a few more steps as a fox will, but it was a slight, satiric revue.

Lilly put the mask to her face. She saw him through fox eyes. Weaabinakaabo nodded to her. Yes. We are good fools. Good-bye.

He said goodbye to each man, smiling, but with growing disinterest. He would begin the long, muddy walk east, pulling his sled loaded with guns, flints, powder horns, fish hooks, knives, hatchets, kettles, needles, mirrors, bells, and little tin thimbles. He yearned to see his family. He hoped his sons would forgive him. Tin thimbles are nothing to laugh about: many whitemen will fit into a tin thimble.

𝕏𝕏𝕏𝕏𝕏

Early one morning, Magnus Brown was lying awake in his hammock when he heard thunder rolling over the snowy banks of Rupert River. Then he heard, distinctly, someone walking on the icy, corn-kernel snow. He got out of bed, opened the door, and saw Des Groseilliers just before he disappeared on snowshoes into the woods.

Magnus Brown dressed, took his gun, and followed.

Jimmy Frost, already dressed, stole some shot for his gun and slipped out in Brown's tracks.

Des Groseilliers could wait no longer. If Pierre does not cross the river today, he will have to stay on the other side until the flood recedes and we can fetch them in a boat. They must be travelling to the east, inland, away from the goose flats, where the ice might be more stable. He would soon know what trade they'd made and on what terms. This was his role as a free man and not a mere servant of the English merchants. Pierre-Esprit would return alive, that he knew for certain. But of the others, who could guess?

He followed the shore of the river, walking east-southeast with his heart in his mouth. If she is alive, what will he do with her? What a stupid question, Médard, you old fool. You don't do anything with a woman like that. You survive love, if you are a free man.

Des Groseilliers heard Magnus Brown lumbering after him and he forked to the west, following the mysterious divination of the hunt, an instinct that never failed him. Soon he heard nothing but early sparrows in the brush. He had outrun Governors before.

Magnus Brown searched for signs of the French Explorer, and by the grace of God he found his trail: the twigs were broken downward, and so they marked the passage of a man, not a bear.

On Brown's tail scurried Jimmy Frost. Frost, light of foot, overtook Brown and slipped past, over a slight hill, giggling to himself. Private trade. Jimmy Frost in private trade. His thin chest choked up with excitement.

Weaabinakaabo was returning to his family. Without his white companions, he moved swiftly, even with a heavy load, singing under his breath. He'd recently dreamed a moose. If he'd dreamed correctly, he'd cache the meat for his sons and blaze the trees for them to track back to fetch it. But for now Weaabinakaabo simply wanted to move.

He spotted a spruce grouse, a female, plain slate brown, waddling through the underbrush. Some moose, old man. He took his pole snare from the sled.

He was sliding the snare over the grouse's head when the bushes snapped nearby. Perhaps a moose after all. He turned too late when a gun fired through the trees. The explosion threw him backward, his fall strangling the bird. He played dead for several moments, stalling, and then tried to rise. The gun fired again, at closer range. This time, Weaabinakaabo spun and fell heavily, thrown on top of the bird.

Jimmy Frost scrambled out of cover. He walked cautiously around the Indian's body, admiring the blood in the snow. The Indian's eyes were unseeing. Frost went to the sled and unwrapped the trade goods there, whistling over the guns and metalwork. Worth a fortune.

Frost shouted in fear when he heard Weaabinakaabo's song. It was the same plaintive, eerie sound the Frenchman had made. He ran to where Weaabinakaabo lay in a widening pool of blood. The Indian looked right through him, singing. An animal complaint. Frost shot him as fast as he could load his gun.

The Indian's sled weighed at least ten stone; its runners kept catching on bushes and deadfall. Frost hadn't gone more than ten yards when he saw Magnus Brown standing in the striped light of a stand of white birch.

"I heard thy gun," said Magnus Brown. "I see thy Devil's work." He raised his gun and gestured with it back over the trampled snow, to where Weaabinakaabo's body lay.

"A heathen gone back to Hell, Gov'nor. And a thief. Would've killed me first. Come, look at all that the savage was stealing from you. Come. I'll show you."

"Perhaps he was no thief. Perhaps he made honest trade with the Company." Brown lifted the gun to his shoulder.

Frost put his hands before him and patiently wheedled, "Now, that's something I've been wanting to discuss with you, Gov'nor. The trade."

"Do you understand what you've done?"

Frost looked briefly confused, then mildly exasperated. "The Frenchman and the King's whore, see?" he explained. "Them, with the old man and the Earl — do ye see what I'm saying, Master Brown? All four rogues in private trade. And with only Jimmy Frost here to protect Company interests."

Magnus Brown shook his head with an agonized moan. "The Voyage is ruined. Under my watch."

"Ye be distressed, I understand, o' course, when a little whore can get the better of you. But I've got her now, and I give her up to you, Master Brown. She thought she'd pull the wool over your eyes. But she didn't, did she now? Not with Jimmy Frost here to look out for you."

Des Groseilliers emerged from the bush behind Brown. Frost's face brightened uncertainly when he saw the Frenchman. Des Groseilliers walked past Brown and, ignoring Frost, looked into the pack of trade goods on the sled. "I heard gunshot," he said.

Frost vigorously nodded. "You've an ear, Mr. Gooseberries." He jerked his thumb. "The savage come at me, but God be praised, I'm a quick shot. Saved myself, but what's more important, I saved the Company from a sizable loss. As you can see. Something sizable."

Magnus Brown approached Frost. "You must leave this place," he said.

Frost appealed to Des Groseilliers. "The little whore is at bottom of this, to be sure. Nothing but wagtail wiles." He nervously licked his lips. "Trust a whore to have a nose for business."

Brown swung his arm with the gun and struck Frost with its barrel. They heard the skull break.

Des Groseilliers raised his eyebrows and looked at Magnus Brown. Then he stooped to watch Jimmy Frost's death spasms until they ceased.

Des Groseilliers built a cairn over Frost's corpse. Magnus Brown watched him for a while, too stunned to move. Then he began to help. It was hard work, unearthing stones still half-frozen into the deep moss of that place.

They placed Weaabinakaabo on a frame of green aspen that Des Groseilliers built, with Brown's assistance, to preserve the body for burial. Des Groseilliers decorated the wood with feathers from the grouse, and then he walked east a short distance, blazing the trees to mark the path for Weaabinakaabo's sons. The cairn for Frost was close to the chief's body; it might be known, thereby, that the debt had been partially paid. He cached the guns and trinkets and marked the site with Weaabinakaabo's snare pole.

Magnus Brown sat down again while the Frenchman finished. He didn't pray to his God to forgive him. He wouldn't be so craven as to expect that. He'd long ago accepted his role as fugitive, stranger, vagabond. There was the keer of a hawk overhead and the smell of spring. In many ways, these past months, serving the merchants in England, had been the worst imprisonment he'd ever known. If there is a Judgment Day, he may yet learn that he has been condemned to Hell.

But right now, Magnus Brown looked up and saw the way the wings of a hawk were perfectly balanced by the wind.

Thirteen

Prince Rupert's almost fantastically long legs in deep plum hose pressed hard on his horse, the high-spirited gelding surging forward to an easy canter. Charles fell behind and then caught up, surprised at his cousin's impatience. The night was wet, the road deeply rutted by carriages. There'd been sleet for a fortnight.

Now and then a traveller would pass quickly with indrawn breath. Rupert and Charles were dressed incognito, but if a stranger were to raise a torch to view them better, he'd know from the richness of the oiled woollen cloaks, from their fine equipage, that he'd met men of quality. So they rode hurriedly and saved their words for the hearth at the Cormorant Inn at Gravesend.

Charles's spies had brought news of the *Wivenhoe*, and Charles had promptly had the messengers imprisoned lest the news spread around London before he and Rupert had had time to assess the situation. It was said that the ship had briefly put in at Plymouth for repairs on her way to Gravesend. It was also said that she was laden with furs. Within a week the bookkeepers would be swarming the ship, weighing what they saw against what had been recorded in the ledger of Magnus Brown. Charles would quietly arrange that the figures published in the *Gazette* would be substantial. He already had a figure in mind.

No word had arrived of the *Prince Rupert*. And it was not publicly known who was aboard either ship.

The cousins were so excited that it was hard not to gloat. They made terse, ironic remarks. Rupert was gratified to see that his plan was already working: Charles was coming out of himself.

It had been a hard year. Charles's beloved sister was dead, her chocolate poisoned (or so Charles was convinced) by her husband or by her husband's lover, the Chevalier de Lorraine. In losing her, he had lost the last person on earth, the last person of any significant power, other than Rupert, whom he could fully trust.

His beloved Henriette-Anne was dead. Bart and Lilly were most likely dead. Charles didn't care to let anyone, ever again, tempt him to great affection. It was not only that Lilly and Bartholomew were gone — he was troubled by the suddenness of their departure. Charles had been caught off guard, torn open, saddened too deeply. His pleasures tasted insipid, and he suspected that this is how most men live, by necessity, as animals cursed with consciousness and long life. Skepticism had once made life vivid. Now, he, too, truly disbelieved in the value of mankind.

Rupert sympathized with Charles's melancholy. He worried that the monarch would lose that part of himself that made life in the Kingdom worth living: the King's amoral tolerance, his fondness for error. Rupert decided that Charles needed to focus energetically on a single enemy, to distract himself from such dangerous disaffection with the entire population.

Now they rode, giddy with surprise at how quickly the stakes will change. "Outflank him, Charles," Rupert said. "We shall outflank the foe."

"Well, we'd better be prepared to give the ass wide berth."

The foe in question was Sir George Rose. Rose of the widening thighs, the multiplying chins: a squat boar with a genius for creating and maintaining cabals critical of King Charles's every move. Treacherous, tremulously fat, and, despite a rabid, freakish hatred of Catholics, oddly successful, Sir George had extended his influence beyond the peers and raised speculation among the citizens that Charles had double-crossed England in making secret treaties with France. Very low, *beneath* low. And Rose was all *tally-ho* for the capture of the murderess, Lilly Cole, King's whore, the powerful witch who had run off with the drunken poet, the Earl of Buxborough, aboard the Adventurers' ship. Rupert's plan was to be first to greet the *Wivenhoe* and thus pre-empt Rose. Further than that, he wasn't yet prepared to say.

Rupert and Charles reached the Cormorant shortly after one. They woke up the household, and the innkeeper offered that his wife would stay awake all night to serve them, but Charles said, "No. Leave us. Leave us with a good bottle or two of claret, some bread and cheeses." For the cousins were exuberant and did not plan to sleep at all.

The inn looked out toward Lower Hope Reach. Many times, Charles left his place at hearthside to search for signs of the ship, though he could see nothing through such heavy rain.

"Come and sit," said Rupert, filling Charles's glass. "I have something to tell you."

XXXXX

Three weeks earlier, the *Wivenhoe* had lain off the harbour at Plymouth. October 3, crescent moon. She'd been labouring, taking on water since coming through a storm northwest of Ireland, and they'd made the last three hundred miles with timbers bracing her hull, arriving at Plymouth at long last, where they waited offshore until they could find a good shipwright.

Besides, Magnus Brown wanted to send a message to Prince Rupert. He had already sent the shallop to shore with a letter to his mentor, a long, subtle letter, for all Brown's plain speech.

Lilly had called her son James, which struck her as a name that could never know poverty, and which struck Magnus Brown as a canny choice, being the name of Charles's brother, quite possibly the heir to the throne. She and little James were playing ball with Sparrow's yarns in Magnus Brown's cabin.

It was crowded, in a pleasant way, in Brown's cabin, with Brown at his desk, writing in the ship's log, and Sparrow cross-legged on Brown's bunk, knitting a sweater for the baby.

Sparrow was thinking about the cold black sea just a few feet from them all, how it seeped into the ship, slowly gaining on the pump. Sea and night conjoined and surrounded them. Sparrow was afraid; his life or his nature seemed to have discarded him, and he was lonely and frightened, though of course he hid this from everyone, obliging Lilly with grand-fatherly clicking noises from his crooked jaw every time she looked to him for astonished approval of the baby's antics. He'd never felt so conscious of a ship before. He knew how terrible it was for the people of Atlantis when the waves rose up and drowned them, when all was lost to the indifferent sea, who is the mother of us all, and who is death.

It was as if he no longer took breathing for granted. He thought, Maybe it's time to have a garden. Lilly looked up at him quizzically. There was only lantern light, but John Sparrow saw her in the sun, as if she were seated on a sunny green leaf, smiling at him from her own future, eager for life.

The child was nearly seven months old. He could sit up and fumble with the ball of yarn. A strong, wiry baby, he couldn't seem to put on weight despite Sparrow's efforts with oatmeal mash. The striking resemblance to his father, so evident at birth, had diminished somewhat: he was himself. James was affectionate equally to all, but he treated his mother to a special, gallant tenderness, not so remarkable in a boy, but — everyone agreed with Lilly here — precocious in a baby.

Lilly rolled the ball of yarn to her son and he squealed in sudden enthusiasm, falling into her lap and pulling at her nose. Radisson came in to tell them all that at dawn they could go ashore while the ship was repaired. He said, "The baby is a scholar even now. He studies the nose to know what way the wind will blow." They laughed. The pump was quiet for a moment while the crew changed hands. Then it was quiet differently. They looked all at once at Sparrow.

And on that night, they committed John Sparrow's body to the sea.

Fourteen

Charles and Rupert finished two flagons of claret and then broke into the pantry, where they discovered a Madeira and some middling brandy. "It is so much to absorb at once," said Charles. He couldn't speak for several moments.

Rupert saw the tears in Charles's eyes and he thought, We have reached an age, my cousin and I, where a man may be perceived by his few dwindling contemporaries as being wise and by everyone else as being effeminate. "More wine?"

Charles's voice was full. "I have a son. A son."

"Governor Brown attests there is no doubting his paternity. The boy is said to be your very image."

"Well. I shall be *very* glad to see him. And his mother. Lilly lives! She brings me a son. Ha!" Charles slapped his chair. "And imagine! Bart! It shall be so splendid to see the pretty scoundrel, how did he manage?" He grew thoughtful. "They survived. They live! Fancy that. Exposed to the cruelties of such a journey." Then proudly: "My son must be a hero." He drank again. "They live. I thank God." With some effort, he composed himself and put down his glass. "They did not find the passage to China, did they, Rupert?"

"No, they did not."

"Are you terribly sorry?"

Rupert gave Charles one of his rare half-smiles. Rupert

looked especially sad when he smiled. He said, "I find that I am seldom sorry about much of anything anymore. Things are, or they are not. And when they are not, we should not be concerned because they soon will become something else." He leaned forward from the waist. "In point of fact, Charles, I am rather happy."

Rupert's long, overly handsome face stirred Charles. Charles admired Rupert beyond any man but Father. He understood that Rupert had purposefully created this evening's occasion; that it had taken careful preparation. He was grateful to him for it. He knew that Rupert had lately been smitten with a lovely actress. It did appear that the Prince had regained his inventiveness.

Rupert continued. "As you know, I had fostered hope in the Governance of Magnus Brown."

"A bit of a Covenanter," said the wily King. "You cannot boil the Presbyter out of a goose." He put down his wine. He did not intend to become drunk.

"No, you cannot," Rupert agreed, as indeed he might have agreed just then that the soul is everlasting and Charles its divine avatar. "Magnus Brown is an unusual man."

"His mother was beautiful," said Charles. He poured himself brandy; it always cleared his mind.

"Yes. I recall. Well, he has inherited some of his mother's skill at contending, if not her delicate bones."

"His father was a huge man."

"Magnus Brown is subtle."

"Built like an armoury."

Rupert nodded in sage remembrance. He folded his hands. "I think we shall have absinthe."

"What? Here?"

Rupert dove into the low velvet pocket of his coat and produced a flask. He handed it to Charles, solemnly stood, solemnly staggered to the cupboard to find fresh glasses. Charles poured two measures. "To England."

"To England," said Rupert. "And Charles. May I add? To Rupert's Land."

"Oh, Rupert, but of course."

"Magnus Brown does not want to be Governor."

"No?"

"Really not."

"How unusual."

"He is an unusual man," Rupert said. "Long life!" He and Charles tossed it off. "I think you'll like this baby," he added.

Charles remembered, in a florid, absinthian moment, that he had a new baby. "Oh — I shall."

"Well. What do you propose to do about him?"

"The baby?"

"James."

Charles burst into laughter. "Oh, I do love it that Lilly is so crafty." Again, he laughed. "James."

"He'll need protection, Charles. From George Rose and his lot. And Lilly will need our protection, too. I assume you wish for her to continue in her role as his mother?"

Charles shrugged generously. "I can't think why not!"

"Brown has made us an offer, Charles. One that I think we might find — persuasive."

Charles blew out. "I don't regret hanging Brown's father," he said. There had been so little hanging. The small vengeance Charles had permitted himself had given him some hope; perhaps it had freed him from lifelong pique. "This is awfully good," he said, tipping his glass to Rupert's. "Thank you, Rupert."

"Charles," said Rupert. "Magnus Brown is very fond of Lilly."

"Really." Charles thought about that. "How daring of him." He laughed. It was so good to laugh. "She is brilliant. And small of build."

"Brown is brilliant too."

"He is. Most certainly very bright." Charles inhaled the absinthe — it was no longer necessary to drink it. In a low voice he said, "He wants to take Lilly and my son away from me. He wants to take them away, and he wants us to help him to do that, provide them a living somewhere. Someplace safe, where he thinks Rose won't find them." He looked up. "Such is Magnus Brown's 'offer.'" Drink often made the King clairvoyant. "Isn't it, Rupert?"

Rupert nodded and loved him.

After several moments, Charles puffed impatiently, decisively put down his glass, and asked, "Why don't I simply have Rose executed instead?"

Rupert tried to conceal his surprise. He waited, then quietly, quite casually observed, "I don't think that kind of thing is possible anymore, Charles."

Charles angrily sighed. "Are the Roses of this world so popular?"

Rupert shrugged. There was nothing to say to that.

Charles reached out to lay his hand on Rupert's shoulder, squeezed hard, and asked, "Does the old Quaker really believe that they can be just — made to disappear yet again? I want to see my son. And Lilly, she is a fine actress, you know. She's wonderful onstage. She should not be hidden in obscurity. It does not fit her."

"There are many marvellous ways to be obscure, don't you think, Charles?"

Charles withdrew his hand. He shivered as if touched by a ghost. "I'll never know," he whispered.

In the silence between them they could hear the innkeeper's wife come downstairs to stoke the fire, muttering some old complaint. She came with her candle and cried out in fear, shocked to see the two tall apparitions seated by her hearth. Hastily, she put the candle down on the floor to tie her apron, curtsying in confusion.

So the night ended and morning began, in darkness, then, daylight without colour and with no sign of the sun. But day. Day.

Fifteen

It seemed to have been raining since the beginning of time. Lilly put a hood over James, but he shucked it off. She liked the feel of his resistance. They battled over the hood. James let her think she'd won, then he shucked it off again.

The *Wivenhoe* had arrived at ten o'clock on a morning darkened by clouds as low as the topmasts of the ships at harbour at Gravesend. Lilly wore a hooded moose-hide jacket, the fur turned to the outside to repel the sleet. James was bundled fitfully in whitened moose-hide blankets. He wore a cap that Sparrow had sewn in the manner of the Moose Cree.

Magnus Brown came up from the chart room. She could feel his radiant heat, standing behind her. She leaned back, pressed against him, and felt renewed surprise at him.

Pierre-Esprit Radisson carried a light pack. He stood awhile looking at them, at Lilly and Brown and the long-nosed baby. His hat pitched rain down his crooked left shoulder. The baby reached for him. "Oh, you cannot come with me, I don't think," Radisson said. "How would we carry on?"

The gangway was laid to the wharf. Radisson couldn't quite hide the anguish he felt on parting. He bit his lip and bounded quickly down to the dock, not looking back.

"Radisson!" Lilly called. "Pierre!"

He stopped. Merde! These people will make me old.

"Goodbye," she said. "I will think of you."

Radisson thought, No, please, now I am old and I will miss you.

Lilly wrapped James with stubborn resolve that so overwhelmed him, he fell asleep. He was sleeping, wrapped in moose hide, when Lilly pulled up her hood and carried him across to the shore of England. It was hard to see clearly in the downpour. As it happened, the King sneezed violently and startled his horse just as Lilly passed. He searched for her but saw only a peasant carrying a load of fur pelts from ship to shore. Some sailor's wife come to retrieve what is probably illegal booty. Charles thought, I shall have to inquire with Hayes, has there been private trade, and how much.

Then Charles saw the unmistakeable bulk of Magnus Brown. The man had grown, could it be so?

The gangway shook and whined when Brown walked toward King Charles, seated on his horse — immobile but for a single black ringlet fallen over his left eye.

Magnus Brown stopped before the gold martingale on the King's horse and lifted his eyes into the rain.

Acknowledgments

I am very grateful to the Canada Council for the Arts and the Manitoba Arts Council for their generous support. Residencies at the University of Winnipeg and at the Winnipeg Public Library made life not only possible but interesting over the years that I worked on this novel. I continue to be nurtured by my association with the University of Winnipeg.

I'd also like to thank my father, Alan Sweatman, who gave me his 1938 copy of Bowditch's *American Practical Navigator*, and whose lifelong talent and fondness for navigating (among many other things) make it so wonderful to be his daughter. Bethany Gibson's brilliant editing and encouragement over several years helped give me the stamina to finish this book. Thank you, Heather Sangster. Thank you, Glenn Buhr and Anne McDermid. I continue to be amazed at my great luck.

Author's Note

The Players was inspired by events that took place in England and North America, primarily between 1665 and 1671. Radisson and Des Groseilliers — two French explorers, two restless men — met the English King Charles II in December of 1665 or early in 1666, and they stayed at Prince Rupert's Windsor Castle apartments. The Plague was still virulent when they sailed up the Thames. In 1668, Des Groseilliers (aboard the *Nonsuch*) and Radisson (aboard the *Eaglet)* set sail from England for Hudson Bay, but bad weather forced Radisson and the *Eaglet* back to Plymouth. Des Groseilliers and the *Nonsuch* made it to Hudson Bay, traded through the winter, and returned to England in 1669. The success of that voyage led to the founding of the Company of Adventurers of England Trading into Hudson Bay and to a voyage undertaken by Radisson (aboard the *Wivenhoe*) and Groseilliers (aboard the *Prince Rupert*) for the winter of 1670–1671.

It may come as a big surprise, but there is no record of a woman aboard either ship.

Lilly Cole, Magnus Brown, and Bartholomew were first inspired by my reading of histories, but they belong solely to *The Players*. Charles II, Prince Rupert, Radisson, Des Groseilliers, and all other characters are dramatis personae for the particular occasion of this novel. Their representation in these pages is intended for entertainment. For historical veracity, the reader may wish to search through the historical accounts.

. . .

The poem on page 171 is from Dante's *The Divine Comedy 3: Paradise*, Canto Two. Trans. Dorothy L. Sayers and Barbara Reynolds, Penguin Books, 1962.

. . .

On page 175, Magnus Brown is quoting from George Fox, *Christian Epistles*, 1650. Fox was an English Dissenter who was considered a founder of the Religious Society of Friends, commonly called the Quakers.

. . .

The madrigal on page 199, 200, and 267 is *"Ohimè dov'è il mio ben*, Roman-esca a 2"* by Claudio Monteverdi; the lyrics are by Bernardo Tasso.

. . .

Research for this novel has taken me far and wide. A full list of my obligations would be too long, but it would certainly include the following:

Ahenakew, Freda, and H.C. Wolfart, eds. and trans. *Kôhkominawak otâcimowiniwâwa = Our Grandmothers' Lives, as Told in Their Own Words*. Told by Glecia Bear. Saskatoon: Fifth House, 1992.

Ashley, Maurice. *Rupert of the Rhine*. London: Hart Davis, MacGibbon, 1976.

Bax, Clifford. *Pretty Witty Nell: The Story of Nell Gwyn and Her Times*. New York: William Morrow & Co., 1933.

Golder, F.A. *Bering's Voyages: An Account of the Efforts of the Russians to Determine the Relation of Asia and America.* New York: American Geographical Society, 1925. Reprinted New York: Octagon Books, 1968.

Defoe, Daniel. *A Journal of the Plague Year Written by a Citizen Who Continued all the while in London [and] A New Voyage Round the World by a Course Never Sailed Before.* Boston: Dana Estes, 1904.

Francis, Daniel, and Toby Morantz. *Partners in Furs: A History of the Fur Trade in Eastern James Bay, 1600–1870.* Montreal: McGill-Queen's University Press, 1985.

Fraser, Antonia. *King Charles II.* London: Weidenfeld and Nicolson, 1979.

Fraser, Peter. *The Intelligence of the Secretaries of State and Their Monopoly of Licensed News: 1660–1688.* Cambridge University Press, 1936.

Glanvil, Joseph. "Philosophical Considerations Concerning Witches." In *Essays on Important Subjects in Philosophy and Religion. 1636–1680,* New York: Johnson Reprint, 1970.

Glover, Richard, ed. *David Thomson's Narrative, 1784–1812.* Toronto: Champlain Society, 1962.

Hakluyt, Richard. *The Principal Navigational Voyages, Traffiques & Discoveries of the English Nation, Made by Sea or Overland to the Remote & Farthest Distant Quarters of the Earth at Any Time within the Compasse of these 1600 Yeares.* Vol. 5, with an Introduction by John Masefield. London: Everyman's Library, 1907, 1926.

Kenyon, W.A., ed. *The Strange and Dangerous Voyage of Capt. Thomas James.* Toronto: Royal Ontario Museum, 1975.

Latham, Robert, ed. *The Illustrated Pepys: Extracts from the Diary.* London: Bell & Hyman Let., 1978.

_____. *The Shorter Pepys.* Berkeley: University of California Press, 1985.

Laut, A.C. *Pathfinders of the West: Being the Thrilling Story of the Adventures of the Men Who Discovered the Great Northwest: Radisson, La Verendrye, Lewis and Clark*. Toronto: William Briggs, 1904.

Montgomery Cooper, John. *Snares, Deadfalls, and Other Traps of the Northern Algonquins and Northern Athapaskans*. New York: AMS Press, 1978.

Mood, Fulmer. "The London Background of the Radisson Problem," *Minnesota History* (Dec. 1935), pp. 391-413.

Morgan, Fidelis. *The Female Wits: Women Playwrights on the London Stages, 1660–1720*. London: Virago, 1981.

Newman, Peter C. *Company of Adventurers*. Vol. 1. New York: Viking Penguin, 1985.

Norman, Charles. *Rake Rochester*. New York: Crown Publishers, 1954.

Nute, Grace Lee. *Caesars of the Wilderness: Medard Chouart, Sieur Des Groseilliers and Pierre Esprit Radisson, 1618–1710*. New York and London: D. Appleton-Century, 1943.

_____. "Radisson and Groseilliers' Contribution to Geography," *Minnesota History* (Dec. 1935), pp. 414-426.

Richardson, Boyce. *Strangers Devour the Land: The Cree Hunters of the James Bay Area Versus Premier Bourassa and the James Bay Development Corporation*. Toronto: Macmillan, 1975.

Skull, Gideon, ed. *Voyages of Peter Esprit Radisson*. Boston: Publications for the Prince Society, 1885.

Tanner, Adrian. *Bringing Home Animals: Religious Ideology and Mode of Production of the Mistassini Cree Hunters*. London: C. Hurst, 1979.

Trease, Geoffrey. *Samuel Pepys and His World*. New York: G.P. Putnam, 1972.

Tyrrell, J.B. ed. *Samuel Hearne: A Journey from Prince of Wales's*

Fort in Hudson's Bay to the Northern Ocean. Toronto:
  Champlain Society, 1911.
Woodcock, George. *The Hudson's Bay Company*. New York:
  Crowell-Collier, 1970.

. . .

Excerpts of *The Players*, in different form, have appeared in
The New Quarterly and *Prairie Fire*.